- You can return this item to any Bournemouth library but not all libraries are open every day.

- Items must be returned on or before the due date. Please note that you will be charged for items returned late.

- Items may be renewed unless requested by another customer.

- Renewals can be made in any library, by telephone, email or online via the website. Your membership card number and PIN will be required.

- Please look after this item - you may be charged for any damage.

Alex Gray was born and educated in Glasgow. She is the co-founder of the Bloody Scotland Crime Writing Festival, has been awarded the Scottish Association of Writers' Constable and Pitlochry trophies for her crime writing, and is the Scottish Chapter convenor for the Crime Writers' Association. Married with a son and daughter, she now writes full time. Find out more at www.Alex-Gray.com.

THE SWEDISH GIRL

Alex Gray

SPHERE

First published in Great Britain in 2013 by Sphere
Reprinted 2013

Copyright © Alex Gray 2013

The moral right of the author has been asserted.

*All characters and events in this publication, other than those
clearly in the public domain, are fictitious and any resemblance
to real persons, living or dead, is purely coincidental.*

A CIP catalogue record for this book
is available from the British Library.

Hardback ISBN: 978 1 8474 4565 0
Trade Paperback ISBN: 978 1 8474 4566 7

Typeset in Caslon by M Rules
Printed and bound in Great Britain by
Clays Ltd, St Ives plc

Papers used by Sphere are from well-managed forests
and other responsible sources.

MIX
Paper from
responsible sources
FSC® C104740

Sphere
An imprint of
Little, Brown Book Group
100 Victoria Embankment
London EC4Y 0DY

An Hachette UK Company
www.hachette.co.uk

www.littlebrown.co.uk

This book is dedicated to
June and George with love

Yet each man kills the thing he loves
By each let this be heard,
Some do it with a bitter look,
Some with a flattering word,
The coward does it with a kiss,
The brave man with a sword!

Some kill their love when they are young,
And some when they are old;
Some strangle with the hands of Lust,
Some with the hands of Gold:
The kindest use a knife because
The dead so soon grow cold.

Taken from
'The Ballad of Reading Gaol'
by Oscar Wilde

PROLOGUE

October

The old man grasped the head of his walking stick, feeling its curve snug within his palm. A glance at his hands might have revealed the yellowing knuckle joints and dark, mottled skin, the fingertips stained ochre from years of rolling his own cigarettes: signs of old age and decay along with the necessary stick. With his free hand he pulled open the green-painted door of the close, letting it fall shut with a slam behind him. For a moment he paused in the shadows of twin hedges that flanked the pathway, fingers fumbling the buttons of his jacket. Then, turning into the street, he blinked, dimly aware of the lamps beginning to glow with a faint amber light against the deepening blue.

Twilight was not his favourite time of day. The setting sun was a glare against the lenses of his thick spectacles, any peripheral vision merely grey-hued shapes leering at him from the buildings on either side. Yet he had to be out; had to make this slow journey from his home to the corner of the street.

Earlier, an insistent voice had made him put on his raincoat, wrench the walking stick out from its place in the hall stand and make his painful way down several flights of stone stairs leading to the street. That same voice had made him swallow down a thin line of phlegm, making him feel the dryness in his throat, inviting him to slake this nightly thirst. It was a voice he always obeyed.

The sound of laughter made him falter for a moment and look up. They were there again, those young hooligans from across the landing, sitting outside the pub as if they owned the place. And, although it was not a summer's evening, he saw that the girls were clad in skimpy blouses, the young men sitting hunched towards them, wavering lines of smoke rising from their cigarettes. He would have to pass them in order to reach the pub door, make a detour around the table and chairs that cluttered up the pavement. For a moment he wanted to raise his stick and shout curses at them, tell them to clear off, but instead he lowered his eyes and shuffled past, hoping they might leave him in peace.

As he passed them he could hear whispers, but not the whispered words. Then more laughter, raucous laughter like crows squawking above a rubbish tip, the sound of it following him around the corner and on to the threshold of the Caledonian Bar. He could feel his heart thumping and, as he imagined their eyes turned to watch him enter the pub, the blood flushed his cheeks into angry spots of colour. But then the loud beat of music from an unseen source drowned out everything as he peered into the gloom, searching for a vacant seat. Even before he took his customary place in the corner the barman was pulling his first pint.

'There, Mr McCubbin. A wee packet of crisps as well, eh?' Ina, the barmaid with the purple hair, was smiling down at him, laying his pint mug carefully on the paper mat. 'What d'you fancy the night? We've got in some nice ham-flavoured ones,' she went on, shaking her head as the old man chose to ignore her, lifting the glass to his lips and drinking deeply.

'The captain's in one of his moods,' Ina remarked sourly to

2

Tam, the barman, who merely nodded at the old sailor and directed his glance at the next customer with a tilt of his chin that served as a question.

Derek McCubbin sat still, his back to the window, listening to the familiar jangle from the taped music, sighing into the night as distant images from seafaring days long gone flitted across his vision. For it was more than a mere physical thirst that drove him here night after night; the drink helped him to forget his age and infirmities, old memories smothering this present wretchedness, memories that could almost make his bitter lips twist into the grimace of a smile. They would replenish his glass a few more times during the evening before the old man made his way back along the street, tapping his stick against the cold hard stones.

Outside the pub Kirsty Wilson shivered.

'Want to go in?' the other girl asked her, running her fingers down Kirsty's bare arm, making goose bumps appear along her friend's skin.

'Och, it's just that old man across from our flat,' Kirsty replied. 'Gives me the creeps.'

Eva Magnusson took her hand away, reaching up instead to smooth her own fine blond hair as the wind began to blow the dust around their feet. 'Thought you were cold,' she remarked.

'You feart of Mr McCubbin?' the big red-haired boy opposite them laughed suddenly, stubbing out his cigarette on the metal ashtray. 'He couldnae hurt a fly, that old codger.'

Kirsty wriggled uncomfortably. Rodge was right, of course. The old man was just that: an old man who didn't see too well and who needed a stick to amble along the street every night.

'You shouldnae be like that, Kirsty,' another of the boys protested mildly. 'D'you not feel sorry for him, all on his own like that?'

3

'Och, he's probably got other old men he meets in the pub every night,' Kirsty said, sensing an argument beginning and knowing she was going to be worse off if she didn't capitulate right away.

Colin shook his head, pressing home his point. 'He's always on his own. I've seen him,' he added thoughtfully.

'Poor old Daddy No Mates!' Eva pulled a face then laughed and the others laughed with her as they always did.

Kirsty sighed quietly. Eva was the acknowledged favourite of their group whom everybody adored. Even the girls from uni didn't bother trying to compete with her because what was the point? Colin, Gary and Rodge pretended that they were cool about living in the same flat as Eva Magnusson but Kirsty knew fine that any one of the three would hop into bed with Eva given half a chance. Especially Gary, she thought, watching the dark-haired English lad narrowing his eyes as he smiled over his glass. Colin and Rodge weren't Eva's type at all: Rodge was like a great bear, more at home on the rugby pitch than in the classroom. Or the bedroom, come to that, she grimaced, remembering a recent drunken night that neither of them ever spoke about. And Colin Young was just too nice for a girl like Eva Magnusson; too nice and too normal. *The boy next door*, Eva had called him once when the two girls had been discussing the lads, and she had made it sound like a sort of insult. No, Kirsty told herself, that wasn't fair. Eva was never unkind about anyone; that was what was so endearing – and maddening – about her. You might envy her Scandinavian blue eyes and silvery blond hair but you simply couldn't dislike her.

'You've just got a suspicious mind, Kirsty,' Gary told her. 'Like your old man.'

'Aye, well, maybe,' Kirsty agreed. Having a dad in the police force was what had swung it for her in getting a place in Eva's flat, she was sure of that. Mr Magnusson had been well impressed when she'd told him that her father was a detective sergeant in Strathclyde Police.

'Ever think of joining him?' Rodge asked. 'Not a bad job for a lassie nowadays.'

'No.' Kirsty shook her head. 'I'm more like my mum. Definitely going to be in the hospitality business. Preferably somewhere warm.' She shivered again and looked up at the darkening clouds.

'You should be your own person, Kirsty!' Eva said suddenly. 'Don't let your parents dictate your life for you.'

'Aye, you get a wee place on the Med and we'll all come for holidays,' Colin joked, glancing from one girl to the other, eyebrows raised in surprise. But the Swedish girl's smile was back almost at once, her sweet expression belying the vehemence with which she had spoken.

'Come on, let's go back to the flat,' Eva said, getting up and looking for the pink cardigan that had slipped off the back of her chair and was lying on the ground.

'Here.' Colin scooped it up and wrapped it around her shoulders, a simple gesture that would have impressed Kirsty but that Eva only acknowledged with a faint smile as though it were her due.

'Five go to Merryfield Avenue,' Colin murmured as he fell into step with Kirsty, Eva and the others already several paces ahead of them.

Kirsty looked at him sharply. Did he think they were kids playing some sort of a game? Well, if that's what he really thought, he was happy enough to take part in it, wasn't he? Or was his remark directed more towards Eva? Kirsty followed her flatmate's wistful gaze. There was no doubt in her mind that Colin Young was well and truly smitten and for a moment she felt sorry for him.

'C'mon,' she said, linking her arm in his. 'I'll stick the kettle on and make us all a cuppa. Okay?'

Colin grinned at her suddenly. 'Know what, Kirsty Wilson? You're going to make someone a great wee wife one of these days.'

CHAPTER 1

Detective Sergeant Alistair Wilson drained his mug of tea and gave a satisfied sigh.

'Good day?' Betty asked with a smile.

'Aye,' her husband replied, leaning back on the kitchen chair. 'Just like old times,' he murmured.

'Fancy having Lorimer back in the division again,' Betty remarked. 'You were all pleased to see the back of Mitchison when he got his transfer, but I bet none of you ever guessed who his replacement would be.'

'No. Thought Lorimer would be up in Pitt Street for a good while longer when he made detective super. Cutbacks.' Alistair shrugged as though that single word explained away the myriad changes within the Strathclyde Police. He picked up his empty mug.

'Another cuppa, love?' Betty asked.

'Aye, why not,' the detective sergeant nodded. 'Hear anything from our Kirsty today?' he asked.

Betty Wilson shook her head. 'She's awfully busy. All these assignments. Wasn't like that in my day. We had a lot more practical stuff to do.' She wiped the table top idly with a flick of her cloth, folded it neatly then laid it across the side of the kitchen sink.

7

'Well if she turns out to be half the cook you are, pet, she'll be doing fine.' Alistair patted his wife's ample bottom affectionately as she passed his chair.

'Don't know if that's what our Kirsty wants,' Betty replied. 'Think she has her sights set on something more to do with the hotel trade.' She bit her lip. Kirsty had been glowing with enthusiasm on her last visit home, telling her mum all about the opportunities for graduates that lay overseas. Although it was still only October she had already applied for summer jobs next year in hotels as far apart as Mallorca and the Channel Islands. It was something she hadn't told Alistair yet. Kirsty was his darling, their only child, and the thought of her spending months away from Scotland would hit him hard, she knew.

'Well, she works all hours at the weekends in that hotel to pay her rent, doesn't she?' Alistair replied. 'And look at the tips she gets from some of those visitors!' he added, a note of pride creeping into his voice. 'Ach, she'll do well, will Kirsty, wait and see.'

'Penny for them,' Maggie Lorimer said, looking at her husband who was gazing into space as they sat on either side of the kitchen table, the remains of their Sunday dinner between them.

'Just thinking that it was good being back amongst the old crew, actually,' Lorimer said, stretching his arms behind his head and yawning. 'You don't realise how much you've missed them till you go back.'

'And *they* welcomed *you* with open arms,' Maggie chuckled. It was no secret that her husband was popular with the other officers in the division.

'I think so,' he said lightly. 'Anyway, now that the posting's been confirmed that's them stuck with me.'

Maggie Lorimer picked up the newspaper she had been reading, the smile still on her lips. His promotion had been well deserved even if his career path had been somewhat circuitous.

After serving in his divisional HQ as a DCI, William Lorimer had been promoted to detective superintendent and seconded to the Serious Crimes Squad at police headquarters for the first half of the year. However, massive changes to the structure of the force and budgetary constraints had resulted in the decision to mothball the unit, and he had waited for several anxious weeks to find out if he was to be posted back to his old division in place of the outgoing detective superintendent, Mark Mitchison.

I'll see what I can do, was all that Assistant Chief Constable Joyce Rogers had told him. But it had been said with a knowing smile and a tap to the side of her nose. Och, it was as good as his, Maggie had insisted, back in the summer when they had taken their annual trip up to Mull for a much needed break. And she had been right.

Now he was back in Stewart Street it was as if he had never left the place.

Maggie thought about the city centre police headquarters for a moment; a squat low-level building huddled amidst tower blocks yet standing out with its bright blue paint and that customary chequered strip. It was close to the motorway on one side and to the top of Hope Street on the other, yet Maggie Lorimer had never once set foot inside A Division, preferring to meet her husband after work in one of the small bistros that were a short walk away. *You don't want to see what goes on*, Bill had said to her once when a high profile prisoner had been detained there. And he was right: Maggie listened to what her husband told her, accepting that there would always be a lot left out of any story involving serious crime and glad that she saw a different side to the man who dealt with criminals in his working life.

What neither the detective superintendent nor his school-teacher wife could have guessed at that moment was the effect that one particular crime would have on them both.

CHAPTER 2

July: three months earlier

Twenty-four Merryfield Avenue was not considered an especially prestigious address, yet it was still unusual for a student flat to be found within its red sandstone walls. The avenue was too close to the bustling street around the corner to have any real cachet as a leafy residential area, yet once it had been the residence of the well-to-do, many of whom were still there, living out their twilight years, remembering better days. The tall fair man stood with his hand resting gently on his daughter's shoulder as they gazed up at the top flat. The large bay windows twinkled in the afternoon sunlight, their lower panes still retaining the original yellow- and amber-stained glass that dated from a different century.

Henrik Magnusson took a set of keys from the pocket of his fine suede jacket and held them out for a moment. 'Here,' he said. 'It's all yours, Eva.' Then he smiled his slow smile as the girl's face lit up.

She clasped her father's arm, her face brushing the soft material. 'Best dad in the world,' she murmured, pulling away again and trying not to grin as she looked up at the top storey of the building once more. Then, turning back, Eva took the keys from his outstretched fingers and together they walked across the road and entered the narrow path marked out by hedges on either side. As she stepped up to the front door, the girl's attention was caught by a pale cream-coloured cat sitting on the window sill of the ground floor flat. It was looking at them intently, its golden eyes curious at the arrival of strangers. Then, as if it had come to a decision about them, the cat slipped noiselessly from its perch and was at the girl's side, rubbing its soft fur against her leg and purring loudly. Eva smiled and nodded, acknowledging the gesture as though it were a good omen, a welcome from this feline resident.

'Shall we let him in?' She turned to her father.

Henrik shrugged. 'I don't see why not,' he said. 'It obviously lives here.'

As she put the key into the lock, Eva noticed a row of names, some badly faded, printed to one side of the doorway, tiny grilles beneath. She nodded, recognising the security entry system.

'We'll need a bigger space for all the names once I get some flatmates,' she observed, looking at the blank space right at the top of the list. Then, pushing open the heavy wooden door, they entered the close. Eva took off her designer sunglasses and looked around.

Inside was surprisingly light. A short corridor to the rear of the building ended with a glazed door, and the half landing above them had a long window that provided another source of daylight. Henrik Magnusson followed his daughter up the stone stairs, smiling as she exclaimed over the arrangements of carefully tended potted plants on each landing, the shining brasses and etched glass on the front doors on either side, the storm doors painted in cheerful shades of red. It was an old property, but one where the existing residents evidently took a pride in their homes. Henrik had asked the estate agent questions about the people who lived at number twenty-four and the man had been surprisingly knowledgeable about some of them. Several were retired people and others would be out at business during the day; there was a residents' association and each of the owners had to pay their share of repairs to things like slates falling off the roof or damage to the stone steps. It was a far cry from the modern blocks that Henrik owned in his native Sweden, where factors took care of everything, charging the tenants sweetly for the privilege.

'Here we are!' Eva turned to her father with an excited grin as they reached the top storey and turned to the door on the right.

'Go on then,' Henrik told her. 'Open up your new home.'

There were two doors to the flat: a heavy storm door that Henrik hooked back into a latch on the wall and an old-fashioned inner door, framed in dark mahogany with opaque glass set in from waist height. Eva Magnusson turned the set of keys in her hand until she found the one that matched the Yale lock.

The door opened noiselessly and she stepped over the threshold, marvelling at the spacious hall within and the adjacent staircase that wound its way upwards.

Eva grinned over her shoulder. 'It's huge!' she said, then laughed out loud, turning to one room after the other, exclaiming at their particular features.

'Any place looks big when it's empty.' Henrik shrugged, but even he was impressed by the proportions of these apartments now that the previous owner's furniture had been cleared out.

'Wow! Look at this!' Eva had reached the end of the hallway and was standing in the kitchen gazing upwards at a set of false beams, her blue eyes twinkling with delight.

Henrik nodded. So. They had left them after all. The plants

cascaded down from their hooks on the wooden beams, making the entire ceiling appear to be a hanging garden. The Swede had haggled and offered a bit extra but he had been given the impression that the owner wanted to take her late mother's precious plants away. Perhaps, after all, there had been no room for them in her own home? Well, his daughter was happy with them as Henrik had known she would be.

'We'll need to find at least one tall young man to reach up and water them for you,' Henrik joked.

Eva made a face but it turned into a smile again almost immediately. 'How many should I be sharing this with?' she asked. 'Another girl and a boy, maybe?'

Henrik shook his head. 'There is enough space for five of you,' he said. 'Three bedrooms on this floor and two upstairs. And,' he shrugged again, 'you can have it all girls if you like but I think a mix would be better.'

Eva did not reply, simply nodding her agreement as she always did.

They turned together as a train rattled past, momentarily shaking the kitchen windows. Eva walked across and looked out over the kitchen sink to where a line of trees marched away beyond the railway line. Looking down she noticed that there was some sort of a yard between the tenement buildings and the railway. Several vans were parked side by side and she could see a heap of used tyres piled untidily into one corner. As she watched, a man in dark blue overalls crossed the yard and opened the door of the van at the end of the row. He was quite unaware of being observed by the girl from the top flat above him, Eva realised. He was simply going about his business. She took a deep breath, savouring the moment. Life was all around her, real life, from the work going on in the yard to the day-to-day business of people on every floor of the building. And now she, Eva Magnusson, was a part of that life.

She wandered back into the hall and immediately entered the main reception room, recognising the bay windows she had admired earlier from the street below. Sunlight poured into this room as the windows were almost ceiling height. Eva's eyes followed the line of coving: the egg and dart plaster mould was perfectly intact, as was the ornate rose in the centre of the ceiling with its grey coil of electric flex ready and waiting for whatever her father might choose in the way of a light fitting. Before she knew it, her feet had taken her right up to the windows where three tired-looking boxes on the sill outside held a few hopeful pansies. She would plant them up as soon as she could, put in scarlet geraniums instead. Eva looked across the street at the houses opposite and blinked, a sudden memory surfacing. It was a painting she had seen in a gallery. What was it called? *Windows on the West*, that was it, where the artist had captured moments in the lives of folk in a tenement flat, just like this. And for a moment she frowned at the idea of someone staring across at her, seeing into her own life.

'It's darker on the other side of the house,' she remarked, hearing her father's footsteps come into the room. 'I think I would like a bedroom with less light. You know I can never sleep when the sun streams in my window.'

The girl kept staring out of the window even when she felt the pressure of Henrik's fingers close upon her shoulder. She smiled, seeing the reflection of her face in the glass, as she calculated how many weeks it would be before she would be here as a student, free from the constraints that had held her for the past nineteen years of her life.

CHAPTER 3

Colin Young picked up the dishcloth and wiped around the edges of the industrial-sized sinks. God knows how many times he had cleaned up after the chefs since the start of his shift, but he supposed that was what his job was, kitchen hand. It had been all that Colin could find as far as a summer job was concerned and he needed the money if he was going to get anywhere decent to stay next session. His face brightened suddenly as he remembered the appointment with the Swedish man, Larsson, or something. No, he was confusing him with one of his childhood football heroes, Henrik Larsson. *Magnusson*, that was his name, Henrik Magnusson. It was the Henrik bit that had muddled him up. Colin's smile broadened as he cast his thoughts back to when he had been a wee lad eagerly following his dad and big brother, Thomas, up the slope to Parkhead football stadium. The boys' Celtic strips had been worn with the kind of pride that was hard for those outside the game to comprehend. Then there was the singing; thousands of voices raised along with the green, gold and white scarves, a sound to make the hairs on his neck stand on edge even thinking about it so many years later.

Well, perhaps this other Henrik would come up trumps for him. The monthly rental was okay, so the flat was bound to be fairly basic, plus it was out at Anniesland, not exactly on the doorstep of the university and he'd have to factor in the cost of a bus or train on top of everything else. Colin gave the stainless steel sink one final rub then put the used cloth into a plastic tub full of bleach before stripping off the industrial rubber gloves that the boss had insisted he wear.

No fur your benefit, son. It's in case ye tak us tae a tribunal if ye get dermatitis, ken?

Colin had nodded, understanding the man's aggrieved tone. There had been so much red tape involved at the beginning of this summer job, forms to fill in, things to sign. And he was only a kitchen hand, after all. It was not as if he was handling any of the stuff out of the ovens, like some of the other young lads, or being yelled at by the head chef.

He untied the greasy apron from around his waist, hung it on the peg behind the door and slipped out into the lane that ran behind the restaurant, the sudden daylight making him blink. A couple of the older chefs were lounging at the corner, taking a quick fag break now that the lunchtime rush was over. They barely glanced at Colin as he walked along the cobbled lane and crossed over to the car park that separated Ashton Lane from the university buildings. But that was fine. Nobody usually gave Colin Young a second look. *The sort of guy who would be lost in a crowd*, one of his pals at school had said. The rest of them had laughed, Colin with them, but afterwards, looking in the wardrobe mirror in his bedroom, he had wondered about that remark. There was nothing wrong with his appearance: at seventeen he had reached his full height of five feet eight in his stocking soles, a slim verging on skinny teenager with a pale face that was the result of too much late-night study for end of term exams.

Now, three years on, little had changed. He was still slightly

17

built, his mid-brown hair cut shorter and better styled than it had been in his schooldays but there was nothing unpleasing about Colin's appearance. Whenever he smiled his eyes would crinkle at the corners and one could almost believe his was an attractive sort of face. It was when he spoke that people turned to give him a second look, this young man with that unusual lilt in his voice that came from being born to a Lewis woman whose own speech had been peppered with Gaelic words and phrases.

The students' residence office was situated over the hill and along one of the streets that criss-crossed the area between Great Western Road and University Avenue. Colin glanced at his watch and quickened his pace. He'd have to hurry if he was to pick up the details of the other flats he'd been offered before catching a bus out to Anniesland. The afternoon sun beat down on his head as he turned into Great George Street. Well, at least he had a decent break before his evening shift and maybe there was even the chance of lounging about in the park, watching the skateboarders, letting the heat soak into his skin.

The bus stopped with an ear-splitting squeal of brakes and Colin descended onto the pavement, his eyes turning immediately to the street on his left. There was a pub just around the corner from Merryfield Avenue, he noticed, where afternoon drinkers were enjoying their pints outside in the Glasgow sunshine. A couple of blue and yellow parasols that boasted the logo of a well-known brewery made the place almost festive and Colin paused for a moment, wondering if this might become his local, if he were lucky enough to get a room in the flat.

There was the usual line of names by an entryphone buzzer and Colin saw the name Magnusson right at the top. Typical, he thought, raising his eyebrows, every student flat he knew was on the top floor. He pressed the bell and waited. There was a crackle followed by a man's deep voice: 'Hello?'

'It's Colin Young. I've come about the room.' Colin bent forward, his mouth close to the intercom.

There was a pause then a click. 'Come up. Top right,' the voice said and Colin pushed open the green-painted main door, his eyes blinded for a moment by the change from bright sunlight into the comparative gloom of the close. A few blinks dispelled the dullness and, as he made his way up the stone staircase, Colin could see that this was a smart place. Not only were the stairs in good nick, but each landing seemed to have a collection of huge plants, the residents here evidently taking some pride in their property.

'Up here,' an echoing and disembodied voice called down and Colin sprinted up the last few stairs to come at last to the doorway of Henrik Magnusson's house.

His first impression was of the man's height: six four at least, Colin guessed. He was a handsome man, Colin saw, taking in the tanned face, the shock of pale blond hair and a pair of piercing blue eyes that commanded his attention. But there was something stern about him that made the younger man want to flinch.

'Come in,' Magnusson said, holding open the door and stepping aside.

Afterwards, Colin tried to describe number 24 Merryfield Avenue but it was hard to remember every detail of the flat. The smell of new carpet lingered in every room as Colin was given the guided tour of everywhere, except the bedroom next to the kitchen, his eyes feasting on the antique furniture in the hall and lounge and the pictures hanging on the walls. *It was not*, he told his brother later, like any student flat he'd ever been in before. They had ended up standing beside a huge black lacquered table in the spacious kitchen, Magnusson staring at him as he threw one question after another: was he a smoker? *No.* What were his political leanings? A doubtful shrug and *Scot Nat, probably.* Did he make time to see his own family? *Oh aye,* but not that often since he didn't have a car and it was a bit of a trek out to Armadale in West Lothian; the train took hours to get there. Nothing about his course at uni, no wonderings about his future career at all, but plenty of questions about his likes and dislikes. Football, the occasional drink, no he didn't do drugs (reddening at the directness of the question), no girlfriend at the moment (nosy beggar, but maybe this was worth it if he could manage to secure a room in this amazing flat).

'You'll be sharing the flat with my daughter and three other students,' Magnusson said at last. Then, the very ghost of a smile as he offered his huge hand in a firm grasp. Ah, his daughter, thought Colin, remembering the room with the closed door.

'That's it?' Colin said, surprised. Then he smiled too, a smile that turned into a grin of genuine delight.

'You can choose one of three rooms,' Magnusson told him, leading the way back into the hall. 'The one next to my daughter's.' He waved a hand as they passed the large bedroom next to the communal bathroom. 'Or one of the two upstairs. The front bedroom has already been taken.'

Colin considered for a moment, entering the square room that looked down over the railway. It was airy enough and had the advantage of being near the front door so he could come and go without being heard, should he manage to keep on the evening shift at the restaurant. Like the other three bedrooms he had already seen it was furnished with a smart modern desk and a decent-sized bed (probably IKEA, but top of their range), as well as a brand new wardrobe and a comfortable-looking Lloyd Loom chair painted in a shade of pastel green to match the duvet and curtains. An empty pinboard hung above the desk and there was a green desk lamp placed to one side. The other rooms upstairs did not have an old-fashioned lamp like this and Colin nodded, imagining himself writing here late into the night, his fingers flying over the keys of his ancient laptop.

'Yes,' he said, 'I'll have this room, thanks.'

'A decent young man, I'd say, and the girl is definitely going to be an asset.' Henrik Magnusson lifted his wine glass, eyes twinkling over its rim as Eva looked at him enquiringly. They were dining tonight in the Chardon D'Or, a quiet restaurant in the city centre that was handy for Magnusson's hotel.

'How do you mean?' the girl asked, head tilted to one side.

'Well,' Henrik began, 'she's at Caledonian University and is taking a degree course in hospitality management. She was *very* taken with the kitchen.' He smiled broadly. 'I imagine you will not starve with Miss Wilson at Merryfield Avenue.'

Eva frowned, then her brow cleared. *Frowning gave one lines* was the mantra that her home tutor had dinned into her. 'Just because she is doing a hospitality course doesn't mean she will be a good cook,' she reasoned.

'She said she *loved* cooking,' Henrik replied firmly, taking up one of the tiny pastries from his plate and nibbling on it. 'The mother's a professional cook,' he added, as if to underline his point.

'And the father?'

'A policeman.'

Eva nodded, her eyes lowered towards her plate as though she were more interested in the *amuse-bouches*. 'She sounds suitable.'

There were no further questions from his daughter and Henrik appreciated that. Eva respected his judgement, after all, and the students that he chose to live in his daughter's flat would be ones who would bring something positive into her life. Kirsty Wilson was a nice enough girl, a little on the podgy side, but with a cheerful, open manner that had endeared her to the Swede. Eva would like her, he was certain of that. And the young man, Colin, he would add something to the flat too, a steadiness of purpose. He had not missed the gleam in the lad's eyes as he looked at the pale wooden desk and the antique lamp. He had arranged for the interview to take place between work shifts, too, so he was a grafter, not the kind to laze about taking handouts from the State. Tomorrow Henrik was to interview several other candidates for the vacant rooms at Merryfield Avenue, but tonight he and Eva would spend time together, enjoying the pleasures of fine dining before taking a stroll around the city. Glasgow had many good things to offer, Henrik knew, from his business trips here, and he looked forward to showing them to the girl who sat opposite, a ready smile on her lips as soon as she caught her father's eyes looking at her.

What Henrik Magnusson did not see, would never see, was the girl's fingers clasped tightly together, the nails of one hand pressed hard into the palm of the other as though to stop her from screaming.

CHAPTER 4

'You'd have to see it to believe it,' Rodge insisted. 'The place is stuffed full of paintings, and there are these wee spindly chairs, their seat covers all embroidered. You know the kind I mean, dead fragile, not really for sitting on.'

'In a student flat?' one of the boys around the table asked, putting down his beer mug and wiping the froth from his lips.

'Won't suit you then, Rodge!' another exclaimed, heralding a peal of laughter from around the table.

'Aye, not what you'd expect, eh?' Rodge beamed as though he had won the lottery instead of simply being given the keys to a duplex flat in Anniesland.

'So no parties at yours this year then?' the first boy grunted.

Rodge's grin faded as he took in the blunt statement. Last year had seen loads of the lads from the rugby club descend on one another's places for nights of steady drinking and revelry that were always followed up by days of clearing rubbish and trying to mend whatever had been broken in the weekend jollities; or explaining things to the landlord.

'No, I suppose not,' he murmured, the shine of the moment suddenly taken from him. 'You should see it though,' he continued, remembering the upstairs room at the end of the corridor with its skylight window and the view over the rooftops. But the conversation had turned to new signings in the Scottish Premier League and Roger Dunbar sat back, wondering for a moment if the flat at Merryfield Avenue had been such a good idea after all.

He shifted in his chair, feeling his knees pressing against the pub table, a spasm of annoyance creasing his usually good-humoured face. The boys were right, of course. A big lad like him had no place in a flat that contained so many antiques and delicate valuables. He'd probably knock into them just going down that spiral staircase; *accident prone* his stepmother always said with that wee laugh that made Roger wonder if she was getting at him or not. Why had that Swedish man been so keen to have him as a tenant, then? He was a big lad an' all, easily Roger's own height of six five. But there the resemblance ended. Mr Magnusson had the sort of aura that only very wealthy folk had; his suede jacket looked as if it was old but it oozed class, and the plain white cuffs of his shirt had been fastened with what looked like solid gold cufflinks, some fancy monogram engraved on them. Roger's jeans and rugby shirt were clean enough, but the older man had made him feel a bit scruffy. Still, he had been interesting to talk to and the engineering student had listened as well as given answers to the list of queries the man had ready for him, questions that he guessed were tailored to finding the right folk for the flat.

Roger might look like a great big teddy bear with his shock of red hair and friendly countenance but he wasn't stupid and could usually see past appearances to the person within. Magnusson had struck him as a bit of a loner. It was obvious that he was dead wealthy, and had he said something to suggest he was a success-ful businessman? His new tenant thought so but there was something else about him that Roger Dunbar had noticed. How could he describe it? The aloofness that bordered on downright

24

rudeness – all these bloody questions! – had slipped the moment he had mentioned his daughter. The man had simply glowed as if someone had lit a candle inside him. Roger had nodded, a bit embarrassed, but he had stored away the memory, seeing the man's vulnerable spot and realising he had been chosen not for his academic record or his sporting prowess but for something to do with the Swedish girl whose flat he would be sharing. Had the father seen a big lad who might be handy around the house? Or was it something else?

Roger supped his pint, nodding as the lads roared back and forth in protest at the shenanigans of certain football managers. He had the sense that he was moving on. Yes, there would still be the nights with the lads, yes he'd still be keen to keep his place in the first fifteen but the session ahead seemed to beckon with the promise of a different sort, a time that involved the finer things of life, perhaps.

Had he known it then, sitting on that sunlit evening in a pub in Byres Road, known that his life was soon to change for ever, Roger Dunbar might have taken the signed lease of 24 Merryfield Avenue from his back pocket and torn it into tiny little pieces.

CHAPTER 5

September

The hills swept before him, swathes of green on either side of the road, a distant line of conifers marching across the skyline. He was only an hour away from the city but this landscape, devoid of any habitation, could have been hundreds of miles from anywhere. The journey had taken Gary more than five hours and, although he had stopped only once to refill the petrol tank and gobble down a quick hamburger, it felt as though he had been travelling all day. Already, home seemed not just far away but far behind him in the choices he had made. He was on his own now, independent at last; he could go anywhere and do anything he wanted. The thought gave him a sudden giddy feeling, as though he were standing on the edge of a precipice, waiting to fly off into the unknown.

Gary grinned, taking the bend through the hills a little more carefully. Daft notion! He was simply transferring from one university to another, taking the chance to be away from home for the next few years. Or for good? a little voice asked him, making Gary Calderwood's grin fade a little. He was the cherished only son of a mother who was on her own now, and in spite of the way she

26

kept telling everyone that *Gary must make his way in the world* he knew she would miss him badly. Dad's death last year had given them all a jolt. Gary's smile faded as he remembered. He had dropped out of university for a year, staying at home to help Moira over the worst of the shock, doing all the things that needed to be done.

His glance fell on the dashboard of the new Mini Cooper and his face lit up once more. It had been a welcome surprise to find in his father's paperwork that he and his mother had been left very comfortably off. Dad had never thrown his money about and he'd had this terrific work ethic, encouraging his son to earn money, never giving him handouts, so that Gary had not realised quite the extent of the family's wealth. Ah well, he thought, swinging the car around a bend that curved into a long stretch between bracken-clad hills, everything seemed to be working out now. When the chance to transfer from Birmingham to Glasgow University had arrived, Gary had grabbed it at once. He didn't know much about Scotland but it was an opportunity to begin afresh, away from the memories that still haunted him. Yes, Mum would miss him, but the description of the flat in Merryfield Avenue had cheered her up enough to tell all her friends and neighbours about it. And, although Gary hadn't actually made any promises, he thought that Moira might come up and visit once he was settled in.

The sun came out from behind a cloud as the car emerged from the shadow of the hills and Gary reached for his sunglasses. He had given a nod to the Scottish Saltire as the Mini Cooper had crossed the border from England into Scotland: it was the first time he had ever driven up as far north as this, his previous trips to Glasgow having been made by plane. Mr Magnusson had been really helpful on the last visit when he had confirmed his tenancy of the flat. It had been almost too simple, really; Gary's late father had known the Swede through business, and a mutual acquaintance had mentioned that the young man was looking for a place to rent in Glasgow. He'd been asked all sorts of questions, of course – and had lied about his smoking habit – but the Swede seemed to have taken a shine to Brian Calderwood's son. It wouldn't be long now, he thought, glancing at the road signs; the city would soon be in sight and before the sun set over the horizon he would be meeting his flatmates, including the Swedish girl who was to be his landlady.

Eva closed the door behind her and dropped the carrier bags onto the floor. She had thought it might be fun to rummage around in the second-hand shops, purchasing stuff that made her look like every other Glasgow student, but her wanderings had taken her further than she had planned after one shop assistant had given her the addresses of several boutiques specialising in designer clothes. The excitement she had anticipated about merging into the Glasgow scene had all but evaporated once she had taken the time and trouble to select garments that she knew would look good on her. It was just like being back in Stockholm, being waited upon by the staff at Nitty Gritty, choosing clothes to wear that would meet with her father's approval. Henrik always liked his girl to give him a fashion parade, twirling in front of him to show off any new outfits.

Eva had thought ... well, what had she thought? That an old mended cardigan would give her the freedom to be herself for a change? Sighing, she picked up the bags again and turned into the room at the back of the flat that she had chosen for her own. It was cooler in here after the sultry heat of the city streets and she took several deep breaths, smelling the woody scent from last night's candle. The window was open wide and the cream-coloured muslin curtains moved sideways as a draught of fresh air entered the room. Outside, a pigeon cooed its velvety note, a sound that was at once calming to the girl. She stood motionless by the window, looking out at the trees and the sky, wondering what she would do once this place was full of the noise of other people coming and going.

A quick glance at the antique porcelain clock on the mantelpiece told her that she had barely three more hours of solitude. Tonight, 24 Merryfield Avenue would be occupied by young men and women intent on discovering each other's personalities, trying out conversational gambits on one another, jockeying for position with the one person who would rather they were not there at all.

Eva Magnusson sighed. Perhaps they would be nice. Perhaps she might even find friendship with the girl, Kirsty, though she doubted that they would have much in common. Her lips moved in a practised curve: she would be gracious and friendly towards them all, never allowing any one of them to see past the smile that she had learned to put on for every single person in her young life.

CHAPTER 6

The old man stood behind the door, watching through the crack as the last of them pulled his baggage over the top step and stood on the threshold of the house next door. This one was a tall lad with a shock of red hair, broad shouldered, too. Derek McCubbin couldn't see his face but he had glimpsed a rugged-looking countenance as the young man turned into the doorway. His eyes flicked across the boy's bare arms but there were no disfiguring tattoos there to make him snort with disapproval. In his day a single anchor had been enough. Nowadays their entire arms were a mess of ink, like the scribbles on a teenager's school jotter.

At the sound of the bell the Swedish girl opened the door and Derek stood still, hardly daring to breathe. His new neighbour smiled up at the red-haired lad and in moments the door was closed to his prying eyes, but not before he'd had yet another peek into that familiar hallway with its high, proud ceilings. Oh Grace, why did you have to leave me?

Then he shut his own door, hearing the soft click, and sank into the ancient chair that was placed next to the hallstand. Derek's heart raced suddenly, making him experience that choking sensation again, and he clasped his arms across his chest, feeling his whole body shake with emotion. It was necessary to sit quietly until it passed, he told himself, taking deep breaths in and out like that slip of a nurse had told him. It would pass, he told himself, then he would be strong again.

He could hear the rattle of a train on the track slowing down as it reached the station. Then a car passed by on the street below. The clock in the hall ticked on, beat after beat. Derek listened, realising that with each second that passed he was nearer to an eternity that gaped like a dark maw ready to swallow him up. He fiddled with the hearing aid in his right ear, the one closest to the door, but there was no sound at all, no voices from the flat across the landing, no laughter or merriment to make him scowl from under his bushy grey eyebrows.

'Well, let's have a toast,' Gary said, raising the flute of sparkling wine that Eva had insisted on pouring out for them. 'To Eva, for sharing her fabulous flat with us all!'

The blonde girl blushed and tilted her head but her smile seemed to reassure the four people who raised their glasses and then clinked them one after the other.

Kirsty Wilson took a step backwards until she felt the base of her spine rest against the Belfast sink. As she sipped the bubbly stuff (was it real champagne?), Kirsty had a moment to suss out her new flatmates. She had been first to arrive and had spent a quiet half hour chatting to Eva Magnusson, during which time she had decided that the girl was probably a little shy. She had shown Kirsty around the flat after she had dumped her luggage in her spacious new bedroom. *This used to be the dining room, I believe*, Eva had said as the girls had stood there looking out to the tenement flats across the street. She had a lovely voice, Kirsty thought, soft and melodious with the sort of accent that folk described as

Transatlantic. Her English was, of course, perfect and Kirsty had found herself warming to the Swedish girl's hesitant but well-mannered attempts at making her new flatmate feel at ease.

She's never done this before, Kirsty told herself, watching as Eva smiled and listened to the three boys discussing their university courses. It was, Eva had admitted earlier, the first time she had been away from Sweden to study and now Kirsty found herself wondering if it was the girl or her father who had decided that buying this flat in Glasgow was a good idea.

'How about you, Kirsty? What are you studying?' One of the lads, Colin, had detached himself from the group and wandered over to her side. He was a nice-looking chap, pale faced with a slick of mousey brown hair that he kept flicking back from his forehead.

'Oh, I'm doing a course in hospitality management at Caledonian,' Kirsty replied. 'So you'll be all right for Sunday roasts,' she laughed.

'With Yorkshire puddings?' he asked hopefully, smiling back.

Kirsty grinned and nodded, liking the lad immediately and seeing something reassuring in his honest, open countenance. She felt herself relaxing for the first time since coming here. Colin would be okay, she thought to herself. He was ... how would she describe her first impressions of this lad? *Safe*. Yes, that kind of summed him up and Kirsty was glad that one of the boys at least made her feel comfortable.

'How about yourself?' she asked, taking another sip of the bubbly stuff. (Flippin' Nora! It *was* champagne!)

Colin made a face. 'Och, I'm doing the bog-standard Arts degree course. Managed to get into Junior Honours to do English Lit.' He shrugged.

Kirsty heard the self-deprecating tone and nodded again. It was typical of the Scots to make light of something big and this nice young man seemed no exception.

'What d'you want to do after?'

'Write,' Colin replied immediately. 'I've always wanted to be a writer. I've had a few things published, poetry and stuff ... ' He tailed off, glancing round as though he hoped the other boys weren't listening.

'Great,' Kirsty enthused. 'Maybe you can show me them some-time?'

'Yeah?' Colin's eyebrows rose in surprise. 'If you like,' he said. 'But you know what I really want? To write a novel. I fancy trav-elling a bit. Australia, maybe. Pick up some work here and there.'

Kirsty noticed the dreaminess in his eyes as he looked away from her. Yet it was a good dream, after all: jobs here were hard to come by and these days an Arts degree wasn't a passport to a defi-nite career.

As the girl stood in a corner of the kitchen she had the advan-tage of watching the small group drinking their champagne by the big black kitchen table. Roger had already finished his drink and had put down the glass flute; now he was standing over the other pair, hands stuffed in his pockets, listening as Gary explained the connection between his late father and Henrik Magnusson. He'd be happier with a pint in his great fist, Kirsty thought as she observed the big red-haired lad, then wondered if Roger Dunbar would really fit in with the rest of them in this flat with its pretty furnishings. She caught him glancing over at her and for some reason this made Kirsty look down and blush as though he had guessed what she'd been thinking.

Rodge folded the last of his clothes and tucked them into the bottom drawer. The room wasn't at all bad, he mused, looking around. No dreadfully steep coombed ceilings to contend with, so there must still be a fair old bit of attic space somewhere up there. The bed was a decent size, too; that wee bed in his previous digs was something he had found hard to bear, his feet perpetually cold on winter mornings, thrust out of a duvet that never properly covered him up. He wandered over to the skylight window and opened it, gulping in the chill evening air. Someone down in the street was singing, a maudlin sort of sound that made Rodge grin. The pub was just around the corner and it was probably closing time. He'd noticed the assortment of tables and chairs on the wide pavement as he'd arrived earlier this evening: that would be a good howff for them if he could coax the Swedish bird away from her posh drinks. The other girl looked as if she enjoyed a few beers; Rodge hadn't missed those swelling breasts under that baggy tunic top. Looked a nice enough lass and he'd laughed at her stories of college when they'd eventually moved into the lounge.

They'd sat there for ages, Eva topping up their drinks. Thank God she'd produced bottles of Staropramen from one of the fridges! Then she'd lit these big square candles on the hearth and their faces had gleamed in the flickering light, especially Eva's. Rodge thought about that face now as he looked out at the darkened street. How could he describe her to his mates without sounding like a total prat? How did you talk about a girl who was so bloody perfect? He remembered how her flawless skin seemed to glow in the candlelight, her eyes grave as she listened to them talking, and her hair ... Rodge sighed. He'd give anything to run his big hands through that stream of pale golden hair. Ach, who was he kidding? A girl like Eva was way out of his league and he'd do well to remember that and not moon after her. Besides, he told himself, as he closed the window and flopped down on the bed, it

34

didn't do to have these sorts of relationships with your flatmates if you were to get along happily all year.

'It's me,' Eva said. She was lying on the bed, mobile phone tucked against her ear. 'Yeah, they seem okay. How about you?' She listened as the voice on the other end of the line replied, his familiar tones making her face light up, the smile softening her lovely features. 'Sounds good. Anyway, when are we going to meet up?' Eva's fingers strayed absently to the ends of her hair, twisting the strands as she waited for the reply.

'You're a sweetheart,' she said at last, sighing deeply. 'See you tomorrow, then. Sleep well.'

The girl clicked the phone shut then clutched it tight as she rolled over onto her side, staring out into the darkness of the Glasgow night.

'Thank God,' she whispered to herself. 'There's one person in my life who understands.'

CHAPTER 7

November

The train station at Anniesland was very close by, handy for Kirsty and Eva to get into the city centre and their respective classes. The boys usually took the bus or, if it fitted in with his own timetable, cadged a lift with Gary in his Mini Cooper.

'Phew! Glad we got these seats!' Kirsty exclaimed, flopping down opposite the Swedish girl. Already she felt hot and uncomfortable after running up the steps to the platform to catch the train but, looking across at her flatmate, she saw that Eva didn't even seem to have a hair out of place. Sure, there was a faint rosy glow to her cheeks but maybe that was simply the reflection from the pink cashmere scarf that was draped around her neck. The girl sat back against the seat, hands folded on her lap, smiling her usual smile. Kirsty grinned back but for a fleeting moment she experienced a twitch of envy as she regarded her friend. How did she manage to look like a supermodel in that plain grey coat and cream lacy tights? Was it the classy leather boots in that ox-blood colour that matched her satchel? Kirsty let out an involuntary sigh as the train pulled away from the platform. She would never, in a hundred years, manage to look as well groomed as Eva

Magnusson. Maybe it was something about being Swedish, she thought, glancing at her reflection in the window. Weren't they all gorgeous and blonde?

As the ticket inspector came to check their tickets, Kirsty caught him pausing to smile down at the girl opposite, though he barely gave *her* travel pass a glance. It was as though Eva could cast a spell over anyone she met, Kirsty Wilson thought to herself. Then she gave a mental shrug and pulled out one of her textbooks and rested it on the edge of the table top that separated them both. But try as she might, the words were a blur as her thoughts turned to the students who lived in the Anniesland flat.

Last night Betty Wilson had phoned and Kirsty had enthused about the flat, trying to show how much fun she'd been having. Since the beginning of the new term they had established a sort of routine, she'd explained to her mother. Didn't Kirsty mind her role as the flat's Mummy? Betty had asked, a slightly resentful note in her voice as though these students had been taking advantage of her daughter's good nature. Oh, no, Kirsty had replied. She enjoyed preparing and cooking for them most nights, and there was always someone to chat to, standing by her side peeling and chopping to her instructions. More often than not it was Colin, whose classes finished early in the day, but she hadn't mentioned this to her mother for some reason.

Kirsty had found herself more and more in Colin's company and at first she had suspected that the lad had only sought her out for the goodies she produced from that wonderful oven, but gradually it had become a habit to sit and chat over endless mugs of coffee, putting the world to rights. There was something relaxing about spending time with Colin: yes, he'd be good boyfriend material but Kirsty preferred his friendship. Perhaps it was the way they always managed to open up to one another, as if they'd been friends for years rather than weeks?

Funny how they had all got into a routine so quickly, Kirsty mused. It was flattering how the others wanted to come home in time to share whatever she had decided to cook each night, and then they would spend most of their evenings together. After the lads had stacked the dishwasher – strangely it was never Eva who did this – they'd often go round to the pub, strolling back home by ten o'clock to watch the evening news on the television.

'Kirsty, we have arrived at Queen Street,' Eva said, breaking into her reverie and making her stuff the book hastily back into her bag and join the queue waiting to get off the train.

The platform was jammed with commuters disembarking, at this time of day mostly students heading for one of the city's universities. A quick ride in the underground from Buchanan Street would take the Glasgow Uni students to Hillhead or Kelvin Bridge but it was a short walk for both Eva and Kirsty from Queen Street station to their morning classes at Strathclyde and Caledonian universities.

Kirsty followed her friend to the automatic barrier then slipped her ticket in the slot, watching it being swallowed up. Then they made their way out of the press of people and headed uphill towards Cathedral Street and the spot where their paths diverged.

'Hey, d'you want to meet up for lunch?' Kirsty suggested. 'I've got a space between twelve and one.'

Eva's smile was still in place as she shook her head, Kirsty noted, but there was something different about the girl today; she had hardly said a word since they had left the flat and there was a faraway look in those blue eyes as if she were harbouring a secret that she wanted to hug to herself.

'Okay. See you tonight, then!' she called out cheerfully and Eva gave her a desultory wave before disappearing among a stream of students heading up Montrose Street.

The Swedish girl glanced at the familiar figure of a tall young man who loped past her, his eyes raking her face for any signs of recognition, but she looked straight ahead again as though completely unaware of his interest, her smile drooping a little lest he think she wanted to engage in conversation. He reminded her a little of Colin, that longing look in his eyes like a spaniel waiting for a titbit from its master. She was used to it now, this attention from young men in her orbit. After the first few weeks of the term it had become tedious though she was always careful not to show it, smiling and talking politely, giving them the brush-off so nicely that they didn't even realise what was happening.

At least she could tell her secret friend about it all, giggling sometimes as they chatted together on the telephone late into the night.

Eva breathed out a long sigh as she came to the crest of the hill. It was evident that Kirsty had no idea just what she had been up to these past few nights. Her smile broadened as she thought what the other girl's reaction might have been. Shock? Maybe. Envy? Well, she wasn't so sure about that: Kirsty was a fairly contented soul who seemed happy enough just to remain friends with everyone she met. But that was not enough for Eva Magnusson, she told herself. She had always wanted more and it was a delicious discovery to find just how easy it was to have it all, especially when it was spiced with the thrill of being hidden in the darkness.

CHAPTER 8

Gary crept back up the spiral staircase, his bare feet brushing each tread of carpet as he listened. There was no sound, however, only the thickness of his breath as he left the lower floor of the flat and headed to his own room again. A sudden flurry of rain pattered against the skylight window as he reached the top of the staircase, making the young man pause, one hand on the curve of the banister rail. Winter storms had been forecast for the remainder of this week and so Moira had called to postpone her visit to Glasgow till nearer Christmas. That was fine with him, Gary thought, a grin creasing his handsome features. His nights were taken with so much fun that he would be hard put to stay awake in class let alone trail his mother around the sights of the city.

The white-painted door gave a creak as he pushed it wide then he was inside and closing it carefully behind him. He rubbed his groin gently, groaning a little as he felt the raw and tender flesh. God! It was true what they said about Swedish girls after all! Gary slipped into bed, relishing the cool sheets against his warm body. He would find it difficult to get to sleep, visions of their antics still hot and hard in his brain. And she was probably asleep already, little minx! Anybody seeing her at breakfast morning after morning would never guess what sort of sexual gymnastics she'd been putting him through, leaving him yawning over his cornflakes. Kirsty had asked him only yesterday if he was coming down with a cold. Gary snickered to himself. He'd managed to keep a straight face, only glancing once at Eva, but the girl had been intent on mixing some of her home-made muesli and had not even acknowledged his presence in the kitchen.

The grin on his face turned to a frown as he began to wonder why the Swedish girl had been so insistent that they keep their affair a secret from the others. Then, as though the thought was too much for his sleepy brain, he closed his eyes and visualised that creamy white body stretching upwards in an arc as he knelt before her.

CHAPTER 9

December

Kirsty turned the key in the door and closed it behind her with a sigh. The hall was in darkness and there was no sound coming from the living room. Her shoulders moved up and down in a shrug of resignation; she was alone in the flat again. Then she remembered. Wasn't there some party that Eva had mentioned? They'd all be there, wouldn't they? Pulling off her thin raincoat and hanging it on the old-fashioned wooden coat stand, Kirsty sauntered into the bedroom next to the front door, unbuttoning her jacket. It was fair handy having this big room to herself, especially when she was working late shift at the hotel. Nobody would be disturbed by *her* comings and goings. She took off her shoes and tossed her jacket, bag and mobile phone onto the bed. Oh, it was good to be home. A wee cup of hot chocolate and some of her own gingerbread would go down well, she thought, already imagining her teeth sinking into a thick slab of treacly cake.

She stopped for a moment, listening. There was a swish then a click as the front door opened and closed again. Then, nothing.

'Colin? Is that you back already?' Kirsty wandered out into

the hall, her bare feet sinking into the pile of the hall carpet, still thick and soft despite all their winter boots tramping back and forth. Eva's father had spared no expense in doing up this flat for his daughter and Kirsty Wilson was grateful for those small luxuries that were absent from most of her friends' student flats.

'Colin?' She stopped again, hovering outside Colin's bedroom door, listening. It was firmly shut and there was no sound from within. Where was the boy? He was the only one likely to return home early from a party. She turned to look at the front door but it was shut fast. Had she not closed it properly? And had the wind blown it shut?

Frowning slightly, Kirsty padded down the unlit corridor, one hand out ready to flick on the light switch as she reached the kitchen. But something made her turn left into the living room instead, just to see if anyone was at home after all.

At first she imagined the girl had fallen asleep, sprawled out in front of the television.

'Eva?'

Kirsty moved forward and bent down, expecting the girl to sit up and yawn. One hand reached out to touch the back of her head but then she drew back as though guided by some inner instinct.

She stood up again and stepped around the recumbent figure, unaware that she was holding her breath.

Then, as Kirsty saw the expression in the dead girl's eyes, the thin wail escaping from her open mouth turned into a scream of terror.

Detective Superintendent Lorimer crouched over the body, aware of the sounds of voices coming from the hall. The dead girl was lying on her back, one arm flung out, the fist curled tightly in the moment of death. Her head was bent to one side, blond hair partly obscuring her features, but Lorimer could see enough to make him wonder about the cause of death.

'Manual strangulation?' he asked, glancing up at the consultant pathologist who was kneeling on the other side of the girl's body. The on-duty pathologist tonight was his friend, Dr Rosie Fergusson. He glanced at her with his usual admiration for her calm efficiency, knowing how different she could be at home as a doting mother and as the wife of Professor Brightman, an eminent psychologist and sometime criminal profiler who had worked with Lorimer in the past.

'Looks like it,' Rosie murmured, her gloved hands smoothing the hair from the victim's face, letting Lorimer see for the first time what Kirsty Wilson had found earlier that night.

Eva Magnusson still had that ethereal quality in death that had captivated those who had gazed upon her: Lorimer saw the perfect oval face with flawless skin and bow-shaped lips that were slightly parted as though she had been taken by surprise. He watched as Rosie reached out to close the dead girl's eyelids, seeing for the final time those pale blue Scandinavian eyes staring out at a world that had proved less than kind.

'It's not her only injury, though,' Rosie went on, turning the girl's head to one side. 'Someone's whacked her skull with a hefty object. Feel that,' she offered, showing Lorimer a contusion towards the back of the victim's skull.

The detective superintendent stroked the lump under the swathe of pale blond hair, nodding his agreement, trying to visualise just what had taken place in this room. Had someone broken in? Had it been a burglary gone wrong? There was still plenty to examine in this crime scene before a post-mortem even took place, providing them with more answers.

44

'Is *she* okay?' Rosie jerked her head towards the lounge door, listening to the renewed sound of sobbing.

Lorimer looked at her and sighed. 'I doubt it. Being a cop's daughter hasn't given her any immunity from this sort of horror.'

'Alistair still here then?'

Lorimer nodded. He had taken his detective sergeant's call less than two hours ago, minutes after Kirsty Wilson's hysterical phone call to her father. Like any crime scene, 24 Merryfield Avenue was now cordoned off at street level and the SOCOs had been quick to respond. Several white-suited figures had already come and gone from the lounge area, photographing the body and its immediate surroundings; now they awaited others who would come to take samples that would be sent to the labs at Pitt Street for forensic analysis.

Strictly speaking this was not a case that would usually be handled by an officer of his own rank but Alistair Wilson was more than just a colleague. The night shift DS from A Division who usually acted as scene-of-crime manager hadn't demurred when he'd arrived to find Detective Superintendent Lorimer and Detective Sergeant Wilson already in the Anniesland flat. DI Jo Grant was already on her way at Lorimer's request: she would take over as SIO once she arrived and caught up with everything.

'When do you think you'll ...'

'Do the post-mortem? Well, I expect it'll be later on today. I'm on call all this weekend, as you know.' Rosie made a face and then grinned. 'Just as well your Maggie takes her godmotherly duties seriously, eh?'

Lorimer smiled back. He and Maggie had tried and failed at the parenting game but since Abigail Margaret Brightman's arrival last year, that gap seemed to have been filled to everyone's satisfaction. The baby was a one-year-old bundle of fun as far as

Maggie Lorimer was concerned, and with no sleepless nights to spoil the image of her beloved goddaughter, Maggie had taken to her role with relish. Abby's father, Professor Solomon Brightman, would be attending a conference at the University of Newcastle later today so Maggie was needed to look after Abby until one of her parents returned home again.

Lorimer straightened up as the officers came into the room carrying the body bag. Soon they would carefully transfer the corpse into the black container, zipping it up so that it became one more anonymous cadaver on a stretcher. The sigh that escaped him held an involuntary tremor, as though something deep inside wanted to cry out in protest at the sheer waste of a young life.

Then a real cry of '*No!*' made the hairs on the back of his neck stand up as a young man burst into the room. A uniformed officer struggled to hold him back, but not before Lorimer had time to see the sheer horror on the newcomer's face.

'Eva?' he whispered, his mouth open as he looked at the shapeless form lying on the floor. Then the boy slumped sideways against the door jamb as though his legs had suddenly decided they were too weak to support him and the officer had little difficulty in bundling him back out into the hallway and into the kitchen.

'Who's that?' Lorimer asked.

Rosie shrugged. 'Must be one of the students who live with Kirsty and our little friend here,' she nodded, her voice tinged with regret. Dr Rosie Fergusson might be well used to examining the dead, young and old alike, but she had never become so hardened with practice that she could not understand the pain that surrounded a sudden death like this. 'Poor boy,' she sighed. 'At least he was spared seeing her close up . . . '

Lorimer gave her a pat on the shoulder before leaving the room and following the officer into what was a large, square kitchen. He looked up at the array of plants cascading down from a set of false beams, ducking instinctively lest his six-foot-four frame knocked against them.

Kirsty Wilson was sitting at a big black table, her arms around the young man's heaving shoulders, and Lorimer hesitated for a moment, reluctant to disturb the pair. He watched as Kirsty sought to calm her flatmate, her voice murmuring something in a soft gentle tone, and the policeman was struck by the girl's evident maturity: she, who only a short time ago had been stricken with shock, was now capable of administering some tenderness towards another rather than seeking a shoulder to cry on for herself.

'It's okay, Colin,' she was telling him, 'it's okay.'

Lorimer pursed his lips into a grim line. It was anything but *okay*, but what words could you use to console a young man in such hellish circumstances?

The boy looked up then, his pale face streaked with tears, eyes already bloodshot.

'Who're you?' he said, straightening up as he looked at Lorimer.

''S okay, Colin. This is Mr Lorimer,' Kirsty told him, stroking his sleeve as though he were a small child.

'Detective Superintendent Lorimer,' Lorimer said, coming forward and putting out his hand.

Colin Young took it and as he gave it a perfunctory shake Lorimer could feel the trembling and sweat on the boy's palm.

'This is my flatmate, Colin,' Kirsty continued, looking up at Lorimer. 'Colin, he's my dad's boss, the one I told you about.' She turned back to the boy and grasped his shoulders a little more tightly.

'Oh,' Colin said, still staring at the tall policeman standing above them. Then he swallowed and Lorimer could see his Adam's apple bobbing in his throat. 'I didn't know . . .'

But what it was that Colin Young did not know was never uttered, for at that same moment Betty Wilson swept into the kitchen, arms outstretched.

'Oh, Kirsty!' she cried, and in a moment the girl was enveloped into Betty's embrace, leaving Colin Young looking suddenly bereft.

Lorimer slipped behind the table and sank into the chair beside the boy.

'Is there anyone you should be calling?' he asked.

Colin tore his gaze away from the mother and daughter for a moment and looked at Lorimer in a dazed fashion.

'Do you want us to contact anyone in your family? Arrange for them to take you home for tonight?'

'Why?'

As Colin shook his head Lorimer could see that he was utterly bewildered, still deeply in shock.

'There will be scene-of-crime officers all over the flat for hours to come,' he explained gently. 'You won't be allowed to stay here tonight.'

'What about the others?'

'Others?'

'Gary and Rodge. They're still at the party . . .' Colin's voice quavered and stopped and he looked down at his hands as though to prevent a fresh outburst of weeping.

'I can have officers here to take all three of you to your family homes later on, if that's what you'd like,' Lorimer continued.

'Gary's home's miles away. Down in England,' Colin gulped.

'We'll be taking statements from you all before you are allowed to go,' Lorimer said. 'But we'll want to know where you are. Is there a friend or a relative who could put you all up, perhaps?'

Colin shrugged, clearly overwhelmed.

'DS MacPherson is the scene-of-crime manager from Stewart Street police station who is in charge of everything right now. He'll explain what will happen over the next few days.'

Colin Young frowned. 'What d'you mean?'

'You can't stay here, Colin,' Lorimer said again. 'You'll be allowed to take some of your things once the officers in charge have obtained all available evidence but it'll probably be a few days before you're allowed back here again.' He smiled encouragingly. 'Forensics takes ages, you know? You've probably seen it all on *CSI*, eh?'

'I can't believe that she's dead,' the boy whispered, looking towards the hall through the glass door. Lorimer followed his gaze to see the Swedish girl's body being carried out. He saw Kirsty clutch at her mother's hand as they watched the two undertakers, suited and masked like all the other officers, carry her friend out of 24 Merryfield Avenue for the very last time.

It had been as a friend as well as his senior officer that Lorimer had arrived so quickly on the scene, Alistair Wilson's plea for help rousing him out of sleep. Whether he could be of any more help remained to be seen but, as Lorimer sat in that kitchen, watching Eva Magnusson being taken away, he vowed to spend some time with Kirsty, if only to soothe her with words of reassurance that the Swedish girl's killer would surely be caught.

CHAPTER 10

The Sunday papers were full of it, headlines proclaiming about the Swedish millionaire's daughter who had been found dead in her Glasgow flat. The city had come in for plenty of stick, Lorimer thought grimly, as he read the column inches about knife crime and drunkenness, with statistics to back them all up. With a sigh he pushed the papers from him and looked down at his breakfast, still untouched.

Maggie had already finished her grapefruit and toast and was bending over the dishwasher, stacking plates away. He bit his lip; she made such an effort to make these Sunday mornings a special time for them both.

He began to scoop out the pale pink flesh from his grapefruit, eating and swallowing but tasting little as his eyes fell once more on the page he had been reading.

Eva Magnusson was a student at the University of Strathclyde, studying for a degree in business and economics, Lorimer read. *The only child of property tycoon, Henrik Magnusson, Eva had been expected to take an active part in her father's business.*

Well, the poor man would be quite alone in the world now, Lorimer thought, reading the details of the man's life. Maggie had shaken her head in sympathy when he had read out the bit about the wife having died giving birth to their only daughter. *What a tragedy*, she'd said sadly, *to lose both the people in the world that you love the most*. And she'd put a protective hand upon his shoulder for a moment, as if to intimate what she and Lorimer were to one another.

'That coffee'll be getting cold,' Maggie said wryly. 'Shall I make us another pot?'

Lorimer looked up from the paper, a sheepish smile on his face.

'Thanks, love. That would be great.'

Yet, even as he nibbled the buttered toast, forgetting for once to spread it liberally with the last of Maggie's home-made marmalade, Lorimer's thoughts turned once more to his detective sergeant and the shocking murder that had taken place in Kirsty Wilson's Anniesland flat. Betty and Alistair had taken the girl home to West Kilbride that night and he had heard nothing from them since. It wasn't his shout, Lorimer told himself; his current responsibilities didn't include being SIO in a case like this and he had decided to let DI Jo Grant take this one on. He had to leave his DI space to get on with it. She knew where he was if she needed him and he knew that she would keep him informed at every stage of the investigation: she was a bright cookie and had experienced a variety of roles within the force, including work as an undercover officer.

Still, he couldn't help but be intrigued by the Swedish girl's murder. The lad, Colin, had gone with both of the other students from the flat; one a tall, ginger-headed boy, the other a good-looking lad with a Brummy accent. Lorimer had been leaving just as they had arrived, noting the expressions of dismay on both their faces as they had been held back at the cordon. Then uniformed officers had taken them into the van outside to talk to them and what little chance Lorimer had had to see their reaction to the terrible news about Eva Magnusson confirmed that they seemed equally shocked as Colin Young.

So, what on earth had happened? Had the girl brought some-one back to her flat as some of the Sunday papers had speculated? Someone who had been aggressive enough to choke the poor lass to death? *A moment of fury and a lifetime of regret*, was the way Lorimer remembered one judge expressing it as he had handed down a sentence in a previous case.

Rosie would have done the post-mortem by now but Maggie had not brought back any information after babysitting at the pathologist's home yesterday other than to confirm that the Swedish girl had indeed been strangled. It wasn't his case, Lorimer told himself again, biting his lip, but still he wanted to know what else Rosie might have found. The Brightmans would be spending today as quietly as baby Abigail allowed them, Rosie's mobile switched on in case she was called out again. Weekends tended to be fairly busy, given the level of drunkenness and violence that marred the city – the papers weren't wrong about that, he thought sadly – and there was a real chance that the pathologist would be back at another scene of crime somewhere in Glasgow before long.

So, when the phone rang, Lorimer was a little surprised to hear Rosie's voice.

'Hi, thought you'd want to know the results so far, in case Jo or Alistair discuss this with you,' she began.

'Yes, thanks. I appreciate that,' Lorimer told her.

'Well.' Rosie took a deep breath before continuing. 'We were right about the manual strangulation. But there are no fingerprints or sweat traces from the neck area so whoever did it wore gloves.'

'Hm.' Lorimer nodded, still listening intently. Not a moment of fury, then, but possibly a premeditated killing.

'In all probability she was attacked from behind with some-thing like a club. We've got photographs of the contusions but it's hard to tell what might have made that mark. We're working on it, though. And the other main thing to say is that she'd had sex some time in the evening. We've got good samples so our friends up at Pitt Street will be rejoicing about that.'

'Any signs of bruising in that area?'

'Nope. I'd say it's been consensual sex. Her knickers were still on, remember, and there was absolutely nothing to suggest that she had been hurt in any way.'

'Other than being choked to death.'

'Other than that, yes,' Rosie agreed drily.

There was a moment's silence while Lorimer digested the facts. Had it been his case, he would have wanted to know all about the girl's movements earlier that night but he trusted Jo Grant to have handed out actions that would result in answers to such questions. He would have to be careful not to interfere in another officer's case, especially at this crucial stage in an investigation.

'Well, thanks for that,' he said at last. 'You will let me know straight away if there are any developments, won't you?'

'Of course I will.'

'What about the girl's family?'

'Oh, the father's coming in to see me tomorrow. Couldn't get a flight from Stockholm any earlier. Not looking forward to that,' Rosie sighed.

'Okay, good luck,' Lorimer said. 'Want to speak to Maggie?'

He handed over the telephone to his wife who had been listening to the exchange, her Sunday supplement discarded on the table in front of her.

While the two women chatted, Lorimer sat back and thought about the case, and for a moment he wished for the days when he was a detective inspector, experiencing the familiar adrenalin rush that a new murder case always brought.

53

CHAPTER 11

Jo Grant ran her slim fingers through her dark hair, feeling the short gelled ends and wondering for the hundredth time why she had given that hair stylist such leeway. But it was a damn sight easier to wash and dry every morning and there would be no grubby little ned to grab a handful of her long hair as he was going out of the interview room. She could still remember the drug addict's breath in her face as he'd lunged at her before being carted back to the cells.

Great job, being a polis, her pal Heather had said as they'd met for drinks. *Good pay and early retirement*. Aye, right, Jo had been tempted to reply. You don't know the half of it. And you wouldn't want to.

It had been one hell of a weekend, from the call-out in the wee small hours of Saturday morning to the post-mortem she'd attended later that same day, and now she was back at Stewart Street at her desk, rummaging to find the files she had begun on the four students from Anniesland. They'd given statements on the night, of course, but some of these were a bit incoherent. Kirsty Wilson had been stunned into silence and at least two of the boys had seemed too drunk to focus properly.

Only Colin Young's statement had been clear and to the point.

Eva had been at the same party over in Kelvinbridge but she had left before the rest of them. He had been in the bathroom at the precise time she had left and had remembered looking for her, only to be told that she had gone home. Someone had made the usual joke about her turning into a pumpkin so he knew it must have been around midnight. When asked how she had gone home he had replied that Eva usually took a taxi back whenever they were out late.

The time she had left the party fitted nicely, Jo realised. If the girl had left just after midnight then she could easily have been back in the flat ten minutes later. And it was after one a.m. when Kirsty had found her lying in the lounge. Plenty time enough for someone to attack and kill a slip of a girl like that.

After giving what statements they could, the boys had all agreed to stay at a hotel in the city centre and come in with Kirsty Wilson this afternoon 'to have another talk' as the scene-of-crime manager had undoubtedly phrased it. 'Helping the police with their enquiries' was way too official and off-putting for four youngsters who had seemed deep in shock at the murder of their flatmate. Well, she'd really been their landlady, Jo mused, flicking through the thin pile of papers she had been given. Though the father had probably bought the place for his daughter, Eva Magnusson's name was definitely on the title deeds. They'd uncovered those, and other papers, in a large bureau in the main lounge.

What else did she know about the deceased? White female, about a hundred and five pounds, five feet three and a half inches, blond hair and – Jo bit her lip, remembering the girl's body before the post-mortem had begun – she'd had a face like an angel's.

'Stick to the facts,' she growled under her breath as she read her notes. Born in Stockholm to Maryka and Henrik Magnusson, mother dying shortly after the birth. How unusual in this day and age, Jo frowned. No siblings. So Daddy hadn't remarried, then? Not quite twenty years old. She put the first sheet aside and looked at the details of the girl's education. Home tutored, apparently, then summer courses at Jönköping International Business School before applying to study at the University of Strathclyde for a degree in business and economics.

Jo shook her head, wondering. Poor kid had hardly been out in the real world until she'd left home to come to Glasgow. She sighed. Eva Magnusson hadn't had much of a chance to spread her wings. Had her sheltered upbringing made her a vulnerable sort of creature, then? Prey to some of the more dangerous elements in this city? Well, she'd soon be finding out answers to these, and other questions, once the Swedish girl's flatmates came in to see her.

Kirsty Wilson stood in her old bedroom, a heap of clothes scattered on the floor at her feet. What the hell did you wear to a police station to discuss your friend's murder? A manic laugh threatened to escape as she realised the absurdity of her thought. All of yesterday Kirsty had veered between weeping and an awful numbness that had developed into a band of tension across her forehead. Mum had given her a couple of paracetamol at bedtime and she had been astonished to find that she had slept soundly until almost ten this morning.

Most of her clothes were still at the flat since Mum had practically bundled her out with only her jacket and bag lifted from the bed where she'd left them. Kirsty felt a surge of gratitude as she caught sight of the thick black tights and clean knickers placed over the back of the bedroom chair. Ever practical, Mum had washed them out for her, but somehow Kirsty could not face putting on the same clothes she had worn when she'd found Eva's body. There were her old black Levi's that were too tight for her now, but maybe she could yank the zip halfway up, hiding her stomach under a baggy jumper? She sighed. Mum and Dad would expect her to be a bit smarter than that, though, wouldn't they? Well, she could just keep her jacket on. Anyhow, who was going to bother about what she looked like? She bit her lip again. Did it really matter what sort of impression she would make for that detective inspector?

Colin had texted her earlier to ask when she was going to Stewart Street and she'd called him back to say that her dad was willing to pick them all up if they wanted. He'd sounded strange on the phone, bone weary, his voice heavy as though he had been doped up with something. And maybe he had, Kirsty thought, wondering how the three boys had coped together yesterday. Saturdays at the flat were normally great. Sometimes she would do a great big fry-up for them all, even Eva who would tuck into her French toast or scrambled eggs. Then one of them would race downstairs to the newsagent's for a paper and they'd spend ages deciding whether to see a film or stay in to watch *The X Factor*. It had all been so *normal*, Kirsty thought. So how could it have gone so wrong?

Kirsty and the three boys got out of Alistair Wilson's car and made their way to the main entrance of A Division, a three-storey build-ing surrounded by modern blocks of flats. The blue building was dwarfed by the high-rise tenements on several sides but it still managed to make an impression, the thistle badge sitting proudly over the front door.

Colin Young lagged behind the others, his hand sliding on the steel rail, his feet reluctant to follow his flatmates into the building. Yet, even once inside the foyer where there was nothing that ought to have intimidated him, Colin told himself, why did he have this peculiar sensation of dread? *You know fine*, a little voice whispered in his ear. *You're feart in case the other lads tell the police what happened at the party*. The glass doors and that blue mat were welcoming enough and Pete the Penguin with its jaunty police cap should have made him smile the way it had for Gary and Rodge who were pointing at the poster as they waited for someone to come for them. Colin's eyes were on other things, however: the bit of pale blue material that looked like a discarded curtain and those two polystyrene cups, one inside the other *sitting at an angle as if waiting to be taken away*. Colin composed the words in his head. Was there a story to tell from these objects? Even as his mind skirted their possibilities a woman in a blue overall emerged from behind the sliding doors and lifted them off, flicking a weary duster over the wooden seats.

It was comfortable enough sitting with his back against the dark wood, curved to make waiting less of a drag, he supposed. Some clever engineer of ergonomics had no doubt won a prize for that design. But the chairs curved around the wall were fixed firmly by bollard-like tubes, making Colin wonder about the need to secure the fixtures and fittings against vandalism. His musings were interrupted by the sound of footsteps approaching from the adjacent corridor.

'Miss Wilson?' A pleasant-faced constable had appeared through the wooden doors and then Kirsty was being ushered out, leaving the three boys alone in the reception area.

'I just don't understand it,' she whispered, her hands clasped around the glass of water that DI Grant had given her. The policewoman had been kind but efficient, asking questions slowly and writing down the answers as though everything that Kirsty said really mattered. But it didn't, of course. Nothing that she said would ever bring Eva back again.

'Did Eva have a boyfriend, do you know?' the DI asked.

Kirsty shook her head. 'Och, she could've had her pick. Boys were always falling over themselves for her, but there was no one special,' she replied. 'Not that I know of anyway.'

There was a silence during which she sensed a disquiet from the police officer. She frowned. 'What is it?'

Jo Grant gave a sigh. 'Eva's post-mortem examination shows that she had had sexual intercourse some time before she was killed,' she said at last.

'Dad never told me!' Kirsty exclaimed.

'He can't discuss the case with you, Kirsty. You are one of our main witnesses and so anything you say about it should be to us. You know that, don't you?'

Kirsty nodded silently.

'So, given that she was supposed to be at a party, can you think of anyone with whom Eva may have had sex?'

Kirsty shook her head. 'Better ask the boys,' she said shortly. 'I wasn't there. I was working, like I told you.'

'I will,' Jo said gently, holding out her hand. 'And I'm sorry to have to ask you things that are so upsetting, Kirsty. But sometimes girls confide things in one another, know what I mean?'

Kirsty nodded, feeling the tears begin to smart under her eyelids again. Had Eva ever confided in her? They'd talked, all right, for hours sometimes, but even in the months since she had met her, Kirsty had only gleaned little bits and pieces about the Swedish girl. And now even these were about to be laid bare in this bleak interview room.

*

'Roger MacDonald Dunbar,' the tall red-haired young man said, his fingers clasped nervously on the desk between them.

'And your date of birth, Roger?'

'Eighth of July, nineteen ninety-three.'

Jo Grant glanced up at the boy who was visibly sweating although the room was not particularly warm. He was a big lad, looked a bit like a farmer's boy in that waxed jacket, but the green eyes that met hers held a keen intelligence that warned Jo not to underestimate him. She tried not to give a second glance to the huge fists: they might easily have strangled a small girl like Eva Magnusson with not a great deal of effort. But why? Why would one of her friends kill her then go on back to continue partying the night away? Besides, Lorimer had hinted that each one of the boys had seemed genuinely shocked at their flatmate's death when he had seen them.

'Right, Roger, I'm DI Grant and I am the senior investigating officer in charge of the case,' Jo told him briskly.

'But I thought Kirsty's dad's boss . . .' Roger trailed off, his face colouring pink in confusion.

'Detective Superintendent Lorimer, you mean?'

Roger nodded, clearly uncomfortable at having made a gaffe right away.

'We are all under his authority,' Jo conceded, 'but it's quite normal for a detective inspector to carry out enquiries in a case like this.'

She could see the lad swallow and guessed that he was coming to terms not only with Eva's death but with the whole police procedure.

'Now, Roger, I need to ask you a few questions about Eva Magnusson and the night on which she was killed,' Jo continued in a no-nonsense sort of tone that she saw had an immediate effect on the lad. Roger Dunbar straightened up and the fidgeting fingers became still. He looked at her gravely, watching her face as she asked questions about the location of the party, who had been there, whether he had seen Eva slipping off with anyone.

Jo Grant felt her pulse quicken.

The young man had taken his time to consider most of her questions, thinking hard as if to visualise the scene. But when she asked that last question she could see him immediately stiffen.

'Eva left the party with someone?' Jo asked.

The boy licked his lips and swallowed again. As he began to reply, Jo could see the faint impression of marks on his lower lip where he had bitten off an immediate reply.

A shrug was all the reply he gave but Jo was not to be put off so easily.

'Come on, Roger, you can do better than that. Surely you remember a pretty girl like Eva getting off with someone, eh?'

The boy's hands were under the desk now and his shoulders were raised in twin peaks of tension.

'No.' He shook his head vehemently. 'No, I didn't see anyone with her. I would probably have been drinking in the kitchen with my mates,' he continued, a glint of bravado appearing in his eyes as he shrugged again. 'I was pretty out of it later on anyway,' he mumbled, looking down to avoid the DI's steady gaze.

Jo tried not to make a face. It was true that the lad had been drunk as a skunk. He'd thrown up in the street, narrowly missing the floor of the police van, one of the officers had told her. And yet … he was no fool and even a night's hard drinking hadn't made him forget everything that had happened at that party. His reaction to her questions had told her that at least. And now there was a stubborn cast to his mouth that the DI recognised as a decision on the student's part to clam up.

This wasn't going anywhere. She was certain from his body language that Roger Dunbar was lying to her and she was pretty sure that she knew why. Whoever had left the party that night with Eva Magnusson might well have been the last person to see her alive.

Rodge breathed a sigh of relief as he stepped out into the cold air. Someone had escorted him out of a different door from the way they had come in and, as he walked past the cars parked tightly together under a canopy, he realised that his initial impression of the place had disappeared. He and Gary had looked at all the posters on the walls of the reception area – anything to take their minds off why they were really there – laughing at the daft penguin, impressed by the well burnished plaque that mentioned a fallen comrade. It had given him a sense that the people working in this place shared a sense of pride in what they were doing. Was DI Grant proud of her methods? She hadn't believed him when he'd told her that he couldn't remember much. Why hadn't she just left it at that? Roger Dunbar scowled to himself as he walked up past the Piping Centre and waited for the lights to change. He'd given her his version of the events as he wanted to recall them and as far as he was concerned he was sticking to them.

Gary Calderwood was a nice-looking young man, smartly dressed in a polar fleece that looked like it had come straight off its clothes rail in the shop and jeans so new that they almost creaked when he moved. Plenty of money, DI Jo Grant decided, taking in the young man's appearance at a glance. He'd evidently gone out yesterday and bought himself some new clothes. Was he trying to make a good impression for his visit to this divisional headquarters? Or had he wanted to cast off any memory of Friday night? Maybe he was just a tad vain, Jo thought, watching as Gary smoothed a cowlick from his forehead. As the student entered the interview room Jo had caught a strong whiff of expensive aftershave. Eau Sauvage, she decided, remembering the brand her dad had used all his life. Now, leaning back in his chair, arms folded, she was aware of him watching her as she wrote down the date and time on her report sheet.

'Right, Mr Calderwood, thanks for coming in. I'm Detective Inspector Grant, the senior investigating officer in this case. You may remember me from Friday night, though we were all pretty similar, weren't we?' she joked. It may have been a frightening sight for the students, seeing all those figures, suited and masked, their gloved hands holding clipboards or bags for forensic equipment. Plus, the boys had been given the news about Eva Magnusson in a fairly brutal manner, arriving in their street to see the close mouth cordoned off and several police vehicles with blue lights flashing.

'No, sorry, I don't,' Gary said, then, leaning forward, he surprised Jo by sticking out his hand.

'How do you do, Inspector,' he added gravely.

Jo took the lad's hand, noticing his firm grip. This one was not a bit afraid of coming into a police station. A cool customer, then, and possibly more able to cope with Eva's death than the others.

'I know you gave a statement to DS MacPherson on Friday night, but there was a lot going on and I wanted to have the chance to chat to you,' Jo told him in as casual a manner as she could adopt.

'We were all a bit wrecked,' Gary replied ruefully, his expression apologetic.

'Yes,' Jo agreed then flicked through the file in front of her as if to find something important. In truth, she knew exactly where

Gary Calderwood's statement was, but it helped to give an air of gravitas to the proceedings, especially as the DI was conscious of the young man's eyes boring into her.

'I've got most of your details here, Mr Calderwood. You are a student at the University of Glasgow studying economics, is that right?'

Gary Calderwood nodded and Jo noticed him sitting back again in a relaxed fashion, his arms folded across his chest.

'The main point of bringing you all in to see me today is to find out what we can about Eva's movements on the night she died,' Jo continued, jumping into the interview with less of a preamble than she had intended.

A slight lift of his dark eyebrows was the only reaction displayed by the young man so Jo ploughed on.

'Can you tell me just what you remember about the party from the time you all left the flat until the time you arrived back again?' she asked, swinging her pen idly in her fingers as though she might or might not take notes from what Gary told her.

He sniffed then let his eyes wander above him as though thinking through an answer.

'Hm,' he said at last. 'Well,' he began slowly, still considering a spot high up on the opposite wall, 'we left the flat about ten o'clock and went round to the pub for a carry-out then caught a taxi to Kelvinbridge.'

Jo nodded encouragingly.

'Well, I don't recall much about what actually happened at the party. Lots of loud music, some of it pretty dreadful if you want to know the truth.' He smiled suddenly, showing a set of perfect white teeth.

'Was Eva with anyone in particular?'

Gary frowned. 'You mean one of us?' he said sharply. 'Not

really. I mean she hung about with us a bit, saw her dancing with Colin at one point. If you could *call* it dancing.' He gave a short laugh. 'Oh, that boy has no sense of rhythm at all,' he said with a smile.

Jo glanced up at him and saw the lips curve in an almost sneer that transformed his face for an instant. Then it was gone and the handsome young man was back again, his expression wholly respectful.

'When did Eva leave the party?'

Gary shook his head. 'Sorry, I don't know. Wasn't wearing my watch as it happens,' he added, tapping his wrist. Jo looked at the chunky Rolex, her eyes widening. That, she thought, must have cost someone an arm and a leg.

'It was my dad's,' Gary said softly, staring at her as though he had read her thoughts. 'I was given it after he collapsed and died last year.'

You're no stranger to sudden death, then, Jo thought. She had wondered at his calm exterior: now perhaps it could be explained. This one was maybe more mature than the others, having already experienced the death of someone close.

'Good idea not to wear it to a rowdy party, then,' Jo agreed. 'You picked it up from the flat that night?'

Gary nodded. 'They let us go up to take some of our things . . . eventually,' he said. As he tailed off, Jo could hear the beginnings of strain in his voice. Friday night must have been all sorts of hell for these students and this chap was making a good show of holding his emotions in check.

'Any idea who was with Eva when she left, then?' she asked.

The young man sat back in his chair and let his eyes wander across the ceiling once more, but this time Jo detected a shift in his manner. This, she thought, was a delaying tactic as she watched his eyes flick back and forth as though searching for the right lie to tell.

'Didn't she go home on her own?' he asked eventually, shrugging as though he had no answer to give.

'That's what we're trying to find out,' Jo told him sharply.

'Maybe the taxi driver would know,' he said.

Jo gave him a wintry smile. 'We're already investigating all of the taxi firms in the area,' she told him. 'What makes you so certain that she took a cab anyway?'

Gary Calderwood's eyebrows took another lift upwards. 'Because that's what she always did,' he said simply.

CHAPTER 12

It was warm in the office where they had asked him to wait, but Colin simply could not stop himself from shivering. The hotel bedroom had been small and stuffy, too hot for sleeping, he'd thought, though he must have dozed off at some point because when he had woken up this morning daylight was streaming in through the window. He'd forgotten to flick shut the blinds last night, preferring to sit at the window and watch the lights from the traffic below, anything to keep out the memory of the past two days and nights.

It seemed like hours since Mr Wilson had arrived to whisk them off to the police station. *A Division*, Kirsty had told him, as though that might mean something to him. He had been waiting in that reception area for ages, watching the shadows of officers behind the frosted glass screens, looking up every time a figure emerged from the wooden doors, following them with his eyes when they went out into the streets, wondering if they were police officers or not. Plain clothes? Undercover? Some of them looked so ordinary he simply couldn't decide.

Kirsty had been first to go, then Rodge and then Gary, leaving him alone with his thoughts.

Colin stood up and wandered across to the square window of

the office that looked out onto the street. A thin drizzle still fell, the grey pavements slick with rain that had been falling all morning. He could see a couple hurrying along under a huge golf umbrella, their faces hidden by the way one of them held it, slant-wise against the driving drops. For a moment he let his mind wander, making up a story about them, giving them a history, a shared past that had brought them to this moment on a Glasgow street. If he had been at home, his laptop open on the desk, then perhaps these strangers might have come alive under his imaginative fingers. Then the thought of home, the flat in Merryfield Avenue, brought Colin back to why he was here, waiting in this room inside the vastness of a Strathclyde divisional headquarters.

The jittering began in his face as though his cheeks had become icy cold.

Putting his hands out against the window sill, Colin tried to remember what Kirsty had told him about breathing against these rising panic attacks that she had witnessed back at the flat. He gulped air into his lungs, held it there for a count of four then exhaled as slowly as he could, feeling the shivers gradually subside. A numb sensation crept over his nose and mouth and Colin turned to grasp the back of the chair. Breathe, breathe, he told himself, but with every gulp of air he took, he could see Eva's lifeless face, all her breath snuffed out for good.

'Mr Young?'

Colin looked up sharply as the woman came into the room, the sudden motion making him feel light-headed and nauseous.

'Detective Inspector Grant,' the woman said. 'Would you like to follow me, please?'

Colin stood up, forcing his feet to walk across the floor and out into a corridor. The ringing in his ears subsided as he tried to match the dark-haired woman's stride, the sound of their footsteps unnaturally loud. They passed several doors, one marked VIPER, another FORENSIC DRYING CABINETS, before the woman stopped and turned towards him.

'In here, please.' DI Grant was smiling at him encouragingly, her hand raised to indicate that Colin should enter the door marked INTERVIEW ROOM 3.

Taking another deep breath, Colin walked into the room. His first thought was of all the real criminals who had been here, quizzed about their terrible misdeeds. A throbbing began in his temple. Was that tension headache returning, or was it that the very air shimmered with the lies that had been spun like spiders' webs over the years?

'Mr Young? Are you all right?' DI Grant was taking Colin by the arm now, sitting him down in that blue padded chair by the table. 'Would you like a drink of water?'

Colin nodded then licked his lips and swallowed. 'Please,' he whispered.

She was gone and back in less than a minute, returning with a bottle of mineral water and a plastic beaker. Not glass, Colin realised, imagining a mad thug smashing a tumbler and hefting it across the woman's face. He winced, the image was so real, then took the bottle and poured it into the beaker, watching his hand shaking all the time. She must see that too, Colin realised, grasping the beaker and taking deep gulps of the water.

'Better?'

Colin nodded and stifled a sigh. Glancing up, he looked at the detective properly for the first time. Detective Inspector Grant was quite a pretty woman, her dark hair cut short in a way that suited her elfin face. She had little make-up on that he could see and the tiny silver earrings shaped into knots were her only adornment. Colin's gaze fell onto her fingers. No rings. Not married, then, he thought, trying to sum her up as best he could. Her rust-coloured shirt and dark brown suit were smart but not intimidating and he had noticed her high-heeled shoes tapping a beat along the corridor before him. A stylish lady, he would say were he asked, but not the sort of woman he fancied.

Her grey eyes were looking into his face as he regarded her and Colin blushed, suddenly aware that he was staring.

'Okay, well, thanks for coming in today, Mr Young. We know it's been a pretty traumatic time for you all these last couple of days so we do appreciate your being here.'

Colin looked up over her shoulder, seeing a uniformed officer for the first time standing by the door. Of course there had to be a second person there, hadn't Kirsty told him that? They needed to corroborate any witness statement, didn't they? Or was it in case one of the people being interviewed turned nasty?

'... want you to tell me about the party,' DI Grant was saying, her words cutting in on Colin's thoughts.

'Party?' He gave his head a little shake as though to clear it. 'Oh, right. What can I tell you?' he asked, his hands clenched together under the table where he hoped she could not see them.

'What can you remember of Eva's movements that night?' the detective asked.

They were dancing together, Eva's hand clasped in his when he pulled her closer, smelling the sweet scent of her hair, feeling her body mould itself to his. Did she notice his hardness? She'd smiled up at him as though it were the most natural thing in the world; a cat's smile of satisfaction, he remembered. Then his arms were around her and they were kissing, moving into a darker corner where he swayed to the music, wanting her, wanting her...

'She was dancing quite a lot,' Colin began, swallowing hard and avoiding eye contact with the woman opposite.

'With anyone in particular?' Grant asked, her tone sharp, reminding him that this was an official enquiry.

Colin shook his head, not trusting his voice to add to all the years of lies that smothered the air in this room.

'Can you remember when she left the party, perhaps?'

Sleep must have overtaken him afterwards, for when he eventually did awaken, she was gone, leaving him shivering and alone. Had he imagined that too? Had that longing translated itself into a dream or reality? Wandering back into the main room his eyes had peered through the gloom, trying to catch a glimpse of her in that pretty frock, hoping that she wasn't one of the couples necking in a corner. And then, when he was sure she had gone, stumbling down the front steps and walking all the way back to the flat. He had walked for the best part of an hour, in a daze, holding onto the magic of the night like a fragile balloon that might blow away at the first tug of a freakish wind.

'Mr Young?'

'Sorry, think I was out of it,' Colin shrugged. Would she take his diffidence for embarrassment that he had been too drunk to know what had been going on?

The DI laid down her pen and clasped her hands together, resting her chin upon them. 'Can you tell me what she was like, Colin?' she asked, startling him by the use of his first name.

'She was beautiful,' he blurted out before he could stop himself.

Then, to his horror, Colin Young began to cry.

CHAPTER 13

The plane flew through a bank of pale grey clouds blotting out the dull green landscape that had been visible moments before. Henrik Magnusson sat by the window, staring out, too afraid to catch the eye of any person on this flight lest his weeping begin once more. Even the kindly smile from the purser as he had entered the cabin had made him bite his lip to control his emotions, though he wasn't to know that the woman had given each and every passenger the same friendly greeting.

It was so different from last summer in Glasgow when he and Eva had been doing up the flat during the summer vacation. A year ago they had still been together, spending the Christmas holiday skiing at Klosters, he remembered, seeing once again that flag of blond hair streaming behind her as Eva had swished down the slopes beside him. Even then he'd had such plans for her! After university she would return to live in the family house in Stockholm and he would begin to introduce her to the ins and outs of the Magnusson Corporation. She was destined for great things, Henrik had said proudly to anyone who would listen, never tiring of telling people how much she had meant to him. But now there was a different story that the world would tell about the fate of Eva Magnusson.

As the plane banked, Henrik gripped the armrest, steeling himself not for the landing but for what awaited him beyond the confines of the approaching airport.

Dr Rosie Fergusson picked up her briefcase and pulled her coat from the peg on the back of her office door. It was another lousy day, dark and foreboding as only days in the depth of a Scottish winter could be. Then, remembering the man she was about to meet, the pathologist gave a rueful grin. Bet they have gloomier days than we do, all the way up into the northern climes, she thought. No wonder the suicide rate was so high in places like Sweden if you had to wait months and months for a glimpse of sunshine.

Outside, the rain had stopped and a weak band of light was showing in the east, but the dark clouds above surely held more bad weather, maybe even the first snows, Rosie told herself, pulling the coat collar around her neck as she slipped into the front of the Saab. It was a short ride across town to Glasgow City Mortuary where Rosie kept her other office and where Eva Magnusson's body lay stored in the wall of refrigerators. The Swede had intimated that he wanted to come straight there from the airport and Rosie remembered the terse email letting her know when he expected to arrive.

God! How she hated this part of her job, meeting the relatives of the dead. For some reason it had become worse since Abby's birth, something that Solly had tried to explain to her in terms of psychology. Before her pregnancy Rosie had been well able to keep all of her emotions in check, always the consummate professional when dealing with her work. But now it was as if some fairy creature had stolen away her old reserves of ... what? Stoicism? Objectivity? Or had she just been a hardened bitch back then? Nowadays the pathologist's head was filled far more with thoughts about the relatives of the deceased and she seemed to have

73

developed a keen empathy with the bereaved to the extent that she found it difficult sometimes to keep her own tears in check.

As she entered the small parking place at the back of the mortuary, Rosie noticed the familiar blue van, its back doors opened wide and empty indicating that some other fatality would be awaiting her attention this Monday morning. A recent accident, perhaps? A sudden death, more than likely, but not one that had necessitated calling her out in the middle of the night, so probably not murder.

She smiled at the undertakers as the empty trolley passed her. They had a job to do and so had she, and if that job was all about the dead, then so be it. They were owed as much care by the pathologist and her colleagues as any sick patients in hospital, yet a different sort of caring, since it was too late for them to speak of whatever had brought them to this place.

And what had happened to the Swedish girl whose body would shortly be taken to the viewing room? That she had been strangled was quite evident. The death had probably been quick enough, but even those last suffocating seconds must have been terrifying. Whoever had committed this crime must have been strong enough to overcome the girl. Small and slight as she was, she had had youth and vigour on her side, not to mention the adrenalin rush that would have caused her to try to fight back. And the traces of semen ... now had that come from the perpetrator? The victim had had sex with someone shortly before her death, a fact that was already written in the pathologist's report. *Oh, dear Lord*, Rosie sighed, knowing that this was something else she was dreading having to tell the father.

The taxi stopped at the lights, letting Henrik see a different part of Glasgow from the business district with which he was familiar. Everything here looked dark, cold and dreary and, as if to underline his impressions, scraps of litter rose in a gust of wind then fell into gutters already lined with detritus. He wrinkled his nose in disgust. If he had known that parts of the city were like this ... he dashed a gloved hand across his eyes. Of course he had known exactly what Glasgow was like, had even argued a little with Eva when she had made her choice to go to Strathclyde. Buying her that flat in Anniesland was meant to have protected her ...

The lights changed and the taxi turned into a side street where, facing them, he saw for the first time the High Court of Judiciary in all its glory. Then the cab turned once more and drew up outside a small grey Victorian building. Taking a deep breath, Henrik Magnusson stepped out into the cold of a Scottish December and made his way to the front door of Glasgow City Mortuary.

He was a huge bear of a man, thought Rosie, ushering the Swede down the corridor to the viewing room where Eva Magnusson's body lay. Apart from his immense height – maybe even taller than Lorimer – she noticed he was a handsome man, his blond hair cut into a smart style, his lambskin coat hugging a body that was strong and muscular. His eyes startled her they were such a vivid shade, making her remember the moment when she had drawn the dead girl's eyelids down over their unseeing blue. That the Swedish girl's father had the same eyes should not have unsettled her like this, but somehow it did.

Magnusson had remembered the ordinary courtesies, even at a time like this, removing his heavy leather gloves to shake hands with this woman who had performed the post-mortem examination on his beloved daughter.

She had taken his outstretched hand, told him how sorry she was for his loss, and now that these preliminaries were over they were standing side by side at the window that looked down on the body lying on top of the trolley. A sudden intake of breath and the sense that the man by her side had stiffened was all the reaction that Rosie noticed, though she stole a sideways glance at the bereaved father just to see if he wanted to speak. But there was only silence as he stood there, staring at his daughter; silence and a sense of sheer disbelief. Rosie's eyes strayed to Magnusson's fingers as he fiddled with his cuffs, straightening the solid cufflinks as though it was an unconscious habit. It's stress, she thought. He needs to control even the tiniest things around him right now.

Then, 'Did she suffer?' he asked quietly.

'The post-mortem results suggest a quick death,' Rosie replied briskly. Her answer had been ready and came perhaps a little too easily to her lips. 'She would have lost consciousness in seconds,' she added a little more gently.

He nodded at that, still staring as though unable to take it all in, needing perhaps to see in order to believe.

Then, as though some unspoken decision had been made, Magnusson turned away from the window and began walking back towards Rosie's office.

'When can I have her back?' he asked gruffly and Rosie glanced at him again, noticing him swallowing hard, trying no doubt to refrain from showing any unmanly emotion. It took some men like that, she knew, the ones who didn't want a stranger to see their grief, while other men simply broke down and wept, sometimes on her shoulder.

'We'll let you know, sir, but until the Procurator Fiscal decides that it may be released your daughter's body will stay here with us,' she said. 'There may be a need for further examinations and so we have to keep Eva here in the mortuary.'

'And now, Dr Fergusson, you will do me the courtesy of telling me exactly what you know about my daughter's death.'

Henrik Magnusson had stopped right outside Rosie's office, his blue eyes bearing down upon her and a look on his face that brooked no refusal.

He was a strong man, Rosie thought suddenly, probably ruthless in his business dealings and maybe he considered himself strong enough to hear the plain unvarnished truth that the pathologist was writing in her full report.

'Come in,' she said, pulling the door back and indicating a seat on one side of her desk. She eased herself past him and sat behind the desk, a weak light filtering through from the glazed window behind her. Eva Magnusson's notes were in a file right in front of her, but the pathologist preferred to look this man in the eye as she told him what she had found, not hide behind the safety of an already prepared document.

'We know a fair bit about what happened,' Rosie began, 'but as yet the police have not identified the perpetrator. Nor,' she added, 'do we know why anyone might have done this to your daughter.'

For a moment the Swede's expression was so bleak that Rosie almost put out her hands to clasp his across the desk. But the long habit of professionalism stopped her.

'Eva suffered manual strangulation from a person unknown,' she continued. 'Someone who was wearing gloves.' She looked at his eyebrows, noticing that they were raised as she spoke.

'It was a very cold night, so the wearing of gloves might or might not suggest a premeditated attack,' she added. 'There was nothing on Eva's body to suggest that she had managed to resist the attack and, as I told you earlier, she would have lost consciousness very quickly.'

Magnusson nodded, his face still a mask of despair, his fingers twisting and turning the solid gold cufflink at his wrist.

'There is something else, however,' Rosie went on, drawing a deep breath before she continued. 'There is evidence in the post-mortem that shows your daughter had sex some time before her death.'

Magnusson's eyes widened but although his lips parted slightly, he did not utter a word.

'We are hopeful of obtaining a DNA match from this trace evidence, naturally,' she said. 'But that will not necessarily give us the identity of her assailant.'

The man sat there staring at Rosie, then began to shake his head as though this extra piece of information must somehow be incorrect.

'Are you trying to tell me my daughter was raped before she was murdered?' he said thickly.

'There was no bruising around the vaginal area or anything like her clothes being removed that would have indicated it had not been consensual sex,' Rosie murmured. 'Plus the toxicology tests have not given any signs of a drug that might have been administered to render Eva comatose.'

Henrik Magnusson continued to stare at her, his brows drawing together as if he were trying to figure something out.

'A date-rape drug, you mean?'

Rosie nodded. 'There was nothing like that in your daughter's blood tests and only a minimal amount of alcohol,' she said.

There was silence for a long moment.

'She did enjoy an occasional glass of champagne,' Magnusson said at last, his eyes wandering past Rosie as if he could see his daughter once again. And, as his expression softened and the tears filled them, Rosie felt a pain in her chest that came from a desire to let herself weep for this big man's loss.

CHAPTER 14

'I think we've got him,' Jo Grant told the detective superintendent, her hands leaning upon Lorimer's desk, her shining
face a picture of anticipation.

'Thank God for that,' Lorimer replied, his breath exhaling in a
long sigh as he sat back. For each and every one of the few days
since Eva Magnusson's death his DI's case had been preying on
his mind and now he experienced a certain sense of relief.
'Anyone we know?' he continued, motioning her to take a seat.

Jo nodded and sat down. 'DNA results came back this morning,' she told him. 'They match the sample we took from one of
the students.' She paused then went on, still regarding him carefully. 'It's Colin Young.'

'Really?' Lorimer's eyebrows shot up in surprise as a sudden
memory of the student's troubled face came back. 'He hadn't
impressed me as the violent type,' he went on hastily as Jo's brow
wrinkled in a frown of annoyance.

'There's absolutely no getting away from these sorts of facts,' she
said. 'He was definitely the one who had sex with the deceased
and . . . ' She hesitated. 'I had him weeping in the interview room
after only a few questions. Total remorse, if you ask me,' she added
with that firm manner that Lorimer had come to respect.

'Well, you know the procedure,' Lorimer said. 'A Section Fourteen. Bring him in and hope that he'll confess. Makes it much easier all round than having to go through the entire trial-by-jury scenario.'

He steepled his fingers under his chin, watching Detective Inspector Grant nod in agreement as he considered how so many cases ended up dragging out for months in the courts. They'd both seen it plenty of times, though a lot of hardened criminals were savvy enough to cough up and plead guilty if there was evidence stacked up against them. A guilty plea carried a lesser sentence and they all knew it. But what of a student like Colin Young who had no previous police record? If he had strangled Eva in a moment of rage would he be remorseful enough to get it all off his chest to the police? Or would fear make him try to spin a web of lies concerning the girl's death? And there was the aspect of the gloves. Lorimer sighed. Did that suggest a premeditated act or had the lad simply worn his gloves on that freezing night?

'Did you find any gloves among Young's possessions?'

'No.' Jo shrugged. 'But I bet he was forensically aware enough to ditch them somewhere. All these kids know the score nowadays. *CSI* syndrome,' she added, rolling her eyes to heaven. The much-watched American cop show, *Crime Scene Investigation*, had made a huge impact on viewers and the interest in forensic medical science had rocketed.

'Right, you better get a warrant for his arrest,' Lorimer said, watching his detective inspector rising from her seat. 'Good luck.'

'Thanks, sir. But don't think I'll need it,' Jo replied with a grim smile on her face.

All the way back down the corridor Jo felt a spring in her step. To get a result so quickly was ace! And having a quick collar for a case that had threatened to become high profile was exactly what she had wanted. No having to waste time with the ladies and gentlemen of the press, no fannying about with a whole lot of student interviews and best of all, closure for the poor father. Still, she had to bring the lad in first as a detainee for twelve hours, during which time she'd aim to wring a confession out of him. Pausing by the office door for a moment to gather her thoughts, Jo hoped against hope that Colin Young hadn't gone and done a runner.

'You awake, son?'

Colin opened his eyes to the darkness of the room and for a moment he was at a loss to know just where he was. Then, as he recognised the familiar objects of his old bedroom at home – his worn brown desk with the stack of poetry books that had gathered over the years, the wardrobe with the right-hand door that never closed properly, its inside mirror reflecting the narrow band of light from the space between the curtains – he remembered why he was here and all the events of the past few days came flooding back.

'Is that you, Dad?' he yawned, flexing his arms before tucking himself back below the duvet once more, huddling sleepily into its warmth.

'Aye, son.' There was a pause, then Alec Young moved closer and sat on the edge of the bed.

Colin's eyes were closed and so he did not see the rush of tender concern that filled his father's face as he looked down upon his boy. And was he even aware of that small sigh filling the space between them before Alec spoke?

'Son, there's a couple of polis here tae see ye. Think ye better get up, eh?'

Colin sat bolt upright, grabbing the edge of the cotton cover to hide the fact that he was naked. 'What?' He blinked stupidly. 'To see *me*? Why?'

Alec shifted uneasily, looking down at the floor now and not at his younger son. 'Don't know, Col. They jist said to get you up. Think they want you to go intae Glasgow again with them.'

Colin shivered as the cool draught from the open doorway reached his skin. 'Okay. Give me a minute to get dressed. Tell them I'll be right there,' he said.

For a moment their eyes met and Colin wondered what was going through the older man's mind. There was no reassuring smile, just a sort of watchfulness as though his father was appraising him, trying to see something in this boy of his that Alec Young had never seen before.

Then Colin reached out and took his father's hand, feeling its calloused roughness. 'It's all right, Dad. I haven't done anything wrong. I'm jist helping them, ken?' he added, slipping back into the familiar vernacular of his childhood.

His dad nodded then sighed. 'If yer mither wis here . . .' he began.

'Dad,' Colin said sharply. 'C'mon. I've got to get up. Okay?'

Alec rose from the bed and left the room, closing the door behind him. For a moment there was silence, then Colin could hear the sound of unfamiliar voices coming from the living room.

Gathering up the clothes he had discarded the night before, Colin hastily pulled on a T-shirt, only pausing to rummage through his rucksack for a fresh pair of underpants and clean socks.

Why had they come? They'd said that they wouldn't be needing him any more, but maybe they had found something . . .

Colin stopped, his hand on the buckle of his belt, wondering. What if they'd found something in the post-mortem? A shudder went through him.

Trembling, he glanced desperately at the small square window of his room. It had been stuck fast for years except for a couple of inches where you could ease it up for air in the summertime. Bloody death trap, his brother Thomas had said often enough. *Death trap.* The words in his head resonated as though someone had actually spoken them out loud.

His shivers continued as he fastened his belt and yanked a jersey over his head, eyes emerging to stare at the door that separated him from the people who were waiting to take him away.

There was no way out. No way to escape whatever was waiting for him behind that door.

As if in a dream, Colin left his old bedroom behind, the place that was filled with so many childhood memories, then walked into the hall, seeing the ancient carpet, its red and yellow leaf pattern worn and faded now from so many feet over so many years. Nothing had been changed since Mum had died, despite the boys' efforts to persuade their father to smarten the place up. Now, for the first time, as a vision of his mother's laughing face came back to him, Colin understood why. It was seeing familiar things like this scabby old hall carpet that kept some of the memories alive for Alec Young.

Behind the living room door Colin could hear the voices and his steps faltered for a moment. His hand turned the door knob and he stepped in to see three faces turned towards him, staring silently as though he had been the subject of a conversation that had abruptly stopped the moment he had entered the room.

Then Colin Young heard words that he had never expected to hear in his life as a uniformed officer stepped forward to enclose his wrist in that cold hard cuff: ' . . . detained on suspicion . . . '

It was all happening too quickly. There was no protest from the father who stood there, arms limp by his sides. Colin tried to see what was in Alec Young's expression. Mute amazement? Horrified disbelief?

Then the moment had passed and he couldn't look back to see any more as he was being led out of the front door, leaving his dad behind them.

A small crowd of people had gathered several paces away, watching the little drama, eyes feasting on the handcuffed figure being led towards the police car. Colin searched in vain but there was no friendly face that he recognised amongst their stares. One of the police officers put his hand onto Colin's head as he was helped into the back seat and clipped into his belt, then the car began to move away from the pavement.

Someone in the crowd called out but the words were lost in the sound of the car's engine and all Colin could see as he twisted around to look out of the window was his father's face, white and strained, as he stood framed in the doorway of their home.

Perhaps he could write a poem about it once they realised their mistake, Colin thought. He was sitting at a well-scrubbed Formica-topped table in an interview room that was almost identical to the one he had been in before, but he had nothing with him to write down any thoughts, not even a pencil stub, and his notebook was back home in the rucksack that he'd been carting about for days ever since he had left Merryfield Avenue.

They had arrived at the back of the police station this time and Colin had been led up a sloping metal pathway barred on each side and through a red door to the Charge Bar, where a man behind the counter had asked if he wanted to call his legal representative or not. Colin had shaken his head, still bewildered at the turn of events.

'You need to have someone with you, son,' one of the uniformed officers who had taken him from his home explained. 'We can get you a duty solicitor if you like but if there's anyone you know, like a family solicitor ...?'

Colin had shaken his head and mumbled, 'We don't have one ...' and that had made the man bark out, 'Duty solicitor then, Sergeant!' Then he had been taken through a maze of corridors until they had reached this interview room.

The uniformed police officer standing guard by the door didn't look much older than he was, but looking at his closed expression, Colin did not feel inclined to engage the other man in conversation. Detective Inspector Grant would be with him shortly, he had been told, and that must have been at least quarter of an hour ago, Colin thought, glancing at the watch he'd remembered to slip onto his wrist. He fingered the metal strap, recalling the morning of his eighteenth birthday when he had opened up the slim parcel and found it inside. A good-looking grown-up watch, something he'd wanted for ages, something that would last him a lifetime.

Colin hung his head as the thought of a lifetime twisted itself in his brain. Eva. She'd had such plans for the rest of her life, hadn't she? And now none of them would ever come to pass. He swallowed hard, blinking away these treacherous tears. What on earth would that detective inspector think if she came in and found him crying again?

The sound of the door opening made him look up and there she was. Colin glanced at the police officer, his mind setting out words to describe her as though she were a character in one of his stories. Today she wore a dark charcoal trouser suit, nipped in at the waist, and a pair of high-heeled ankle boots. The open-necked shirt revealed a single line of pearls at her throat. *Pearls are for tears*, he remembered his mum telling him, and the memory of her voice made his throat ache with a renewed desire to weep.

Just behind the detective inspector was another woman, older and more careworn, wearing a simple black suit over a black and white striped shirt and carrying a matching black briefcase. She came forward looking at him seriously.

'I'm Mrs Fellowes, the duty solicitor. You may request to have your own legal representative here if you wish, Mr Young,' the woman said, standing by the side of an empty chair as though waiting for Colin to make a decision.

'No, that's all right,' he said, an innate politeness making him wish for this stranger to be at her ease. She came around the table and sat in the empty seat next to his – not close, he noticed, but near enough for him to be aware of her presence.

'You remember me, Mr Young?' DI Grant had seated herself opposite them after fiddling with a box over near the wall, something that Colin recognised as a recording machine of some kind. Colin nodded. His head felt muzzy as he listened to her words, unable to really make out what they meant. Then a peculiar sensation came over him, as though he were outside looking down on these people instead of being one of the figures himself. Small details seemed to loom large, like the piece of sticking plaster curled around the detective's index finger where she must have cut herself; the way the lawyer's hair curled around her tiny shell-like ears, and his own sweating hands clasped tightly together as though ready for prayer.

DI Grant introduced herself and Mrs Fellowes to the tape machine and gave the date and time then turned to face Colin.

'You know why you're here?' she asked.

Colin nodded, letting himself be part of this dreamlike state.

'Speak for the machine, please,' she told him crisply.

'Yes,' Colin said gruffly, then cleared his throat.

'Yes,' he said again, more loudly this time, and as if the utterance of the word had broken a spell, he was suddenly aware of the padded seat pressing against his back and the coarseness of the material under his buttocks as though he had landed from a great height.

'It's to do with Eva,' he continued helpfully.

DI Grant leaned forward slightly. 'We have had results from our laboratory, Mr Young,' she began, then gave a small smile of satisfaction. 'DNA results that show that you were the person who had sex with Eva Magnusson shortly before her death.'

Colin nodded once again.

'Please speak for the machine,' DI Grant said again with a sigh that made Colin feel awkward and ashamed.

'Yes, that's right. We did have . . . sex,' he mumbled, feeling his face reddening, not wishing to discuss intimate things in front of these two women. Suddenly he was angry. What right had she to peer and pry into his private life? Looking up he could see DI Grant's smile continue, though her eyes were hard and cold.

'We'd done nothing wrong,' he protested, then swallowed hard, hearing his own voice come out small and shrill.

'Consensual sex?' DI Grant persisted. 'Or did you force the girl against her will? Hit her hard to make her more compliant? Eh?'

'Detective Inspector—' Mrs Fellowes began but Colin could see the police officer wave her hand brusquely in the air as though to simply brush aside any possible protest.

Colin's mouth opened in astonishment, then he closed it again. She didn't know. How could she? Well, he wasn't going to be the one to tell her what had really taken place. Eva was dead. It would do nobody any good to reveal to anyone what life had been like for him over the past few months, especially to her father.

He sat back in his seat, suddenly exhausted as though the last vestiges of energy had drained out of him.

'No comment,' he said at last, forcing his eyes to remain

focused on his hands that were bunched together on his lap, fingernails digging into the palms and making them bleed.

'Here's what I think happened, Colin,' DI Grant continued, leaning forward so near to him that he was aware of a pungent scent that might have been tea-tree oil. 'I think you fancied Eva, fancied her a lot. A pretty Swedish girl whose warm sunny nature makes her popular with everyone she meets, a girl way out of your league, Colin. Wouldn't you say?'

'No comment,' Colin whispered to his hands again, the scent emanating from the woman's fingers making him feel sick.

'Speak up, please.'

'No comment,' Colin said again, anger with this stupid woman and her stupid machine making his ears burn.

'See, Eva could have had her pick of the lads, so why pick you, Colin?'

He kept his eyes down, refusing to rise to her bait, refusing even to answer.

'Did you force her to have sex? Or was she so sorry for you that she let you have your way? And what happened afterwards? Did you come too quickly? Did she laugh at you? And then did you have a moment of utter rage when you hit her on the head? Such overpowering rage that you had to take her throat and squeeze it so hard that you killed her?' Grant's voice grew louder with every question.

'No!' Colin sat up suddenly, thumping the table between them. 'I didn't kill her! You can't believe that I did!' he gulped.

'Sure about that, Colin?' The woman was smiling at him still, her cats' eyes gleaming as though she had scored a point by making him answer her at last.

'Of course I'm sure,' he said, clasping his hands together to stop them trembling, eyes cast down to avoid the detective inspector's stare.

'You see, we think that you did,' DI Grant continued. She paused for a moment and he looked up despite himself to see her regarding him thoughtfully.

'We think that you killed the girl in a moment of . . . what shall we call it, a moment of madness, if you like. Some killers do tend to use that particular phrase, you know,' she said drily.

Colin wanted to turn to the solicitor in mute appeal but a sudden thought made his skin prickle with sweat. She had made no noise of objection on his behalf. Was she part of the 'we' that the detective inspector was referring to? Was this some kind of conspiracy against him?

Colin shook his head again. 'I did not kill her,' he said slowly, enunciating each word as though to make the detective understand. 'I don't *have* a temper. I'm not that sort of person.'

The detective inspector shared a wry smile with the other woman, one sardonic eyebrow lifted as though to say, *Well what was all that shouting about then?*

'No? What sort of person are you then, Colin?' She was sitting back in her seat now, arms folded, looking at him with interest.

'You're so sweet, Colin,' Eva had said, tracing his lips with one finger. Her eyes had looked into his, melting him with that blue gaze. He had smelled her scent, something that reminded him of gardens after the rain, fresh and lovely, just like Eva herself. He had run his hands over her hair, gently, caressing her—

'What sort of person do you think you are?' the woman said, rephrasing her question.

'Don't know,' Colin shrugged. *Not a killer, not someone who would ever have hurt that girl, any girl,* he wanted to scream. But all he needed right now was to get out of this room and away from the persistent voice that was accusing him.

'Okay, let's try again,' DI Grant said, folding her hands upon the table between them and staring at him intently. 'Let's begin at the beginning when you first met Eva Magnusson.'

Colin opened his eyes, hoping that he was wakening from the nightmare that had engulfed him. But what he saw as he looked around the place reminded him that it was all too real. Although the sky was dark, the white-painted walls glowed from the street lights outside and the metal toilet gleamed in the corner of his cell. Something smelled stale and sour and Colin realised with a sense of shame that it was coming from his own unwashed body.

He had slept fitfully on top of the blue mattress, trying hard not to let his emotions get the better of him, hearing voices calling in the nearby cells, often accompanied by banging against the blue metal doors. Once he could have sworn he had woken himself by crying out, for an officer had opened the door and asked if he was okay. Someone seemed to stop by that door at regular intervals, always disturbing his sleep. Tomorrow he would be taken from this place to the court where his defence – Mrs Fellowes? – would try to get him released on bail.

'Don't bank on it,' the solicitor had told him quietly. 'This is a grave charge and you might be refused bail, even though you have no previous record.'

He had stared at her, wide-eyed from all the hours that he had spent being quizzed by that detective inspector. His head had been aching afterwards and the cold calmness of being alone in this cell had come almost as a relief. What would happen next? Would he be taken from the courts and allowed to go home to his father? Colin Young squeezed his eyes tightly shut, forcing himself to discount any other possibility.

CHAPTER 15

'I can't believe it!' Kirsty Wilson slumped into the armchair, looking at her father's face as though he were making some sort of sick joke. 'It can't be true! Colin wouldn't hurt a fly!' she protested, the tears suddenly springing back into eyes that she thought had wept themselves dry.

'Sorry, love,' Alistair Wilson murmured, coming to sit on the arm of the chair and pat his daughter's shoulder.

'Well, what does he say? He hasn't confessed, has he?'

'No.' Alistair shook his head and frowned. For the umpteenth time he wished that his professional life had not impinged on his family, especially Kirsty. It was bad enough that work had made him miss so many special occasions in the past, but now to have his wee girl involved in a murder case that was being investigated on his own patch, well that was just too much.

'I don't believe he did it. Something must be wrong,' Kirsty protested. 'Anyway, where is he now? At home again with his dad?' she asked hopefully.

'No,' Alistair replied with a sigh. 'He was refused bail.'

'Oh, no!' Kirsty's hand flew to her mouth. 'Where is he?'

'Barlinnie,' her father answered. 'On remand.'

Kirsty shook her head. 'That's awful, Dad,' she said, looking up at him as his hand grasped hers in a consoling squeeze.

'I know, pet. I'm sorry,' Alistair said.

'But isn't there anything we can do?'

Kirsty saw her father turn his face away then and at that moment the girl experienced a sense of loss greater than she had ever known in her life. They were divided, father and daughter. Detective Sergeant Wilson would always take the part of his professional colleagues over the feelings and sensitivities of his daughter, wouldn't he? She slipped her hands out of his grasp and stared straight ahead.

'You've always said I'm a good judge of character, haven't you? Listen, I know what Colin's like, Dad,' she said quietly. 'And I know that he's not a killer.'

The horse was the first thing he saw as the transporter trundled through the gates of HMP Barlinnie Prison. For a split second Colin thought he must have been hallucinating: a horse? Here inside a prison? But as he had craned his neck to look more closely he recognised the sculpture as something similar to the heavy horse made out of barbed wire that looked down over the M8 motorway. This one had horse brasses around its neck, tufts of plaited mane sticking up and a plough trailing behind it. Colin remembered the tiny seed of hope that had been planted in him as the horse left his view, the transporter turning on the grey tarmac beside the prison gardens: maybe it wouldn't be too bad here after all, if there was something creative going on?

The rest of his admission was now a painful blur; blubbering like a child in front of the nice nurses who had insisted he had to be strip-searched, hanging his head in shame as one of them patted his back, telling him that it was okay, everyone felt like this at first. Then that awful clang as the door of the cell closed behind him.

Colin Young fingered the lapels of the faded blue shirt folded neatly on his narrow bunk. His clothes had been taken away and, although one of the prison officers had mentioned that someone would be allowed to bring his own stuff from home, Colin was not sure when or if that would actually happen. On arrival he had been handed a pair of red tracksuit trousers and an orange fleece; hideous but probably necessary to identify him as a new entrant to this penal system. Now they lay in a garish bundle at the foot of his bunk.

The chubby-faced prison officer had told him that he was to be taken to the prison block that would be his home until the time came for his trial. One hundred and forty days, someone had said, but Colin had doubted this, hoping it wasn't true. How many different men had worn this particular garment, he wondered. The shivering was as much from that thought as from the fact that he was standing in only a T-shirt and underpants. These, at least, had been in a plastic packet and looked brand new. He pulled his arms through the sleeves and buttoned up the shirt, looking at the dark blue jeans that still lay on the bed. They too were faded with many washes yet still stiff from the dryer. There would be no putting out of a wash here, he suddenly realised, no billowing lines of laundry like the ones in the back greens at home. It would be all done by machinery somewhere in the bowels of this enormous place.

For a moment Colin remembered the black and white engravings he had seen in the People's Palace, old Glasgow, where women came from all parts to spread their linen out to dry on the famous Glasgow Green. When would he ever be able to walk across that swathe of grass again?

Before he realised it, Colin was dressed and ready for whatever this new day was to bring. He had spent the night alone in this cell, a much smaller one than the large sparse cell back at Stewart Street, sleeping in fits, disturbed by the prison officers on their rounds, sliding the square viewing panel up to check that he was all right. This was a special block – one that was reserved for men coming into prison to enable the prison officers to orientate them into the ways of the system. Or so he had been told. Colin had tried hard to listen to everything, taking in what he could, but his mind had been numb with the fear of it all and the reality that he was actually inside a prison, accused of a capital crime.

'I didn't do it,' Colin had whispered, confiding to the prison officer who looked older even than his own father, hoping that the kindly eyes that swept over his quivering body would understand. 'I didn't do what they said I did,' he had insisted quietly.

'Aye, they all say that, lad,' the man had said with a tired smile. And at that moment Colin knew that his very presence here in this prison had given him a different status. He was a suspect, a male on remand, a killer in the eyes of each and every one of these officials. That he lived in a country where one was supposed to be innocent until proved guilty didn't seem to matter now. The very idea of voicing that thought had made Colin suddenly weary. From the moment he had left his home two mornings ago it was as if all the energy had been leached from his body and soul. Now he felt a dull ache all the time, as though he were battered and bruised, though nobody had laid a finger upon him.

Outside he could hear the clanging of doors as the prison officers made their way along the upper corridor of the remand block in Barlinnie. The sounds grew louder, making Colin stare at the cream-painted door that separated him from the new prison world that awaited him. Thoughts of other inmates and their brutality rushed through his brain. Would he be a victim of assault? Or was that just something that cop shows and paperback thrillers tended to suggest? He had been protected here on his first night, told that he would be sent into the main prison today: A Block, he thought the officer had said, whatever that meant.

Colin stiffened as the heavy metal door swung open. A thickset man in a black uniform stood clutching a bunch of keys in one meaty hand, looking at him without a trace of emotion in his large moonlike face.

'Young. Come this way,' he grunted, and motioned for Colin to follow him out of the cell where a second officer was waiting.

Above them Colin could see that the sky was still dark through the glass roof that arched overhead. It was nearing the shortest day, he remembered, and every day would be as gloomy as this one. Inside, though, the artificial lighting made the whole place a cavern of light and space, intensified by the echoing sounds from the metal stairs as he followed the prison officers down the steep flights right to the ground floor. A simile came into his head then: the stairs and the upper corridors were like ribs in a sunken ship ... could he fashion something into a poem about his incarceration?

Then he was at a door and another, keys turned, bolts shot back and Colin found himself breathing fresh air once more.

Outside, the rain was just a memory in the wind, a faint damp-ness that cooled Colin's upturned face, though he was glad of the rough blue windcheater that he had put on. The three men walked in silence, Colin between them, past high grey walls that loomed up into the winter sky. He listened, but there were no birds here, no singing before the dawning light, only the sound of their feet stepping onto hard ground.

*

It was a bit cheeky, perhaps, but Kirsty Wilson had decided that it was the only way that she could see to make things happen. She'd known him since childhood, of course, admired him from afar, listened to her dad as he told tales that made her shiver. William Lorimer had been in many dangerous situations in his police career, Kirsty knew; he had faced some of the most horrible criminal types, *the mad ones as well as the bad ones*, as her dad was fond of saying, and yet Kirsty had never seen a cynical hardbitten side to the tall detective superintendent.

It was dark in the late afternoon and, despite the light pollution from nearby street lamps, Kirsty was able to make out a few early stars as she walked down to the house where the Lorimers lived. Looking for the numbers on the houses, she pulled her scarf tighter as a gust of wind crept under her hood and across a bare patch on her neck. Some had names, others numbers but there were a few with neither and Kirsty had been counting the odds and evens since she had turned the corner into the avenue.

It was easier to spot than she had realised. The detective superintendent's big silver Lexus was parked on the drive in front of a single garage and the house number was fixed to the wall at the side of the front porch. As she approached, a security light flooded the entrance, illuminating a swathe of greenery beside the doorway, the tiny yellow flowers of winter jasmine a warm note of colour in these darkest days of winter.

She pressed the bell but could not hear a sound from within, though there was a light shining from behind a thick curtain. Was anybody home? Had she steeled herself all the way over here just to find it had all been a waste of time? For a moment Kirsty felt a sense of disappointment tinged with relief. She wouldn't have to do anything after all. Would she?

Then, as the door opened, she started, heart beating wildly as the man stooped down a little to see who was there.

'Kirsty?'

And as soon as Lorimer spoke her name, the girl knew for a certainty that there was no going back now.

'Come in, come in, it's freezing out there,' he said, opening the door wider and ushering her into a place that was bathed in warmth and sparkling light.

'Oh!' she exclaimed, catching sight of a Christmas tree on the upper landing.

Lorimer followed her gaze and smiled. 'Maggie likes to put it up every year.' He shrugged. 'Some of the decorations are as old as the hills; stuff from our childhood,' he said, looking up at the twinkling fairy lights.

'We didn't put ours up,' Kirsty said in a small voice. The long sigh that followed was enough explanation. Who would feel like celebrating in the wake of a friend's murder?

'Come on through,' Lorimer said. 'Fancy a coffee? Maggie's not in at the moment but I do know how to boil a kettle,' he joked.

'Thanks,' Kirsty replied, following the tall man into a big open-plan room. A long stretch of breakfast bar divided the kitchen area from what looked like a study-cum-sitting room. An open laptop sat on a desk near the front window and Kirsty suddenly felt guilty that she had disturbed this man from whatever he had been doing. She trailed after him into the warmth of the kitchen, unbuttoning her coat and pulling off the scarf that had been wound around her neck, her eyes flicking over the neat cream-coloured cupboards and a shelf full of cookery books. She moved across to stand beside the glowing oven, bending down a little to see what was inside.

'Smells good,' she offered, seeing the cast iron casserole inside.

'Maggie's a great cook,' Lorimer said, switching on the kettle and turning to give Kirsty a smile. 'Think we're in for one of her goulashes tonight,' he added. 'You can stay for dinner if you'd like. She'll be back in an hour or so.'

Kirsty shook her head. 'I'm working tonight,' she told him. 'And it was really you I wanted to see anyway.'

He had turned away to spoon instant coffee into a pair of porcelain mugs decorated with pictures of cats, so Kirsty failed to see the thoughtful expression on his face but he stood so still that she imagined that he must realise just why his detective sergeant's daughter had come to visit on a Saturday afternoon.

'Your dad says you've gone back to the flat. Isn't that a bit hard for you?'

'I s'pose so.' She bit her lip. 'But I keep mainly to my own room and the kitchen.'

She could almost hear that unspoken question: 'How can you bear to enter that room again?'

Lorimer turned to look at her, a teaspoon held aloft. She saw the pity in his eyes but all he said was, 'Sugar?'

'Two please,' she nodded, then they were sitting opposite one another beside a low coffee table, sipping the hot drinks. Kirsty noticed how Lorimer took his plain black and unsweetened, and now the policeman was looking at her intently, as though waiting for her to begin.

'It's about Colin,' she said at last. 'I wanted to see if you could do anything...'

Lorimer's frown made her heart sink. Was he annoyed at her for coming to ask?

'He's not guilty,' Kirsty said suddenly, lowering her mug of coffee onto a coaster. 'I *know* Colin. He simply isn't capable of something as terrible as that,' she told him earnestly, looking up to meet his blue gaze.

Lorimer gave a sigh. 'Oh, Kirsty, I'm really sorry about this. But tell me, honestly, can you really say you know a person that has only been your flatmate for what . . . barely three months?'

The girl nodded vigorously. 'Yes, I can. I've got to know Colin Young better than all of the others,' she insisted. 'He's a gentle soul, wouldn't hurt a fly, never mind . . . what someone did to Eva.' She bit her lip, terrified still to utter the dreadful words. 'Colin's a writer,' she went on. 'He's into poetry and things like that. A bit of a dreamer at times.' She smiled as though she were already a grown-up mother remembering a favourite son. 'He's a *nice* person, Mr Lorimer. I just know he couldn't have done it!' she repeated.

Lorimer looked down at his coffee cup for a moment as though considering her words, leaving Kirsty to bite her lower lip, tense with hope.

'What did you imagine I could do, Kirsty?' he asked at last, his voice so gentle that the girl felt tears prick behind her eyelids.

'I thought . . . ' She sniffed then gulped. 'Thought you could investigate a bit more and see that it was all a mistake,' she said quietly. But even as she spoke her words sounded foolish.

'I can't do that, Kirsty,' Lorimer continued. 'Now that Colin's been charged it's up to a court of law to decide if he's guilty or not. Besides, I'm not even the senior investigating officer in this case. It would be quite impossible for me to go against a colleague,' he explained. 'And anyway, what grounds do you have for thinking that further investigation is needed?'

'I know the sort of lad Colin is!' Kirsty blurted out. 'I just know he couldn't have killed Eva. He . . . he really liked her,' she stammered, colouring as though she had suddenly said too much.

'Your loyalty does you credit, lass,' Lorimer told her, 'but if all you've got to go on are your feelings, how can that stand up in a court of law?'

Kirsty shook her head, too full of emotion to speak.

'Listen,' Lorimer continued. 'If you really want to help Colin, then find something to substantiate these feelings.'

Kirsty looked up, a sudden hope flaring in her heart.

'There would only be grounds for a further investigation if there was some kind of new evidence that pointed away from Colin. D'you understand?'

Kirsty nodded, looking at him intently, searching the light blue eyes for any sign that the detective might agree to help her. But there was only an expression of sympathy there, pity for a young woman who could not believe the worst of her friend.

Lorimer sighed as he rinsed out the mugs under the tap. She was a nice kid. Alistair and Betty had done a grand job with their only daughter, he thought, realising what courage it must have taken for Kirsty Wilson to have visited on the boy's behalf. And it was quite her own idea; that much he believed. There had been no contact between the two flatmates since Colin Young had been taken to Barlinnie prison but Kirsty must have felt completely miserable to have lost not one but two friends so tragically. No wonder she was trying to salvage something from that emotional wreckage.

But it was absolutely true what he had told her: there really was nothing he could do for the boy now that he was on remand.

He laid the mugs on the draining board and picked up a towel to dry his hands, his eyes staring out at the darkening midwinter sky. There was something in that girl's plea that gave him pause for thought. What if they'd got it wrong? It wouldn't be the first time someone had been wrongly imprisoned, would it? Lorimer cast his mind back to a case where he had interviewed a young woman in Cornton Vale prison. That had been a hard one to decide, hadn't it? But justice had prevailed in the end. It was all they could do, as police officers; bring the perpetrators of crime to the courts of law and let a judge and jury make the final decision.

CHAPTER 16

The path outside the front door was slippery and Henrik had to put out a gloved hand to steady himself, catching hold of the edge of the wall before his feet gave way. For a moment he stood still, his breath coming in clouds before his face. Was this what it felt like to become old? Would he always feel this uncertainty beneath his feet, the lack of power in a body that was ageing day by painful day? The very air seemed to tremble as Henrik stood there, cold seeping into every pore of his being. Then, with a sigh, he pulled off his right glove to rummage in his coat pocket, and inserted the key into the big keyhole in the green door.

Even as he made his way up, Henrik Magnusson could feel his heart beating in his chest as though it was an effort to climb those flights of stairs. Was he coming down with some sort of an infection, perhaps? Marthe, his housekeeper, was forever telling him that air travel was notorious for spreading germs. But when had he last suffered any illness in his life? Henrik stopped suddenly on the landing below the flat, remembering. It had been shortly after Eva's birth; he had fallen ill with a severe dose of flu, caught perhaps by standing at his wife's graveside in the driving snow. He had taken to his bed, leaving the baby in the care of the woman who was to become Eva's nurse throughout her child-hood. He had not seen Marthe since the news of his daughter's death: the telephone call to tell her had made him feel a physical pain as he heard the woman weep and Henrik was reluctant to repeat such an experience just yet. Perhaps grief did that to a man, he thought, made them weak and vulnerable, prey to any sort of virus that sought a host. He swallowed, feeling a rawness in his throat that seemed to confirm his thoughts, then, placing his hand on the ancient wooden banister, he pulled himself up the last few steps.

Kirsty was barely awake when she heard the door opening with a click. For one wild moment she sat up in bed, supposing it to be Colin, then the memories of what had happened came flood-ing back. Had it been the wind that night? Or had she been only feet away from the person who had killed her friend? Kirsty shiv-ered, snuggling deeper below the duvet. She'd imagined it, right? That was what the senior investigating officer had implied any-way.

And right now it was probably Rodge or Gary coming back, and she wasn't up to talking to either of them just yet.

'Hello?'

The voice made Kirsty slide out of bed and grab her fleecy dressing gown from the peg on her door.

'Mr Magnusson!' Kirsty gasped as she padded into the dark-ened hallway. Then she stepped forward, seeing the big man slouched on one of the antique chairs. 'Are you all right?'

She touched his coat sleeve, feeling the cold wrinkles of the sheepskin as she bent to look at him more closely. The handsome face was pale and gaunt, his brow beaded with sweat.

'My God!' she said. 'You're not well! C'mere. Let me help you.

103

I'll make you something hot to drink.' She tucked her hand under his elbow as if to assist him up from the spindly chair.

'Kirsty,' he whispered, turning his face up to hers, and she could see the tears in his eyes as Eva's father swallowed hard, unable to speak. But there was no need for words as the girl bent to hug the stricken man, feeling how cold his cheek was as she put her face to his.

Oh you poor, poor man! Kirsty wanted to say but she only sniffed back her own tears, determined not to upset him any further.

'Come on through to the lounge,' she told him. 'I'll light the fire and you can sit and get warm while I find you something to make you feel better. Okay?'

She watched intently as the big man heaved himself out of the chair and leaned against her.

'C'mon, now, take it easy,' she whispered, helping him along the hallway and into the big airy lounge at the far end.

'Here,' she said, ushering him into the wing chair nearest to the fire. Henrik sank into it heavily, his eyes refusing to meet her own. Was he embarrassed to be suffering this moment of weakness in front of a girl who was only his tenant? Perhaps it was her nightclothes, Kirsty thought, pulling the sash tighter around her body. What on earth must he be thinking, seeing her in those flannelette pyjamas decorated with cartoon cats and the white fleecy dressing gown that made her look like a big fat snowman?

She knelt down and lit the gas fire, turning the flame up to its highest before turning to check that he was all right. He sat as before, slumped into the chair, his face white and drawn, staring into the fire that had begun to burn quietly in the hearth.

It was almost a relief to be in the familiar kitchen, filling the kettle, rummaging in the cupboards for some paracetamol and looking in the fridge to see if there was anything she could give him for breakfast. There were sausages – past their sell-by date – and bacon and probably some eggs still in the crock over by the window. Kirsty stood still for a moment, her tongue protruding from one side of her mouth as she considered. Scrambled eggs, she decided, then set to work.

Henrik stared into the fire, afraid to look up and see the rest of this room. It had been such a short time ago that the place had been full of workmen, painting and decorating to his commands, then fitting the rich, ruby-red carpet and setting his choice of furniture wherever he directed. And it was here, he knew, that Eva's life had been taken. Didn't the girl realise that, he wondered in a sudden spurt of anger, but the feeling passed in a flash as he acknowledged that Kirsty Wilson was simply doing what any woman would do, seeing to the needs of someone in distress. She reminded him of Marthe, he thought. Not that this dumpling of a girl resembled the tall, slender woman in any physical way, but there had been that same quality of warmth and care in her voice that recalled his housekeeper to mind.

At last the man raised his eyes and looked around the room. Little had changed, he thought, seeing the fine furniture against the walls: an antique cabinet that was full of books, the table by the window covered in trailing plants – his choice from that big garden centre, he remembered – and the low coffee table beside him with a few large glossy books pushed to one side. He drew his finger across the surface of the topmost book, seeing the trail left on its dusty surface, and gave a sigh. Why would he have imagined that the students might have any interest in such volumes as these? It was obvious from their pristine condition that the books on history and aviation had been of no interest to the young people in this flat. He sighed, the sound becoming a groan as his eyes refused to look down on the carpet.

'Here you are,' Kirsty said and Henrik looked up as though surprised to find the girl standing in front of him. She set down a tray on his lap and Henrik took it carefully, noting the steaming cup of coffee and scrambled eggs beside a glass of water.

He looked at her and shook his head. 'I don't think I could eat anything,' he said.

Kirsty bit her lip and shrugged. 'Och, don't worry. See what you can manage. I think you should have these anyway.' She handed him two white capsules. 'You look terrible, by the way,' she blurted.

Henrik managed a rueful smile. 'Thank you, Kirsty,' he said. 'I'll try not to look in any of the mirrors then.'

'Okay, well, um . . . I think I better go and get dressed,' Kirsty said, dithering by his chair then, much to Henrik's relief, she was gone again, leaving him to swallow the pills and contemplate the breakfast before him.

As she came out of her bedroom, dressed hastily in jeans and a warm sweater, Kirsty stopped to turn up the central heating on the wall next to the front door. She was the only one of them to have returned to Merryfield Avenue so far but Rodge had texted her to say that both he and Gary would be back some time today. The boys had been put up by Roger's pals for several nights now and Kirsty wondered just what the future was going to hold for them all here in the Anniesland flat. Well, she told herself, pulling back her shoulders and preparing to stride through the hall, the very man who could tell her that was here right now.

'Oh, you managed . . . ' Kirsty smiled as she saw the tray lying on the coffee table, the plate empty and the knife and fork laid neatly across the middle. 'Can I get you anything else?' she asked, bending down to lift the tray away. But a movement from the man made her pause.

'Kirsty, leave that just now, will you?' he asked quietly. 'I would like to talk to you, if I may.'

This was it, then, she thought sadly. He was going to ask them all to find somewhere else to live. Couldn't blame him, though, she told herself. How could he keep this place on now?

She shrugged then tried to smile but failed. 'Well, I guess you won't want us hanging about here after all that's happened,' she began.

Henrik frowned. 'You think I am going to evict you, Kirsty? Why on earth would I do that? I am perfectly happy that you remain here, if you want to, that is. You have all signed a lease for the year and I would not dream of asking anyone to leave!' he exclaimed.

'Oh, I thought . . . ' She bit her lip and looked at him again. 'Well, I *do* want to stay here, Mr Magnusson. It was lovely till . . . ' She broke off then breathed in sharply, trying to compose herself for what she wanted to say. 'And I think Rodge and Gary will too. And Colin, when he comes back, of course,' she added in a rush.

The big man sat back, his eyebrows raised in a moment of total astonishment.

'You expect that he will come back here?' His voice rose in a credulous note.

Kirsty nodded silently.

'But he has been put in prison for killing my daughter!' Henrik protested. 'How can you say such things! My Eva, who was so perfect until . . . ' He stopped, one hand across his eyes as though he were trying to blot out some terrible memory.

Kirsty shivered, a sudden chill coursing down her back. What did he mean? Was he talking about Eva's death? She frowned, biting her lip.

'Mr Magnusson,' she began, trembling slightly under the man's stern gaze, 'I really don't think it was Colin who killed her. Honestly I don't.'

'But the police have evidence that he was the last one with her—'

'They have evidence that he and Eva had sex,' Kirsty told him bluntly. 'That shouldn't be the same as thinking he killed her as well. Making love isn't a crime,' she went on, then stopped, remembering for a fleeting moment her own rough and tumble upstairs with Roger Dunbar.

'See, I really got to know Colin quite well since we all came here,' she told him earnestly, leaning forward and hugging her arms around her chest. 'Colin's a nice lad, a bit bookish, perhaps, but a gentle soul. He would never have hurt Eva,' she said, shaking her head. 'He was so very fond of her, you know.' She sighed.

'And she liked him too, did she?' Henrik asked, shaking his head in puzzlement as though it had only just occurred to him that there might have been something he did not know about his daughter.

'I think so,' Kirsty said, mentally crossing her fingers. Why had they been together that night? Oh, Eva, if only you were here to tell me!

'You think the police have got it wrong?'

'Yes,' she said simply. 'I can't speak to my dad about it but I did see Detective Superintendent Lorimer yesterday.'

Henrik nodded, encouraging her to continue.

'Well, the police can't do anything more for Colin unless some new evidence comes up to show that he was innocent.'

'And? How is that going to happen?'

He was frowning again and, Kirsty thought, a bit annoyed at her. But she wasn't going to achieve anything unless she was brave enough to plunge ahead.

'Could I have your permission to go through all of Eva's things? There's still stuff that the police have left in her room,' she explained.

'Kirsty.' Henrik reached out and took her hands in his. When he spoke again his voice was husky. 'I can see you have been a friend to my girl and you are obviously a friend to this young man.' He heaved a huge sigh that threatened to bring tears to his eyes and Kirsty looked away, too afraid to see this big handsome man break down in front of her.

'You have my permission to look around, yes. I trust you to do this,' he told her. 'But only you, Kirsty. Take the key to Eva's room, my dear, and keep it safe, will you? Then,' he paused for a moment, 'when you are sure that you have done all that you can, I will come back and we will pack up all her things together, yes?'

Kirsty nodded again, then on an impulse she rose from the chair beside Henrik's to give him a hug. She could hear a sigh as she held him for a moment. Then, as she pulled away, she could see through her own blurred eyes the streams of tears that were coursing down this stricken father's cheeks.

CHAPTER 17

'No, I don't have any wholemeal bread, you're just gonnae have to have plain white like the rest of us!' Corinne Kennedy gritted her teeth as she pulled the loaf out of the plastic bread bin, noting for the umpteenth time the yellowing tape that held its broken lid together. Everything in this bloody house was falling to bits, she told herself, shoving the hair out of her eyes. She yanked a couple of slices off the end of the packet, muttering to herself as she pushed them into a toaster that had once been chrome and white but was now stained with scorch marks like the smudges of nicotine on her father's old fingers.

'Just you wait, see if I cannae find you a wee place out in the country,' she hissed quietly. 'Then we'll a' hae a bit of peace.'

Corinne slammed the cutlery drawer shut, listening all the while for the tap tap of the stick that might herald the old man coming through from the living room to stand and girn in her ear. It had been like this for more than a week now, ever since that poor wee Swedish lassie had copped it. At first Corinne had tried to show her elderly father a modicum of kindness; he'd had a bad fright, right enough. But after the first couple of days his whining and demands and that incessant '*What?*' that made her practically shout at him to be heard had got on her nerves. And why should she be nice to him anyway? she thought, fingers closing over the bread knife. He'd been the one to chuck her out when she'd fallen pregnant, hadn't he?

The toast popped up with a dull ping and Corinne slapped the pieces down on a plate, buttering furiously. He didn't like her sort of butter, he'd told her; preferred that expensive Danish stuff. Well Derek McCubbin was in *her* home now and he'd just have tae take what he was given, Corinne told herself, scooping up some watery raspberry jam from the bottom of a jar. Maybe she could bring up the subject of rent? He wanted to stay on here, she knew that fine; but maybe she should hold her tongue a wee bit longer till she had worked out just what her father's future was to be. Then it would be payback time for all the years she'd suffered. She smiled to herself as she sliced the toast into neat triangles. Once the Anniesland house was sold it would be easy enough to work on him.

With a sigh that came from too many years of scraping along on cheap food and cut-price everything else, Corinne Kennedy put the plate onto a melamine tray along with the pot of tea that had stood stewing till it was black enough for the old man's liking, and strode through to the living room of her third-floor flat. Her father was sitting where she had left him, in the most comfortable chair opposite the television, a rug spread across his knees.

Corinne blinked for a moment. Where had the time gone since she had left home with his words ringing in her ears? *You've made your bed now you can lie on it*, he'd shouted at her, no sympathy for her advanced state of pregnancy or for the hasty marriage that had ensued in the register office. Margaret McCubbin had said nothing, but Corinne could still recall the tears in her mother's eyes when her only daughter had left Merryfield Avenue for good, the poor soul wringing her hands on the hem of that old flowered apron.

'Here ye are, Faither,' Corinne said, placing the tray onto the old man's lap. 'Watch an no' spill the tea, okay?' She put out a tentative hand to pat his shoulder but withdrew it suddenly as he turned his face to scowl up at her.

'Where did you learn to speak like that, woman?' he growled, his gimlet stare pinning her to the spot. 'After the decent education we gave you! Too many years in this slum of a place, that's what's wrong with you,' he snarled bitterly before turning his attention to the pieces of toast.

Corinne bit her lip and retreated to the kitchen once more. Her hands were shaking as she held onto the lip of the sink. He could still do this to her, make her feel like some inadequate. Well, if it all worked out, she'd be having the last laugh. A place in the country, she told herself, thinking about the neat little bungalows spread out in Carmunnock, not this wee space inside a tenement shaped like a cereal packet in the sprawl of houses that was Castlemilk.

Anyhow, he'd been a right auld misery since his next-door neighbour, Grace Smith, had passed away, Corinne thought, standing up straighter and pulling a dry tea towel off the radiator. Grace's daughter had sold the flat in Merryfield Avenue last summer and taken bits and pieces of her late mother's things back to her home in St Andrews. Corinne had dropped plenty of hints that Derek should sell up, leave his sad memories behind and move in with her to somewhere nice but until now he had stubbornly refused to consider such a thing. *Grace was my friend*, he'd told her, *I can remember her best if I stay where I am*. But that was before. Now that poor wee Swedish lassie had been found dead in the same flat that Grace had died in everything was going to change, she thought, wiping the dishes and stacking them back in the cupboard.

Corinne Kennedy swept a disgusted glance over the grey cupboards – 'catkin', the brochure had called them, but they were still just a dull indeterminate shade of grey – to the window beyond where a weak sun was trying to emerge from behind the edge of the buildings that blocked her view of the skyline.

Her expression hardened for a moment. Aye, everything would change now and she was going to make damned sure it was a change for the better.

Kirsty Wilson waited behind her bedroom door, listening. Outside there was a low hum from the traffic making its way along Great Western Road and she could hear the swish of wet tyres down below her window. There was no sound from upstairs, but that didn't mean that the boys were asleep yet. Either of them could be lying in bed with their ears full of music downloads. She heaved a sigh. Well, if she was ever going to find a time to search in Eva's room it was now. The December darkness had filled the flat since well before the afternoon was over and now it was almost midnight. Kirsty shivered, not from cold but from the anticipation of making that diagonal walk across the hallway and unlocking the door to the dead girl's room.

A sudden thought of Colin made her straighten up and take those few steps along the corridor. He would be sleeping in a narrow bunk in a cold cell, wouldn't he? There was nothing in the girl's experience to give her a visual idea of what that might be like, only ancient TV sitcoms like *Porridge*, but Kirsty reckoned that any kind of incarceration had to be pretty bleak for a sensitive soul like Colin Young.

The keys that Mr Magnusson had left were in her dressing gown pocket and she pulled them out, feeling the cold metal in her fingers, seeing a piece of white fibre that had attached itself to the smallest. She picked it off and held the key up to the light. Aye, that was Eva's, all right. Her father had shown her the markings on the small Yale key so that she would recognise it again.

The door opened smoothly and Kirsty entered the room for the first time since the Swedish girl had died. Her hand found the light switch and the room glowed warmly under the soft pink light from the overhead lantern. Everything was there, just as Eva had always left it. Even the searches by the police and forensic folk hadn't disturbed the usual neatness of the girl's bedroom. The curtains were open to reveal the emptiness of the night sky, a dark rectangle that only reflected her image, a tubby figure lurking uncertainly in the doorway. Kirsty turned the handle to close the door, fearful of hearing the tiniest click, then moved to the space beside Eva's bed. Where to begin? She turned slowly, considering her options. There was a wall of cream-coloured sliding doors opposite Eva's bed and Kirsty pulled them slowly aside, holding her breath lest they make any sort of sound and alert the boys upstairs. It was an odd place to start, perhaps, but the girl was curious to see if the police had left her friend's things the way she'd liked them. She nodded to herself as she saw the colour-coordinated garments hanging in double rails, shoes arranged in boxes below, each turned end-on to show a picture of their contents.

She'd gasped the first time that Eva had pulled aside these doors and now Kirsty recalled the Swedish girl's uncharacteristic frown as she noticed her flatmate's reaction. Kirsty had wanted to blurt something out about it, but had held her tongue instead: *It was completely anal*, she'd muttered later in the sanctuary of her own room. But Eva Magnusson had explained sweetly that she had been taught to keep her clothes tidy and it was easier to find something if it was arranged in a colour scheme. Kirsty had tried it for a bit but after a week the jeans and sweatshirts were back to their usual higgledy-piggledy mess, over the back of a chair or lying in a corner of the room.

Reaching out, Kirsty touched the cashmere cardigan that Eva had worn so often. She let the soft garment slip off its hanger then held it to her face, breathing deeply. The inhalation ended in a sigh as she recognised the girl's favourite perfume, and with it the memory of that first night when they had all sat in the lounge drinking vintage champagne in the candlelight. The air had been redolent with that scent of sweet lime and cedar; it was the smell of new beginnings and autumn leaves. But now the perfume simply reminded Kirsty of death and decay. She shivered again, ready to leave the room undisturbed, to admit to herself that there was nothing she could do to change what had happened. With a sigh she put the cardigan back on to its silk padded hanger and replaced it on the rail next to a chiffon blouse of palest pink scattered with tiny embroidered rosebuds.

This wasn't what she had come for but it was almost as if the dead girl's influence still reached out from beyond the grave, her fey beauty beguiling the policeman's daughter. Eva had fascinated her, an ordinary girl from Glasgow, there was no denying it, Kirsty knew. *You were a good friend to her*, Henrik had claimed, and Kirsty had nodded, but was it true? Had she been a good friend? Or had she merely acted as the house mother, cooking up lots of great food for them all, keeping Eva company whenever she wanted a girl to chat to? Blinking back tears of remorse as she looked around the room, Kirsty wondered for the first time if she had ever really got to know the Swedish girl at all.

Colin had known her, certainly in the biblical sense. Eva was – not was: had been, she told herself crossly – what? A gorgeous girl

115

who might have enjoyed the odd sexual fling with her friends? Had she really fancied poor old Colin? Or had that been just something that had happened at a party? No boy had ever come up to the flat since they'd moved in, Kirsty realised, though God knows Eva could have had her pick of any boy at Strathclyde. Unless ...? Who had been in the flat that night after the party? Not Colin; no, not Colin, she told herself, firmly. That was something she had to hold onto, that belief in the lad's innocence. Had Gary or Rodge seen her with another lad? Surely they'd have said something to Detective Inspector Grant?

As the thoughts swirled around her head, Kirsty moved around the room, patting the lace-edged pillows, picking up and replacing the matching boudoir cushion, checking the bookshelves for something, *anything* that might provide a clue to what had really happened that terrible night. Trouble is, she thought gloomily, I don't even know what I'm looking for.

'Kirsty?'

'Oh my God! You gave me a fright!' Kirsty put her hand to her throat as she saw Roger standing frowning in the doorway.

'What are you doing?' he asked, nodding into the room. 'Thought that was all locked up after the police ...?'

'It's okay, Rodge, Mr Magnusson said I could come in and sort Eva's stuff out,' Kirsty reassured him.

'Funny kind of time to do it,' Roger remarked, eyeing her askance.

'Well, I didn't want to disturb you or Gary ...' Kirsty began lamely. 'Hey, seeing we're both up, d'you fancy a cup of tea?'

Switching off the light and locking the door behind her, Kirsty followed the large figure of her flatmate into the kitchen, slipping the key back into the voluminous pocket of her dressing gown.

*

He would find it hard to get back to sleep now, Roger Dunbar realised, and it was nothing to do with all that tea swilling around inside his stomach. He closed his eyes but all he could see was the shape of a stretcher between the two undertakers as they carried Eva's body out to the waiting van. Rodge had never understood that word 'closure', feeling it to be just so much American psychobabble, but now he felt an overwhelming need to see Eva just one more time, just to say goodbye to her. Was this what it meant, then: closing a door on images that refused to disappear behind tired eyelids? Seeing the room downstairs, that room flushed pink like a girl's cheeks after sex ... Bloody hell! What was he thinking? And why had that image suddenly come into his head?

Remember the good times, Kirsty had told him kindly. Though, God! It must be just as hard for her, harder, maybe, since she was adamant that Colin had nothing to do with Eva's death. Yet he'd seen him with his own eyes, hadn't he? Slipping out of the door not long after the Swedish girl had upped and left the party. He hadn't told that police inspector woman, had he? And he'd bottled it tonight as well. Couldn't bring himself to tell Kirsty that wee Colin had gone out after Eva, following her all the way home. Nobody had said that Roger Dunbar would be called as a witness so he didn't have to worry about telling any lies, did he? Even if this was, perhaps, a lie by omission.

So why, lying here in his bed under the rooftop, was he feeling such a sense of guilt?

CHAPTER 18

'Your daughter came to see me the other night,' Lorimer said, watching the man's face to gauge his reaction.

'Oh.' The word dropped like a stone as the detective sergeant grimaced and looked down at his feet. 'She's still on about Young being innocent then? Look, I'm sorry she bothered you ...'

'It's fine, don't worry about it,' Lorimer said, putting a reassuring hand on the other man's shoulder. 'But I did want you to know. If anything should come up that suggests the presence of a stranger in the Anniesland house then the Fiscal would definitely want to take another look. And I wouldn't want another team being involved.'

'Kirsty had no right—'

'She cares about the lad,' Lorimer interrupted the older man firmly, 'and what do we know about the relationships that went on in that flat? Kirsty is far better placed to make judgements of that sort. And besides,' he broke off thoughtfully, 'I reckon your girl is pretty sorted. She's not the dramatic, emotional sort, is she? Struck me as a young lady with her head screwed on. And she has the knack of getting under the skin of the people she meets.'

'Aye, well, neither Betty nor I go in for any kind of histrionics. And Kirsty was always a sensible lass.' DS Wilson frowned for a moment. 'There isn't anything we can do though, is there? I mean, Jo Grant's got it all done and dusted, hasn't she?'

'No, you're right.' Lorimer's mouth twisted into a rueful smile. 'Unless something new appears, it looks as though Colin Young will have to face a trial in a few months' time.'

The prison library was a lot smaller than he had imagined it would be, just a few shelves of books, really, when all was said and done. The librarian wore an ordinary jacket and trousers, a simple lanyard slung around his grey V-neck sweater, unlike the uniformed officers with bunches of keys attached to their belts who attended him throughout the day. The other inmates seemed to know the pack drill so Colin watched as they lined up at the little desk with their returned books. The librarian was perhaps in his late thirties, a thin man whose pallor was not helped by the harsh fluorescent light shining down on him from the ceiling. He reminded him of Mr Armitage, one of his history teachers at school. As the librarian chatted to each of the prisoners, Colin noted the way he swept a hand over his thinning hair from time to time, a nervous gesture that his history teacher had repeated during every lesson. Once all the boys in his Higher class had mimicked this but Armitage had been in full and eager flow about the Battle of Leipzig and hadn't noticed a thing.

'You're new,' the librarian said as Colin came forward at last.

'Yes.'

'What do you like to read?'

Colin shrugged, unsure how to answer this. Didn't the man know anything about him, then? He'd assumed that all the staff would know every detail about him by now. Like at school where the Guidance teachers had a file on you. But perhaps it didn't work like that in prison.

'I'm a student ...' Colin began.

'Just in on remand,' the librarian said, meeting Colin's eyes and nodding. 'Yes, I think the deputy governor mentioned you. English Lit at Glasgow, isn't it?'

Colin nodded again, reddening. 'I shouldn't really be here,' he whispered. 'It's all a mistake.'

The librarian did not even acknowledge Colin's remark but instead looked down at once and flicked a couple of papers on his desk.

'We're going to get in touch with the university, see if we can keep you going with lecture notes and such.'

Colin's eyes widened. 'You can do that?'

'Oh, yes. You're a registered student. It would be just the same as getting hold of stuff to read up if you were on a long-term illness. In fact' – he stopped flicking the papers and held one up for Colin to see – 'just got instructions this morning.' He waggled the paper with the prison name at the top. 'Straight from the boss. Asking me to liaise with the university.'

There had been no difficulty getting hold of a notepad and pen. All the inmates seemed to be in the habit of letter writing but none had access to a computer or laptop so the prison was full of men penning letters the old-fashioned way. Snail mail, Colin thought to himself. And that phrase suited prison life where everything went at a snail's pace. Day after endless day passed in here, the whole place trembling with the effort of waiting till a term of imprisonment or a period of remand was finished and life in the real world outside could begin again.

He would write to Kirsty, he thought. She was one of the people he had listed as potential visitors, but would she come to see him? He wanted to tell her how he was doing and ask what was happening back at the flat. Would they still be there? He paused for a moment, pen poised over the blank page, wondering. Well, he would send a letter anyway, in the hope that a forwarding address would have been arranged.

Half an hour later Colin Young was still sitting on the edge of his bunk, the notepad's pages turned over where he had tried to scribble down his thoughts. It was no use, he told himself bitterly. Everything he'd wanted to say had turned out like a whine. And he didn't want a girl like Kirsty Wilson to think he, prisoner number 201316, was wallowing in self-pity. If only he was back in the flat, sitting tapping on his keyboard. The words would flow easily then, surely?

It was then, in the quiet of the late evening, that the idea took hold. Colin smiled to himself. Taking up the blue biro pen once more, he began to write.

Kirsty wasn't used to snooping around in other people's rooms but she had found herself alone in the flat that afternoon and somehow her feet had taken her across the corridor and into Colin's bedroom. The curtains were still drawn across the window to the back of the house and she automatically walked over to draw them apart, even though dusk was beginning to fall over the city. It was quiet in here, but no doubt a train would rumble past soon enough on its way to Anniesland station. The room was very tidy, Kirsty saw. Had the scene-of-crime officers left it like this? She'd only glimpsed Colin's room from the corridor, his desk usually piled high with notes around his ancient laptop, a second-hand IBM ThinkPad that he'd been given by an uncle. Now the desk was empty of Colin's stuff, the laptop having been taken away by the police, and only the green lamp was there. It was just as it had been when Kirsty had first looked around the flat, she recalled.

'Oh dear,' she whispered, though there was nobody to hear her. Suddenly, for no particular reason, Kirsty found herself flopping down on the single bed, staring up at the ceiling. How often now had Colin stared up like this, waiting for inspiration for one of his stories or poems?

Kirsty's fists clenched tightly in a moment of anger. He should still be here, writing these things ... if it hadn't been for Eva! It was all *her* fault, that perfect face, perfect figure, perfect everything!

A whimper escaped her lips and Kirsty screwed her eyes shut, appalled at her thoughts. And, as her breath exhaled in one enormous sigh, the girl's fingers relaxed until they were limp by her sides once more.

She felt the vibration under her body as the train rattled past. How had Eva and Colin put up with that? She'd never once heard either of them complain so she guessed that it was something they'd become used to pretty quickly. There would be no vibration under his prison bunk, she thought, fists clenching once more by her side. What sort of hell was he going through in that awful place? With a tiny shake of her head, Kirsty swung her legs over the edge of the bed and stood up. These sorts of maudlin thoughts weren't getting her anywhere and she'd be better having a look next door in Eva's room while she had the chance.

The dead girl's room was considerably larger than Colin's but not as big as Kirsty's own, the airy, former dining room that looked out over the street. As before, Kirsty was aware of the scent of Jo Malone perfume; a woody, citrus sort of smell that reminded her so forcibly of the dead girl. She took a deep breath, closing her eyes to conjure up Eva's smiling face once more. When she opened them, it was almost a surprise not to see the Swedish girl standing there, blue eyes looking quizzically at her, wanting to know why Kirsty had intruded in her room.

'Your dad said I could,' Kirsty whispered into the air as though something was listening. 'Oh, Eva, if only you could tell me what really happened,' she sighed, then bit her lip as she felt the tears well up.

The officers must have taken lots of the dead girl's possessions, Kirsty realised, after she had spent a fruitless hour looking for things like her mobile phone, address book and the Apple Mac notebook that Eva had carried back and forth to lectures.

Och, it was no use! She ought to give up now and just get back to her own room. There was plenty of course work to do, after all. This was still the first term but already Kirsty had a couple of essays outstanding and loads of background reading to cope with. With a sigh she closed Eva's door and locked it, returning to her own bedroom across the corridor.

She had begun to flick over her notes when she caught sight of something scribbled in a margin. The sight of the emerald green ink made Kirsty smile. Jackie, her pal at Caledonian, always used these bright gel pens. She'd meant to copy down the girl's new mobile number into her own phone but had completely forgotten. She'd do it now, before she forgot again.

It was as she was fishing in her handbag for the mobile that Kirsty suddenly stopped and stared into space.

What if . . . ? The thought propelled her out of the seat by the window and before she had time to think Kirsty was turning the key to Eva Magnusson's room once more.

The Swedish girl had been methodical in all aspects of her life, Kirsty thought, seeing the shelves beside her desk full of ring binders, as if someone had made that shelf specially to fit. And perhaps someone had, she thought. Money had been no object for

123

Eva, after all. She hunkered down and pulled the whole lot from their place by the pale pine desk, letting them fall with a thump onto the carpet.

'Right, let's see if there's anything here,' she muttered, pulling the first file towards her and opening it.

She sat back on her heels, taking a quick breath, as she saw the girl's familiar writing. It was so perfect, a neat copperplate hand, sloping prettily over the lines, the phrases copied down and attached to printed notes by a metal paper clip. Business management might have been interesting to the Swedish girl but skimming through the notes, Kirsty wrinkled up her nose: it was definitely not the sort of subject that she would have chosen to study.

She read to the last page and closed the file. Nothing. With a sigh, she picked up the next one, a red ring binder with Eva's name printed on a label inside.

It seemed to Kirsty as she flicked through the notes that her flatmate had approached her subjects with the same degree of organisation as she took to colour-coordinating her wardrobe. *It makes it easier*, she imagined Eva's voice telling her and she turned with a guilty start as if the dead girl had actually walked in behind her.

Don't be silly, she scolded herself. She can't hurt you now.

Kirsty frowned at the oddity of the thought. Had Eva ever hurt her? What a silly thing to pop into her head. Eva had been incapable of hurting a fly. And yet she had to rub her arms suddenly, as though a chill had entered the room.

'Look at the darned files,' she breathed aloud, turning her attention to the folders once more. As her eyes ran over the perfectly ordered pages, Kirsty sighed. She could just picture Eva sitting in her classes, earnestly taking down notes, concentrating on the lecturer's every word.

She had almost finished searching through that folder when she stopped and smiled. Gotcha! There it was, a wee bit of writing standing out from the black and white page. Kirsty could see it right at the foot of one of the printed sets of notes where Eva must have added something of her own. The lecturer's name and email address were there for all his students to see but now there was more: a telephone number written in pale blue ink. And beside it, a hasty scribble that was different from Eva's own writing. Kirsty took a deep breath as she noted a date and time.

She blinked and read it again then sat back on her heels, mind in a spin. If Eva Magnusson had not been killed on the night of that party then she would have been meeting someone at eight o'clock the very next evening.

Dirk McGregor had not intended to follow his father's footsteps into the world of academia. No, his path was to have taken quite a different turn, though by the early years of the new millennium, Dirk had to admit that gaining a degree in business studies and the lectureship that followed was a huge relief. A sudden lunge across a wet football pitch by a defender on the opposing team had put him out of the beautiful game for good, cutting short a career that one or two pundits grudgingly agreed might have taken him to international stardom. Or perhaps not. Dirk had been a reasonably skilful footballer, usually making the first team in a club that hovered somewhere in the middle of Scottish First Division football. Sometimes, when he had been a little too long in the staff club of a Friday night, Dirk was wont to become somewhat maudlin, lamenting the freak accident that had destroyed his career, a career that would surely have blossomed given half a chance.

Now he was ensconced in his shoebox of a study, glancing up at the clock: ten more minutes of peace and quiet until the next lot of students turned up for their seminar. His desk was covered in a pile of essays to return, a dirty coffee mug and an open laptop. To one side was a digital photoframe, its screen blank for the moment. Sometimes Dirk liked to watch the slide show, glimpses of his life like visual sound bites: Fran and the girls in the garden, his father and mother – before the Alzheimer's took hold of the poor old girl – and several of himself in a black and white strip, action photos salvaged from his glory days.

The sound of his mobile ringing made Dirk frown in annoyance: Fran knew fine she shouldn't call him at work; what the hell did the stupid cow want now?

Thrusting his fingers into the right-hand pocket of the cord jacket slung behind his chair, Dirk pulled out the phone and snapped it open.

'Yes?' His tone, even to him, sounded irritable. But the small silence that followed, then the unfamiliar voice asking that terrible question, made the lecturer suddenly ashamed.

'Who is this?' he demanded.

Dirk listened to the continuing silence then the question was repeated.

'Yes, this is Mr McGregor. What are you doing calling this number?'

His hand shook as he waited for an answer, but again, the woman simply reiterated her first question. 'Are you Dirk McGregor, the man who was seeing Eva Magnusson?'

Dirk let the silence continue for a moment then, as the door to his study opened to admit his first student, he closed the phone and switched it off, dropping it back into the pocket as though it were a burning coal.

*

Kirsty sat on the floor of her room, trembling. She'd had all night to think about this, after all. It wasn't as though she'd called him on the spur of the moment. What the heck had she done? The man had sounded really, really alarmed. Frightened, even. Well, maybe he had good reason to be frightened if he had been seeing a girl who was one of his students, a girl who had ended up dead in her own flat.

Kirsty blew out her breath in a huge sigh. She really ought to report this to somebody. DI Grant? She made a face. No. That one had Colin tried and convicted already, hadn't she? Her dad? Kirsty thought about it for just a heartbeat then shook her head. Not Dad either. Lorimer? He hadn't seemed to mind her turning up before, had he? Even suggested that she poke around a little. Well, she had, and now there *was* something to report, wasn't there? Kirsty leaned forward and pulled her handbag off the edge of the bed. She'd put it somewhere, inside her uni diary, most probably. Aye, here it was; a card with another number that she ought to have listed in her phone.

The girl sat back against the radiator, trying to decide. Was it too soon to bother him? Or would he welcome the call? It was Detective *Superintendent* Lorimer now, she remembered. He had been promoted a while ago but had been away in Pitt Street before coming back into her dad's divisional HQ. *He's a very busy man*, Alistair Wilson had warned her when he had called to talk last night.

What were her options? To go over to Strathclyde and seek out this man, Dirk what's-his-face? Or to ask for Lorimer's advice?

Eva had never said a word about meeting this man, McGregor. Well, maybe it was all completely innocent. But a Saturday night at eight o'clock? Hm, Kirsty huffed aloud. No way. She'd been up to something, hadn't she? Arranging to meet one of her lecturers –

a married man, perhaps? – the day after a party where she had been having it off with poor wee Colin.

Kirsty Wilson blinked hard as though trying to clear the fog that was misting up her brain. There was a lot she had not known about Eva Magnusson. And for the first time, she began to wonder just what other secrets the Swedish girl had kept from her friends.

'Hello, Lorimer speaking. Oh, Kirsty, it's you. How are you?'

The tall man leaned back in his chair, stretching his long legs out in front of him.

'No, it's fine. I'm on my own right at this moment but I will be going to a meeting in about quarter of an hour. What can I do for you?'

Lorimer listened, not interrupting once as Kirsty recounted what she had found in Eva's notes and how she had acted upon that, calling up the business studies lecturer.

'He hung up on you?' Lorimer nodded, wondering, as the girl continued.

'What if . . . ?' Kirsty began but then broke off, not really knowing what she wanted to say.

'What if this man had been having an affair with Eva? Is that what you've been thinking?'

'Yes. Look, I know this sounds horrible, but Colin just wasn't Eva's type. She was a sophisticated girl, you know? She'd travelled, mixed with all sorts of important people – famous, some of them. It just didn't make *sense* for her to have a relationship with an ordinary bloke like him.'

Lorimer sighed before he spoke. 'I have a colleague who would say that this simply endorses the suspicion that Colin Young killed your friend,' he said at last. 'If he wasn't Eva's type then perhaps he had been rebuffed by her before raping and strangling her.'

128

There was a silence between them and Lorimer suddenly felt an immense pity for the girl. She was doing her best and he had given her a little encouragement, after all.

'Was it rape?' she asked quietly.

'Ah, now that is a good question,' Lorimer said, wondering just how he could begin to answer this without compromising the case in any way.

'There was no sign of rape, was there?' Kirsty insisted.

'No,' Lorimer admitted. 'But that doesn't mean it was consensual either. Eva may have been forced into something she didn't really want but had decided not to resist.'

'Well, what about this man, this Dirk McGregor? Shouldn't we be doing something about him?'

Lorimer smiled to himself. The girl was so eager to clear Young's name that she obviously felt that she had entered into some sort of liaison with the senior police officer. Perhaps she had. And it would do no harm if he made a discreet call to see the lecturer. Just to chat about Eva?

'Kirsty,' he said, making up his mind even as he spoke, 'leave it with me. It might be nothing at all, something completely innocent. Okay?'

'Okay, Mr Lorimer,' she mumbled, clearly disappointed that she was not being asked to join him in an investigation.

'Oh, and Kirsty . . . '

'Uh-huh?'

'Keep looking in Eva's room.'

'What am I supposed to be looking for?'

'Who knows? But you'll know when you find it.'

CHAPTER 19

'Sir?' Jo Grant stood uncertainly in the doorway of Lorimer's room, her lips parted as though she had wanted to say more.

'Sit down, Jo.' Lorimer gestured to the chair opposite his own.

'Sir,' she replied dully, folding her arms over her chest in a gesture that the detective superintendent recognised as protective.

She's assuming that I am about to reprimand her for something, he thought guiltily.

'Jo,' he began again, 'I have something to tell you that you aren't going to like.'

'You're taking me off the case?'

The detective inspector dropped her arms and looked at him in astonishment.

Lorimer shook his head. 'No, no, nothing like that,' he assured her. 'Actually, I have a huge apology to make to you, Jo,' he said slowly.

The woman frowned and tilted her head, clearly puzzled.

'It's about Colin Young.'

'What about him?' Her face cleared and there was a trace of a smile as she asked, 'Don't tell me he's confessed? Oh, boy, no flaming court case, after all—'

'No, he hasn't,' Lorimer broke in. 'It's nothing like that at all. In fact,' he said, 'he might even be released if things develop the way I think they could.'

'Oh?'

Lorimer heaved a long sigh then bit by bit recounted the whole story of Kirsty Wilson coming to see him and the strength of her conviction about the man who was in Barlinnie.

'I knew this would come as a blow,' he went on. 'You imagine you've got the right man then fresh evidence appears to make you wonder.'

'But why didn't anyone tell me right from the start?' Jo blurted out, her face tight with suppressed anger.

'When Kirsty Wilson came to me I couldn't be sure she was doing more than wanting to express her feelings. And I didn't want to offend you.'

'And you're telling me now that you think I messed up?' The woman had turned white with fury and Lorimer held up a placating hand.

'I'm not saying that at all. Maybe I should have told you as soon as the girl came to see me but, if I had, would you honestly have been prepared to reconsider your initial stance?'

Jo did not reply, pursing her lips in a discontented moue instead.

'So, what now?' she said gruffly.

'I want your cooperation on this,' Lorimer told her gently. 'The last thing I want is for us to fall out as colleagues. But' – he raised an admonitory finger – 'I don't think you want to see an innocent man go down for something he didn't do any more than I do.'

'And the grounds for reopening this case . . . ?' The arms were folded again as she looked him in the eye.

'It's entirely up to the Fiscal, of course,' Lorimer told her. 'But let's just say that, thanks to Kirsty Wilson, we are beginning to find out a bit more about Eva Magnusson and the people around her.'

'But you still haven't persuaded me that Colin Young couldn't have killed her,' she protested. 'This lecturer guy, she might just have been going to see him about her studies.'

'On a Saturday night?' Lorimer's twisted smile was sceptical.

'I still think it was Young,' Jo insisted.

'But why?' Lorimer leaned forward, staring right at his DI. 'Can you honestly say what motivated an otherwise mild-mannered young man to commit such an act?'

Jo still had her arms folded across her chest and was staring straight at him, her mouth closed tight.

'Okay.' Lorimer raised his hands in mock surrender. 'I can see you're not happy and you think I'm taking up precious time right now, but I really felt I had to tell you what we've been doing.'

'And Alistair Wilson doesn't know a thing about it?'

Lorimer smiled thinly. 'You had to be told first. I think he'll have Kirsty's guts for garters when I tell him. You know we have to wait for approval from the Fiscal and then if anything else comes up that provides a new lead in the Magnusson case we will keep him informed.'

'And meantime you want me to do what, exactly?'

Lorimer stared back at her, wondering if she would have the grace to add 'sir'.

'Your job,' he said stiffly.

Jo Grant clenched and unclenched her fists as she marched back to her own desk. It was beyond belief! Why the hell would a detective superintendent risk so much just on the off chance that the wrong man had been arrested for murder? What kind of evidence did he think he had? She had been with Young, watched him break down, hadn't she? Besides, his DNA profile was right there for anyone to see, so why go off on a tangent with something as unreliable as a tenuous date in the victim's social diary?

Okay, so maybe she had got the wrong man, she fumed to herself. It had happened before and the norm was for police to close ranks, protect their own, wasn't it? What a court and a jury of fifteen men and women did thereafter was up to them.

She sat down at her desk with a thump, staring angrily at the computer screen. Then a small voice of doubt crept into Jo Grant's thoughts. What if she *had* been wrong? What if Colin Young was innocent after all? It meant two things, didn't it? First, a guiltless student was being held in Barlinnie prison, undergoing who knew what sort of deprivations, and second – a thought that sent chills shivering up her spine – Eva Magnusson's killer was still out there.

Lorimer held up a list of the names of those interviewed in the aftermath of Eva Magnusson's murder. He was grateful for Jo's cooperation, however grudgingly she had given it, and now he was looking once again at the entire procedure of the case. If Jo had got it all wrong there was a chance that the powers on high might well put in a review team to examine the case, officers from a different division crawling all over their own patch who might make Jo Grant feel small and inadequate. Whereas, he reasoned, this way he could repair some of the damage without her losing too much face.

The names and addresses of neighbours were near the top of the list and Lorimer frowned as he read them. Kirsty had mentioned the neighbour across the landing, a deaf, grumpy old man, she'd told him. Why hadn't his name been there? Surely, he

133

thought, Mr McCubbin would have been questioned by the police.

He dialled his DI's extension and waited until she picked up.

'Jo? Lorimer here. Just a wee question. Derek McCubbin, the next-door neighbour. No sign of a statement from him. Wondered why.'

'He was away that night,' Jo replied sharply. 'At his daughter's in Castlemilk. He's selling up anyhow,' she added.

'Okay. Thanks.'

An old deaf man would probably not have heard anything anyway, Lorimer reasoned, even if he had been in his flat that particular night. And who could blame a protective daughter for wanting her father to leave the place after what had happened?

Still, perhaps he would pay the old man a visit some time, just to see what he could glean about the comings and goings at 24 Merryfield Avenue in the days before someone took the life of his lovely young neighbour.

CHAPTER 20

For a December day that was creeping towards the winter solstice, the morning appeared with a freshness that made Professor Solomon Brightman smile. The first faint flush of rose spread across the horizon, the sky above palest lemon, a brightness that dazzled his eyes even as the sun struggled to pierce the early mists. Life, he thought to himself, was very good indeed: his life, at any rate, with so many blessings for which to give thanks. There was Rosie, of course, and baby Abigail; not quite such a baby now, her first birthday behind her and developing at such amazing speed that Solly was almost afraid to leave the house each morning lest he miss something vital. Abby had taken her first steps two months earlier and had begun to utter discernible words even before that. Both he and Rosie were looking forward to the Christmas holidays and seeing their little girl's face on Christmas morning.

Abigail Margaret Brightman was a determined little lady, not at all bashful at asserting herself if there was something she wanted. Like the shiny red bauble that he had placed just out of her reach. Solly smiled, remembering the previous night when Abby had systematically stripped the tree of the painted wooden baubles, gathering them all to her tiny chest like so much treasure. His heart ached to give her everything she wanted but his wiser self knew that his little daughter had to learn what was safe to touch and what might harm her, like a glass sphere that could shatter into deadly shards or an electric socket that was left without its safety plug.

They were both still asleep; Abigail back in her cot and Rosie in the warmth of the big sleigh bed that he had slipped from only minutes before. The temptation to crawl back in beside her was strong: there had been yet another night of broken sleep, Abby leaving both her parents feeling shattered. But it was Saturday morning, there were no classes demanding his presence and Rosie was not on call, thankfully, this particular weekend. Morag, the wonderful nanny who had been an answer to all their prayers, would not be in until Monday morning so he had two whole days to spend indulging his little family.

Standing back from the window in his study, Solly's gaze was drawn to his laptop. There would be emails to deal with, but somehow he could not bring himself to spoil this moment of quietness, the stillness within the flat as yet unbroken by a child's demanding cry. Yet, as if the very thought itself had broken a spell, the psychologist found himself seated at his desk, tapping in his password. There were eighteen emails in his inbox, several of which he recognised as coming from his colleagues and post-graduate students. He deleted the junk mail as he scrolled down, eyeing the list with increasing indifference. Then his hand paused, hovering over the cordless mouse as he read the familiar name. *Lorimer.*

Solly's bushy eyebrows rose and he smiled at his own reaction, a delighted eagerness to read whatever it was that his friend had deemed important enough to send late on a Friday night.

It was not, Solly saw, really from Lorimer at all but a forwarded email from a girl who called herself KirsWil3@gmail.com. The appended note from Lorimer was brief and to the point.

> Kirsty Wilson wants to clear Colin Young's name, Solly, and I'm afraid I encouraged her to look a bit into the Magnusson girl's background – more in the hope that she would decide to give up, really. But she may actually have found something so I have agreed to forward this on to you for your opinion, and, I trust, sound advice. I will be letting Jo Grant know what has been found, of course.
> Lorimer

Solly gave a sigh and nodded. It was a rum business, this Swedish girl being murdered in her own flat. And DS Wilson's daughter mixed up in it, too. He scrolled down and read the forwarded message.

> Dear Professor Brightman,
> I am really sorry to bother you but I'm very concerned that a miscarriage of justice may be about to take place and I wanted to talk to you. You see, I feel very strongly that my flatmate, Eva, was not killed by Colin Young, as the police seem to think. Would it be at all possible for you to spare me time to talk about this?
> Best wishes,
> Kirsty Wilson

Solly sat still, reading the message over again. The tone was polite, deferential, even, but there was a directness about it that he found appealing. 'You see', the girl had written, as though she actually wanted him to see what she saw, to share her viewpoint.

But did she want more than that? 'A miscarriage of justice' was a phrase that brooked no argument. Also she had used the word 'very' twice as if to underline her obvious concern, something that might even hint at passionately held feelings. Did she have any sort of romantic attachment to Young, the chap who had been charged with the Swedish girl's murder? Solly placed his hands behind his head, amused at the extent to which Kirsty Wilson had already wormed her way into his thoughts. Yes, he decided, he would see her, if only to put her mind at rest that the police had done what they had to do.

He frowned suddenly. What if ...? Jo Grant was a bright woman, but if she *had* made a blunder in this case, then her career path might come to a dead end.

'Daaa-daaa!' a familiar little voice called out, making Solly stand up and turn towards the nursery, a grin on his face. It seemed that, after a restless night, Abigail had decided that breakfast time had finally arrived.

The message from Kirsty Wilson stood out on the screen, waiting for a reply, but for now the psychologist had another young lady demanding his attention, one who simply would not be prepared to wait a moment longer than necessary.

Across the city another father was sitting down to breakfast, the Saturday edition of the *Gazette* propped against the cereal packet that separated him from the tousle-haired woman sitting across the table. Upstairs, all was blissfully quiet. Amanda and Catherine were still asleep and, listening to her incessant chatter, Dirk McGregor heartily wished that his wife had decided to stay in bed as well.

'We could take off on the Tuesday and be back in time for the girls' disco on the Friday. What do you think?' Fran McGregor tried to push a stray curl away from her forehead but it tumbled back down again across a brow etched with permanent frown marks.

Dirk gave no reply except to make a grunt, his usual ploy when pretending to listen to his wife.

'Sharon says we can stay over, no problem. The cottage isn't let out at that time of year so we would have the whole place to ourselves. Dirk? What do you think?' she repeated, this time with more of an edge to her voice, a sign that Fran McGregor was not prepared to be ignored for very much longer.

'Aye, fine, whatever you say,' Dirk replied testily, trying to concentrate on the leading article about yet another political career in turmoil.

'We could share the driving,' Fran persisted, her tone a shade doubtful.

With a sigh that was deliberately audible, Dirk lowered the newspaper and glared at his wife.

'I'll drive,' he said shortly. 'Just you make sure there'll be enough grub for, how many days did you say?'

'Three nights,' Fran replied, beaming now that her plan had been accepted by her irascible husband.

Dirk grunted again and lifted the paper as though to signal the end of that particular conversation. But somehow the article he had been reading had lost its appeal and the memory of that woman's voice on the telephone returned to haunt him.

Eva Magnusson! Beautiful, naughty little Eva. God! What he would give for her to be back in his life again! And yet . . . Dirk clutched the sides of the newspaper, remembering.

The pale limbs stretched upwards, the way her back had arched under his heaving body . . . oh God! How could he have let himself be led into a situation like that? But he had, Dirk thought.

And it had been oh so easy for her to seduce him, hadn't it? The ego of an older, jaded man had been flattered by a little beauty like the Swedish girl. Dirk blinked, realising that his eyes were filling up, thankful to be hiding behind the newspaper.

It had always been going to end in tears. But he hadn't wanted it to end like *that*.

Fran was talking again, going over all the things they would need for a few days away up at Malcolm and Sharon's cottage. The girls stopped their private school more than a week before Christmas so there would be no problem in taking off to the Highlands. And maybe it would be good to escape for a while, Dirk thought, biting his lip. Though at that precise moment the lecturer could not honestly say just what it was that he wanted to escape from.

'No, Dad, I'm no' gonnae put it off another day. We have to see the estate agent an' get this all settled.'

Derek McCubbin pushed the spoon around the bowl of corn-flakes, watching the thin milk sopping the tan-coloured cereal into a soggy mess. Bloody semi-skimmed! Why could she not buy the full cream that he liked? Derek had always insisted he had the top of the milk at home, *the breadwinner's prerogative*, his wife used to remark fondly. Well he was still the man who was providing the wherewithal, wasn't he?

'You don't really want to go back to Anniesland, now, do you, Dad?' Corinne wheedled. 'Not after everything that's happened, eh?'

Derek shook his head, a silent answer that seemed to satisfy his daughter.

'Right, want some toast?' Her voice softened a little now that she had got her way.

He nodded without looking up, too afraid to meet her eyes. No, he would not return to Merryfield Avenue or to the memories of those hooligans across the landing. Good riddance to the lot of them! Yet, as his hand lifted the spoon to his mouth, Derek felt a trembling in his fingers and lips so that a gob of cereal fell onto the table.

'Tsk!' Corinne swooped onto the mess with a cloth, snatching it up, then wiping his lips in one quick movement.

Her father looked away, ashamed. Was this his fate now? Was he becoming an old helpless man? It was something he had tried to resist for so long. Derek had listened to their whispering, imagining them making cunning plans to take him away from all that he held dear and put him into some kind of home for the elderly. 'God's waiting room', some called it. The old man breathed a sigh of relief. It wouldn't come to that, now. Corinne would look after him. The flat would be sold and he would live out his twilight years in a modicum of comfort, away from the noise and bustle of the city.

He pushed the bowl away from him and slumped into his chair, his appetite quite gone. There would be no more jaunts around the corner to the pub on Great Western Road. But then he wouldn't have to suffer those flights of stone stairs, his leg aching with the effort to climb back up to his beloved home. It was a different sort of ache that Derek McCubbin was experiencing now; an ache in his heart for all the yesterdays he had spent so carelessly and that could never be given back.

CHAPTER 21

'Ready?' Lorimer watched as Maggie bustled about the kitchen, testing the back door to see that it was locked, gathering up her capacious handbag and the plastic bag with Abby's present.

'Aye, all set. D'you think she'll like it?' Maggie asked, lifting the fluffy duck out of the bag and regarding it doubtfully.

Lorimer grinned. 'Course she will! She loves the ducks in the park and once she gets the hang of pressing the bit that quacks she'll drive her parents crackers!'

'Or quackers,' Maggie quipped, slipping out of the front door while Lorimer held it open for her.

They had been for a ramble down at the RSPB centre at Lochwinnoch, just after sunrise, to watch the flocks of wading birds on the loch. The soft toy was one of many bird species that made an accurate sound when pressed and Maggie had been unable to resist the duck as a present for her godchild.

They were both used to early rises even in this dark time of year when the sun was a reluctant visitor; Lorimer was punctilious about being at his desk in Stewart Street by six every morning and Maggie made a point of spending time with her husband at breakfast. The extra time before setting off for Muirpark Secondary School was used for preparation and any last-minute corrections, giving the English teacher a head start to her day. So when the weather forecast showed that Saturday was to be dry and wind-less, they had decided to pay the waterfowl a visit. Seeing the first burning rays of sun coming up over the hills, spreading golden layers across the water, had been well worth the sacrifice of a lie-in. And now little Abby was to have a new toy, something that the godparents hoped would encourage her growing interest in birds.

'Oh, this is nice,' Maggie sighed, looking out of the window as they drove across the river. The familiar landmarks of the city stood out sharply against a pale winter sky: the spiked tower of Glasgow University, the white spire of Trinity and the newer, modern buildings that hugged the banks of the Clyde. The river below was a streak of pearly grey, coursing out towards the misty west where it would eventually widen into the Firth and join the Atlantic.

Lorimer nodded, his eyes on the road ahead, his thoughts not on the sky or the river but on the message he had sent to his friend. Would Solly be willing to take an interest in the case? And if so, was there anything to be found? The senior policeman frowned. Jo Grant had been pretty tight-lipped when he had told her what Kirsty Wilson had discovered. And perhaps his own will-ingness to see Kirsty Wilson had undermined that loyalty already? The information about McGregor was in the Fiscal's hands now and they would just have to wait to see if anything changed.

His thoughts returned to Alistair Wilson's daughter. There had been something very persuasive in the girl's manner, casting the tiniest shadow of a doubt in his mind. What if they had got it wrong? There was a celebrated defence lawyer in the city whose mantra was that it was better that ninety-nine guilty men went free than that one innocent man was wrongly convicted. Lorimer, like so many of his police colleagues, didn't hold with that at all. They would rather every guilty person was convicted and all the innocent set free. Yet he could see the lawyer's point. What if Colin Young had been wrongly charged? Well, there would be fifteen men and women on a jury at the High Court some time next year to see that justice was done, he told himself. Jo Grant had done what she had to do, given the existing evidence, and they would continue to discuss between them how best to take this forward. His DI was still insistent they had the right man. Yet the frown that had settled between Lorimer's eyes as they drove along the riverside persisted, despite his efforts to assure himself that they really had apprehended the Swedish girl's killer.

Every day here was exactly the same and Colin had to make a real effort to remember what day of the week it was. Christmas was not too far off, a mere matter of days, but Colin wanted the occasion to pass him by as quickly as it could. The other prisoners all seemed to be sports enthusiasts, taking off for the gym at every opportunity in the hope of winning one of the prizes on offer for the festive competitions, but Colin had come into the system too late to enter for anything and he simply didn't have the energy to be bothered anyway. Dad had been in once, bringing his clothes and other stuff he had asked for, and he knew he would be in again this afternoon.

He'd told him about Sam, the tall white-haired man who had slipped him a Mars Bar and offered him good advice. *Get yer da tae nip ower tae the vending machines tae get ye stuff soon as he comes in tae visit, right? He cannae afford tae wait in thon queue else ye'll never hae time tae talk thegether, mind an' tell him, son.* Sam had been a decent sort, nice to him and friendly, and Colin had felt a huge relief that someone was looking out for him.

Colin sat on the side of his bunk, fiddling with his pen. Oh how he missed having his mobile phone! It was like part of him had

144

been taken away, like a limb, leaving him with that phantom pain that amputees talked about. All his pals were the same: a click of a button away from a voice or a text, communication guaranteed. But they were forbidden in here and he could only use the telephone down the corridor occasionally. Still, Dad would update him on things, wouldn't he? Tell him how Celtic was doing, for instance, though the fate of his father's favourite football team was of little interest to Colin. What he really wanted to know was how the lawyers were getting on with his case and if anything new had come to light that would allow him to return to the life he so missed. And it was the wee ordinary things that Colin Young missed, things he'd taken for granted; like having a hot shower whenever he wanted it, going out for a walk when the notion took him, making himself a cup of decent coffee . . .

He rolled over to face the far wall. He was on his own again, the young ned who'd shared his cell having been taken off somewhere else last night. He hadn't asked any questions, but the sly grin on the other boy's face had left him wondering.

He closed his eyes and thought about Merryfield Avenue. If he tried very hard he could pretend he was back there lying on his own bed, listening to sounds coming from the kitchen . . . Perhaps Kirsty would be up and about already, cooking French toast with blueberries and cinnamon, one of her Saturday morning favourites. The remembered taste of it made the saliva curl around his tongue. In here . . . no, he wouldn't even think of the food in here . . . *basic and nourishing*, the pantryman had told him sharply. Remember the good times, he'd told himself over and over, then he wondered what Oscar Wilde would have thought about in Reading gaol whenever he'd had time to pause from the hard labour prisoners were set in those days.

*

Fiona Travers jogged along the pavement, dodging bits of Friday night's litter, the discarded pizza boxes picked clean by crows, and bottles rolling about in the wind. It was daylight now but the leaden grey clouds shifting across the sky threatened rain. Just ahead the girl spotted the opening to a narrow lane. She bit an indecisive lip as it drew closer. It wasn't a route she liked to take because of all the dog poo underfoot and the gloomy overhanging trees. Still, if she took a wee shortcut down this path and watched her feet maybe it wouldn't take so long to get back before the heavens opened.

There were no dog walkers out this morning, just a lone figure walking beneath the line of ancient elms that skirted the footpath. Fiona took a deep breath and increased her pace, determined to reach home before the rain began.

She did not even glance at the man as she passed him by, eye contact with strangers an unwritten taboo.

The sound of her trainers thudding on the beaten earth was the only sound and yet some inner instinct made Fiona half turn as though she had heard something behind her. She twisted around, just in time to see the man's glaring eyes and the upraised arm holding a hefty stick.

She had to run faster. Had to get away. Had to duck out of his reach . . .

The movement made her stumble then slip on a patch of mud, giving him the advantage he needed.

Fiona opened her mouth to scream as the stick came towards her brow but all that issued from her lips was a small whimper of pain and disbelief. She was on her knees now, one hand held to her bleeding head.

And so it was that the girl did not see the man bending over her, fingers stretched out towards her throat.

CHAPTER 22

'Shame about the weather,' Maggie remarked. She was standing at the huge bay window that overlooked Kelvingrove Park, watching the rain sweep across the paths. 'It was so nice first thing as well.'

'Never mind, Abby was up a lot last night so missing a walk to see her beloved ducks won't give us too much grief.' Rosie smiled wearily. 'Anyway, now that she's settled, let's have that special hot chocolate I promised you.'

The two women wandered through the lounge to the spacious kitchen, their husbands ensconced in Solly's study.

'Kirsty Wilson contacted Solly, did Bill tell you?' Rosie began as she set out the four Christmas mugs on the counter then reached for the tin of Charbonnel et Walker.

Maggie shook her head. 'I knew she'd come by last weekend to see him,' she said slowly. 'D'you think she'll get into trouble?'

Rosie raised her eyebrows and sighed. 'Don't know. She's entitled to poke around if she's certain there's something to find, I suppose. But I have a horrid feeling that Kirsty is only storing up a lot more grief for herself over that boy.'

'She's sweet on him, then?'

Rosie shrugged as she spooned the chocolate powder into a big jug of milk and put it into the microwave to heat. 'Don't know. But why else would she be so keen to see him exonerated of a crime like this?'

'Maybe because she knows him well enough to believe he couldn't have done it,' Maggie said slowly, remembering. Hadn't she once championed a friend accused of something dreadful? So why jump to the conclusion that Kirsty was romantically attached to Colin Young?

'I don't know,' she continued. 'Remember what happened at Muirpark with Eric?'

'Yes,' Rosie said, 'hard to forget that case. I suppose you must think of it a lot, working there every day.'

'No, just sometimes,' Maggie replied. 'Usually I'm far too busy to think of anything but the next lesson or the continuing assessments.' She said ruefully.

'Oh, guess who smelled the chocolate,' Rosie laughed, seeing her husband and Lorimer appear at the kitchen door. 'D'you want—' She broke off as Lorimer's BlackBerry rang and the policeman retreated into the lounge.

'Okay, we'll just have it here, shall we?' Rosie shrugged, spooning mini marshmallows onto the surface of each drink.

Maggie's eyes were on the empty doorway, however. Could this be a call that would leave her here alone with the Brightmans? She looked up as Lorimer entered the room again, resignation settling onto her features as she saw his expression. Something had come up.

'It's serious, I'm afraid,' Lorimer told them. 'The body of a young woman has been found over near Jordanhill. Uniforms just called it in.' He turned to Maggie. 'Can you . . . ?'

'It's fine, I'll get the underground into town and a train home, don't worry,' Maggie said firmly.

'Who's on call this weekend from your lot?' Lorimer asked, turning to Rosie.

'Dr Dan,' Rosie told him.

Maggie's eyes had been fixed on her husband's face as he spoke, searching for some sign that he was about to impart information to them. But the tall policeman simply nodded and pocketed his BlackBerry. They would find out the details soon enough, she supposed. Detective Superintendent Lorimer was required at a scene of crime and there was no time to waste on needless explanations.

The icy rain was driving against his face as Lorimer fought against the wind, making his way down the path that was now cordoned off at one end at the main road. Already water had formed large puddles across the path and he could see the silver metal treads spaced out between them, leading to the locus. The sides of the tent were being whipped by violent gusts, making the whole thing look as if it could take off at any moment, exposing the body within. The on-duty scene-of-crime manager, clad, like Lorimer, in a white protective suit, waved him through.

'Pathologist here yet?' Lorimer asked him, wiping the rain from his brow.

'No, sir. Dr Dan was supposed to be on call but he's called in sick so we're waiting for Dr Fergusson.'

Lorimer suppressed a grin. Maggie might well be staying on at the Kelvingrove flat to keep Solly company and help with little Abigail. And it was no hardship to learn that Rosie and he were to work together on this case.

'What do we know so far?' he asked the detective sergeant, as both men stepped carefully inside the tent.

'A dog walker called 999 on his mobile, uniforms got here and we set up the necessary as soon as we could, sir. The victim has no ID on her, I'm afraid,' he added as they looked down at the body lying spreadeagled on the wet ground.

'Not even a mobile phone?' Lorimer's brows lifted in surprise under his white hood. 'Thought youngsters never went anywhere without them,' he murmured.

'We found a wee set of earphones in one trouser pocket,' the DS told him. 'But no MP3 player.'

'You saying she was mugged?'

The DS regarded Lorimer carefully. 'No conclusions as to that, sir. Better to wait for the doc to come before we can ascertain the likely cause of death.'

Lorimer hid a smile once again. It was well known in the force that the detective super was a stickler for insisting that no officer ought to jump to conclusions. As an illustration there was a favourite story he liked to tell during lectures at Tulliallan about the death of a drunk man outside a Glasgow pub. The on-duty doctor had pronounced the dead man's demise as heart failure but after he had left the locus the cops had turned over the body only to discover a huge knife sticking out of the man's chest.

His smile faded when he looked down at this body, however. The young girl was lying on her front, her head bent to one side, long blond hair escaping from a black hair-tie. How old was she? Eighteen, twenty, maybe? A student, perhaps, out for a jog, he reckoned, looking at the mud-covered trainers. Her arms had been flung out as though to break her fall and so Lorimer could see that there were no rings on any of her fingers. Taking a pen out of his pocket, he drew back her left sleeve. A slim gold watch encircled the wrist.

Lorimer glanced up at the DS. 'If it was a robbery, the mugger missed this little beauty,' he remarked, peering closely at the watch face to identify the brand. 'And hopefully that might help identify her, if someone doesn't call her in as a missing person.'

The girl's face was still, in death; calm, almost peaceful, as though she had simply dropped off to sleep on this damp patch of ground, except for the fact that her eyes were wide open, vacant and unseeing.

'Blue eyes,' Lorimer murmured to himself. Then, as he bent down to see her more clearly, he was suddenly struck by the memory of another victim. Perhaps this girl was merely pretty, whereas the other had been a real beauty. But there was no escaping the similarity between this young woman and the Swedish girl.

Something made him stand up and look towards the door of the tent. It couldn't be more than five minutes' walk to Anniesland Cross from here. And Merryfield Avenue was practically around the corner. Lorimer blinked hard as though the thought that had taken hold was forcing him to peer through a fog of indecision. Could Kirsty Wilson be right, after all? And was Eva Magnusson's killer still out there while Colin Young languished in prison for a crime he did not commit?

'Lorimer, we really must stop meeting like this,' Rosie grinned as she ducked into the tent. 'Right, give me a bit of room, you two. Let's see what we have here.'

There were other footsteps out on the path and Lorimer pulled a flap aside to see the scene-of-crime officers assembling by the side of the path, some already in their protective suits. But soon he was back inside the tent, watching as Rosie Fergusson began to examine the corpse, her expression softening as she regarded the young girl.

'Not been dead long,' Rosie remarked, after a body temperature had been taken. 'Less than a couple of hours, I'd say.'

Lorimer waited as she turned the girl over onto her side, gloved hands gently probing the victim's head and neck.

'Bit of blood on her scalp.' She pointed to a contusion that had so far been hidden from their sight. There was a momentary silence as they watched the pathologist examining the victim's neck and throat. 'Aye,' she nodded to herself. 'I thought so. She's been strangled, poor lass. See?' She sat back on her hunkers, letting the officers look down on the girl's neck. Sure enough, red welts sat up on either side, the shadowy marks of a pair of strong hands.

'Let's just hope we get prints,' the DS growled.

'What's up with Dan?' Lorimer asked, bending lower so that Rosie could hear him above the sound of the wind whining against the thin canvas walls.

'Bad oysters by the sound of it,' Rosie muttered. 'Kind of disrupted my weekend, eh?' She twisted around and wrinkled her nose at Lorimer. Yet there was not a trace of annoyance on that pixie face, rather an eagerness to resolve the problem that lay there before them.

'Well someone sure as hell disrupted hers,' Lorimer sighed, nodding towards the corpse. 'If only it had started raining earlier she might not have decided to come out for her run,' he added quietly, almost to himself. Then, standing back to allow the SOCOs entry to the tent, he looked again at the dead girl. A student, perhaps, he had surmised. Same age as Eva Magnusson? The ideas were coming thick and fast and with them so many possibilities.

Afterwards, as he sat in the Lexus, Lorimer knew he had some decisions to make. If the MO was the same then perhaps they had charged the wrong man for Eva Magnusson's murder. But where could he begin to tackle this? They were still waiting for the Fiscal's decision on whether more investigation was required. Lorimer guessed that Iain MacIntosh would tell them to dig deeper: if nothing was done and it came out during a future trial, there would be mayhem.

There was no question that Lorimer knew what he should do. *Each case demands teamwork*, he'd always drummed in to new recruits to the force. *Don't try to be a hero by flying solo*, he'd insisted. And it was true. Kirsty Wilson might have been encouraged to go looking into Eva's things – and he was glad he had done that, no matter how irregular that might have been – but now it was up to the team at A Division to take control. Was this poor girl's murder related to Eva Magnusson's? This was a question that needed to be asked at the next meeting back at HQ. He needed Jo Grant on his side, not working against him, especially if he was to help Colin Young.

CHAPTER 23

'Andy, where's Fiona?' The girl with the short red hair walked into the kitchen, bleary-eyed with sleep. Kim Travers yawned and hugged herself more closely into her camel dressing gown, blinking sleepily at the young man sitting at the table, a pile of weekend papers spread in front of him.

'Don't know,' Andy Harrison replied with a shrug. 'She went for a run earlier on and hasn't come back. Maybe went into town?'

'Aye, maybe.' Kim yawned again. 'I'll give her mobey a ring. We're supposed to be going home later today. Cousin's engagement party,' she explained.

'That the one who met the woman in New York and asked her to marry him three weeks later?'

'Naw, a different cousin. This guy's been with the same girl for ages.' Kim moved forward towards the cupboard and peered at the selection of clean mugs before selecting one without any chips.

'Maybe she's forgotten?' Andy suggested.

'Fiona? Forget a party? I don't think so,' Kim scoffed. 'More likely she met someone and went for a coffee. I mean, who'd want to run in this?' She jerked her head in the direction of the kitchen window where rain was streaming down, battered by the ferocity of the winter wind.

Kim Travers shuffled slowly out of the kitchen only to return a few minutes later.

'That's weird,' she said with a frown. 'She's not answering her phone. It's just ringing out.'

Her flatmate looked up and saw the worried expression on the girl's face. Kim and Fiona were as unlike in appearance as it was possible for sisters to be but there was a strong bond between the pair. Andy Harrison put down the paper he had been reading, all thoughts of the state of the Scottish Premier League gone from his mind.

'D'you think she's maybe had an accident? Slipped and hurt herself?' His eyes followed Kim's as they both turned towards the window, now hearing the sound of hail battering against the glass.

Kim sat down heavily beside him, staring into space. 'I don't know,' she answered. 'But I've got a horrible feeling that something isn't right.'

'Hello?'

'It's Lorimer. Can we meet up somewhere?'

'Oh.' Kirsty Wilson stood looking out as the rain continued to drive across the bay windows of her room. Her heart quickened. Had they found something? Was Colin going to be released? Why did he want to meet up? 'Okay,' she replied, trying to sound less flustered than she felt. 'Where are you just now?'

'Crow Road. Not far from your flat.'

Kirsty thought for a moment. She didn't want him coming here and she suspected he had too much sense to revisit the scene of crime without a genuine pretext. 'What about the pub on the corner? The Caledonian Bar,' she suggested. 'You know where that is?'

'Yes. Right. See you there in ten minutes.'

Kirsty looked down at the mobile in her hand. Had she started something that was going to get the detective superintendent into trouble? His voice had sounded terse, not angry, just restrained as though he was holding something back. Hastily she threw on her duffel coat, grabbing the gloves and scarf that were hung on a peg behind the door.

Outside on the street the wind seemed to have redoubled its strength and Kirsty had to battle against it all the way along to the corner, gusts pulling back her hood and spilling her hair all ways in front of her face. It was cold too, a real north-easterly, holding the threat of snow or hail.

There were no café tables or chairs on the pavement now, just double doors on the corner swinging open as she approached, a couple of men in green and white football strips barging out, no doubt on their way to the match at Parkhead. Kirsty shivered seeing their bare, tattooed forearms. How could they not feel the cold on a day like this? Mad, she told herself, then grinned. Och, listen to her! She was beginning to sound just like her mother. Kirsty made her way into the heart of the pub past crowded tables and the huge bar that was festooned in loops of silver and pink tinsel. She peered into the deepening gloom, searching the corners to see if he was there. A sigh of relief escaped the girl as she caught sight of him, sitting alone by the fire, a glass of something tawny already in his hand.

'Good spot. Surprised there wasn't anyone else here,' Kirsty said, nodding towards the roaring fire as she plonked herself down beside him.

Lorimer smiled at her. 'Actually, they just left,' he said. 'Couple of Celtic supporters. Right, what can I get you to drink? I can't stay too long, I'm afraid.'

'Oh, not anything cold,' Kirsty told him, still shivering from the short walk along Merryfield Avenue. 'They do coffees in here as well. So . . . a latte, maybe?'

She watched as he rose from his place and strode towards the bar. He was a striking figure of a man, Kirsty thought, and it always surprised her how tall he really was, something that was emphasised by the wee man standing patiently beside him now, waiting for his pint to be pulled by Ina, the purple-haired barmaid. They were talking, Lorimer and the wee Glasgow man, and though Kirsty couldn't hear what was being said she expected it was something to do with either the weather or the afternoon's fixture list.

It is so strange how complete strangers can strike up a conversation in this city, Eva had once observed. It was as if she was right there, speaking to her, Kirsty thought, hearing the Swedish girl's voice in her mind. Sudden tears came unbidden then and Kirsty had to search in her coat pocket for a hanky, glad that Lorimer was not sitting there to see her being such a fool.

'One latte.' Lorimer set it down in front of her and brought his chair a bit closer around the small table.

'Thanks,' Kirsty said. 'What do I owe you?'

Lorimer shook his head and made a face. 'Think I might owe you quite a lot,' he began. 'Anyway, we'll see.'

'What's happened?' Kirsty cupped the hot drink in her hands, waiting for him to begin.

'I've just come from the scene of what appears to be another murder,' he said quietly. 'Young woman, maybe about the same age as your flatmate, long blond hair . . . attractive girl . . .'

'So you think there's a serial killer on the loose?' Kirsty breathed excitedly.

'Whoa, steady on, now. The first thing any officer learns is not to jump to conclusions, okay?'

'But you think there might be similarities?'

'Could be,' Lorimer said. 'On the other hand this poor city of ours has more than its fair share of homicides. Could be a strange coincidence. And anyway, this one was outdoors, unlike your friend's.'

'Oh.' Kirsty was visibly deflated by this piece of information. 'So you don't think ... ?'

'Kirsty, listen to me, will you?' Lorimer looked at the girl intently. 'I can't raise any hopes, okay? But there is something ... ' He paused as she stared back at him, a flicker of expectation lighting her eyes. 'We've approached the Procurator Fiscal to see if there's anything that merits reopening the case. But there isn't a hell of a lot to go on so far. There's your feeling about Colin and the aspect of Eva's lecturer to consider. Now this new victim has got me wondering ... ' He heaved a sigh. 'Call it a policeman's instinct, call it fear that we've got it wrong, I don't really know. But now this has got a hold of me and I'm not prepared to let it go.'

'What can I do to help?' Kirsty asked.

Lorimer shrugged. 'Just what you've been doing so far. Searching in those areas of Eva's life that we might have overlooked. Reporting anything, and I mean *anything*, back to me. I can't involve you too much, Kirsty but what I want to propose is that you and I talk to Professor Brightman about visiting Colin.'

Kirsty's eyes widened. 'What will you say to Dad?'

Lorimer gave a hollow laugh. 'Oh, your dad knows. Says I'm mad to listen to you. Hasn't he said anything to you yet?'

Kirsty shook her head, a worried look crossing her pale features.

'Don't fret. I told him you were doing a good job, okay?'

Kirsty raised her eyebrows in an expression of doubt.

'No, it's true. Listen, since your discovery about Dirk McGregor, and with this morning's affair, we're going to begin asking questions of various people.'

'Not just this lecturer?'

Lorimer shook his head. 'I've spoken with DI Grant and we have agreed that what we would like to do is have you visit Barlinnie and speak to Colin Young.' He hesitated. 'It might be better if you and Professor Brightman go together. Colin will have to request that he is added to his visitors' list, of course. What do you think? Could you do that?'

Kirsty Wilson raised her mug of coffee as though to salute him. 'I don't think you're mad at all, Mr Lorimer,' she said. 'Of course I'll go and speak to him. I'll write to him today.'

Then, turning away before the policeman could see the tears starting in her eyes, she pretended to bury her face in the coffee mug.

Oh, Colin, Kirsty thought, what will you have to tell me?

CHAPTER 24

'I've called everyone,' Kim wailed. 'Even the A&E departments of the local hospitals!'

Andy Harrison sat opposite his flatmate, holding her hands between his own. Her fingers were so cold. Poor circulation, the scientist in him thought, then he chided himself immediately. The girl was distraught, panicking even. It was hours now since Fiona had left the flat for her daily run. And although Kim could be a bit of a drama queen at times, Andy felt that she was genuinely upset as though she instinctively knew something was wrong.

'What about the police?' he said quietly.

Kim choked back a sob. 'I couldn't . . .'

'D'you want me to ring them?'

The red-haired girl nodded, fishing a crumpled hanky from her cardigan pocket.

'Okay. Sorry, Andy, I'm probably being silly, but . . .'

'No, it's all right,' the young man replied. But, as he left the kitchen to make the telephone call, the science student had to admit to an irrational sense of foreboding in his heart.

The woman on the line was pleasant but firm, directing his call through to the local police station where an officer took Fiona's name and other details, promising to call back if there was any news and assuring Andy that there was probably no need to worry. People went missing all the time and usually turned up again safe and sound within twenty-four hours.

'Fiona Travers. Lives in a flat up near Jordanhill station with her sister and another fellow. Left the house early for her usual run. Description: long blond hair, blue eyes, approximate height five feet five, slim build, aged twenty. Think she's the one?'

The detective sergeant looked up from his clipboard at the uniformed officer who had relayed Andrew Harrison's call.

'Could be. Timing's right. So's the location. Better ask the sister if she can come down to the mortuary.'

The uniformed cop nodded. This was one aspect of the job that they all hated. Giving bad news to relatives was such a crap thing to have to do. Still, there was a young bloke in that flat, too, so maybe he'd accompany her?

Kim clung on to Andy's sleeve as they entered the front door of Glasgow City Mortuary. The rain had stopped but the Glasgow streets were still awash with water gurgling into the gutters. She felt Andy's hand on her back as he guided her into the place, hardly heard the lady pathologist's words as she was led towards the viewing room. It was, Kim thought, like a bad dream where all sense of time and place was blurred at the edges and you knew that you would wake up at any moment, shaking off all the horrid images.

She was to look at a television screen, not at a real body, after all. It was okay, she told herself over and over again. It wouldn't be Fiona, but some other poor soul lying in this cold place. Fiona would be fine, she'd be okay ... sitting having coffee with someone she'd forgotten to ring, or having sex with a boyfriend she'd kept secret . . .

Only it *was* Fiona there on the white bed; Fiona with her hair spilling around her sweet face as though she had simply fallen asleep.

And it was Kim's own wail that she heard echoing through the corridors of Glasgow City Mortuary.

'Tired?'

Rosie nodded, her head sunk into the soft cushions of the sofa. A broken night's sleep followed by a day on call had left her feeling completely drained. A huge sigh escaped the pathologist as she sipped the mug of mulled wine that Solly had warmed for her.

'It's such a shitty thing to happen. Poor girl caught by some sick bastard. God! You should have seen the state her sister was in!'

Solly stroked his wife's hair, listening as Rosie told him about the post-mortem, wincing a little when the details became a little too grisly for his delicate stomach. It wasn't like her to react so emotionally, he thought to himself. She had become far more sensitive about the victims of capital crime since Abby's birth and the psychologist suspected that there was a proper hormonal explanation for this. Though, to be fair, lack of sleep probably had a lot to do with her state of mind.

Solly remained silent as Rosie's conversation tailed off and he heard her breathing become deeper. He'd let her sleep a while beside him before insisting they both set off for bed. But for now Solly was content to mull over the events of the day. Maggie Lorimer had left for home by the time the young girl had telephoned. Kirsty was to come in to his office tomorrow afternoon and he wondered just what she would tell him. There had been only that insistent note in her voice that Colin Young was innocent of the Swedish girl's murder. And of course she was hoping that this latest tragedy would exonerate her friend. The psychologist sighed. In his opinion it was unlikely to be the same man. A jogger in the woods suggested a random attack by an opportunist, whereas Eva Magnusson had probably known her killer. Lorimer wouldn't like it when the psychologist spelled it out in his next report but he would have to see that the patterns weren't the same.

The rain had stopped now and the wind that had battered against the bay windows earlier was spent. Solly gazed up at the winter sky; it was like a black canvas against the pale window frames. Somewhere there would be stars sparking in the night, looking down on a humanity that included the good, the bad and those damaged by life's vagaries. And somewhere there might be a tortured soul seeking consolation for the terrible deed that he had committed. Or maybe not. If Fiona Travers's killer was a person with a psychopathic personality then there would be no question of remorse, rather the possibility of a renewed urge to kill again.

Colin could hear the boy weeping silently in the bunk above his own. There was little that separated them, little that allowed for privacy and he had kept quiet, hoping to give the lad a bit of space. Colin still hadn't found out why his previous cellmate had been transferred out from A Block. He'd overheard one of the other inmates talking about it, the name *Brogan* being uttered then a shifty glance was thrown his way causing a silence that had excluded him from their conversation. The chance to breathe the air on his own had been short-lived, however, before the door had swung open again. Darren had given him such a look when he'd been admitted to the cell; a look that was meant to be all big-man bravado to conceal the fear in his eyes. At first sight he didn't think Darren was any more than eighteen, a thin wee runt of a lad with a weaselly countenance and eyes that darted here and there, suggesting that he might be under the influence of some substance or other. So it had come as a surprise when he'd told him he was twenty-six.

'Ye either get auld in here or it keeps ye lookin' young,' Darren had told Colin, a defiant chin in the air. He had form, he'd boasted, knew the place inside out.

'Jist a matter o' time till ah'm sentenced an' back oan the workshoap. Makin' furniture fur thae garden centres, like,' he'd told Colin. But now, under cover of the inky darkness that permeated the cell, Colin could hear the real agony in the other prisoner's soul.

'You have to leave your mobile phones behind,' Lorimer told them, looking in turn from Solly to Kirsty as they sat in the psychologist's office at the university. 'It's like going into another country,' he said, a half smile on his lips. 'Just remember to take your passports or some other form of visual ID for the duty officer at the reception desk, okay?'

'How long do we get with Colin?' Kirsty asked.

'Fifty minutes, max. Less if there are as many as three folk visiting. They don't allow more than three at any one time,' he explained.

'Did you think to call his father?' Solly asked the girl.

Kirsty shook her head, an anxious expression on her face. 'Should I have . . . ?'

'Don't worry. It's a working day today so I would doubt if Colin's father is able to make the trip over from West Lothian anyway.'

'What do I say to him?' Kirsty bit her lip, looking more troubled than ever.

'The truth,' Lorimer said simply. 'But I wouldn't go trying to raise any false hopes either, d'you understand me, Kirsty? Just because another girl's been strangled doesn't mean that Colin is innocent of his charge.'

Kirsty nodded, tearing her eyes away from the tall policeman's stern blue gaze. He was right, of course. There was always the chance that she was making too much of what she believed about Colin. And what if he had changed? What if the person she was about to see was a different young man from the one she thought she had known so well in Merryfield Avenue?

Fridays had always been favourite days of his on the outside, the week ending with the promise of good things ahead. But here, as a prisoner on remand, there was little for Colin Young to look forward to, weekends marking extra visits from families and the collective atmosphere of despair that followed them. It was hard to remember he had been here less than a month yet already Colin had become used to the daily routine and its occasional high spots. The next library visit was not until Thursday and then only for a limited time. He'd already browsed the bookshelves, finding a preponderance of crime fiction novels. Was that homework for the lags? Or did they simply like to read a novelist's made-up version of reality and laugh derisively?

He'd be able to go over to the gym later on, Colin thought, once he'd been allowed the hour's exercise out in the yard. A scatter of thin hailstones flung against the barred window made him look up towards the grey wall of E block opposite his cell. He stood up on a chair and looked out over the exercise yard of 'The Wendy', a special unit where disruptive prisoners spent time in solitary, to the huge wall beyond, seeing the white-painted numbers of cells from 43 to 39. Sometimes voices shouted across the space and he could hear answering laughter.

Today marked the winter solstice, the turning point of the year. The daylight was so limited anyway and dark rain clouds would scowl down on these figures marching around, beating their arms to keep warm. Yet being out and shivering in the open was better than being cooped up all day.

Darren was away to court this morning, leaving Colin guiltily appreciative of having the cell to himself once again for a while. It gave him time to think, though that in itself was a two-edged sword. How he would present himself to a jury when the time came was something his dad had tried to talk to him about last weekend and Colin knew that this ought to be at the forefront of his mind. Only it wasn't. The thoughts of what was happening outside kept returning to him over and over again. The restaurant where he'd worked would be extra busy now with festive bookings every night. Colin could imagine the place, lit up with rows of starry lights swung between the buildings along Ashton Lane, customers laughing as they made their way into the warmth of the place. He closed his eyes, conjuring up the sights and smells of the kitchen: the fragrant aroma of good coffee wafting in as the door to the dining area opened and closed, the delicate scent of honeyed almonds from the dish that was made up daily and – Colin's favourite – the roasted meats turning slowly on that great spit over the charcoal-burning fire. He breathed in deeply, as though to savour the memories.

The noise of the cell door clanging open made him look up suddenly, the illusion vanishing in an instant.

'Time for you to see your visitors,' the prison officer told him, opening the door wider. 'Mr Popular, aren't you?' the man added with a grin.

Colin looked towards him to see if he was making fun or being sarcastic but the officer's eyes had slid away from his as though it had been instilled into them that making any human contact was a bad idea. Colin didn't even know the man's name, hadn't bothered to ask even though it was the same person who came regularly to lock and unlock his cell. Somehow it seemed safer not to indulge in small talk. After the first time, when his attempt to find a little sympathy had been rebuffed, Colin had sworn to keep his emotions to himself. Still, he felt a surge of expectation to see the man Kirsty was bringing with her to Barlinnie.

The large windowless room where visitors came was cheerfully painted in bright apple green, furnished with sets of numbered tables and chairs. There were two people at the far end sitting in the blue visitors' chairs and Colin's face lit up with pleasure when he recognised Kirsty. It was funny how this girl was already like an old and trusted friend, yet he had only known her since September. His gaze shifted momentarily to the other figure, a dark, bearded man with a long multi-striped scarf that was wound around his neck. Was this the professor he had heard so much about? Colin's step faltered as he approached the single green chair opposite them.

Professor Solomon Brightman had watched the young man from the moment the door at the back of the hall had opened and Kirsty had whispered, *That's him!* His first thought was that the slightly built figure coming towards them looked nothing like the stereotypical image of a killer. But then, as he knew all too well, superficial appearances could deceive. He was only a little taller than Kirsty Wilson herself, pale faced and with mid-brown hair that looked as though it could do with a wash.

167

'Colin!' Solly watched as Kirsty gave her friend a hug then stepped back, looking into his face, unaware of the prison officer who was staring at them almost rudely. Lorimer had told him about how prisoners could get drugs from their womenfolk: *a quick kiss, transfer the wad, a swallow and it was done*. Colin had already taken his seat opposite, obviously used now to the regimen required for visits. Was he pleased to see her? Solly wondered, looking at the boy's hands clasped tightly together, his eyes devouring the girl's face.

'This is Professor Brightman,' Kirsty said, and Solly offered his hand across the table. The hand he clasped for a brief moment was damp with sweat and clammy-cold. Nervousness could manifest itself in many ways and for many reasons, Solly knew, guilt being only one of them.

'Hello, Colin,' Solly said firmly, holding the boy's gaze with his eyes. 'We haven't met before,' he added.

'Like I said in my letter, Professor Brightman is here to see if we can help you, Col,' Kirsty said, softly, so that her words might not be overheard.

'Help me? How?' Colin Young frowned and in that moment Solly saw a lad ill at ease, more embarrassed at being in the situation he was in than anything else. Seeing Kirsty here was not what he wanted, Solly realised as Colin shifted uncomfortably in his seat. She was part of the good times in his life, not part of these bad days spent in Barlinnie. Hadn't she thought of that? Their relationship might well become tainted through this visit.

'I've been doing a wee bit of poking around,' Kirsty continued, unaware of the boy's discomfiture. 'I don't believe for a minute that you did what they say you did,' she went on, then lowered her voice. 'And Lorimer has asked the Procurator Fiscal to reopen your case as well ...'

'Detective Superintendent Lorimer would have liked to come today but it's not possible.' Solly shrugged, giving Colin an apologetic smile. 'He's known by too many people here and if we are to make any headway in the case then he has to keep a very low profile.'

'Lorimer? But I thought DI Grant was in charge of the case?' Colin looked from one to the other, clearly confused.

'She still is, nominally. There are things coming to light that might be useful to your agent once the case comes to trial,' Solly continued. 'Sadly we can't divulge too much to you here.' He glanced around as though there might be hidden microphones recording their every word. 'But Kirsty has, as she says, been looking into aspects of Eva Magnusson's life and has uncovered some interesting things.'

'But I don't understand,' Colin said. 'What can you do? Why did you want to come here?'

'I sometimes work for Strathclyde Police,' Solly said. 'But the day job is in the department of psychology at Glasgow University.'

'Oh.' Colin's frown cleared then he nodded, a trace of a smile on his thin lips. 'Yes, Kirsty told me,' he went on. 'Didn't you write that book about profiling?'

Solly nodded, a shy smile of pleasure flitting across his face. Then he became serious again. 'As to your other question: why am I here? Well the answer is that I want to find out as much as I can from you about Eva Magnusson.' He sat back and opened his hands in a frank gesture.

'I thought it was criminals you profiled,' Colin said slowly.

'Amongst others, yes. But if we are to help you in any way, then I need to begin to know the victim first.'

The two men regarded one another for a long moment and

Solly could see the doubt in the prisoner's eyes. Then, as though the psychologist had passed some sort of a test, Colin breathed a long sigh and glanced down at his hands. 'Don't know why you should bother . . . '

'Because we believe in you,' Kirsty insisted. 'Colin, you could-nae hurt a fly, never mind . . . ' She tailed off, her smile drooping as the words remained unsaid.

'There isn't much time.' Colin glanced around at the clock on the wall. 'And it's hard to know how to begin,' he said.

'Begin by telling me about your own relationship with the girl,' Solly said.

'*My* relationship . . . ?' Colin bit his lip and looked from one to the other, redness blossoming onto his cheeks.

'Yes,' Solly replied. 'It's something I need to know if I'm to be of any help to you.'

'Okay,' Colin sighed, then licked his lips nervously. 'Kirsty . . . ' He broke off, obviously embarrassed. 'How much did you know about Eva's . . . ' – he swallowed hard – '*habits?*'

'How d'you mean?' Kirsty frowned.

'Colin's asking what you knew about Eva's sex life,' Solly said, making it sound like something purely academic.

The relief on the boy's face made Solly realise something else about him: Colin Young was a shy lad, maybe a little inexperienced with the ladies, and Solly suddenly wondered if the boy had been completely out of his depth with a beauty like the Swedish girl.

'Well, she never really seemed to have any boyfriends—' she began then broke off at Colin's snort of derisive laughter.

'What?' she asked, turning to look at Solly as though he could provide an answer.

'Eva didn't have time for *boyfriends*,' Colin told her, holding

170

out his hand and touching her fingers gently. 'She was too busy having one-night stands and breaking hearts.' His light tone belied the bitterness of the words themselves and Solly could see the strain on the boy's face, a pain that told him several things. Colin Young had cared for the Magnusson girl all right, but there was part of him that despised her too, and maybe there was a deep-seated jealousy underlying it all. A Counsel for the Prosecution might well make a lot of this to the prisoner's detriment, he thought to himself, wondering just how Colin might come across in court.

A glance at the detective sergeant's daughter made him blink suddenly: Kirsty Wilson was staring open-mouthed as though in shock and Solly guessed that the girl was having to swiftly reassess her opinion of her dead flatmate.

'Sorry, time's up.' The prison officers were there suddenly, bunches of keys jangling from their belts as they stood either side of Colin, making him rise from his seat.

'Kirsty tells me you write,' Solly said, leaning forward. 'Send me anything you can about Eva,' he added. 'But only the truth, understand?'

'*You* don't believe me?' Colin hissed.

Solly smiled at him. 'I only believe what I can see to be true,' he said. 'Remember that psychology is a science after all,' he added gently.

'And what *do* you see?' Colin whispered.

But there was no time for an answer, the prison officers motioning their charges towards the far door.

'I'll come again,' Kirsty said, a catch in her voice.

Colin only nodded, refusing to meet her eyes, then he turned away, walking between the two guards, not looking back at them.

'Come on,' Solly said, taking Kirsty's arm and tucking it into his. 'I really think we need to get you out of here.'

'Awright, my man?'

A small man stared at him as he entered the cell, his narrow, weaselly face full of the sort of sharp angles that told their own particular addict's tale.

Colin didn't reply as the door to their cell clanged behind him, throwing himself onto the bunk and turning his face to the wall. He didn't want to talk to anyone, especially to yet another new prisoner. Seeing Kirsty like that had been a shock. He'd forgotten what she looked like; in the flat he'd seen her stomping around in her old woolly dressing gown, not a trace of make-up on her apple cheeks. Here, clad in that dark coat, her face had seemed thinner, paler, her eyes tired despite the layers of thick black mascara, and there was something else. The old Kirsty, the one who chatted, joked around, even made him feel like he had a big sister in the flat, had disappeared. In her place was this stranger who had protested his innocence and made him feel utterly ashamed.

Then there was the psychologist. Colin could sense his cheeks burning as he thought over what he had said and how he had failed to recognise the celebrated Professor Brightman! How could he have forgotten what the man looked like, a man who had such a high standing within the university and beyond? Okay, he wasn't studying psychology, but Brightman's photo was always appearing in the student newspaper, connected to some high-profile case or other. The professor must have thought he was a bit simple, surely? Colin closed his eyes. What did Brightman think about him? Was he able to translate his body language into something spectacular? See beyond the cringing embarrassment to the quivering wreck he had become in here? Or did his analysis give him a different take altogether? Was he even now transforming his impressions into words to sum up a character that was guilty as charged?

'Hey, wee man, fancy a game?'

The voice beside Colin's bed had an edge to it and the boy rolled over and sat up, seeing the other prisoner's face creased into a grin as he shuffled the pack of greasy playing cards.

'Name's Joseph, by the way. What's yours?'

'Colin. Colin Young.'

'Awright, well, young Colin, here's the score. Nae messin' wi' ma stuff and ah leave yours alane, get it?'

Colin nodded silently. He could do this: go along with the life in here, marking time until his trial. Then, what? As he accepted his cards and fanned them out, Colin tried to prevent that reckless feeling that sought a way to surge through his heart and mind. He would not, could not let it master his resolution; but it was hard to forget Kirsty's eager face and the words she had spoken, words that were meant to make him hope.

'What's he like?'

Solly looked up from his dinner plate. Abby was still bashing her spoon against her empty dish, having gaily tossed the last bit of her dinner overboard onto the plastic mat below.

'Troubled,' he replied, shifting his glance from Abby to Rosie who was leaning across to wipe their little girl's face. Abby struggled under her mother's ministrations, turning her head away as Rosie tried to dab the damp muslin onto cheeks and chin.

She looked at him directly, a question in her eyes. *Was he guilty?* her expression seemed to ask. But Solomon Brightman was not yet ready to deliver such a verdict on the young man who languished in Barlinnie prison. Guilt was there, oh, yes, but of what was the prisoner guilty? Having sex with a girl who had been out of his league both socially and . . . and what? There was something bothering Solly about the Swedish girl. She hadn't had regular boyfriends but Colin Young had intimated that she enjoyed sexual encounters simply for their pleasure. Promiscuity was not an offence but the boy had made it sound like some sort of sin. Murderers could and had killed women in brutal acts that were meant to expunge all traces of sexuality from their victims. But Eva Magnusson's body had shown no wounds to her genital areas, or anything that would indicate an impassioned and frenzied attack. Had he dropped her body in a moment of terror? Afraid at what he had done?

Solly tried to imagine the scene as Colin Young sat back on his haunches, looking at the hands that had strangled the Swedish girl. A smile twitched above his dark beard as the image refused to come clearly into focus. He really could not *see* Colin Young as the murderer after all. The impressions he had so far gleaned from the meeting in Barlinnie had served to come to this initial conclusion. No, like the Wilson girl, Solly Brightman did not believe that the boy was capable of such an act. He replayed the interview in his mind, seeing once again the moment when Colin Young had reached out and touched Kirsty's fingers. He had wanted to make a connection, show his concern for *her*, Solly thought. He wanted to protect Kirsty . . . from what? The truth about Eva Magnusson, perhaps? And what was that truth?

Kirsty had been brave, stepping out of the safety of doing and saying nothing, even to the point of coming to Barlinnie to speak to him today. Was that why Colin had shown a moment of protectiveness towards her? Or did he have other feelings for the girl, feelings that a man guilty of a capital crime might have been incapable of expressing back there in such a situation? No, he told himself again, if he were a member of Colin Young's jury at this moment in time, Solomon Brightman would not be able to offer a guilty vote.

So, he sighed, ignoring the wails from his daughter as she was lifted out of her high chair by Rosie, who else might have had a reason to kill Eva Magnusson?

CHAPTER 25

'There are several things missing,' Lorimer told the officers assembled in the incident room. 'Her mobile phone, a Nokia' – he turned to point at the enlarged picture behind him as it came onto the screen – 'and this MP3 player,' he said, indicating the next picture that suddenly came up below it.

'There was also a green leather wallet containing her bank cards and student ID plus around ten pounds or so, according to her sister.' Lorimer paused, looking at the attentive faces regarding him. 'She isn't sure just how much money Fiona had on her, but didn't think it was a lot as she had already done all her Christmas shopping and had let on that she was pretty skint.' The detective superintendent tried to conceal his feelings but his lips twisted in a moue of disgust. A young girl mugged and killed for a mobile phone and a few quid!

'So what we need is to get out there pronto, scour all the known pubs for druggies trying to make a quick deal, see if anyone has spotted these items. As for the wallet, she'd got it as a gift, apparently. And her sister says it looks something like this.' He clicked the button so that an artist's image appeared behind him.

'Any luck with forensics?' a voice asked.

Lorimer gave a wintry smile. 'Well, they got prints off her body, as it happens. No match on our database, unfortunately, but still, something to go on if we get a suspect.'

There was a murmur of approval from the other officers. Christmas was only days away and there might well be someone trying to flog a mobile or an MP3 player round the pubs. Every snout worth his salt would be chased up by the officers from the city centre division in the hope that whoever had murdered Fiona Travers would not be at large to enjoy his Christmas dinner.

'And there are enough traces to give us a sufficient amount of DNA should we need it,' Lorimer added. 'Fingerprints and bodily fluids, including mucus.'

'So all we need is a druggie with a bad cold,' Jo Grant murmured.

Lorimer glanced at his DI but said nothing. He could see she was still smarting from the possibility she had got Colin Young's charge all wrong.

'Right, you all know what I want from you so let's get out there and see if someone can shine a light on this.'

Lorimer looked up as his door was knocked on then opened.

'Jo, what can I do for you?'

His DI came forward and rested her hands on the edge of the table.

'This thing with Kirsty Wilson. It could make me look really stupid, you know. Sir,' she added, her cheeks flaming into twin spots of colour.

'Jo,' Lorimer said kindly. 'You did what you felt was right on the basis of what evidence you had. Any good officer does that. But new evidence comes to light all the time. And it won't help matters if you appear to be intransigent about Colin Young, will it?'

'No, sir,' Jo replied stiffly.

'He has to remain on remand for now, though. And unless any concrete evidence appears he will remain there until the case goes to trial.'

Jo Grant nodded.

'And good work to all of you on the Travers case. Things are looking more positive there.'

A grudging smile appeared on the woman's face as she nodded. 'And, as you said, there appears to be enough DNA to nail the bastard whenever we get him,' she said grimly.

'Good.' Lorimer nodded, fiddling with the pen in his hands. 'Well, I'll let you get on. Just keep me informed, will you? We're not going away over Christmas so I'd be grateful to know what progress you make.'

'Oh.' Jo cocked her head to one side. 'Not going up to Mull for New Year, then?'

'No, afraid not. Your aunt's wonderful cottage is fully booked over the season, but not by us, I fear.'

The DI nodded. She had been instrumental in introducing the Lorimers to Aunty Mary's cottage in Mull several years back and it had become a favourite escape for Lorimer and his school-teacher wife.

'Right, sir, I'll be off, then,' Jo said, giving the detective super-intendent a quick smile.

Lorimer watched her leave then gave a sigh as the door closed behind her. It would be excellent if DI Grant were to make a quick arrest and have the certainty that Fiona Travers's killer was behind bars. Try as he might, Lorimer could not convince himself now that his officer had got it right with the arrest of Colin Young. But wasn't he to blame as well? After all, he hadn't disagreed at first when Jo had decided on the young man's guilt. However, if the accusation against Colin was to go completely awry, then having a collar for *this* case would go some way to alleviating Jo Grant's ensuing embarrassment and his own guilty conscience.

The scene-of-crime tape tied to the tree trunk still flapped in the wind as he passed down the lane. The tall man stopped for a moment, looking at the flattened patch of earth where the girl's body had lain. She had looked out at him from every newspaper in the land these past few days, a smiling blonde girl, younger than the creature he remembered, panting down the beaten track, ears full of that trashy music. His fists clenched as he recalled the moment when he had swung the stick, feeling once again the sickening impact, hearing it anew as he recalled the sound of wooden club on flesh and bone.

He stepped to one side, leaning against the tree trunk, a weak feeling melting his insides. He glanced at his bare hands, seeing the dark hairs on the wrists, the protruding knuckles then, in one swift movement, he thrust them deep into his coat pockets as though to banish that other image.

The man closed his eyes and a thin whimpering sound escaped from his parted lips. Try as he might, he could not rid himself of that recurring moment when he had gripped her around the neck, squeezing the very life from her.

CHAPTER 26

'Thank goodness!' Maggie slumped into her favourite chair, her bags and her unzipped leather boots discarded around her. 'Oh, Chancer,' she said as the orange cat sprang up onto her lap causing a smile to light up her tired face. 'Two whole weeks off! Bliss!' She pulled her scarf off and let it drop onto the floor, sighing with pleasure at the thought. It had been a hard term of prelim exams, ending with the usual round of school concerts, dances and other evening activities that ate into her free time, leaving the staff exhausted and thankful for the Christmas break.

Maggie Lorimer sighed again, letting her body slip back further into the cushions. Bill would take a bit of time off between Christmas and New Year, leave that he had saved especially to be with her. They planned to spend Christmas Day together, just the two of them, feasting on a crown of turkey ordered specially from the butcher and a couple of good bottles that she had put away for the occasion. Then an evening sat slumped in front of the telly or reading some new Christmas books ... the prospect made her smile in anticipation as she tucked her legs under her, lifting the cat and settling him further onto her lap. They had no shortage of invitations to join friends but Maggie had refused them all with a gracious 'no thank you', relishing the thought of peace and quiet. The Brightmans were heading south this year for a family gathering so there would be no wee god-daughter for Maggie to spoil on Christmas Day. Besides, this was one of the few precious times she could enjoy with her busy husband. Detective Superintendent Lorimer was to work right up until Christmas Eve, then take off what time that he could. Oh, if only he was off for the entire holiday! 'Two whole weeks,' she murmured, her caresses on the cat's warm fur becoming slower and slower as her heavy eyelids closed.

Outside, darkness had fallen but the coloured lights on the Christmas tree throbbed rhythmically as though to unheard music, their reflection cast against the windows banishing the gloom of the winter solstice.

Lorimer turned the car into the drive, sensing the iciness beneath the tyres, glancing at the temperature gauge. It had already plummeted to minus three degrees and the surface of the pavements glistened with an early frost, giving the entire avenue a Christmas card appearance. He switched off the engine yet sat on for a few minutes in the warmth of the Lexus, considering the days ahead. Maggie had expected them to spend a fair bit of time together, but once more she was to be disappointed. There was no way he could take too much time off when they were in the middle of such serious cases.

Rosie and Solly were heading down to London tomorrow to spend the week with Solly's family. Jewish traditions there did not preclude a visit from Father Christmas, Maggie had assured her husband when she had finished wrapping Abby's presents and, yes, Ma Brightman had put up an enormous tree in the Wimbledon house.

What would it be like for lads like Colin Young this Christmas? Torn from the security of friends and family, uncertain of what the coming year might bring, it could only be a bleak Christmastide for prisoners such as him.

'He's a shy lad,' the psychologist had said, 'but I believe he's well aware of what's going on.' Then he'd muttered softly, 'Perhaps *too* aware. Sensitive,' he'd concluded, nodding his head and stroking the dark beard that made him look so much like a prophet from Old Testament times.

Heaving a sigh, Lorimer opened the car door and got out. The windows of his home beckoned behind the curtains, a light shining to welcome him, Maggie somewhere inside. She would understand, he told himself; she always did.

Dear Professor Brightman, Colin wrote, then paused. His last letter from the psychologist had suggested that he simply write down his thoughts and feelings, forgetting that the words were destined to be read by another. But it was hard. What was Brightman doing with his letters anyway? Studying them to search for clues into his own character? Or was he really delving into Eva's personality as he had said?

I'm sure that Eva's plans for the future didn't include me, but it wasn't important back then. Just being with her and seeing her smile was enough. Then of course it all changed. That night, that wonderful night ... He drew in a deep breath.

The exquisite joy of their lovemaking had been his lasting memory of her.

Who was to know that Eva and I would never be together again in this world? When I held her that night it was like something beyond my wildest imaginings. Then she left me. But how could I have ever known it would be for ever?

Roger closed the door behind him, pulling the storm door shut as Kirsty had insisted. Then, as he bent to turn the key in the lock, a movement behind him made the young man turn.

'Mr McCubbin!' he exclaimed. 'I haven't seen you in ages. Everything all right?' he asked politely, straightening up to his full height, towering over the old man who stood uncertainly in his own doorway.

The old man's eyes slid past him to the closed door. 'All gone away, then?' he asked, his voice rasping in the chill night air.

Roger nodded. Then, seeing that the old man had made no attempt to return to his flat, he stepped forward hesitantly. 'You *do* know what happened here, sir?' he asked.

'Aye.' Derek McCubbin nodded then looked down at his feet. 'Bad business, bad,' he muttered.

'Are you spending Christmas alone here?' Roger ventured, feeling a sudden pity for the figure before him, bent with age, a stick clutched in one hand.

'Nobody's business where I spend it, is it?' Derek growled, his chin jutting out as he glared at the young man.

'Well, have a nice time, wherever you get to, eh?' Roger said, forcing a smile. Then, shouldering his rucksack, he headed on down the stone staircase, glancing back once or twice, aware that the old man was watching him from the landing above.

'Dad! What on earth are you doing out there? Come on in before you catch your death of cold,' Corinne scolded, bustling to the front door and drawing her father back into the warmth of the hallway. 'Right, that's nearly everything packed. You shouldn't need anything else for a good while, eh?' she told him, patting his arm.

Derek McCubbin gave a grunt and allowed himself to be led back into the flat. Corinne had become bolder of late, ordering him to do this and that, arranging for the estate agent to come, even beginning to thrust brochures into his gnarled hands to see what sort of home they would purchase once the big flat in Merryfield Avenue was sold. The old man felt the creak of leather beneath him as he sank into his fireside chair. It was for the best, he supposed, though whether he could ever be happy in a new place was a moot point.

'Better off out of here, eh, Dad?' Corinne said, her hands full of the linen that she had been folding. 'Away from all that dreadful business next door,' she insisted.

But Derek McCubbin did not deign to reply, staring instead at the empty grate and the cold ashes within.

CHAPTER 27

The church officer switched off the lights and pulled the security door closed before locking the main door to the church. 'All is calm, all is bright ...' The words of the carol resonated in his head, making him smile as he pocketed the bunch of keys and headed towards the car park behind the building. Tom stopped for a moment and looked up. Through the naked branches of the trees he could see the myriad stars scattered across the night sky, Jupiter twinkling as brightly as that first Christmas star must have done so long ago. His breath of satisfaction was a plume of mist before his face, evaporating into the darkness. It was a perfect night for Christmas Eve, one where a little child could almost believe in the sound of sleigh bells coming over the clear night air.

Everyone had gone home now after wishing one another a 'Merry Christmas', the spirit of goodwill that the midnight service had engendered lingering on. Only Tom was left now and he was glad of the peace and quiet. Christmas week was a frantic round of Sunday School parties and events, culminating with the midnight service. Now he would have a bit of a rest, Tom decided; at least until next Sunday morning when he would rise early to prepare for the day.

A movement in the shrubbery and a swishing noise made him

look to his right. But there was nothing to see. A fox, maybe, out hunting for some small night creatures.

Tom opened the door of the car and slipped inside, already thinking about the bottle of Glayva that awaited him back home; his wee nightcap would be well deserved after the work he had put in tonight. He switched on the engine and the car headlights then looked over his shoulder, preparing to turn the car around to face the exit.

Tom frowned. Had a sudden wind blown up? Or was there some large animal thrashing about in the undergrowth next to the car park? Though situated not far from the city centre, theirs was almost like a rural parish, the church surrounded by woodland. The man bit his lip as a sense of anxiety grew in him. Another high wind might well cause more damage to the roof, an expense that he didn't relish after the recent December gales. But the trees above him were still, and the stars still shone through the tracery of twigs, assuring him that all was well.

Tom had just changed gear to drive off when a figure crashed out of the darkness, arms flailing, white hair streaming behind her. He braked suddenly, a scream dying in his opened mouth at the horror of her bloodied face before her body fell across the bonnet with a sickening thump.

'It's always the same on Christmas Eve,' the police officer assured his younger colleague. 'You'd imagine peace and goodwill to all men? Nah, for loads of folk it's just another excuse for a piss up. Then we get to clear up the mess when a drunken party gets out of hand.'

'D'you reckon that's what happened?' PC Gregor McLafferty whispered, hunkered down next to the woman lying where they had wrapped her in blankets.

'Och, who knows? Can you not smell the sick off her? Too much of the sauce, I'd say. But that's not what caused this,' he said, pointing to the injuries on the woman's face. 'Someone's given her a right doing.'

'Where's that church officer?' PC Graham continued. 'Thought he was going to open up so we could get her inside out of the cold?' He shivered suddenly.

'Here he is,' PC McLafferty replied, seeing the man emerging from a side door of the church.

'Okay, pal?' PC Graham asked as the older man approached them.

The younger policeman rose to his feet, ready to help lift the injured woman from the car park and into the relative warmth of the church.

Just then the faint rise and fall of a siren could be heard and all three men turned to see the flashing blue lights as an ambulance appeared round the bend in the road.

'Once they've taken her to A&E we'll need you to give us a statement, sir. Okay?' PC Graham said, looking hard at the man who stood before him, his face blanched white in the glare of two sets of headlights.

Tom nodded. He still couldn't believe what had happened, the image of that woman coming at him out of the darkness a thing that he knew would haunt his dreams for many nights to come.

'She's still unconscious, I'm afraid,' the doctor said, nodding to the two police officers who were standing outside the curtained cubicle. 'There are signs of internal bleeding and once we have some results from downstairs we will decide if she requires immediate surgery.'

'Will she live?' PC McLafferty asked, concern clouding his young eyes.

The doctor shook his head. 'Too soon to tell. If she hadn't happened upon that man outside the church ... ' His shrug made the young policeman shiver. He'd only been in the force for five months and was yet to be inured to the terrible things that human beings did to one another. It would come, his ex-cop father had told him gruffly. After a while the whole thing became routine.

PC McLafferty turned away from the woman's cubicle and walked smartly along the brightly lit hospital corridor after his colleague, unsure if he wanted to rid himself of the horror he had seen this Christmas Eve or to have his senses numbed by such things for ever.

Maggie slipped out of bed, glancing at the form of her husband hunched beneath the duvet to make sure he was asleep. It was still the middle of the night, still Christmas Eve, as far as she was concerned, though the clock on her bedside cabinet registered three a.m.

Silly, aren't we, she told herself, sneaking next door to the upstairs lounge where their Christmas tree sat robed in darkness. Two old woollen stockings that were normally tucked into stout climbing boots hung limply across the arms of two squashy armchairs, waiting for someone to do the business of filling them with tiny gifts. It was still a tradition between them both to put an apple, a tangerine and a coin into the toe then stuff as many wee presents as they could manage into the rest of the sock. Maggie couldn't remember a time when she hadn't managed to wake up first. But her early morning task was always rewarded, much later, by Bill telling her to stay in bed while he took his turn to fill her own stocking. Did other childless couples go through all this rigmarole? Maggie wondered, stretching along the floor to switch on the tree lights. Or did they jet off to warmer climes, quaffing champagne for breakfast in some luxury hotel, far from the cold of a Scottish winter?

Maggie Lorimer grinned as she retrieved the big bag of parcels from behind the sofa. It wasn't easy to find time to do Christmas shopping but with Bill working such long hours she had allowed herself the luxury of trawling the internet for bits and pieces that she knew her husband would like. She picked up a small square parcel, recognising the chocolate orange: that would go down after the fruit and the two-pound coin that she'd laid aside, then some music collections and a slim, but expensive, bottle of aftershave, followed by some sweets, a new velvet bow tie for formal occasions, and a couple of books. Last of all she picked up a bulky parcel that had been the very devil to wrap because of its awkward shape. The high-definition binoculars from the RSPB were simply wonderful and Maggie felt a slight pang of conscience as she pulled the neck of the stocking to make space for the present, not just at the price, but because she would enjoy using them on their bird-watching trips too and it felt a bit like self-indulgence. Ooh well, they were great and he'd love them.

There. She sat back on her heels, a warm glow inside her at the sight of the bulging stocking. Was this how it felt for parents creeping around in the middle of the night, playing Santa Claus to their wee ones? For a moment there was the familiar pang of regret for all the poor babies who had left her struggling body far too soon, rendering them childless. But there was also a little bit of sadness that Abigail, Rosie and Solly were away from Glasgow and that they would not be sharing their godchild's Christmas this year. It was a reminder that the little girl was not always part of their family circle.

Yet, in that same moment, Maggie's mind flew to a different thought entirely. That poor young boy who had been Kirsty Wilson's flatmate. Was he really guilty of the crime? Jo Grant seemed to believe it, but she had seen lately that Bill had his doubts. What, she wondered, shivering, would Christmas be like for Colin Young?

He was awake long before the door clanged open at the usual unlocking time. It was something that seemed to have happened to his body clock since he had come here, as if the precious hours of the night when sleep would have been most welcome had deserted him, leaving him tired and listless by early evening. This should have been a special day but Colin doubted that it would be much different from every other day in Barlinnie. Dad and Thomas were not allowed to visit but they would be here tomorrow and Thomas had joked that he had been in training to get to that vending machine first this time. It was bitter for them too, Colin knew, and sometimes he wondered if he was the luckier one being in here away from all the catcalling and snide remarks that Thomas told him about. How people could be so cruel to a man who had lived a blameless life was simply wrong and it wracked Colin with guilt to think how much suffering he had caused his father.

But there would be time later to escape from it all, wouldn't there? Colin's mouth twitched into the ghost of a smile as he thought about how he had found his get-out-of-jail card and now every day the student looked forward to a bit of time spent writing in his notebook. Professor Brightman had said to describe Eva and at first he had found himself shying away from attempting that, his guts churning with a real pain whenever he thought about the dead girl. But making up a story about her was different and already he had formed the structure for an opening chapter that he had entitled '*I Meet Eve Magnusson*'.

It was her father who impressed me most, Colin had begun. *A giant of a man, like some Norse god stepping straight out of a myth.*

Henrik had such authority and bearing that I was expecting some tall queen-like creature to be his daughter. Perhaps I had been thinking about the Valkyrie? Anyway when I did finally meet her I was surprised at how demure she was. Yes, demure is the word I am using here and that was just how she seemed; quiet, polite and friendly but not overly so, more as though she was hosting some event and we were her special guests for the night. Except of course we weren't. Kirsty had arrived before me so we spent a while together chatting in the kitchen before the lads came up. Eva was nice, but a bit reserved as though politely brought up Swedish girls didn't fraternise too closely with their tenants. I was a bit disappointed, to tell the truth. But, oh, dear God, that didn't last long, did it?

Colin felt his face burn as he reread the passage that followed. That would have to go, he thought, scoring out several lines where his prose had begun to gush. He could rewrite it, couldn't he? Then a spasm of anger surged through him as he thought of the laptop back in his home in Armadale. Or had it been taken by the police? Oh, how he could do with the ability to delete stuff or cut and paste to his heart's content! Instead he had to make do with this reporter's notebook, line after line telling his story about Eva to Professor Brightman.

He was a long way from writing about the night of the party, and Colin half dreaded, half yearned to get to that chapter. Instead he was at the part where he first knew about his own feelings for the slim blonde creature who had so beguiled him.

She took us all for granted, especially Kirsty. But did any of us mind? Not a bit! It was as if she had cast a spell over us, like some fairy creature from a different world. And, yes, there was a kind of other-worldliness about her at times. Fey, that's the word I used to think about as I watched her face in the candlelight at night.

Colin stopped and thought again about the first moment that he had longed to hold her. They had been at the pub around the corner and he had picked up her cardigan. Had she said thanks? He couldn't remember. But the way she had turned, smiling, had given him a jolt, as if some surge of electricity had been shot through his body. It was as simple as that. *She was suddenly the centre of my universe,* Colin had written, then scored that out too as being so flaming clichéd. He wasn't going to sacrifice good prose even though the exercise was supposed to be about the professor seeing into Eva's character and the psychologist probably couldn't care less about how the facts were written down.

A stirring in the bunk above his made Colin close the notebook and slide it beneath the mattress, out of sight.

'You awake, pal?' There was a creak as the other prisoner rolled towards the edge of his bunk then Joseph's thin arm shot down towards Colin.

'Merry Christmas!'

Colin grasped the other prisoner's hand, feeling it warm and slightly moist.

'Aye. Merry Christmas to you too,' he replied, shaking his cell-mate's hand then letting it go before wriggling back under his own covers. Joseph was in the habit of relating snippets from what he had done outside in those precious minutes before they needed to get up and dressed and Colin did not expect that today would prove any different.

He waited for the stories to begin within the darkness, stories of a different kind that made his own life seem burgeoning with privilege, stories that made him feel somehow ashamed that so many things were outside his own experience.

And, as he listened to Joseph's rambling accounts of his life, punctuated by the vibrations made as the man's anxious hands bumped against the side of his bunk – the obsessive compulsive disorder a feature that Colin had seen in several of the inmates here – he found himself wondering which stories were real and which were imagined. Yet he made no comment nor offered any reciprocating insights into his own past, simply waiting until the lights went on and the doors to the cells were unlocked on what he expected to be this bleakest of Christmas mornings.

DI Jo Grant unwound the thick scarf and tossed it to the back of her chair. God! What a cold morning to have to come into work at Stewart Street. Despite the decorations everywhere, the division seemed cheerless now that Christmas was actually here. Or, Jo reflected, perhaps it was her? That assault to severe injury last night had come her way and already there was a small team of forensic scientists examining the injured woman's clothes. Christmas Day might be a day off for the majority of the population but there were plenty who simply had to be at work, Jo grumbled inwardly, folk like herself, seeing to the messes that human beings made of their world.

She switched on her laptop and waited for the machine to go through its preliminary routine, rubbing her hands together to warm them up.

'Coffee,' she muttered. The usual coffee shop en route to work was closed, natch, and so she would have to make do with the machine along the corridor for today. With a sigh, Jo watched the screen, trying to decide whether she could be bothered to go along and get a cup or simply wait for one of the other officers to do it for her.

'Merry Christmas, ma'am.' DS Alistair Wilson appeared in the room as if by magic.

'I bring you tidings of goodwill from the woman back home and a wee something to go with our breakfast,' he grinned, shoving a plastic box onto Jo's desk.

'Coffee?' he asked, hardly waiting as Jo nodded, her face splitting into a grin as she opened the box to find a large pile of Christmas pies, still warm from Betty Wilson's oven in West Kilbride.

'How *did* you find an angel like that?' Jo asked. 'And where *does* she find the time to bake at this ungodly hour ...?' But Wilson had disappeared out of the room, whistling something that was meant to sound like 'We Wish You a Merry Christmas'.

Half an hour later, six on-duty officers were gathered around Jo's desk, their coffee cups binned and the plastic Tupperware box empty except for a few pastry crumbs and a festive serviette.

'We've got a name for her,' Jo told them. 'Lesley Crawford. Aged thirty-four, works for the Royal Bank of Scotland. Lives in Bearsden but was at a party in Jordanhill not long before the attack took place.' Jo looked up at the faces regarding her. 'Christmas Eve party. Too much to drink and yet the silly cow tried to drive herself home.'

'How did she come to be at that church, though?' Wilson asked.

'Seemed she had stopped the car and fled into the bushes to throw up. The uniforms who called it in had a recce and found where she'd vomited. They reckon the attack must have happened just as she tried to walk back to where she'd parked the car.' Jo stretched her back as though she had been at the desk for hours. 'That's how we found out her details. Handbag was still on the passenger seat so whoever mugged her wasn't after her stuff.'

'Was there *anything* missing, ma'am?' one of the detective constables wanted to know.

Jo shrugged. 'Don't know till we talk to her. She lived on her tod, apparently. But since she's still on the critical list there isn't a lot more we can find out from her. Still,' she went on, 'one of you is going to park their bahookie at Gartnavel Royal Hospital until she does wake up. Okay? Any volunteers?'

As five hands shot up, Jo laughed. Hospital on Christmas Day was a pretty good option for a police officer, even hanging about in the high-dependency unit. They would be treated to endless cups of tea and cakes as visitors and staff brought their boxes of goodies into the wards.

Later, once she had the room to herself again, Jo drew out the file on Fiona Travers. Despite their best endeavours the team investigating the young woman's murder had drawn a complete blank. Jo's lips narrowed into a thin line as she slid the student's photo onto her desk. Such a bloody waste. A young life so full of promise with hopes and dreams ahead of her. Bloody good-looking too, the DI thought, letting her eyes flick over the smiling face.

Then she frowned. Hadn't she seen that girl before? And quite recently? For a moment Jo sat still, thinking hard. What had she been looking at this morning, other than the productions that had been taken from Lesley Crawford's handbag? She straightened up with a sudden jolt. That was it, of course. There were copies of the injured woman's documents lying in a manila envelope right under her nose, including her driver's licence and an ID card for a swanky gym.

Jo opened the envelope and the thin photocopies spilled out.

'Good God in Govan!' she exclaimed as she took a closer look at the woman's photograph. Long blond hair curling over her bare shoulders and a twinkling smile that showed a set of perfect teeth. Laying the two images side by side, Jo Grant felt an involuntary shiver like cold water trickling down her spine.

They could have been sisters, the Travers girl and this Crawford woman. And there was surely no denying their similarity to the beautiful Eva Magnusson. She looked up and out of the window where daylight had begun to show as streaks of salmon pink across a slate blue sky. Lorimer was so fond of telling them that he didn't believe in coincidences, wasn't he? She heaved a sigh, wondering just what the detective superintendent would make of this one.

Christmas would never be the same, Henrik told himself, slipping out of the bed he had shared last night with one of his oldest girlfriends. Helena reminded him of his late wife whenever he thought about her, but between the sheets she was a completely different woman. She had left not long after midnight, kissing him on the cheek, whispering 'Merry Christmas' as he drowsed in the aftermath of their lovemaking. There was a husband for Helena to return to, a financier who was not entirely blind to his wife's occasional infidelities but who pretended to himself that they simply did not matter. Henrik slouched on the cream satin bedsheets, staring into space. Outside, the world was still robed in white; even the fir trees were completely covered in snow so that they looked like strange triangular growths emerging from the snowdrifts.

He had cancelled the ski trip, too sick at heart to contemplate the usual crowd and face their questioning eyes. Instead Eva's father had ordered in enough supplies to last him well into January and beyond. He had ordered the housekeeper to take her break, telling her that of course he would manage on his own, didn't he always? He had been unnecessarily sharp with Marthe, then felt so bad about it that he had signed a large cheque and stuck it in her Christmas card, hoping that would assuage his guilt. It hadn't, of course, and now Henrik Magnusson was alone on Christmas morning feeling as though everyone he had ever loved had deserted him, leaving him with only memories and photographs for consolation.

The portrait on the walnut bureau smiled out at him: Eva, hair tousled, laughing as he had clicked the shutter. The picture always brought back the moment before when he had whisked off her ski hat and demanded that she *smile please for Daddy.*

And of course, she had. Now that smile was his for ever, a reminder of her youth and beauty. And innocence? He had thought so at the time, but now, looking at the portrait, Henrik wondered just how much he had known about his daughter. He had never hidden his lovers from her, but somehow Eva had hidden some secrets from him, like the boy who was now imprisoned for her murder. Had they been sweethearts? Or merely lovers? And, most important of all, had the Scottish police really found the man who had snuffed out the lovely face that looked out from the frame, its smile wavering as the tears spilled over from his eyes?

*

If he had to write about the best thing that had happened to him since coming into prison, it would have to be this, Colin thought, marching behind the men dressed in red and blue fleece jackets. He gazed up at the dark wooden ceiling then his eyes misted with sudden tears at the Christmas tree lights blazing from the front of the huge chapel. Somewhere music was playing soft, familiar carols that made him wipe his hand across his eyes. The moment was so utterly full of memories: going to morning service with Mum, Dad and Thomas on Christmas mornings, dressed in his best clothes, carrying one of the toys that Santa had left for him ...

He was ushered to the front of the chapel and Sam passed along the row, handing out hymn sheets decorated with rows of green fir trees and little yellow bells.

'Ye awright, Colin?' Sam asked him and Colin nodded back, glad to see a friendly smile on the old man's face.

Christmas Day here in Barlinnie was turning out to be a lot different from his expectations, Colin realised. First there had been an extra special breakfast with the promise of a really good feast at lunchtime. Joseph had been in prison at this time of year before and had enthused about the great grub, and now his cell mate was sitting next to him, hands and feet moving rapidly up and down as usual. He tried to ignore his twitching as they stood to chant the first hymn, male voices rising in one accord, the acoustics making the sound rise right to the top of the barrel-vaulted roof.

He breathed in, almost expecting the whiff of incense to hit his nostrils, but there was only the clean fresh smell of open space and an understanding of it for the first time in his life as he sang the phrase 'joy unconfined'.

198

CHAPTER 28

Lorimer glanced back at the house as he drove off. The candle branch lights twinkled from the upstairs window and he envisaged Maggie sitting in her rocking chair, Chancer on her lap, as she continued with her favourite Christmas reading. A new Alexander McCall Smith had been one he knew she would like; something to take her away from the workaday world of home or school. With McCall Smith's characters to keep her company, Lorimer felt a little less guilty in deserting Maggie to pursue the Swedish girl's case.

Jo Grant's latest bit of news had arrived as an email just this morning. Despite the holidays, forensics had been hard at work and there was no mistaking the excitement in his detective inspector's tone as she wrote.

> Good news. We have a match between the traces on
> Fiona Travers's clothes and those of Lesley Crawford. Have
> a look at the jpgs attached and let me know what you think.
> Team going all out to see what we can find re perp.

The likeness between the two women was all the more marked when seen side by side, Lorimer realised. He thought of the image of Eva Magnusson that he would soon place next to these others. It was uncanny how closely they resembled one another. He had watched Jo Grant's face last night as he voiced the opinion that the three murders might be linked, and seen her expression of relief when he had admitted that there had to be more evidence, something concrete to tie them all together.

There was no request to have him cut short his holiday and come in. No, Jo was too wise an officer for that. This was her case and although she needed to keep her boss informed, she could handle it. Lesley Crawford's photograph had been splashed across the daily newspapers – THE TRAGEDY OF CHRISTMAS EVE, one headline had read, as though the poor woman was dead already. But she remained in intensive care and under police supervision; when – if – she awoke, perhaps she could throw some light on the identity of her attacker. Lorimer pursed his lips as he drove across the city. Knowing that his victim was still alive might only serve to drive her attacker underground. He sighed, wondering if one of his theories was dead in the water: there had been no mention whatsoever that traces found on the two women matched anything of Eva Magnusson's. Had they even looked? Lorimer wondered. And if not, could he sneak into the labs for a quick word with one of his forensic pals?

As ever, Lorimer felt a sense of pride as he crossed the Kingston Bridge, glancing to his left where the skyline boasted familiar landmarks like the syringe-like spike beside the science centre, the white arcs of the newer bridges crossing the Clyde, and that dark outline of the university tower. This was his city and with all its faults and battered dreams, it still gave his spirits a lift to see it etched against the cold blue winter sky. Minutes later he had parked beside his old office in Pitt Street and was looking up at the red-brick building with a pang of nostalgia. This could have been such a good unit, he thought, had it not been for the budgetary restraints that had forced him to renew his acquaintance with A Division. Still, he mused, giving the receptionist a nod as he passed the front desk, he wouldn't have been able to do much to help Kirsty Wilson if he had still been commanding the Serious Crimes Squad, would he?

'Calum, how are you? Drawn the short straw, have you?' Lorimer stood in the doorway of the lab as a white-coated man turned around and smiled back at him and shrugged. Someone had to man the place during the Christmas break, his expression seemed to say. 'Mind if I come in?' he asked.

'Course not, grab a coat, there's a clean one on that hanger.' Calum Uprichard pointed at the lab coat and nodded for Lorimer to join him at his lab bench where he resumed peering into a scanning electron microscope. Lorimer pulled on the white coat and buttoned it up. Donning a lab coat before entering a working area was all part of the scrupulous routine: a stray hair or piece of fluff from an overcoat could contaminate a production, laying waste to weeks of work.

'What brings you here, Detective Superintendent?' Calum asked, not taking his eyes off whatever was proving to be so absorbing to his eagle eye.

'Hm, on a bit of a quest, really. Wondered if I could have you look into something in a couple of unrelated cases,' he admitted.

'Oh? That sounds interesting.'

'I think so, but this has to be kept strictly between you and me.'

'Not doing anything naughty, I hope?' Calum's grin was infectious and Lorimer gave a laugh.

'No, the Fiscal will likely approve it anyway. Just wanted to test a theory, really.'

'Hm, maybe the less you tell me the better, eh?' Calum sat back, sliding his chair to the left side of the desk to type something onto his open laptop.

'It's the Magnusson girl's murder,' Lorimer told him. 'I wanted to see if there was anyone who could do a check on the productions from the crime scene.'

'Oh?'

'Jo Grant's told me that there's a match between the Travers victim and the assault on Lesley Crawford, the woman who was attacked on Christmas Eve . . . ?'

'Aye, we read about that. Horrible thing to happen. How is she?'

Lorimer shook his head and made a face.

'Bad as that, eh?' Calum sighed. 'Well I can look up the databases right now and tell you,' he said, glancing around the empty lab. He lowered his voice. 'Just as well you came in when it was quiet or there might have been some explaining to do.'

Lorimer waited patiently as Calum opened up file after file, watching the scientist's eyes darting up and down the data on his screen.

At last the scientist turned and shook his head. 'Sorry. Not a sausage. Was there a reason for thinking that the guy they got for the Swedish girl's murder wasn't right after all? Or,' he added, seeing the grim look on the detective superintendent's face, 'shouldn't I ask?'

Kirsty had told him that the English lad would be back down south for the duration of the Christmas holidays so Lorimer was mildly surprised to hear that the other student, Roger Dunbar, was already back in the Anniesland flat and had agreed to meet the detective superintendent.

Merryfield Avenue looked different from his previous visit when crime-scene tape had cordoned off the entrance to the flat and white-suited officers were everywhere. On this late December morning the place was rather pretty, Lorimer thought, looking at the Christmas trees that lit up so many bay windows in the flats. Dark red sandstone provided a warm contrast to the grey streets below and the leaden sky above that now threatened snow.

A large FOR SALE sign dominated the path to the front door. Old Mr McCubbin, their next-door neighbour, was selling up, Kirsty had told him. Looking around at the quiet street, Lorimer wondered how many viewers had already been to see the duplex flat in this desirable part of Glasgow: quite a few, he suspected. If he had to live in the city, this wouldn't be a bad place to call home. Yet the news of a murdered girl might make many reluctant to live in this particular close.

He pressed the buzzer and waited, hoping that the student hadn't got cold feet and decided not to be in when the police officer arrived. But then a crackle came, followed by an unfamiliar voice.

'Hello?'

'It's Lorimer here,' he told the intercom.

'Come on up.'

Lorimer pushed in then stood in the hallway, watching as the heavy door swung shut, hardly making a sound. He tested it, just to see that the door was in fact locked, and it was. And surely Jo and her team had done exactly the same thing, checked to see that the main entry had been secure on the night that the girl had been murdered? Lorimer gave himself a shake: this sort of thought was not worthy of him. He trusted Jo Grant to do a proper job. Still, his policeman's instincts made him work along this line of thought. Someone would have had to gain entry along with a resident, or have been allowed up via the intercom system, just as he had.

In a matter of minutes he had loped up the flights of stairs and arrived at the flat.

The big red-haired lad was waiting for him, standing just inside the doorway, and he stood aside politely as Lorimer came forward.

'Sorry to intrude on your holiday time,' he began as the door shut after them and he walked beside Roger Dunbar along the hallway.

'You don't mind if we go into the kitchen? Only we don't go into the lounge much now,' Rodge said, pausing as they stood at the angle between the room where Eva had died and the door to the kitchen.

'Fine with me,' Lorimer replied.

The big lad seemed nervous, Lorimer thought, as he saw that Roger was keeping his distance from the policeman. Or was he simply a bit embarrassed at this unofficial visit?

'I take it you know why I'm here?'

'Yeah, Kirsty told me what was going on,' Roger muttered at last, looking down towards the ground as though reluctant to meet the detective's eyes.

'I was a bit surprised that you had come back here so soon after Christmas Day,' Lorimer ventured.

'It's quieter here,' Roger answered, almost too quickly. 'I get more peace than I would at my dad's place.'

He nodded towards the kitchen table and Lorimer sat down, his back to the window.

'Oh?'

'Stepmother's got three kids,' Roger told him, pulling out a chair a few feet away from the policeman. 'Noisy wee blighters.' He affected a nonchalance that Lorimer did not believe for a minute. Instead, the slight strain in the young man's voice told a different tale and, although Lorimer simply nodded, he guessed that Roger Dunbar felt like an outsider in the extended family. *My dad's place*, he had said, not *home*.

'Your mum still around?'

He shook his head. 'No. She died a few years back. Cancer.'

'Sorry, that must have been hard.'

Roger bit his lip and nodded in reply.

'Anyway,' Lorimer went on, now anxious to change the subject but still regarding the student thoughtfully, 'you know that we are continuing to investigate Eva's death?'

'Kirsty said something about the Procurator Fiscal,' Roger replied, shifting his gaze momentarily to check out the man who had seated himself so easily at his kitchen table.

'That's right,' Lorimer told him. 'We have to disclose any new information to him. And Kirsty has given us a bit of that.'

'Oh.' Roger Dunbar looked uncomfortable. 'I thought it had all been decided. I mean once Colin had been arrested an' that . . .'

'What if Colin Young has been accused of something he didn't do, Roger?' Lorimer asked gently, leaning forward. 'How would you feel if you had been unable to help him?'

The young man let an indifferent shrug be his only response.

'You're quite prepared to talk to me about Eva and Colin, though?'

'Suppose so,' Roger said, shifting uncomfortably, his long legs stretched out under the table at an angle to Lorimer's own.

'I know this is hard, but can you tell me what you remember about the party that night? Sometimes it takes a while for things to come back, especially after the sort of shock you must have experienced.'

Roger gave a sigh and exhaled long and loud as though preparing himself for some arduous physical task. 'What exactly do you want to know?' he said, risking a glance at Lorimer.

'Did you see them together?'

Roger nodded. 'Aye, they were dancing in the main room for a while then ...'

'Then?'

The boy shook his head, cheeks reddening suddenly. 'Well, I suppose they must have ... they went into one of the bedrooms ... you know?'

'And did you see them afterwards?'

'Well, not really. I mean, I never saw Eva leaving, but someone said she'd gone.'

'Can you remember who that was?'

'Sorry, haven't a clue.'

'And Colin?'

Roger was silent for a moment and Lorimer watched as the boy chewed his lower lip, hands clenched tightly together.

'Roger?'

The boy turned his head away for a moment as though to hide his emotions, then, clearing his throat, he went on. 'See what you said about trying to help Colin?' He swallowed and gave a cough. 'Well, what if I tell you something that *doesn't* help him, what then?'

'I only want the truth,' Lorimer said softly.

'Well,' Roger said, turning to meet the detective superintendent's eyes properly for the first time, 'the truth is that as soon as Colin knew she'd gone he was out that door and after her like a bat out of hell.'

'Why didn't you tell this to DI Grant?'

Roger's cheeks flamed again and he shook his head silently.

'You think Colin followed her here and strangled her, don't you?'

'I don't know!' Roger protested, drumming his fists on his thighs.

'But you kept this to yourself because, like Kirsty, you couldn't bring yourself to believe that he had done something like that?'

'But I *did* believe it!' Roger exclaimed. 'At the time, I mean. I thought he'd found out about me and Eva.'

'*You* and Eva?'

The big lad nodded unhappily then turned a tearful gaze to the detective. 'Aye, we had, well . . . a bit of a . . . sort of a . . . *fling*.' He looked earnestly across at Lorimer. 'Will I get into trouble for not saying?'

It was Lorimer's turn to shrug. 'Nobody's going to blame you for keeping *that* to yourself till now,' he said. 'But I would hope you would tell the whole truth if you were asked it under oath.'

'Will it come to that?' The lad's mouth fell open in a moment of astonishment.

'Unless we can turn up new evidence that points to a different perpetrator or something transpires to prove Colin's innocence or he decides to plead guilty then, yes, the case will go to trial.'

The two looked at one another for a long moment and Lorimer thought he could see something like pity in the red-haired lad's face.

'There's something else . . .' Roger bit his lip and glanced fleetingly at the detective from under his lashes.

'Go on.'

'I heard Eva having a row with someone. At the party.'

'When was this?'

'I'm not sure. Couldn't have been long before she left.'

'Was it Colin?'

Roger shrugged. 'That's what I'm not sure about. You see, I only heard *her* voice on the other side of the bathroom door. There was a lot of noise, you know? Music and that.'

'So how do you know she was having an argument with someone?'

'It was what she *said*.' Roger looked down at his feet, suddenly embarrassed.

'And ... ?'

'She said ... she was shouting ... other folk must've heard her ...'

'Roger?'

'She said, "I'll screw anyone I want!"'

There was a moment of silence as Roger closed his eyes, clearly upset at having to recount this incident.

'Later on ... after she ... well, I thought it must have been Colin,' he said miserably. 'Thought he had found out about Eva ... and ...' He swallowed, his Adam's apple bobbing painfully. 'And me,' he finished in a hoarse whisper. 'I thought that he'd become jealous ... Oh God! And I've been thinking such awful things about him all this time!'

The boy pushed the shock of red hair back from his face, his eyes finding Lorimer's once again. 'But now I don't know,' he said. 'What if Kirsty's right? What if he *didn't* do it?'

'What do you *think*, Roger?'

The boy looked away again, hands clasped thoughtfully under his chin. 'I don't know. Honestly, and that's the truth, I really don't know. I mean, I liked Colin and he was the last person you could imagine hurting a girl, but ...'

Lorimer waited, eyebrows raised in question.

Another sigh followed. 'Don't they say it's always the quiet ones who act out of character?' Roger said at last.

A sound behind them made the pair turn and then Kirsty was there in the kitchen doorway, unwinding her long scarf.

She had opened her mouth as though to speak then caught his glance.

'Oh,' she said, and began to back out of the room.

'It's okay,' the detective reassured her, 'we were just about finished anyway.' Then, catching the expression of relief on Roger Dunbar's face as the student stood up, he put out a hand.

'Roger,' he began, standing up so that the tall student had to look at him, 'Professor Brightman wants to talk to you as well. Will that be a problem?'

Roger hesitated for long enough to let Lorimer see the doubt in the boy's eyes.

'Don't suppose so,' he shrugged at last, slouching away from Lorimer as he spoke, putting as much distance between them as the long kitchen allowed.

'Right,' Kirsty said uncertainly, looking from one to the other. 'I'll make some tea then, shall I?'

'When does Gary come back?'

'Oh, not for ages. Glasgow Uni's term begins the third week of January. Why? Do you really need to see him that urgently?'

Lorimer sipped the tea that Kirsty had made him, not answering. Did he need to see Gary Calderwood? Yes, he thought, suddenly, he did. In fact he would call the student this evening to ask him to come back to Glasgow. Anyone who had known the Swedish girl, and the student arrested for her murder, had to tell them everything they knew about the couple. And that thought brought him back to the Strathclyde University lecturer, Dirk McGregor, who had agreed to meet him in town this very afternoon.

*

209

Princes Square was, on reflection, a terrible choice of rendezvous, having as its only redeeming feature the fact that it was easy to spot a policeman of six feet four inches standing by the balustrade outside Fifi and Ally's tea room. Everywhere, shoppers milled around, the blank expressions on so many faces as though it were some sort of tribal duty to scour the shops for a post-Christmas bargain. Maggie had occasionally ventured into town to shop at the sales but declared that the heaving crowds made finding new clothes a thoroughly unpleasant experience. Even the windows of chichi boutiques were plastered with large SALE notices, obscuring the mayhem within. Looking around, Lorimer smiled to see several men, like him, leaning on the polished wooden rail, waiting resignedly for their wives and girlfriends to return. The place was pretty enough, though, he told himself, looking up at the glass roof and the sun streaming in, catching the swirling snowflake decorations that hung suspended by hundreds of nylon threads. Down below, someone was playing the grand piano, the tinkling music wafting upwards, past the giant crystal shape that represented a Christmas tree, mingling with the babble of women's voices and clinking teacups from the tables behind him.

He had told Jo Grant that he was having this meeting with McGregor. *I think he'll open up more in a less formal place than Stewart Street*, he had told her when she had raised her eyebrows. The boss was doing things his way, her expression seemed to say, and she wasn't one hundred per cent happy about that.

'Lorimer?'

The man stepping off the escalator tapped the detective superintendent on the arm. Lorimer turned to see a man about his own age regarding him suspiciously.

'Mr McGregor?'

'Aye, that's right,' the man said, his eyes boring into Lorimer's own. 'What the hell's this all about? And did I need to come into Glasgow?' he protested.

'You didn't want police at your home, did you?' Lorimer growled back. 'I could always escort you up to Stewart Street, if you'd prefer? I know my DI would just love to meet you.'

The man shook his head and made a face.

Lorimer took him by the crook of his elbow and beckoned him back to the down ramp. 'Come on,' he said. 'It's impossible to talk in here.'

Dirk McGregor shook the policeman's hand off as though offended by his touch but followed him nonetheless.

'Gallery of Modern Art's maybe going to be a bit quieter than a place like this,' Lorimer suggested, glancing back at the lecturer who was scowling at him.

'Thought we might have found a decent pub,' McGregor countered gloomily.

The policeman raised his eyebrows. 'Is this you offering me a seasonal tipple by any chance?'

'Thought you lot weren't supposed to drink on duty,' the man shot back.

Lorimer deliberately ignored the barb. 'GOMA's just around the corner. And it's closer than any pub,' he said, as they came out of the shopping mall. Buchanan Street was heaving with people and Lorimer had to slow his pace to make sure that McGregor did not simply walk away from him.

He glanced at the lecturer from time to time, appraisingly. He was a lean, good-looking man, rakish, with brown hair, thinning slightly on top, and a loping stride that matched Lorimer's own. His long, brown wool coat was unbuttoned to reveal a faded suede jacket over a mustard-coloured open-necked shirt and a pair of

211

highly polished loafers showed below his cord trousers. If Eva Magnusson had been having an affair with this older man then perhaps it may have been a purely physical attraction.

They were silent as they rounded Royal Exchange Square and crossed towards the gallery's entrance. Already the light had changed and the darkness of the winter afternoon contrasted with the gauzy golden net of tiny lights suspended above the square. The statue of the Duke of Wellington astride his horse stood looking down on the people hurrying along Queen Street and for once there was no orange and white traffic cone placed by mischief-makers on the heads of either horse or rider.

Lorimer saw with some relief that the gallery was almost empty. 'Coffee?' he asked and Dirk McGregor responded with an ungracious grunt that he took for assent.

A few minutes later they were seated at a corner table.

'What's all this about?' Dirk McGregor grumbled once again, shooting Lorimer a look of annoyance.

'Oh,' the policeman smiled thinly, 'I thought I was going to ask that question.'

McGregor frowned. 'What is it you want?'

'The truth about your relationship with Eva Magnusson.'

McGregor gave a hollow laugh. 'Truth? Ha! The truth is I was taken for a mug, that's what the truth is, Detective Superintendent.'

'Oh?' Lorimer cocked his head to one side. 'Care to elaborate?'

McGregor shifted uneasily in his seat. 'Look she was just a right little cock teaser, wanted what she could get, that was all, right?'

'So you never had sex with her?'

McGregor looked down at his coffee mug, sighing. 'Never said

that,' he began. 'All right, we did have sex, okay?' he muttered.
He gave a sigh, bit his lip then looked up at Lorimer for a long
moment before shaking his head in a gesture of despair. 'God, she
was the best thing that's happened to me in a long time!' He vio-
lently brushed a hand across his eyes. 'Who would have wanted to
destroy a lovely girl like Eva?'

'I'm trying to find out that very thing, Mr McGregor,' Lorimer
told him softly.

'But I thought you'd caught the guy?'

'Perhaps,' Lorimer said vaguely. 'There are lots of enquiries
still going on into Eva Magnusson's life here in Glasgow, however.'

The other man frowned. 'I see,' he said. 'Well, actually I don't
see ... isn't the case closed?'

'There are lots of background checks to be made,' Lorimer
went on smoothly. 'Loose ends to tie up.'

'I won't have to testify or anything, will I?' McGregor had shot
upright, a look of alarm across his handsome features. 'My wife
doesn't need to know ...?'

'Perhaps not,' Lorimer conceded. 'Now, let me ask you a bit
more about Eva. What was your relationship like?'

Dirk McGregor relaxed a little, sitting back and spreading his
hands across the table. 'What was Eva like?' A smile flickered on
his mouth. 'A real wee firecracker, actually,' he said, preening
himself a little as the memory took hold. 'But she was the one
who started it, Lorimer, not me.' The smile faded as suddenly as
it had appeared, like a rare shaft of sunlight in a Glasgow rain-
storm.

'Go on,' Lorimer said quietly.

'You want to know the truth, the real truth, well here it is.' He
leaned forward. '*She* seduced *me*, Detective Superintendent. So

get rid of any idea that I was the big bad *lecherer* in this story, okay?'

'You didn't happen to be at that student party she was attending the night she died, by any chance?'

The lecturer shook his head. 'No.'

'So where were you that night?'

McGregor gave a hollow laugh. 'At home with the wife and kids. Sad but true.'

'But you had planned to meet up with Eva the day after she was killed?'

McGregor sighed, putting both hands to his head. 'God, if only we had!' He looked up and Lorimer could see the misery in his eyes. 'Do you know how horrible it is thinking you're going to see someone then knowing you'll never ever have the chance again?'

The policeman swallowed hard. Didn't that fate come to everyone at some time or other in their lives?

'Can I ask you something else?' he said instead. 'Did you ever see Eva with anyone else – another man or a boy, perhaps?'

McGregor frowned again, but thoughtfully this time as if Lorimer had struck a hidden chord in his memory.

'She always had her friends about her, right enough. But you're wanting someone special? There was a lad who hung about a lot,' he began. 'Not sure if he was from their course ...' He chewed his lip. 'Thin lad, pale face – yes, now I come to think of it he sat along from her in some of the lectures, followed her out sometimes ... oh, sorry, cannae mind his name. It'll be on a database somewhere, though.'

'This might or might not be important,' Lorimer said, trying to keep his expression as impassive as possible while pinning the man with his stare. 'But when you can find this student's name you will contact me right away?' He took out his leather wallet, picking out a card and sliding it across the table.

'Oh, and there's just one more thing, Mr McGregor,' he continued. 'At some point we will need you to come to police headquarters to make a statement, but we'll let you know.'

Dirk McGregor pocketed the card and sat back. 'Is that it, then? Am I free to go?' The ghost of a smile twisted on his face as he spoke.

'Aye, for now, though I might need to talk to you again soon.'

Lorimer watched as the lecturer walked away from him, brown coat swinging, out of the cafeteria and up to the ground floor of the building. Would Solomon Brightman want to talk to this man? Perhaps not.

Then a sudden memory of the dead girl lying on the carpet at Merryfield Avenue came back to him, blond hair spread across that perfect face. Could the dead still speak across that dark void? And was there anything that a deeper investigation into the Swedish girl's life might tell him?

She brought something like wonder into my life, established a sense that there were possibilities I'd never ever considered. It wasn't just that she was from Stockholm or that they were filthy rich, it was Eva herself. Every day felt new from the time she changed me. You know how spring kind of creeps up on winter? One day the trees and hedges are all bare and full of twisted sticks, stark against the pale sky, then it seems that overnight the air has changed, the sun is out in a blue sky that looks like it's been washed clean and the greening begins. That was what it felt like; something inside me *began to grow and blossom. And I was foolish enough to call it love.*

Colin felt the sting of tears behind his eyelids as he looked at the pages of his notebook and the scribbled heading, *THE SWEDISH GIRL*.

What had she done to him? And how on earth was he ever going to convince anyone that he was innocent of her murder?

CHAPTER 29

It was always the same, Solly thought with a sigh; five days away from home and a list of emails awaited his attention. He scrolled down to see who had been trying to contact him, deleting the spam, taking notes of the details for his forthcoming lecture in Stockholm before pausing at the one bearing Lorimer's personal email address.

Saw Dirk McGregor, the detective superintendent had written, and went up to speak to Roger Dunbar. Think you'll want to see that lad for yourself, though, he had added cryptically.

Solly sighed again. The Christmas break had been a blessed respite from any sort of work and he had not once given the police case a thought, content to be with Rosie and Abby, seeing the little girl being thoroughly spoiled by her grandparents, uncles and aunties. But that interlude was over and now he was back in his Glasgow home, pondering just what he had agreed to take on and whether the entire case would come back to haunt him in later years. If Colin Young was brought to trial and found guilty, would there be some mud clinging to his own reputation if it was discovered he had meddled behind the scenes? Once he would never have hesitated to consider a thought like that, Solly told himself, but now he was a husband and a father, responsible not just to himself but to his little family.

A memory came back then of the boy, Colin, as they had shaken hands before he watched him being led away amongst the other prisoners. He had looked back just once, his eyes searching for Kirsty. And what had he seen in that look? Expectation? Hope? Or simply the forlorn expression of a lad who was desperately trying to put a brave face on his situation?

It was no good, the psychologist told himself, pointing the cursor at Reply, he had to do what he could for that young man, even at the risk of his own reputation.

'Gary's coming back early,' Kirsty said. 'Kept saying he couldn't leave his mum but looks like he's changed his mind.'

Or had his mind been changed for him? she wondered, not voicing this sudden thought. She knew that Lorimer had been anxious to speak to him.

'Soon there'll be the three of us again,' she continued, forcing herself to speak brightly. 'And you'll be back too, Colin. Wait and see.'

Colin imagined her back at the flat, in the bedroom across from his own. Was her ear pressed hard against the mobile as though that would bring her a little closer to him, imagining her friend on the other end of the line? He hoped so.

'Good. Maybe he'll tell them more about Eva,' Colin said, glancing sideways to see if there was anyone else approaching the two phone booths at the end of the corridor.

'What can he tell them that we don't know?'

Colin bit his lip. She didn't suspect a thing about Eva and Gary's relationship, did she?

'Och, you never know,' he replied vaguely. 'Gary's a good-looking bloke. Maybe Eva fancied him?'

Kirsty gave a snort of laughter. 'I don't think so,' she declared. 'Gary just fancies himself. He's like that guy in the Shania Twain song, you know? The one who keeps a couple of combs in his pocket just in case. "Oh-oh, you think you're special",' she sang.

Colin laughed. It was great just to hear Kirsty's voice and she still had the capacity to make him feel better, even in here. Think of nice things to ask her, he told himself.

'How was your Christmas?'

'Och, the usual, you know. Granny Wilson had knitted me a sweater that came down to my knees so I'll probably wear it as a mini dress and shock the poor old soul.' There was a pause before she asked, 'How about you?'

'Not so bad, really. We all got selection boxes at teatime and the meals were good. The staff make an effort, I'll say that for them.'

'Good,' Kirsty agreed, then there was a silence between them as though she wanted to say something but couldn't find the words.

'It'll be all right, Colin, I just know it will.'

'Aye, well, we have to wait an' see, don't we?' he whispered. 'Look, I'll call you again soon, promise.'

He hung up and wandered over to the end of the corridor to the tall bank of windows, glancing behind him to check if anyone was watching. The windows opened inwards and provided a welcome draught of air, but once he had been sharply reprimanded by another inmate for letting in the cold, though why any of them wouldn't want to smell the fresh air was beyond him.

Outside, the afternoon light was fading and he could see the orange points of the street lamps against the green arc of a nearby golf course. If he craned his eyes to the left then he could just make out the towering shapes of the infamous Red Road flats, but usually he let his eyes dwell on the Campsie Hills, trying to remember happier days when he had been free to roam around the countryside, unaware of what a gift that freedom really was.

Dusk was falling now, making shadows where none had been before, obscuring the path that lay below him. The trees had begun to stir, as though they were nocturnal creatures roused from sleep by some unseen force. The chill in the air spoke of a frost forming even as he stood amidst the shrubbery, hidden from the sight of any passer-by. Soon enough the leaves would harden, their edges rimed with white, the whole woodland caught in the grip of a cold wind blowing in from the east.

He could go home, he told himself, back to the place where a fire might be lit and curtains drawn against the night and all its terrors. But warmth of a different kind was what he anticipated: the warmth of flesh and blood under his hands, the warmth that made him feel such power surging through his veins ...

The sound of feet thudding somewhere to his right made him shrink back, his fingers clasping the weapon more tightly, as though to reassure himself it was still there. Then the figure appeared out of the mist, a grey phantom shape, slim-hipped and hooded. His lips parted as he watched her approach. It was a woman, he was certain of that, but was she the right one?

His body tensed for the moment when he would hurl himself at his victim, knocking her to the ground.

She was almost parallel with his hiding place when her feet faltered and she stopped, turned and looked straight at the quivering bushes as though she could see right through them. For a moment she was still, alert like a startled doe. Then, in one swift movement she cast back her hood, revealing a dark ponytail, and pulled out her earphones, letting them dangle in her gloved hands.

He felt his body go rigid as he tried hard not to make a sound, gritting his teeth in disappointment.

Then, as though the woman had decided that there was nothing to see and nothing to hear, she picked up her pace, running along the track towards the road where there would be street lights and traffic and human company.

The man watched her go, blinking away the wateriness that had formed in his eyes. Then, thrusting the weapon into the inside pocket of his coat, he stepped onto the path and prepared to walk the long way back from where he had come.

As Rodge crossed the road to the curve of University Gardens he looked up at the big stained-glass windows of Professor Brightman's office. He'd walked this path hundreds of times on his way to the Queen Margaret Union but today it felt as though he was taking this route for the first time.

Soon he was standing at the large panelled door, wondering why he should be so tense with nerves. The guy was only one of the staff, after all, not some monster to be feared.

Yet when the door swung open, Rodge found he had jumped back a pace, the sight of the bearded man only adding to his discomfiture.

'Roger? I'm Professor Brightman.'

He took the proffered hand, feeling its warm clasp, then he was inside a large airy room that might have been a small library its walls were lined with so many books.

'Come in, come in! Over here to the window,' the professor said, gesturing around a big table in the middle of the room.

'There's a variety of teas and coffees and, hm, maybe a biscuit, though the first years were in just before Christmas, so maybe not . . . ' he muttered into his beard, picking up a flower-patterned plate that bore nothing but crumbs.

'It's okay,' Rodge began, 'I've had my lunch, anyhow.'

'No tea?' The eyes behind that pair of horn-rimmed spectacles lost a little of their twinkle as though the professor was disappointed.

'Oh, but you go ahead, I mean, if you were going to have tea . . . look I'll have a cup if you want . . . ' Rodge felt his face begin to flush and he cursed the gene pool that had given him such a shock of red hair and the complexion that came with the package.

The professor beamed. 'What'll we have? Camomile, mint, rosehip, um, something to make you sleep better . . . ' He flicked through a pile of tea bags in a small wicker basket.

'D'you have any ordinary tea?' Rodge ventured. 'That'll do me, honest.'

'Of course,' Solly replied, triumphantly lifting out a sachet of English Breakfast as though he had conjured it up. 'Now let me guess. Milk and two sugars?'

Roger nodded.

'Right, how much time do we have? You'll be busy, no doubt.'

'It's okay,' Rodge assured him. 'I'm not, really.' Then he bit his lip, wondering if he had missed the chance to fib and leave this interview all the sooner.

The professor caught his eye and smiled and in that moment Roger knew that Brightman was living up to his name: he had sussed him out just like that. So, what did he see? A big lad with nice manners who couldn't even lie about something as simple as having somewhere else to go?

'Thanks,' he said as Solly handed him a mug of tea.

'No, I must thank *you*,' Solly said gravely. 'You didn't have to come to me today, or any other day for that matter. And I appreciate that you are here.'

'Detective Superintendent Lorimer said you'd want to talk to me about Eva,' Roger said.

'Yes,' the professor replied, then stared past the student as though deep in thought. 'Yes, that's right. We have to know a lot more about her if we are to make any progress with this problem.'

'Problem?'

'The problem of the wrong person being charged with her murder!' Solly replied, his bushy eyebrows shooting up as though in mild astonishment that the student had not yet cottoned on to why he was sitting in this room drinking tea. 'You don't think Colin Young killed her, do you?'

Roger shrugged. 'I don't know any more,' he admitted.

'Well, then, we must endeavour to find out who did and to achieve this I think we need to know a lot, lot more about Miss Eva Magnusson!'

The professor gave him a kindly smile and tilted his head to one side as though a question had been asked.

'What?' Rodge asked, feeling the telltale flush of crimson reddening his cheeks.

'Tell me everything about her,' Solly said gently. 'And I *mean* everything.'

The deep brown eyes behind the horn-rimmed spectacles blinked owlishly as the psychologist regarded his notes. It was interesting how writing things down always seemed to clarify one's thoughts, Solly nodded to himself. And, although his next interview should be with Gary Calderwood, he wondered about speaking to someone different altogether.

The three boys had several things in common: they had been selected to share a flat with Eva Magnusson and had fallen for the girl's undoubted charms. Colin's letters hinted at his suspicion that Gary had been in the Swedish student's bed. And everyone knew now about the ill-fated sexual encounter between Eva and Colin Young. Lorimer had not told his detective sergeant's daughter about Roger Dunbar, however, and the more he thought about it the more convinced Solly was that the three boys had been chosen deliberately. For, he reasoned, hadn't they other things in common? Like the fact that each one of them had lost a parent, just like the Swedish girl. A coincidence, perhaps, but somehow Solly doubted that, and his thoughts began to turn to Henrik Magnusson and the reasons behind his choice of tenants for the flat in Merryfield Avenue. Had the dead girl's father some sort of an agenda in mind as he interviewed Eva's potential flatmates?

Kirsty was the house mother, of that there could be little doubt; hadn't she told him herself how the others had loved her home cooking? He pondered on the Swede's choice of Kirsty as the only other girl. Her father was a detective sergeant with Strathclyde Police, good credentials for any prospective tenant, and the dark-haired girl would never have proved any sort of competition to Eva. She had a nice, kind face, Solly reminded himself, but he would be lying if he didn't describe her as a bit on the hefty side: there was nothing of the glamour-puss in Kirsty Wilson. Was that the sort of girl Magnusson had wanted? A homebody? Someone who was bright and friendly, who would make his daughter feel cosseted? A motherly type, in other words, for a girl who had never known what it was to have a mother of her own.

Mrs Young had died of cancer when Colin and his brother were little boys, Mrs Dunbar's death had occurred when Roger was just

224

thirteen. And Gary Calderwood? He did have a mother, that was true enough; it had been the loss of his father that had interested the psychologist. Roger had told him a little about his flatmate, how Magnusson had known the student's late father through business, how Gary had taken time off his university studies to help his mother over their bereavement.

Four little lost children, Solly mused. All put together by a man who wielded power over thousands of his own employees ... Yes, perhaps it was Henrik Magnusson who should be the next person on his visiting list. And maybe his own Rosie could give him an inkling about the Swedish millionaire whose businesses controlled so many lives.

Multiple entries appeared on his screen as soon as Solly googled the man's name and for the next twenty minutes he amused himself trying to fit a personality around the bits and pieces of information that could be garnered so easily on the internet.

The lecture at Stockholm University was to take the psychologist away from home for a day and a night: could he possibly find the time to seek out Eva's father before returning to Glasgow? The thought translated itself into action as he searched through the file that Lorimer had given him, pausing at a sheet of paper with Magnusson's personal details written down. Was this a step too far? Would the Swede be willing to meet him to discuss his daughter's dreadful death? And could he do it all without alerting the officers of Strathclyde Police who were legitimately handling the case?

'What does Lorimer say?'

Detective Inspector Jo Grant shook her head. DS Wilson's question was a fair one. They seemed to have reached an impasse in the case now, despite the slim possibility of the injured woman remembering enough to give them a description of her attacker. William Lorimer was, after all, the most experienced officer among them when it came to matters of multiple murder. And, despite the fact that he had delegated a fair bit to his DI, she still seemed to be simmering over the Magnusson case, Wilson thought.

'Do we have to ask him for every last thing?' she asked, her face twisted in a moment of irritation.

Wilson shrugged. 'Okay, ma'am, I just thought ...' He spread his hands in a gesture of apology.

'Well, don't!' she snapped. 'Just for once can we not manage without running to the great man for advice?'

Once he had turned to leave the DI at her desk, Wilson raised his eyebrows. He could see the woman's point of view all right. It was hard on any SIO to have their authority questioned and it was his own daughter who had opened the can of worms that had led to Jo Grant being on such a short fuse. The officers concerned with the latest case were really up against it now that forensics had drawn a blank. There was plenty to examine, but not a single trace had found its equivalent on any of their databases. The attacker was therefore unknown to the police – something that Wilson found surprising. Often those serial killers with an agenda had previous convictions, sometimes for indecent exposure in their youth escalating later to rape; a one-off murder he could understand, but when there had been Fiona Travers's death and an attempt on a woman's life in the same area, then surely it was reasonable to expect that the perpetrator had appeared previously on the police radar?

At least Lorimer had been thorough, giving the team actions that included interviewing family and friends of the victims and door-to-door searches of the areas where the deaths had taken place, plus loads of the inevitable paperwork. It hadn't been a great Christmas for lots of the officers involved, a quick dinner then back out at the division to trawl more files or tramp the cold winter streets. Still, Alistair Wilson would have felt a lot more comfortable if Lorimer was here instead of upstairs in his office: just being able to run stuff past the detective super would give him the confidence he felt Jo Grant lacked right now.

'Stockholm? That's a surprise.'

'Not really. The lecture has been arranged for several months. But you do have to agree that the timing is fortuitous.'

'Indeed. Have you told Rosie?'

'That I intend to meet Mr Magnusson? No.' There was a pause before the psychologist continued. 'I thought it best to keep that particular matter quiet. After all, she is a potential expert witness in this case and I don't want to give her any more problems than she already has.'

'Okay. Let me know if he agrees to see you.'

Lorimer put down the telephone. Fortuitous, yes, but fool-hardy? Possibly. Keeping this investigation under wraps could prove detrimental to both their careers should it all go wrong.

Kirsty Wilson's voice came back to him then, her earnest tones reminding him so much of his own desires for justice. And she didn't give up easily. Pity she had decided to make her career in hospitality, he thought. Kirsty would have made a good copper.

Lorimer smiled to himself. Was Kirsty Wilson a risk taker? Perhaps. Then his smile faded as he thought about Solly and the very real risks he was taking in meeting the dead girl's father face to face in Stockholm.

CHAPTER 30

'Here's the one I got at the bank,' Corinne said, tossing the thick newspaper onto her father's lap. 'Read through the ones in our area and circle any that you fancy, okay?' She dropped a biro onto the *Glasgow Solicitors' Property Centre* newspaper, nodding in satisfaction as the old man picked it up and began turning the pages.

Back in the kitchen, Corinne turned the radio on, humming along to a catchy tune as she began to wash up the lunch dishes. Oh, it wouldn't be long now, surely? The estate agent had told her there was a possible buyer interested in the big duplex flat and, with prices rising again, they would be looking at over a couple of hundred grand, he'd said, easily enough to get her out of this place and into a nice wee bungalow. Not Newton Mearns, though: too posh for her liking and too dear, anyway. No, a little house in the country out in Carmunnock, or even down the Ayrshire coast ... Corinne smiled dreamily as she invented her perfect home: a whitewashed bungalow with a garden looking out onto fields and hills, far from the concrete mass she'd endured for the past couple of decades.

The doorbell rang, interrupting her thoughts, the little white house vanishing as she scuttled through the hallway, drying her hands on her apron as she went.

'Oh!' Corinne's eyes travelled upwards as she regarded the tall man standing at her door. A good-looking man, she thought immediately, mentally regretting her lack of make-up and her dishevelled clothes. Then, as he produced the familiar warrant card, her eyes narrowed in distaste.

'Detective Superintendent Lorimer,' he told her.

'He's no' here,' Corinne said, folding her arms over her thin bosom. 'Havenae seen him fur years.'

The tall man frowned, puzzled. 'Your father? Mr McCubbin?'

'Oh.' Corinne took a step backwards into the hall. 'I thought . . .' She hesitated. 'You want to see ma *faither*?' Her brow creased in a moment of surprise.

'If he's at home,' the detective superintendent replied politely.

'You'd better come in,' Corinne said reluctantly, opening the door wide to admit the handsome stranger. 'What did ye say yer name was, again?'

'Lorimer,' he told her, stepping into the dark narrow passage. 'Did you think I had come to see someone else?'

Corinne shook her head. 'My man,' she said simply. 'He was always a wrong 'un.' She shrugged. 'In and oot the jail . . . havenae set eyes oan him since the divorce . . .' She tailed off, seeing the dark-haired man looking enquiringly at the door ahead.

'Faither's in the living room,' she continued, lowering her voice. 'Is it aboot thon wee lassie next door tae him?'

'Yes, I'm afraid so. Is he very upset about it?'

Corinne shook her head, looking away towards the living room. 'Hasnae said a word aboot it. So, aye, he probably is. Daft auld bugger. Come away through.' She led Lorimer into an over-furnished room where the decor was predominantly ochre and beige, the worn carpet pocked by ancient cigarette burns.

An old man was sitting facing the television, bent over the newspaper on his lap. White wispy hair appeared above the high-backed chair and, as Lorimer came around to greet him, he saw behind the heavy spectacles hooded eyes, glazed with fatigue (or medication?), and stubbled cheeks sunken into a cadaverous face that had a yellowing bruise along the jaw. Had he fallen, perhaps? Old folk were sometimes unsteady on their feet. As if to confirm his thought, Lorimer noticed a wooden stick lying beside his chair, just close enough for the old man to grab with his gnarled hands.

'Mr McCubbin? I'm Detective Superintendent Lorimer,' he said, putting out a friendly hand for the man to take.

But at first the old man kept his fists clenched over the paper, frowning up at the stranger standing above him.

'Who'd you say you are?'

'Detective Superintendent Lorimer,' he said, louder this time so he could be heard.

Then a grudging hand was raised and Lorimer felt his own taken in a surprisingly strong grasp.

'I'm here to ask you about your next-door neighbour, Eva Magnusson,' he began. 'Do you mind if I sit down?'

'Course he doesn't!' Corinne broke in. 'And I'm sure the super-intendent would like a nice wee cup of tea. You too, Dad?'

'Thanks, that would be lovely.' Lorimer smiled up at her then looked back at the old man in time to see him dart a vicious glare at the woman whose expression hardened before she turned away to the kitchen. It was a brief moment but enough to allow the detective to see that there was no love lost between father and daughter.

'Mr McCubbin, I hope you don't mind my coming here to see you?'

'Hm,' the old man replied, folding the newspaper and slipping it down the side of the armchair. 'What d'you want to know?' He looked across at Lorimer, his eyes unblinking, but watchful as though he was waiting for a difficult question.

'Oh, general things, really. I believe you were here when the incident took place,' Lorimer said.

'Aye,' he said shortly.

'And you've got one of those young hooligans for it, I hear,' the daughter called out.

Derek McCubbin's eyes slid away from Lorimer's gaze, resting instead on the door between the living room and the kitchen where sounds of teacups clattering could be heard.

'Were they a nuisance, then, these students next door?'

'Noisy, bad-mannered lot!' Derek McCubbin muttered.

'Not the sort of place for students. That's what you always said, isn't it, Dad?' Corinne interrupted.

'It's a residential area, for families, decent folk . . . ' The old man tailed off, wiping a bit of spittle from his lips.

'Had you complained to anyone about their behaviour?'

There was no reply, a mere shake of the old man's head.

'Waste of time! Who's going to listen to an old man like him? You thought it was going to be the big fair-haired chap didn't you, Dad? Not a load of students playing their loud music and annoying everyone!'

'Who else might have had cause to complain?' Lorimer countered, looking up at the daughter but inwardly wishing that McCubbin wouldn't let her answer for him.

'The neighbours. There's a residents' association. Keeps every-one informed about what's happening in the close. Repairs needing done and that sort of thing . . .'

'And information about the owner of a newly sold flat?' Lorimer leaned forward towards McCubbin, willing him to speak.

The old man nodded.

'Who owned the flat before that?'

'Och, he had a grand wee neighbour for years, didn't you, Dad?' Corinne came between them, setting down the tray on a rickety coffee table. 'Milk and sugar?'

'Just milk, thanks. Where did that neighbour go?'

'Grace Smith. A right nice wee neighbour she was. Och, she died and the flat was left tae her daughter in St Andrews,' Corinne said, ignoring her father and speaking for him to Lorimer. 'Gave him a bad shock, poor wee Grace going so sudden like that. Anyway, we're going to sell up and find a nice wee place away from the city. Aren't we, Dad?' She smiled, barely turning to acknowl-edge the old man, but Lorimer saw a malicious gleam in her eyes that belied the curve on her lips.

'Grace,' Derek McCubbin whispered. 'They sold her home to that man and his daughter . . .' He trembled visibly as he took the mug from Corinne, cupping his hands around it as though to warm his aged fingers.

'Did the other neighbours complain about the noise?' Lorimer persisted but Derek made no reply so he looked at the woman instead for an answer.

'Must've done, eh? I mean, if Faither could hear a racket with his bad hearing, it had to be pretty bad, right?'

Lorimer nodded politely. Yet there was absolutely nothing in Jo Grant's reports to show that the tenants in the top flat of number twenty-four had been anything other than exemplary neighbours.

232

Perhaps nobody liked to speak ill of the dead? It was a common enough reaction. But still . . . there was something here that didn't seem to add up, and, as he sipped his tea, Lorimer wondered just what that was.

'And you were at your daughter's all of that evening and night?'

'He said he was!' Corinne snapped. 'Can you lot no' leave a puir auld man alone? Why're ye no' oot getting that fellow that attacked these women? Eh?'

Lorimer put down his mug, surprised at the woman's sudden protective ferocity. Perhaps he had been wrong about the relationship between them. Maybe the daughter was closer to the old man than he had assumed.

'Perhaps I had better be going,' he said, aware of the hostility on the woman's face. 'Thanks for the tea.'

He made to stand up and take his leave just as Derek McCubbin pulled out a crumpled handkerchief and blew his nose noisily.

The old man muttered something into his hands as the policeman left the room and Lorimer turned for a moment, unsure if he had heard the word 'Sorry'.

'He's an auld man that jist needs a bit o' peace and quiet,' Corinne explained as she opened the door. Yet, as he left, Lorimer couldn't help feeling there was more reason than that for the woman to avoid his eyes as she ushered him out of her home.

He had no reason to suppose that someone was watching from the upstairs flat, but as the detective walked across the road to where his car was parked, he felt rather than saw eyes boring down on him. A quick glance upward and the merest twitch of a curtain confirmed his suspicions. But who was it looking down: father or daughter?

As he drove away from the rows of pale concrete flats, Lorimer could not help but feel a pang of sympathy for the woman hemmed in by the conglomeration of houses that comprised Castlemilk housing scheme. And, as he turned into the more affluent area of Kingspark where bay windows still displayed twinkling Christmas trees, he reflected on whether Derek McCubbin would ever be happy sharing a home with his sharp-tongued daughter and if, even now, the old man regretted leaving his spacious flat in Anniesland.

CHAPTER 31

'Yes, Detective Inspector, I agree,' Solly said, picking up the cup of herbal tea and taking a sip. 'There is a reasonable chance that the killer has a predilection for victims with long fair hair.' He paused and took another sip. 'How is the poor woman anyway?'

DI Grant smiled. 'The doctors think she's going to pull through after all,' she said. 'We've got a couple of officers at her bedside for when she wakes up. It'll be the best start to a new year for her poor family that I can imagine.'

The psychologist breathed a sigh of relief. 'Good,' he said, laying down his cup on Jo's desk. 'Then it might be possible to catch this man . . . ?'

'So long as he's at large he presents a real danger to women,' Jo declared. 'In my book, men who target lone females are either sad, mad or bad and my feeling from the start is that this one is pretty mad.'

Solly tilted his head to one side thoughtfully. 'A personality type that selects his victim on the basis of appearance is probably relating them to someone from his own past that he wishes to harm. Yes, this man most likely displays a certain sort of behavioural disorder,' he said, nodding his agreement.

'Aye, like I said, mad!' Jo declared, watching with glee in her eyes as the psychologist winced. 'Anyway, Lorimer tells me you've been interfering in my other case,' she said, catching the psychologist's eye and pinning it with a glare.

'Guilty as charged,' he murmured. 'But perhaps Colin Young is not,' he added quietly.

'You know I could report him – and you – for taking steps like this?'

Solly managed a half-hearted smile. 'But you won't, will you?'

'No.' The woman's tight-lipped reply ended in a sigh. 'I have too much respect for him to do something like that.'

Solly nodded, watching the expressions flitting across Jo Grant's face. She was hurting, wasn't she? When he spoke again it was in a gentle, understanding tone.

'And you feel that he ought to have had the same respect for you? And that he should have done nothing that would have upset this done-and-dusted case of yours?'

'He's been totally out of order,' Jo replied. 'But if I was wrong about Colin Young . . . ' She bit her lip, leaving the words unsaid. *How would any decent-minded police officer feel about having an innocent man thrown into prison?*

'You did what you had to do,' Solly told her. 'You believed there was sufficient evidence to charge him. He'd had sex with the girl, he had followed her home, he broke down weeping when you interviewed him . . . '

'But was it enough? Evidence has to be corroborated, doesn't it?'

'And how many folk at that party saw Colin hurrying out after the girl?'

'Plenty,' she replied, 'and once we had his DNA matched it was a doddle.'

'If it's any consolation, DI Grant, I am not of the opinion that Eva Magnusson's case is in any way linked to those others.'

'Oh?' The woman's eyebrows shot up in surprise. 'I thought that you and Lorimer ...'

'We don't always agree on every aspect of a case,' Solly smiled. 'And, getting back to Eva Magnusson, I don't want you to think of that victim in a bad light,' he said. He had already recounted his visit from Roger Dunbar and what he had found out about Eva Magnusson's sex life.

'You don't want folk thinking that she was a wee slapper?' Jo smiled back. 'No, I can see what you've been saying, Professor. And I do get the point that she might have been trying to thwart her father's domination by taking lovers he wouldn't have condoned. Human nature to go after the bad ones,' she murmured, making Solly raise his eyebrows a fraction and wonder if the detective inspector was referring to something in her own past. On this, the thirty-first of December, it was not unknown for sensitive souls to look back at the year gone by, but Solomon Brightman preferred to look forward with hope and anticipation at what was just around the corner.

Glasgow was the poor relation when it came to the great Hogmanay party, Lorimer thought, tucking Maggie's arm into his own as they walked back along the avenue. Over in the capital there would be the biggest party of the year with all its music and revellers thronging the streets. Round the next corner lay their own home and soon they would be sitting like thousands of other families across the land, in front of a television, waiting to catch a little of the fun, watching as the display of fireworks burst over Edinburgh castle.

Drinks with the neighbours had been a low-key affair and it

had been made clear that everyone was expected to leave before the actual bells rang out heralding the New Year to come.

'They don't do all that first-footing now, do they?' Maggie remarked, cuddling in to his side, a warm woolly scarf covering her dark curls.

'I can remember when I was wee my mum and dad used to have all the neighbours in for sausage rolls and sandwiches,' he said. 'The house would be full and nobody went to bed till after five in the morning.'

'It was steak pies in our house,' she laughed.

'Aye, your mum always gave us a rare spread,' he replied. There was silence then as they approached their front door, each reflecting on the families now gone and the sense of loss that this engendered.

As Lorimer turned the key they could hear a loud miaow from Chancer, waiting to greet them.

'Hi, puss,' Lorimer said, bending down to scoop the cat onto his shoulder where he balanced, digging sharp claws into the detective's good overcoat.

'Well at least we have our wee pussycat to welcome us in,' Maggie said.

'But better not let him be our first-foot, eh?' Lorimer chuckled.

Maggie punched him gently on the arm. 'Load of superstitious tosh!' she exclaimed. 'As if a red-haired first foot would bring bad luck!' She lifted her hand to stroke the cat who began to purr loudly. 'You wouldn't bring us any harm, would you, Chancer?' she crooned.

'Come on, woman,' Lorimer said, placing the cat in her arms and shrugging himself out of the coat. 'What about that cold bottle waiting in the fridge?'

Later, as they held their champagne flutes in readiness to

welcome in the New Year, Lorimer reflected on the old superstition. He had been in great demand as a popular first-foot
during his teens, already tall (*and dark and handsome*, his mother
used to add).

'You shivered,' Maggie told him, laying a hand on his arm.
'Goose walk over your grave?'

'Just remembering all those years being pushed out the back
door and having to walk around to the front while the bells rang
and everyone wished each other a Happy New Year. It felt
strange, being the one outside, listening to the boats sounding
their hooters down the Clyde.'

Maggie nestled in to his side. 'Do they still do that, d'you
think?'

'Right, here we go,' Lorimer said suddenly, hauling her to her
feet as the voices from the television counted down to midnight.

The booming tones of Big Ben sounded twelve sonorous notes
then a cheer rang out and Scottish dance music began to play.

'Happy New Year, darling,' Lorimer said, clinking his glass
against Maggie's.

'Good health and happiness,' she rejoined, taking a sip of the
champagne and smiling back at him. 'Will it be a good one, do you
think?'

Lorimer stood at the bedroom window watching as a pale Chinese
lantern floated silently across the expanse of inky black skies. He
had slept for a bit then awoken, aware of the ginger cat between
him and Maggie's sleeping form. He had disturbed neither of
them as he slipped out of bed, Chancer merely stretching out a
paw before returning it to a soft furry place beneath his body.

He was thinking about the old superstition. A black-haired man
coming to your door as a first-foot after midnight was the sign for

good luck whereas a red-haired man was an ill omen. Somewhere out there in his city there was a sick individual whose messed-up brain was telling him to target fair-haired women. What sort of symbolism was there? If any? Solly had spoken to him about different theories concerning symbolic choices and why killers might identify their prey with a person from their past. Did this killer have an issue with some fair-haired person who had abused him? He recalled the case from years back, when he had first encountered the psychologist. That killer had had mental issues, hadn't he? Was Solly remembering him, too? And, perhaps, trying to create a profile that was not unlike that of the man now languishing in Carstairs, the Scottish mental hospital?

'New year, new start.' Mrs Calderwood raised her glass and smiled happily at her son who was sitting at the other end of the long dining room table. The room was bathed in a dazzle of winter sunlight making rainbow kisses on the crystal glasses that were now being clinked as the family members acknowledged the toast.

Everyone was here: Grandma Iris, Uncle Terry and his wife, Linda, plus their two sullen-faced teenage girls who had already fallen out over which of them was to sit next to him at dinner. Miriam, the younger one, was knocking back her Veuve Clicquot like it was so much lemonade and Gary tried not to raise a disapproving eyebrow at her. Eva would never have behaved like that . . .

The thought came to him suddenly, making a lump in his throat; a memory of candlelight and the perfume she always wore.

'Going back to Glasgow, then, Gary?' Grandma Iris was smiling at him, her eyes holding the question that was in everybody's mind but that they were all too polite to actually ask. *Do you really want to return to the flat where a murder took place?*

Gary smiled back, his face hurting from trying to pretend. 'Yes, Grandma, of course. Have to get on with my studies, you know.'

The old woman looked back at him, the crinkles around her eyes becoming almost a wink. 'Hope you are doing more than just studying, my boy,' she whispered, leaning in towards him so that only he could hear. 'Time for some fun, now that you're away from home, eh?'

Gary gave a small laugh. 'Well, we'll see. Got a pile of stuff to do before the exams,' he added, still smiling.

'D'you want to play Monopoly after dinner, Gary?' Esther asked.

Gary nodded. 'Sure, if everyone else does,' he said, noting the smirk on his cousin's face. Esther was thirteen going on thirty, he thought, trying not to show his disgust at the untidy mess of backcombed hair supposedly styled in a bouffant, or the false eyelashes with feathers on the ends and that bright kingfisher blue and opalescent pink that must have taken hours to paint on to her eyelids. His gaze drifted across the table to Aunt Linda with her tight-fitting black dress that showed too much cleavage and not enough good taste.

The memory of a blonde girl draping a pink cardigan around her shoulders flitted across his brain and he took a quick pull on the champagne to hide the sudden tears that stung his eyes. He swallowed the bubbles too quickly and, as he spluttered into his napkin, he saw Esther grinning across at him, amused at his momentary discomfiture. For a moment he wanted to reach out and grab her untidy nest of hair and twist it around her neck. Little cow! He saw the girl's smile fade and wiped his mouth once more on the white damask linen napkin, aware that he had let his guard slip.

'Silly me,' he murmured. 'You'd think all these weeks living in Scotland would have made me a seasoned drinker!'

Esther smiled again as everyone laughed but this time Gary noticed a new wariness in his cousin's eyes and he cursed himself inwardly for the momentary lapse.

'I'm off to bed, darling, thanks for clearing up. You are such a pet.' Moira Calderwood blew her son a kiss over her shoulder as she disappeared up the stairs towards her room. It had been like this ever since he had returned home: Moira would rise late, yawning her head off, yet as soon as ten o'clock struck on the grandfather clock in the hall she was off to bed, never even waiting to catch the evening news. Gary had sneaked into her bedroom just before Christmas while Moira had been at the hairdresser's. The prescription tranquillisers were still there right enough, in her en suite bathroom. It was coming up for two years now since Dad's death, time enough to wean herself off the bloody things! Gary had told himself angrily, shoving the dark brown bottle back onto the glass shelf exactly as he had found it. If Dad hadn't died, Moira would never have become the way she was now, so clingy and wanting his help at every turn.

But, he reasoned, stacking the plates carefully into the Miele dishwasher, hadn't she always been dependent on Dad? His mouth twisted as he envisaged the next three weeks spent fetching and carrying for the woman upstairs who was probably comatose already. A wistful memory came to him of Saturday mornings in the flat, Kirsty cooking up a great breakfast for them all, and in that moment Gary knew he wanted to cut short his visit home and return to Glasgow.

'Tomorrow,' he said aloud. 'I'll tell her tomorrow.' Then, having made up his mind, he dropped a tablet into the dispenser, shut the door and pressed the start button, listening to the machine's gentle whirr, the first real smile of the day appearing on his handsome face.

Did I hate her? I don't think so. Do I hate her now? He sighed, the pen poised above the lines, wondering if he should score them out. What was there to hate? A young girl who had beguiled him? Didn't that happen all the time? Colin's mouth disappeared in a thin line as he looked around his cell. This might be what he had to look forward to for the next couple of decades if he was found guilty; he'd be a middle-aged man when he came out. He closed his eyes, remembering her hair, the way it had swept across his face as her body rose and fell in a rhythm with his own. She would be forever young, he thought, trying to remember a line of poetry. Keats, wasn't it? *Forever wilt thou love, and she be fair!*

Was that to be their lasting testament?

Colin rolled over in his bunk, wishing now that he could rid himself of that other vision in his brain, the picture he had tried so hard to forget, of her body lying so still, so very still on the patterned carpet.

CHAPTER 32

Professor Solomon Brightman stood outside the flat, watching for the girl's shadow to appear beyond the glass.

'Hello,' Kirsty said brightly as she opened the door wide to let him in. 'You're early.'

'Thought I would come up while Abby's having her afternoon nap,' he explained. 'She doesn't keep any particular timetable,' he apologised, 'but she does usually have a sleep some time after lunch.'

'Know the feeling.' Kirsty made a face as she rubbed her stomach. 'Mum's been force-feeding me all holidays as though I've been starving in a garret. I mean, c'mon,' she laughed as she pulled down a baggy jumper to hide her bulging tummy, 'do I look like an underfed waif?'

Solly laughed with her but not before he saw a trace of sadness in the girl's eyes. Had it been hard being the plain Jane here alongside a beauty like Eva Magnusson?

'Cup of tea? I've got camomile or spearmint,' Kirsty went on, leading Solly through the long hallway and into the kitchen. 'And there's some home-made cherry cake as well.'

'Mint tea would be lovely, thanks, but I'll pass on the cake,' Solly told her.

'Ah well, the boys'll just have to polish it off.'

'Boys?'

'Oh, did you not know? Gary came back early. *Said* he had work to catch up on but I guess he was finding it hard going at home just him and his mum.'

'And Roger's been here since just after Christmas.' Solly nodded to himself.

'When are you off to Sweden?' Kirsty asked, cutting a large slice of cherry cake and picking up the crumbs with her fingers. 'Mr Lorimer told me you were going there to deliver a paper.'

'The day after tomorrow,' Solly told her. 'No rest for the wicked.' He chuckled.

'I bet it's lovely there,' the girl said dreamily. 'All snowy and crisp, a proper Christmassy sort of landscape, not like this,' she added in disgust, glancing outside where the wind was driving the rain, rattling in gusts against the kitchen window.

Solly smiled but did not reply. His trip to Stockholm might turn out to be far less pleasant than the idealised picture that was in Kirsty Wilson's mind at this moment.

'You said on the phone that there was something you wanted to talk to me about,' Kirsty went on, fishing a teabag from a green packet and plonking it into a flowery mug.

'Yes, there is,' Solly replied, then paused as they went into the lounge where a warm fire crackled in the grate. He sat down, rubbing his hands before he spoke again. 'I wanted to talk to you about Eva Magnusson. I know I've asked you this before, Kirsty, but what was she like? I mean, what was *your* impression of her?'

'Oh.' Kirsty put down the mug she was holding with a sigh. 'What can I tell you?'

'Just the truth,' Solly said simply.

'She was like no one I'd ever met before,' Kirsty said.

She had chosen to sit on the floor by his feet, her arms wrapped around her knees, hands almost lost under the long sleeves of a shapeless brown garment that might have been a knitted tunic.

'She was the sort of person you would imagine going to the ambassador's party, you know what I mean?'

Solly frowned and shook his head.

'That Ferrero Rocher advert, you know. The one where the flunkey comes in with these gold-wrapped sweeties all piled up high like a croquembouche.'

Solly smiled, still shaking his head.

'Well, you get the idea. She was the sort of girl who could go anywhere, be with anyone and still carry it off. Posh places give me the willies but Eva, no, she was meant for the high life.'

There was no bitterness in the girl's tone, Solly thought as he listened to her. Kirsty Wilson might sound a little wistful for snowy Christmas scenes but there did not seem to be a trace of envy in her manner as she described the dead girl.

'What was she like around her father?' he asked.

'Oh, now you're asking, Professor.' Kirsty nodded over her mug of tea. 'Mr Magnusson definitely brought out a different side to our Eva.'

'Describe that for me, will you?'

Kirsty looked into the middle distance as though trying to recapture a moment lost in time. 'He was always very polite, you know? But it was as if she was standing to attention whenever he was around. Does that sound strange? I mean she was kind of stiff, like a doll, going through the motions just for him. Like she was playing the part of the perfect daughter and doing just what he wanted her to do.'

'Go on.'

'Well, she even dressed differently the couple of times he was here. I mean, Eva had nice clothes, *lots* of nice clothes,' she added in mock gloominess, 'but she'd always put on something kind of demure, you know. Not quite twinset and pearls but the kind of dress that most students would consider pretty old-fashioned.' She twisted the empty mug back and forth in her hands as she spoke. 'Then when he'd gone she would put on something short and flimsy – she had loads of chiffony things, stuff like her Ghost blouse.' She glanced up at the professor's puzzled expression and sighed. It was clear that such niceties of fashion were lost on the psychologist. 'Good designer labels, see?' Kirsty explained.

'And she'd be different in herself, more carefree, less the lady-like doll that her father expected her to be,' she added sourly.

'Didn't you like Mr Magnusson?' Solly asked in surprise.

She shook her head. 'Please don't get me wrong, Professor Brightman, I feel terrible for the poor man, but you did ask me. I really didn't like the way he seemed to ... I don't know ...'

'Dominate his daughter?' Solly suggested.

'Yeah, you could put it like that, though she wasn't cowed or anything, it wasn't as bad as that, just ... Oh, I don't think I'm doing a very good job of explaining what I mean. God! And you should have seen the state he was in when he came up here after the post-mortem! Poor guy!' Kirsty shook her head again silently and Solly was moved by the sight of tears in her eyes.

'When will Gary be in?'

Kirsty smiled. 'Who knows? Depends when he gets away from Detective Superintendent Lorimer. Poor Gary,' she laughed. 'Bet you anything that he's wishing right now he'd stayed at home!'

*

247

He couldn't blame the boy for not wanting to visit A Division again and so Lorimer had agreed to meet him at the pub on the corner.

He recognised Gary Calderwood from the description Kirsty had given him. *He'll be sitting outside on the smokers' bench, a pint of lager in one hand and a cigarette in the other*, she had said with a short laugh. And that was almost true. As the detective superintendent approached the dark-haired young man he could see him nervously picking at a ragged nail, the dregs of his drink on the table in front of him.

'Gary?'

The student looked up, an expression of alarm on his face that was swiftly replaced by a pasted-on smile.

'I'm Detective Superintendent Lorimer. Can I get you another?' He nodded towards the near empty glass.

'Yes, thanks. Pint of Carlsberg,' Gary replied, his eyes never leaving the detective's face for a moment.

Lorimer felt rather than saw those same eyes boring into the back of his head as he left the student sitting there and entered the pub. The bar was a curved old-fashioned affair and so Lorimer stepped around to a space where he could place the order and still see out of the window to where Calderwood was sitting.

As he waited for the drinks to arrive, a quick glance showed him that the student was busy on his mobile phone. Texting or tweeting, perhaps? Or was he letting someone know that Detective Superintendent Lorimer had arrived? The idea took hold as he carried the drinks back outside, Calderwood hastily slipping the phone back into his coat pocket as the detective approached.

'One Carlsberg, one cranberry juice and two packets of cheese and onion. Okay with you?' Lorimer asked cheerfully, laying the drinks down and taking the crisps out from his own pocket.

'Thanks,' Calderwood said, lifting the glass. 'Cheers.'

'*Slainte*,' Lorimer replied with a grin. 'Right, Mr Calderwood. You prefer to sit out here with your fags rather than enjoy the warmth of your flat upstairs?'

'Oh, yes.' Calderwood flicked ash into a sand bucket by his side. 'The tenants aren't supposed to smoke, you see.'

'Bet you didn't let on to Magnusson at the beginning,' Lorimer said, his tone deliberately light, putting the younger man at his ease.

'Course not,' he replied equally lightly, blowing a line of smoke heavenwards. 'No need to upset the apple cart.'

'Okay,' Lorimer began again, leaning forward so that only Gary Calderwood could hear him, 'here's what I want. All the information you can give me about Eva Magnusson from the time you met her until the night she was killed. Understood?'

Gary Calderwood sat up a little straighter and nodded mutely.

'Your flatmate has been arrested on suspicion of murder. That's a damned serious charge, Gary. And we want to find out if there is any reason why it might not stick. Got me?'

The student looked a little doubtful at the policeman's sudden change from affable to bullish.

'But I thought that Colin . . .'

'You thought Colin what?'

'He was charged so he must have done it.' Gary shrugged but there was a new note of doubt that had crept into his voice.

'Tell me,' Lorimer said. 'Start with Colin. What was he like around Eva? What kind of guy was he to share a flat with?'

Gary Calderwood raised his eyebrows in thought before replying. 'Colin was all right. A bit geeky, maybe, but he mucked in with the chores and all that sort of stuff. Had a proper crush on Eva, anyone could've seen that,' he smirked.

'And you?'

'What about me?' Calderwood's chin jutted upwards, defiantly.

'Well, rumour has it that you and Eva were more than mere flat-mates, Gary.'

'Don't know what you mean,' the boy replied.

'Come on, Gary. They all knew about it,' Lorimer bluffed. 'Creeping upstairs afterwards, making sheep's eyes at her over the breakfast table?'

The young man reddened suddenly, more through a sudden surge of temper than embarrassment, Lorimer guessed.

'So, what if we did? No harm in that, is there?'

'None at all,' Lorimer said evenly. 'Nor was there any harm in her sexual relations with Roger or Colin or Uncle Tom Cobley.'

'What . . . ?' Calderwood's jaw dropped as he stared at the police officer.

'She was playing with you, Gary,' Lorimer smiled. 'A beautiful girl like that could have her pick of bedmates. Couldn't she?'

Gary Calderwood ran a hand across his dark hair, rumpling its perfectly gelled style. He seemed genuinely stunned, Lorimer thought. Too egotistic to have contemplated that Eva Magnusson was simply using the boys for her own gratification, Gary had evidently considered that he was somehow special to the Swedish girl. So special that he had become jealous of anyone else?

'You didn't know about what she and Colin were up to the night of the party?'

Calderwood was looking at the ground, now, shaking his head silently.

'You know something, Gary?' Lorimer leaned closer to him. 'I don't believe you. I think you knew fine what was going on in that bedroom.'

The eyes that flicked up to meet his held an expression that

Lorimer recognised as fear tempered with uncertainty. He'd seen this countless times before, this doubt in a man's eyes during an internal struggle to tell the truth or blurt out a lie. Which choice would this young man make? he wondered.

'Okay.' The word seemed to be drawn out of him like a long sigh. 'I did know she was flirting with him, dancing, all that . . . Oh Christ!' He put his head in his hands. 'I thought . . . '

'You thought she was trying to make you jealous?'

He saw the dark head nodding up and down and heard a stifled groan as Calderwood bent forward, eyes closed against having to face a truth that he had previously denied.

'When did you leave the party, Gary?'

Calderwood took his hands away from his head and sat up again, mouth open.

'You don't think that *I* had anything to do with Eva's death, surely?'

'Perhaps I should be asking that question down at A Division,' Lorimer answered quietly. 'We have plenty of time to go down there if you like. And I would also have the facility to record your answer.'

The colour drained from the young man's face as he realised the seriousness of his position.

'You want me to go back there?'

'Perhaps it would be best,' Lorimer agreed. 'I think you might actually have a bit more to tell me about Eva Magnusson than you let on to my colleague DI Grant.'

Billy Brogan tied the white laces together in a simple knot, an expression of regret on his face. These Reebok ERS trainers were pretty nice ones and he'd miss wearing them, but they were a small sacrifice to make for the bigger plan he had in mind. Sam had paved the way with the lad, giving him occasional treats, acting like a kindly uncle, so that Young was completely under his spell. The old man was useful in that way. Now, a wee pressie like the trainers would be a bargaining chip in the negotiation that he had to make with the prisoner in A Block. Brogan grinned to himself. The student thought he had nothing more to do than to sweat it out until his trial but Billy Brogan would make sure that he earned his keep in here, just like the rest of them. Brogan might be inside HMP Barlinnie but his drug distribution business was still ticking over nicely outside.

'It's one of the things that keeps him awake at night, Chancer,' Maggie said, tickling the ginger cat under his chin so that he purred loudly while kneading his claws into her jeans. 'If that boy didn't kill Kirsty's friend, then who did?' she mused, her fingers smoothing Chancer's soft fur as he settled on her lap.

They had lain awake far into the night, Maggie listening as Lorimer unfolded the whole story, not even missing out the parts that involved Dirk McGregor. Gary Caldwell had admitted to having had a fierce row with the Swedish girl at the party. He'd been really upset, Lorimer had told her, especially when he'd admitted it had been him that Roger had heard Eva shouting at in the bathroom. But that had been the last time he had seen her, he had insisted, his lasting memory the bitterness between them.

Again and again, Maggie's brow furrowed with the same thought: who would have wanted to kill a lovely girl like that? Okay, Eva Magnusson might have been a bit promiscuous, but then wasn't that a given in Scandinavian countries? Maggie made a face. Perhaps she'd been reading too much Stieg Larsson lately?

Jealousy was a motive in some crimes, wasn't it? She looked across at the bookshelves groaning with hardback copies of books that they had accumulated over the years. The gold lettering on the spine of a dark red leather book seemed to wink at her: Shakespeare's Complete Works. Maggie thought of the tragedy she was teaching to her sixth years: *Othello, the Moor of Venice*. His life had been destroyed by that green-eyed monster, hadn't it? And who was to say that something lurking in the Swedish girl's life had not triggered a feeling of passionate enmity on the part of a man who had been overwhelmed by feelings of love only for it to become sour and turn into hate?

CHAPTER 33

Henrik glanced around the room, noting how tidy it was, and for the first time in his life he felt the need for something – or someone – to clutter the place up, change the minimalist decor into a homelier place. Even the books were hidden behind pale birchwood doors and he knew without having to look that they were arranged in alphabetical order, dusted regularly by the housekeeper, and only brought out when there was something he needed to consult. It had been no different when Eva had stayed at home: her own rooms were kept just as clean and smart, the dressing room next to her bedroom vast enough to keep all the clothes that he bought for her, orderly and colour-coded just as he wished them to be. Behind him on a sideboard there were several decanters ready with drinks, crystal glasses ranged around them. A refrigerator concealed below held an assortment of beers and soft drinks, everything that could be offered to his guest by a perfect host. There were no decorations, no colourful lights to mark the Christmas season; it might have been any night of the year, the thick damask curtains drawn over the windows keeping out any trace of starlight or lamplight.

The white leather sofa creaked beneath his weight as Henrik

sat down. A glance at his Cartier watch showed five minutes to eight: the professor had said he would arrive at eight o'clock. What would he want to know? Henrik's brow creased in a frown. Surely a criminal profiler sought information about the suspect, not the victim? But then, he acknowledged to himself, there were many things that had not impinged on his consciousness before, the psychology of murder being only one of them.

He was out of the chair and striding into the large hallway as soon as the bell rang, his shoulders raised in tension as he anticipated the person waiting in his porch.

'Mr Magnusson? Solomon Brightman.'

The man with the beard stood beaming up at him, his ungloved hand stretched out in greeting. Henrik took it briefly, surprised at how warm it was given that it was at least minus twelve degrees outside. The man blinked owlishly at him through a pair of horn-rimmed spectacles, but there was a keen intelligence in those dark brown eyes and a kindliness in his face that put the Swede at ease.

'Come in, please.' Henrik gestured the psychologist inside. 'Let me take your coat,' he added, relieving the man of his long black overcoat and a multicoloured scarf that had to be unwound several times before it could be handed over. The professor wore a neat grey suit and a silk tie decorated with myriad colourful butterflies in flight, an interesting contrast between sober and daring that made Henrik wonder for one fleeting moment if there was some sort of deliberate psychological approach to the man's choice of clothes.

He opened the sliding door in the hallway to reveal a spacious cloakroom then hung the garments on a wooden hanger before closing the door once more.

'Please, come in,' Henrik said, ushering the professor into the room he had prepared for this visit.

'My! What a pleasant room!' the professor remarked, looking around him. 'Our house is perpetually untidy, you know. Abigail, our little one, is at the stage where one toy is dropped on the floor in favour of the next one she fancies,' he chuckled.

Henrik looked at him, mildly astonished that the psychologist had the temerity to refer to his child when he was still grieving the loss of his own.

'I'm sorry.' Solomon put his hand on the tall man's sleeve. 'Was that crass of me? You must miss her terribly,' he added softly, taking off his spectacles and sitting down on the edge of a high-backed chair to rub the fogged-up lenses with the end of his tie.

Henrik swallowed hard and blinked back the tears that had come unbidden to his pale blue eyes. 'Yes,' he admitted huskily. 'I miss her every day.'

'Nothing can bring her back,' Solomon Brightman said quietly. 'But your memories of her may be happier ones when the whole truth about this is revealed.'

'Will they? I doubt that,' Henrik said shortly.

The professor shrugged and smiled as though there was something secret and wise that only he knew and somehow Henrik found his mouth forming the ghost of a smile at this quaint Englishman with his dark curly hair and luxuriant beard.

'May I offer you a drink, Professor?'

Solly watched as Magnusson walked across to a sideboard where several expensive-looking crystal decanters winked in the lamplight.

'Thank you, but no.'

'Something soft, perhaps?'

'I'm fine,' Solly said, smiling politely as he watched the man pour a large measure of amber liquid into a whisky glass.

'Do you have any photograph albums of Eva?' he asked just as the Swede sat down.

'Yes, of course, but why?'

'I thought about what we might discuss,' the professor began, folding his hands across his knees. 'It struck me that looking over pictures from the time she was young might help me to form the best impression of Eva.'

Henrik placed his glass on the small table beside him, stood up and moved towards a wall of pale wooden cupboards. 'Yes,' he murmured. 'They are all in here.'

The bereaved father was unaware of the sympathetic eyes following his movements as he knelt down and pulled several thick photograph albums from a bottom shelf. Or of the slightly raised dark eyebrow that caught sight of the uniform pile of brown leather books with their dates marked clearly on the spines.

'Here we are,' Henrik told his guest, placing the books on a glass coffee table that lay between the sofa and the chair where the professor was perched.

The photograph albums lay open now, revealing Eva to the psychologist's discerning eyes. As Henrik turned the pages, he explained each photograph, smiling as the memories returned, boasting a little, as fathers will do, about his child's achievements. Solly was shown the Swedish girl as an eight-year-old, beaming her satisfaction as a tall lady pinned the rosette onto her pony's bridle, or pictured against snow-covered mountains as she grinned into the camera, her blond hair caught up in a bright blue ski band. Then there were the photos of her on holiday: posing on the yacht in Cannes, standing amongst the pigeons in St Mark's Square and turning her attention from eating a meal somewhere, the grey landscape beyond the restaurant windows a view Solly remembered from Montmartre.

'Do you have more recent pictures?'

The tall man shook his head. 'Not like these,' he said. 'Only digital images on my computer. I always meant to have them printed off . . .' He stopped, dashing a hand across his eyes. 'Only there never seemed to be time . . .'

'Any photos of her with boyfriends?' Solly asked. 'You know, at a school prom or something?'

Henrik closed the last album with a snap. 'Eva was home tutored,' he said coldly. 'There were no *proms*.' He stressed the word as though it was something unpleasant. 'Nothing like that. And any boyfriends she had would have been photographed by a professional at whatever function they attended. I doubt she kept them.'

Solly frowned. Did he mean the photographs or the boyfriends? 'I don't understand,' he said. 'Didn't you know who her boyfriends were?'

Henrik had turned away from him so that Solly could only see the man's profile; a straight nose and angular chin that was raised as though in disdain.

'Eva would tell me who was taking her out and if I deemed him suitable then that was as much as I needed to know.'

Solly nodded, wondering just how much information this father had required about any of his daughter's boyfriends; had the property magnate trawled the internet to see the fellow's pedigree? Or was there a private detective following Eva around just in case? Nothing would surprise him, he thought, seeing the man's mouth tighten into a thin disapproving line.

The psychologist took a deep breath before asking the question that had prompted the visit in the first place.

'And how did you choose her flatmates?'

Afterwards, Solly struggled to tell Rosie how he had been overwhelmed with pity for the Swedish man. 'Barren' was the word that had kept coming to the forefront of his mind. A house filled with quietness but no sense of peace; an orderly existence but a life that had been ruptured by chaos; a man whose wealth gave him immense power over others but who had been powerless to prevent the destruction of his daughter.

It was well after eleven when Solly closed the door of his hotel bedroom, letting his briefcase fall to the floor and breathing in the warm air once again. He bent down to open the small refrigerator and drew out a bottle of pineapple juice. Magnusson had offered him a drink back at the huge modern house which he had declined politely but now he was so thirsty that he snapped open the bottle, drinking the juice straight down in gulps. The taste seemed to banish something sour that had formed in his mouth and Solly sighed, wondering if whisky or gin did the same for other men after a difficult meeting.

And it had been difficult. Magnusson had been annoyed at first, asking what business the psychologist had questioning his choice of tenants. But gradually he had admitted that there was some sense in Solly's gentle probing, finding out about each of the students in turn was helping the professor to understand the ways he protected his daughter, wasn't it? Solly had smiled and nodded, but not confirmed this interpretation of his questions. In truth, what he had wanted to find out was why these young people had been chosen and how he hoped it might tell him more about Eva herself.

Gary Calderwood had been the only one whose background had given him the right to a place at Merryfield Avenue, but even he had been subject to Henrik's scrutiny. *The right sort of boy*, he had called him, whatever that meant. And Solly, looking at the Swede, had taken it to mean that he had thought of Gary as boyfriend material. And Roger? *Capable, the type who would look out for her*, Henrik had declared firmly. And take her to his bed? Had that been on Magnusson's agenda? Kirsty, as he had guessed, was the *husmor*, and Colin Young *the boy-next-door* – Eva had called him that herself, Henrik had said, laughing shortly as though struck by the irony of it.

'Did you select the boys as potential sexual partners for Eva?'

Solly blinked, remembering Henrik's reaction: it was as though the man had actually hit him, such was the glare from those cold blue eyes and that mouth opened wide in anger. But then Magnusson's expression had changed to one of anguish, his hands covering his face as he began to wail, 'Oh my God, my God!'

'It was my fault?' he had whispered at last. 'Putting these young men with her? I gave them a chance to be nice, to enjoy her company and yet ...' He had shaken his head again, speech deserting him.

'We cannot know for sure if Colin Young took her life,' Solly had told him, one hand on the man's shoulder. 'Kirsty is certain he didn't and having met him—'

'You met him? How? Where?'

Solly had gone on to relate the prison visit and how he had taken careful note of the young man's behaviour.

'I'm not often a poor judge of character,' he had stated, 'and I would have said that Colin is suffering quite a lot as a result of having been wrongly accused of a capital crime.' Magnusson had listened then, attentive to what Solly had told him.

'I think the boy was very sweet on your daughter,' he added at last. 'In fact, I think in their own way each of the boys may have been a little bit in love with Eva.'

And that, of course, was what this father had wanted, Solly told himself, switching on the small kettle in the hotel bedroom. He had manipulated the students for his own particular agenda, to make sure that if Eva had any sexual relations then they would be with decent young men of his choosing. Solly sighed at the thought: how could any father have imagined that his girl would behave exactly as he demanded, and in a foreign country, far from parental control? Surely, he told himself, it had been asking for trouble to let this girl loose in the mean streets of Glasgow.

As he waited for the water to boil, Solly thought about Rosie and Abby. How different their lives were! To love his daughter was also to give her the freedom to become herself, wasn't it? A surge of pity filled him then for the dead girl. What sort of life had she endured? All the privileges of wealth had been nothing compared to the freedom to make choices that were truly her own. The overbearing love he had had for his daughter: surely that was what had driven her to seek illicit pleasures, like the affair with her university lecturer. And had there been others: secret lovers taken to satisfy an appetite that sought some sort of fulfilment? Colin, Roger and Gary had been her father's choice. He stared into space, ignoring the cloud of steam coming from the kettle as the thought came to him at last.

Had the killer been some unsuitable lover? Someone danger-ous that Eva had chosen for herself? And had she wanted that spice of danger as an antidote to her father's choice of bedmates? But why would she sleep with all of her flatmates unless she wanted to? Sheer promiscuity? Or because her father expected it?

CHAPTER 34

Kirsty stood on the corner of Cathedral Street and Montrose Street watching as the students took their different routes, some to Caledonian and others to Strathclyde. She had left Eva here loads of time last term before heading to her own classes. If only Colin could be released from jail it would almost feel normal again ... but without Eva it was never going to be the same, was it?

Last night she had listened as Lorimer and Professor Brightman had explained what they had found out so far. A secret lover, she mused, thinking of the Strathclyde lecturer whose number she had discovered by chance. And had there been others? God help me, Kirsty thought, Eva had scarcely been in Glasgow four months, yet in that short time the seemingly modest and self-contained girl had managed to hop in and out of so many different beds! Apart from her own drunken scramble with Roger, Kirsty hadn't had one bit of attention from a lad. And how do I feel about that? she wondered. Glad to be alive, a small voice whispered in her ear. And in a funny way, Kirsty felt relieved. Perhaps being so beautiful was what had killed Eva Magnusson. And nobody was going to notice dumpy Kirsty Wilson in a crowd, were they? she thought as she turned up Montrose Street and headed the way the Swedish girl had always gone.

Lesley Crawford blinked from her hospital bed as the sunlight glared through a gap in the curtains, the brightness of the winter sunlight a contrast with this shaded room. She put one tremulous hand to her forehead, wondering for a moment why her hair felt so odd, so coarse … Then the memory of the hospital corridor and other, harsher, lights returned, green-clad figures that had loomed over her vision until the blackness descended. Letting her fingers trace the bandages, Lesley struggled to remember more. An accident. She must have been in some kind of accident, that was it.

The throbbing on either side of her head made Lesley close her eyes against the light as she listened to the muffled roar of traffic coming from somewhere far below. And, as she lay, slipping gratefully back into the comfort of sleep, the woman in the chair beside her gave a small smile of satisfaction.

'She's still on fairly strong medication, Detective Inspector,' the sister told Jo Grant. 'It will be at least tomorrow before you can expect any signs of lucidity. And even then,' she warned in a tone that brooked no disagreement, 'it will be entirely up to Dr Leckie to decide if his patient is fit to talk to the police.'

'Thanks,' Jo replied. 'But we really do need to talk to her the moment she can speak.' She paused, looking at the senior nurse, wondering how much dedication to her patients went on inside that intelligent face, trying to decide just how much to reveal.

'The man who attacked Lesley has to be found,' she said quietly, staring meaningfully into the other woman's eyes. 'You do know what I'm saying, don't you?'

'Of course,' Sister replied, one eyebrow raised. 'He might very well try to attack and kill other defenceless women.' She smiled a trifle wearily. 'It's your job to prevent that, Detective Inspector, and it's mine to care for the health and well-being of my patients.' The woman nodded and sighed. 'I've got your number. I'll call you the moment she is able to talk to you, I promise.'

The lecture theatre was full of students jostling along the narrow rows, haversacks slung in the aisles or under desks as Kirsty filed in with the last of the class. She hurried to the nearest vacant seat at the back, darting anxious glances around, but no one seemed to notice a stranger in their midst. What was it one of her own tutors had told her at the beginning of her degree? *If you drop dead nobody's going to notice.* That had elicited an explosion of laughter but the sentiment behind it was true enough. Was any single student really thinking about Eva Magnusson right now? Probably not. Their eyes were all on the figure walking down the short flight of steps towards the lectern.

Kirsty took a deep breath. Dirk McGregor. She had known it was his class, but somehow seeing him in the flesh made everything so horribly real. The image of Eva's dead body flashed into her mind, then the idea of the Swedish girl rolling in this man's embrace . . .

Kirsty shook her head as if to dismiss the pictures. Concentrate on the here and now, she told herself firmly. Remember why you're here.

If Dirk McGregor noticed a stranger in their midst then he was keeping it to himself, Kirsty thought as she listened to him giving the lecture. He was good, she had to admit, even giving her a wee inkling about business economics despite the fact that she had expected it to be way above her head. And he could make the class laugh. It was obvious that they enjoyed his lectures. She glanced around her at the eager faces fixed on the figure at the lectern, giving a rueful smile as she watched the girls in particular, eyes shining as they drank in McGregor's words; it wasn't difficult to see what the attraction had been for Eva. McGregor was a bit old, right enough, but, looking at his lean body and that charismatic grin, she decided that the lecturer may have been sex on legs in his younger days.

But it wasn't McGregor Kirsty had come to see today. And, as the buzzer sounded for the end of class, she shivered, wondering if what she had planned might bring her any nearer to helping Colin Young end his time in prison.

'Trainers? For me?' Colin looked up at the old man who was smiling back at him.

'Aye, present from an admirer,' Sam chuckled. Then, seeing the alarm on the lad's face he patted his shoulder. 'Dinna you worry, son, it's no' frae ony o' thae shirt lifters.' He tapped the side of his nose and nodded. 'These are frae the big man in E Block.'

Colin was sitting on the bench outside the showers looking doubtfully at the pair of sparkling white trainers in his hands.

'He wants a wee favour off ye in return,' Sam explained. 'Nothing that'll get ye intae bother. Jist a wee help wi' passing oan a message fur him.'

Colin frowned. 'Like on the phone, you mean?'

Sam's smile turned into a grin, his tombstone teeth showing yellow against his pallid lips. 'Naw, son. Jist pass on a verbal tae wan o' the visitors next time ye're in the place.'

'How will I know who to speak to?' Colin looked puzzled. All visits were so closely monitored, prisoners being allocated particular numbered tables where their visitors would await them.

'Ye'll be telt nearer the time, okay?' Sam's smile had disappeared and the old man stood up, clearly irritated at Colin's questions.

'And if I decide not to pass on a message?' Colin asked, looking up.

Sam shook his head slowly. 'Naw, son, ye cannae decide onything like that. Wance the big man asks for a favour, ye do it. Simple as that.' And, looking him straight in the eyes, Sam drew a finger across his throat, turned and walked away, leaving Colin with the accursed trainers on his lap.

He watched as Sam disappeared then closed his eyes. What had he expected; a nice old man looking out for him? This place was full of criminals, Colin reminded himself, men who were adept at gulling the unwary. It wasn't enough, seemingly, to keep his nose clean for the officers who were present at every corner. Now he had to be wary even of people who were incarcerated in a completely different block from himself.

'Hello.' Lesley tried to smile at the woman by her bedside, a nurse of some sort, her white cap edged in lace, her blue uniform different from the nurses who had been in to take her temperature and blood pressure.

'How are you feeling?'

'Tired,' Lesley whispered. 'Sore.'

The sister glanced up at the drip that was attached to the patient's hand.

'If it gets too bad, press this,' she said, indicating a red button a few inches up the plastic tubing. 'It monitors the painkiller and will give you some relief.' She paused, looking a little more closely into Lesley Crawford's face. 'Do you feel up to talking to the police?'

Lesley frowned then let her brow clear when a jolt of pain creased her temples. 'Police?'

'You were attacked, Lesley. The police need to speak to you, ask you questions. Are you up for that, do you think?'

Lesley turned her head away, remembering. Christmas Eve. She sighed and bit her lip, reluctant to let the memories return, to relive again the moment when it had happened.

'I suppose so,' she answered dully.

'Good, I'll let Detective Inspector Grant know. I think she'll be in quite soon to see you.'

Lesley watched as the sister left the room. Then, letting her fingers work their way up the plastic tubing, she found the button and pressed it once, praying under her breath that the drug would quickly take effect.

The slim dark-haired woman who entered her room was not Lesley Crawford's idea of a police officer. Her initial impression was of a young, pretty woman, the sort that Lesley would expect to see in one of the city bars she frequented after office hours. The injured woman's gaze took in the fashionable skirt suit and the flat-heeled leather boots before travelling upwards where her stare was returned by eyes that held an expression of both warmth and sympathy.

'Detective Inspector Grant,' the police officer said, showing Lesley her warrant card before sitting in the grey plastic chair next to the bed. 'The ward sister said you were told to expect me.'

Lesley stifled a sigh. Those keen eyes regarding her solemnly; what did they see? Another woman, like herself? Or a victim of crime? Suddenly she wanted to be left in peace but the police-woman had folded her hands on her lap as though she were waiting for Lesley to take the initiative.

'What do you want to know?' This time there was no masking the sigh that ended in a yawn.

'Everything that you can tell me,' DI Grant replied with a faint smile. 'We need to catch the man who did this to you, Lesley. And we may be able to do that sooner rather than later with your help.'

The woman's voice was firm but kind and Lesley knew there was no way she was going to be allowed to escape reliving the worst Christmas Eve of her life.

'Where do I begin?'

'How about telling me where you had been and what took you to the vicinity of the church car park,' the detective suggested.

'I was at a party,' Lesley began. 'That's where it all started.'

The cafeteria seemed to be the best place to begin, Kirsty decided, following a string of students from the lecture theatre and along to a ground-floor snack bar. She took a deep breath and looked across at a table where some of them had congregated, bags and haversacks slung carelessly on the floor.

'Hi, mind if I join you?'

'Sure.' A girl around her own age pulled out a vacant metal chair then shuffled around to make space for her.

Five pairs of eyes regarded her quizzically.

'Haven't seen you here before,' a dark-haired lad with pencil-thin sideburns nodded at Kirsty, a faint smile on his face. 'New to the course?'

Kirsty drew in a deep breath. Here goes, she thought.

'My name is Kirsty Wilson. I live in the flat where Eva Magnusson was killed.'

There was a silence around the table as the five students stared at her. Then the girl next to her who had offered her a seat leaned forward and placed her hand on Kirsty's arm.

'You poor soul. That must have been awful for you.'

'God, yes!' a pretty Asian girl broke in. 'Poor Eva. That was a terrible thing to have happened. A nice lassie like that, coming over from Sweden . . . '

'You knew her, then?' Kirsty asked.

'Oh, aye,' the first girl nodded. 'Everyone knew her. I mean, you could hardly miss her, could you?'

There was a murmuring around the table and one of the boys coughed, reddening as he caught Kirsty's glance.

'Smashing girl. A real head-turner. Pure shame, really.'

'Aye, a bloody waste of a young life!' another lad with a Geordie accent exclaimed, thumping his fist onto the edge of the table. 'Hope the bastard who did it gets life!'

Kirsty jumped a little at the vehemence in his voice.

'Nobody's guilty till a jury decides,' she said slowly.

'Oh, of *course*, it was a lad in your flat that did it!' the Asian girl exclaimed.

'Or maybe not,' Kirsty said softly so that only the group around the table could hear her.

'But I thought . . . ?' the red-faced lad began.

'See, why I'm here is to try to find out if there was anyone Eva was hanging about with, or anyone who might have, well . . . ' She broke off, unsure how to continue. 'Anyone who fancied her.'

'Only the whole of the university,' the first girl laughed suddenly. 'Including the staff.'

'Come on, she was a pure doll.' The third boy, who had remained silent until then, broke in. 'We all thought so the minute she arrived in class. They were queuing up just to speak to her. She could've had her pick of any of the men she wanted.'

Kirsty looked at the young man, listening hard. Was that an edge of bitterness in his voice? He was tall and lanky with dark curls that tumbled over his pale brow, a pair of rimless spectacles adding to the overall impression of keen intellect.

'But who *did* she pick?' Kirsty asked, looking at each one of them in turn.

The question was met with a silence, the girls looking faintly embarrassed, the boys turning away from Kirsty's stare as though she had asked something way too intimate.

'Look, my friend's in Barlinnie,' Kirsty rushed on, 'and I honestly don't think he did what the police claim ...' She had raised her hands in a gesture of appeal, making them all look her way once more. 'See, if anyone else knew what Eva had been doing in the weeks before she was murdered it could help a lot.'

'So why aren't the polis here asking these sorts of questions?' the lanky lad asked, shoving his specs further up his long nose.

'They've arrested someone,' Kirsty shrugged, mentally crossing her fingers as she spoke. 'Why would they bother?'

'Well I never saw her with anyone special, did you?' the Asian girl asked, sweeping her glance over each of her companions in turn. Heads were shaken and murmurs of assent given.

'Sorry,' the girl said brightly. 'But I think you're wasting your time here. Nobody is going to tell you about a secret romance that never happened, are they?'

Kirsty was breathing heavily as she reached the brow of the hill on Montrose Street, her cheeks still burning with embarrassment. Stupid idiot! What did you think you were trying to achieve back there? She cursed softly under her breath, relieved to be heading back along to Caledonian University and her own comfort zone.

The sound of footsteps drumming behind her made Kirsty step

aside for a moment, then she gave a cry as someone grasped hold of her arm.

'Kirsty?'

The girl jerked free, spinning around to see the Geordie lad who had been in the cafeteria.

'Look, sorry about that, didn't mean to give you a fright.' The lad glanced about as if to check that nobody was following him. 'Is there somewhere we can talk?' he asked, turning back to look intently at Kirsty. 'You see,' he explained, coming closer to her and letting his voice drop into a whisper, 'we weren't telling you the whole truth back there.'

'Okay,' Kirsty said slowly. 'So why did you want to follow me? And what's your connection with Eva?'

The lad shot her a disarming grin. 'Wish I'd had a connection! Lovely lass never gave me a second glance.' He looked intently at Kirsty as though he were trying to gauge her reaction, then nodded and put out his hand.

'James Spencer,' he said.

Kirsty grasped it, feeling the warmth and strength in the young man's grasp. And there was something more, the way his brown eyes held a sort of sympathy for her as though he understood why she had come, that made Kirsty feel that she could trust this young man with the soft Newcastle brogue.

'Thanks,' she said, then dropped his hand, aware that she might have held it a little too long. 'How about walking me across to Caley? That's where I'm heading.'

'You're a student there?'

'Aye. Hospitality management,' Kirsty replied as they fell into step. 'Eva used to devour my chocolate fudge cakes.'

'She didn't look the sort to munch cakes,' James said in surprise. 'That gorgeous figure ...'

'Know what you mean,' Kirsty mumbled, suddenly aware of her own girth hidden under layers of jersey and duffel coat.

'She was quite different from all of the other girls,' James said quietly. 'Seemed older – well, maybe not older, more mature, not as daft as a lot of the lasses. Eva was, well, dignified. You could imagine her giving tea parties in one o' these stately homes, know what I mean?'

Kirsty nodded. She knew exactly what he meant.

'She had plenty of friends, everyone seemed to take a right shine to that lass. Anyway, she did have an admirer,' James told her as they waited on Cathedral Street for the lights to change to green. 'There was a lad used to haunt her wherever she went. Weedy little chap, he was. Or, should I say, *is*. One of the girls back there used to refer to him as Eva's puppy.'

Kirsty nodded encouragingly, willing James to tell her more.

'Brian something his name is. Always sat right behind her in economics class. And I think they were in the same group for McGregor's seminar.'

'Have you seen him since . . . since it happened?'

James Spencer frowned. 'Funny you should ask that, Kirsty, but I don't think he's been around since the new term began.'

'Thanks,' Kirsty replied, then she drew in a breath of surprise as James caught her by the hand and led her across the road.

'There,' he said as they reached the opposite pavement. 'Safely delivered, Miss . . . ?'

'Wilson. Kirsty Wilson,' she told him, laughing despite herself as the lad gave a mock salute.

'And does Miss Kirsty Wilson have a phone number?' James asked, a light of mischief in his eyes that Kirsty suddenly decided she found very appealing indeed.

*

Kirsty walked smartly along the road, wondering if he was standing there at the corner watching and willing herself to be cool; not to look back and see.

They had exchanged mobile numbers. So? She smiled to herself. It meant nothing. He was just trying to be helpful, wasn't he? And, if he could find out more about the mysterious Brian, then that might just lead her a little further along her quest to find out more about Eva Magnusson and who she had been seeing in the days before her death.

As Lesley Crawford closed her eyes, Jo could see tears falling between the girl's lashes. She reached out and squeezed the girl's hand gently.

'It's all right, Lesley,' the detective was telling her. 'We'll get him, I promise.'

Jo stood up and looked at the woman lying in the bed. Her head was swathed in bandages and it was hard to visualise this as the same woman whose photograph lay between the pages of her files back in Stewart Street. Her long blond hair had been shorn pre-surgery and her face was thinner, the cheekbones prominent, reminding Jo of some of the junked-up women she'd seen in parts of the city.

We'll get him. Her words echoed in DI Grant's brain as she headed towards the lifts, her thoughts already back at headquarters and the next stage in uncovering the man who had beaten this woman almost to her death.

CHAPTER 35

'Hello?' Kirsty was standing on the landing below the flat, mobile phone pressed to her ear, wondering at the unfamiliar number on the tiny screen.

'Hello, Kirsty Wilson. It's me, James, your new best friend.'

Her mouth arced in a smile as she listened to the Geordie accent. My new best friend, she thought gleefully.

'Hi, James, how's things?' she replied, affecting a coolness that belied the sudden dryness in her mouth.

'Oh, well, you know...' The lad tailed off for a moment, leaving Kirsty wondering why he had rung her so quickly. 'Completely forgot to tell you about Anders,' he said at last.

'Anders?'

'Aye.' There was a pause. 'He hasn't come back to uni either.'

'Sorry, James, you've lost me. Who's this Anders?'

'Did you never meet him? That's odd.' James Spencer's voice expressed surprise. 'He was a pal of Eva's from Stockholm. Hung about with her a lot, but they were just pals, everyone could see that. Are you sure she never had him up to the flat?'

'James, I've never *heard* of an Anders,' Kirsty replied firmly. 'And there were never any Swedish boys up here. *Worse luck,*' she added in a whisper.

274

'I heard that, Kirsty Wilson,' James said reprovingly. 'Anyhow, do you not think that's really strange? I mean, why would she keep a friend from back home a secret from you all?'

There was silence between them as Kirsty slowly climbed the final flight of stairs to reach the front door of the flat.

Who the hell was this Anders? And why had Eva never mentioned him?

'Does this mystery man have a second name?' she asked.

'Oh, aye, Anders Andersson. Dead easy one to remember, eh? Oh and the other guy, the weedy chap? His name's Brian Hastie.'

'Right, thanks, James,' Kirsty said slowly, fumbling with her free hand to find the key in her coat pocket.

'Not a problem, Kirsty Wilson.' There was a pause as Kirsty listened, waiting for him to say more, hoping that he would.

'Any chance of meeting up some time?' he asked, and Kirsty grinned, liking the wee hesitation in his voice.

'Aye, sure, just not at weekends though, cos I work. But I'm usually free on Thursdays,' she said.

'Great. Can I come up for you then? Take you out for a drink somewhere?'

'Yes. Thanks. That would be great,' she said. 'I'll text you the address, okay? Got to go now, bye.'

Kirsty pulled the door open, trying not to let out a whoop of excitement. A date with a nice-looking fellow! She pulled off her duffel coat and hung it on the back of her bedroom door, heart thudding unreasonably.

'But what the heck is all this about a mysterious Swede?' she said aloud.

And, biting her lip, Kirsty knew the first person she needed to speak to about this was Detective Superintendent Lorimer.

*

Lorimer stood at the front of the muster room, leaning his tall frame against a table. It was the end of the day and the officers gathered for the meeting were all looking towards DI Grant who was fixing a new photograph onto the wall behind her. He would listen to her report first, before sharing what Kirsty had told him.

'There,' she said, turning with a glint of triumph in her eyes. 'Lesley Crawford as she is now.'

'Jesus!' someone said as they all regarded the blown-up photograph of the injured woman.

'Aye, grim,' someone else remarked.

'Well she's lucky to be alive,' Jo said, standing to one side to let them all compare the two images of the young woman; the smiling blonde on the left and, next to it, the puffy face full of bruises and stitches, head swathed in white gauze bandages, no sign of the blond tresses that had been clipped off for emergency surgery.

'I'm just back from the hospital,' Jo told them. 'She remembers her assailant quite well, as it happens. Even though she was guttered and it was dark. She can't give us much about his height, only that he seemed taller than she was. But he was white, about twenty-five to thirty, probably dark haired, though he was wearing a hoodie.'

'Narrows it down a bit,' someone offered, getting a general guffaw from the room.

'She says she can remember what his face was like,' Jo went on, glaring at the offending officer. 'So we've got our artist going up to see her tomorrow morning. Soonest we could manage,' she said, looking at Lorimer. 'And the hospital insisted she had to have a rest tonight.

'So, lads and lasses, you can expect every front page in the country to carry it as soon as the artist and our victim come up with a decent image.

'Meantime, we need to ask questions of the different hospitals and clinics to see if any of their patients have been signing themselves out in the past few weeks.'

'Why's that, ma'am?' a voice asked.

'Professor Brightman reckons that the profile of this man fits someone who has come off medication suddenly.'

'Schizophrenic?'

'Could be. "A sudden cessation of medication can result in dramatic behavioural changes",' said Jo, reading from a paper she held in her hand.

Lorimer hid a smile behind his hand. He could imagine the psychologist's serious tone as he spoke to the detective inspector.

'Ordinarily, patient files are completely off limits,' Jo went on, 'but information about someone who has been taking medication or having treatment then disappearing into the night can be given to us by the medics.'

'And Brightman reckons it's a nutter?' one of the officers asked.

'Well, what do you think?' Jo asked sarcastically. 'Two separate attacks on defenceless women with the same MO?'

'Or three if you count Eva Magnusson,' someone whispered behind their hand out of Jo Grant's hearing. Lorimer had shared his suspicions with them that the Swedish girl's death was part of this pattern. Rumour had it that he was angling for her murder to be investigated again in the light of the current cases and that DI Grant was less than happy about her case being stripped apart.

'But maybe it's just a druggie mugging them for what he can get?' another voice piped up.

'Fiona Travers had her wallet taken, and her iPod,' Jo agreed, 'but nothing of Lesley Crawford's was missing. So we can't assume that was the motive.'

'Maybe the thug heard the church officer and scarpered?'

'Perhaps,' Jo said, and Lorimer could hear the first signs of exasperation in her voice.

'Thanks for that, Detective Inspector Grant. And I'm sure we're all relieved that this young woman is not only fit enough to give us information about her attacker but that she appears to be heading for a full recovery, even though that photograph might suggest otherwise,' Lorimer said, stepping forward to stand beside Jo.

'May I have a word?' he added quietly.

'Sure,' she nodded, scooping up the papers on the table before addressing the men and women in the room once again.

'There's a man out there targeting a particular type of young woman. And we want to get him before he does any more damage,' she said, trying to force herself to sound enthusiastic when she knew they were all as bone weary as herself. 'So, let's concentrate on finding him, okay? See you all tomorrow,'

Lorimer held the door open, watching his detective inspector as she headed towards him. Jo pushed one hand through her short dark hair and he could see that the woman was trying to stifle a yawn. She had been working for fourteen hours straight, Lorimer knew, and was at that stage of tiredness when most of her inner resources had been used up. Would his news pile even more fatigue onto those sagging shoulders? Or had his detective inspector now come to terms with the possibility that someone other than Colin Young was guilty of Eva Magnusson's death? As Jo walked through the open doorway, he looked back at the before and after photographs of Lesley Crawford, a reminder to them all of just why they did this job. Sometimes it was a thankless task and the long winter days seemed to sap what little energy they had, but a result in this case would renew their strength, giving them the impetus that every police officer needed to deal with whatever fate threw at them.

'Brian Hastie and Anders Andersson. Names mean anything to you?'

Lorimer could see the frown between the woman's eyebrows. But she hadn't shaken her head.

'Hastie, yes,' Jo replied at last. 'The party the Magnusson girl was at.' Her expression cleared suddenly. 'It was at his flat. At least, the flat he shared with another two boys. Why?'

Lorimer told her.

'And what was it they called him?'

'"Her puppy",' Lorimer said.

'Some kind of stalker?'

Lorimer shrugged. 'Could be. On the other hand, perhaps he was simply a lad with a crush on an exceptionally pretty girl.'

'We took statements from all the students at that party,' Jo told him. 'Hastie's will be among that file.'

'And what about the Swedish boy?'

'Never heard of him. Didn't appear anywhere on our radar.' She frowned.

'You didn't check the student database? According to this Strathclyde student he was a friend of Eva's from home.'

Jo shook her head, eyebrows raised. 'That name didn't come up on the list Strathclyde gave us. Sorry, he's as much a mystery to us as he seems to have been to her flatmates. Did you speak to the boys or is this just Kirsty's version of things?' she asked, not disguising the acerbic tone in her voice.

Lorimer nodded. 'None of the flatmates has heard of this Swedish boy. And I'm guessing that Dirk McGregor just wants to keep his head down and hope this all goes away.'

Jo Grant raised her eyebrows. Lorimer had already told her how the Strathclyde lecturer had been adamant that he didn't want his wife knowing about his affair with the Swedish girl.

279

'Someone must have known about this Andersson lad,' Lorimer went on. 'And I think I might just make a call to Mr Magnusson, see if he can throw any light on it. And there's something else, Jo, something that Kirsty let slip.'

Jo looked at him sharply, hearing the intensity of his tone.

'It was when we were discussing how often Eva's father visited Glasgow. She made this throwaway remark about how Henrik Magnusson could afford to come back as often as he liked seeing he had his own private jet.'

'We didn't know that, did we?' Jo said slowly. 'There was never any mention about that, was there?'

'No.' Lorimer's jaw tightened. 'Look, I know this whole case has given you a real headache but is there any chance the team can look into Magnusson's movements around the time of his daughter's death? Check the logs at Glasgow airport, for instance? Okay?'

The DI sighed volubly. 'Right, sir. Anything else?'

'No. You go home and get a decent night's kip, Jo. You'll need it before you face the press tomorrow.'

'Thanks, sir, goodnight.' Jo stood up and he watched her as she left his room, a woman on the edge of exhaustion. How many times had he been there himself? Too many, a little voice replied. Maggie would be waiting for him, something good cooked for his evening meal, he thought. What was Jo Grant going home to? A microwaved dinner or a takeaway?

He glanced at the clock to see that it was now approaching seven-thirty. Magnusson could have left his own office by now. One telephone call, that was all, Lorimer told himself, then he too would step out into the winter night and head for home.

'Mr Magnusson, Detective Superintendent Lorimer, Strathclyde Police.'

'Y-es?' A single word, but the voice on the other end of the line sounded anxious.

'Sorry to trouble you, sir, but it has come to our attention that a Swedish student called Anders Andersson was at the University of Strathclyde and we'd like to contact him.'

There was no disguising the intake of breath from Magnusson. 'Who did you say?' he muttered at last.

'Anders Andersson.'

The pause that followed was just a shade too long for Lorimer's liking before the Swedish man replied. 'Sorry, don't know him. Should I?' Then, before Lorimer could reply, Magnusson added, 'Line's breaking up, sorry, can you hear me?' Then there was a click and the continuous loud hum of a disconnected call.

Lorimer put down the phone, staring at the instrument as if it could tell him something. There had been no trace of static or anything else, he thought. The man had deliberately made that up and cut the connection. For a moment he wondered about redialling the number but decided against it. Still staring at the phone, Lorimer shook his head. He was experienced enough to know when someone was lying. And he was sure that Henrik Magnusson had lied about not knowing the mysterious Anders Andersson.

'But why would he do that?' Maggie asked, settling herself into the seat opposite her husband.

'Don't know,' Lorimer replied, spooning the second helping of chicken broth into his mouth. He paused, spoon in mid-air. 'If Eva was trying to keep the lad a secret from her father then she wouldn't have told her flatmates about him either, would she?'

'She didn't want Daddy knowing her boyfriend had followed her to Scotland.'

'Something like that, maybe.'

'You think this Swedish boy's the real murderer?'

Lorimer laughed. 'Whoa! You've been watching too many crime dramas on the television!'

'Well, that's the sort of thing that makes you think, isn't it?' Maggie persisted. 'Stranger in town, secret lover . . .'

'Yet he wasn't a stranger to the other students at Strathclyde, was he?' Lorimer mused, tilting his plate and scooping up the last of Maggie's delicious soup. 'And according to that Geordie lad Kirsty's been speaking to they were merely pals, not lovers at all.'

'And he wasn't at the student party?'

Lorimer shook his head. 'No. There were some of Eva's class there, and other pals of Hastie's flatmates. Plus the three lads from Merryfield Avenue. But no Anders Andersson. We've got a full list of names, addresses and the particular courses the students were on.'

'You know what, though,' Maggie said thoughtfully. 'If this lad was an old friend from back home, Eva would have had his mobile number, wouldn't she?'

'Nothing on it according to the records. It's one of the first things that's checked,' Lorimer replied.

Maggie chuckled.

'What?'

'You have to think like a teenage girl sometimes to get inside their heads,' she said. 'I wonder if Eva had the same scheme going as Daisy Taylor?'

'Who?'

'One of my third years,' Maggie explained. 'Inventive wee besom when it comes down to breaking the rules, is our Daisy. Thought she had cracked the no-mobile-phones-on-school-premises policy till I found her sim card taped inside her Macbeth folder. Wee rascal had her phone going red hot at lunchtimes till then. Charged her classmates sweetly to use it, as well!'

Lorimer stroked his chin thoughtfully. Just how thorough had the scene of crime officers been in scouring Eva's room? And was this just the sort of tiny thing he had wanted Kirsty to find? A spare sim card to keep in contact with Anders Andersson while avoiding her father's eagle eye might answer a lot of questions.

'Here you are, Sir.' The cheery-faced lady handed Lorimer the plastic bag containing Eva Magnusson's phone.

'Just sign here, please,' she continued, handing him a clipboard with a sheet of paper attached. There were already several names and signatures appended for this particular production: it was an essential procedure that every person examining an object taken from a crime scene had to sign his name and give the date on which the object was removed from the store. Failure to do this could have disastrous results. One careless omission from the chain might bring the weight of a defence lawyer crashing down on an unsuspecting officer, the accusation of tampering with evidence throwing an entire trial into disarray.

It took just a few minutes to find what he was looking for. No Anders Andersson. He scrolled up and down, looking to see if there were any other names that might give a clue about the girl's activities, noting any that did not tally against the list of friends from the Hastie boy's party. And texts? What messages might she have kept stored in this phone? Lorimer's gloved fingers moved across the tiny screen, seeking something that could give him a clue. He pursed his lips as he stared at the message boxes. They were empty. Had she been a fastidious girl, clearing every message that had been read? Or, he thought, had she been afraid to keep any messages lest her secrets be

283

discovered? And was there a missing sim card somewhere in the Anniesland flat?

One way or another, Lorimer had the feeling that they needed to find this young man, wherever he was. And, as he re-signed the paper on the clipboard, another name came to mind – one that might just offer some explanations about both Brian Hastie and Anders Andersson.

Strathclyde University was situated to the east of George Square, a conglomeration of buildings that stretched from the old red sandstone of Royal College almost as far as the Royal Infirmary. Livingstone Tower was a rude finger of concrete and glass pointing skywards and, as he craned his neck to watch the clouds scudding past, Lorimer had the momentary sensation that the entire block was shifting sideways through space. He looked down at his watch, blinking to stop the whirling feeling in his head. It was just after ten o'clock, a perfect time to catch the lecturer before he set off for his next class at eleven.

Dirk McGregor's office was near the top of the building. Lorimer squeezed into the lift beside a gaggle of girls who were all clutching laptop bags and chattering away, quite ignoring the tall stranger by their side. Had Eva ever stood here, joining in the gossip? Of course, she must have used this lift countless times, but somehow Lorimer imagined Eva Magnusson keeping a little aloof from the other students, watching them as if from the outside. Once again that face flashed into his mind, the dead girl like a sleeping angel. She had seemed perfect in death but now he was beginning to know the flawed reality so much better, this other Eva whose life had been full of secrets.

The lift doors pinged open and he followed the crowd out into the landing. A sign with room numbers was fixed to the wall and he made his way along a corridor, losing the noisy girls as they turned into a lecture theatre.

'Come in,' a voice called and Lorimer opened the door.

Dirk McGregor stood up suddenly. 'What the hell are you doing here?'

'Nice to see you too, Mr McGregor,' Lorimer replied smoothly. 'Mind if I sit down? Your office said that I might find you here between classes.'

McGregor's face paled. 'You told my office . . . ?'

'That I needed to speak to you concerning some of your students,' Lorimer said, taking a seat opposite the lecturer who had sunk back into his own chair as though winded.

'What . . . ?'

'Two students on the same course as Eva Magnusson,' Lorimer continued, ignoring the man's discomfiture. 'Brian Hastie and Anders Andersson. Neither one of them seems to have come back this term. Thought you might know why.'

'Is that all?' McGregor leaned back, hands behind his head. 'Come in all this way just for that? No wonder our tax bill's so bloody high when a senior officer spends time on such trivial details,' he declared, his handsome face twisted into a sneer.

Lorimer's own expression remained completely impassive, the years of practice interviewing cocksure thugs paying off at times like this. 'The two students,' he said again. 'Can you tell me why they have not returned to the university?'

McGregor was now swinging nonchalantly in his chair. 'That's easy,' he said. 'Hastie's on long-term sick leave with glandular fever. Might even have to repeat the year. And the Swedish lad was an exchange student. Probably not on the main lists you plods looked at,' he added gleefully. 'Only here till Christmas.' He shrugged. 'That all you wanted to know?'

'Their home addresses and any other contact details would be useful,' Lorimer replied mildly.

'Ask the office.' McGregor stood up once more. 'Looks like you're good at doing that,' he snapped.

McGregor was only guilty of churlish behaviour, Lorimer told himself as he walked back across the city. Yet the fear in the lecturer's eyes had been unmistakable. What had he expected from the policeman's unheralded visit? And was the presence of a senior police officer in that office some sort of a threat to his safe little world? He had been anxious that his wife knew nothing of his affair with Eva Magnusson, something Lorimer had managed to contain so far but without any promise that such knowledge would not come out in the future. He gritted his teeth: someone would get the sharp end of his tongue for this. Failing to search all of the student databases was just sheer carelessness.

Kirsty would be disappointed: there were two reasonable explanations for the missing students. Yet there was still an unanswered question about Andersson: why had Eva Magnusson kept him a secret from her flatmates and, presumably, from her father?

Colin slipped back into his cell, used now to its confines, sometimes even welcoming the peace and quiet when his cell mate, or 'co-pilot' as they called them in here, was away on a work detail.

He had dreamed about Eva last night, a dream from which he had awoken with tears on his cheeks. It had felt so real, hearing her voice, as if she were really there again. He slumped onto his back on the bunk and felt under the mattress for his notebook. He had written *The Swedish Girl* on the front and in idle moments had decorated the title with lines and curls, the sort of thing that reminded him of doodling on his school jotters.

Pulling the pen from the spiral binding, Colin began to write.

It is her voice I miss as much as her very presence, he began. *How can I begin to describe that voice?* He paused, hearing the dream in his head once again. *She sounded like a lady,* he continued. *Refined, but not in an English Home Counties sort of way, that was one of the beauties of it. Eva spoke like an actress, as if she had learned to wipe out any trace of an accent.* He smiled to himself, remembering how they had all laughed one morning when the girl had come out with a really Glaswegian expression. What had it been? He shook his head, her exact words failing to return, only the memory of how funny it had sounded coming from her lips.

Hers was a soft voice, melodious, the sort of voice that a singer might have had, though we never heard her sing, not even when there was music playing in the flat. He stopped, pen poised, remembering another time, his cheeks flushing as the images flooded back, unbidden. *And that husky tone,* he wrote, hand shaking slightly, *when she had me in bed, urging me on.*

Colin stopped writing. He couldn't go back there, no matter how much the professor wanted him to describe Eva. He simply could not relive any of that night. Yet the girl's voice was in his head right at this moment in time, like a ghost visiting his brain.

Did the dead hover somewhere up there? Was Eva's spirit still able to make him feel that anguish and pain? And, he thought, putting both hands over his ears, did he really deserve to suffer like this?

CHAPTER 36

'A sim card?' Kirsty's head turned towards the door of Eva's room. 'I could try,' she said. 'Okay. I'll call you back if I find anything.'

Kirsty's eyes gleamed as she put the phone down on the polished hall table. Now at least there was something positive to look for. Taking a deep breath she turned the key in Eva's door and stepped in once again.

If I wanted to hide a wee thing like a sim card, where would I put it? she wondered. Somewhere nobody would find it but a place that would be handy if I used it regularly. Late at night. When I was in my bed . . .

The dead girl's bed had an ornate white carved headboard that matched the little table to one side. Kneeling down, Kirsty saw the pair of electrical sockets just above the skirting board. The bedside lamp was plugged into one, its wire snaking behind the table. The other, hidden by the sweep of pink silken counterpane, held one of those plastic safety covers that her Aunty Joyce used when her kids were wee.

Kirsty blinked, noticing that one side of the plastic cover protruded just the tiniest bit away from the socket. Would the scene of crime officers have pulled that out to have a look?

She held her breath as her fingernails eased it out.

'Bingo!' Kirsty's smile broadened as she turned the cover over to see the tiny sim card taped carefully to the inside of the socket cover.

'This is Detective Superintendent Lorimer, Strathclyde Police. Am I speaking to Anders Andersson?'

There was a short pause before a thickly accented voice replied. 'This is Anders. What do you want?'

'Mr Andersson, I wanted to ask you some questions about your stay in Glasgow.'

'You got wrong fellow,' the man interrupted. 'This is Anders senior.'

'It's your son who was a student at the University of Strathclyde?'

'That's right. Young Anders did a ... what is it ... an exchange, yes?'

'Yes. Can I speak to him, please? Is he there?'

'This about the Magnusson girl?'

'That's correct, Mr Andersson. We are still investigating the circumstances around her death.'

There was a longer pause before the deep voice proclaimed, 'Anders is not here any more. Sorry. Can't help you,' before the click that let the policeman know the call had been terminated.

Cursing under his breath, Lorimer redialled the number but it was already engaged.

He imagined the father calling his son at that very moment, telling him that the Scottish police were looking for him. Biting his lip, Lorimer had a growing feeling that the elusive Anders might really have something to hide. Well, perhaps there was more than one way to find out. Dialling the mobile number he had copied from Eva's extra sim card, he wondered if the father was speaking the truth or if he simply didn't want to become involved.

As the engaged signal rang out from the student's mobile, Lorimer nodded to himself. He would bet a month's salary that he was right and at this very moment father and son were discussing what to do about this call from the Scottish police.

'The initial call to Mr Magnusson was made to his mobile,' DS Wilson told Lorimer.

'And the call was logged at what time, exactly?'

Wilson glanced at his notes. 'It was just after ten a.m. on the Saturday morning, sir. Fiscal had to be informed first.'

Lorimer nodded. 'I've checked out a few things. Magnusson told Dr Fergusson he had to get a domestic flight to Glasgow, but I honestly can't see why he didn't simply use his own aircraft.'

'He has his own plane?' Alistair Wilson's eyes widened.

'Aye,' Lorimer said. 'Your Kirsty told us that. And thank God she did. There's something funny going on and once I've spoken to the good people at Glasgow airport we may just find out what that is.'

'You're going where?'

'Stockholm,' Lorimer told her. 'Pity it's not anywhere near half term or you could have come with me. You deserve it after coming up with that idea about Eva's sim card.'

Maggie Lorimer shook her head. 'What do the rest of the team think of this?'

'I haven't told them all yet,' Lorimer replied. 'Anyway, they're all answerable to me at the moment.' He shrugged. 'It's some consolation being the boss.'

'And Solly?'

He grinned. 'Wondered if you'd ask me that. It depends on what cover he can get for his classes. He'll come with me if he can. He's still working on the profile though. Reckons it's no coincidence that these blonde women are so alike.' He made a face. 'But he still sticks to his opinion that Eva was killed by someone else.'

Maggie laid down her wine glass and looked at her husband. 'Seriously, what do you think you're going to achieve by flying all the way to Stockholm?'

'Hopefully we will be able to speak to the Andersson boy and his father, but they're not the only ones we need to talk to.'

'Oh?'

'No.' His face clouded for a moment. 'It was a remark that Kirsty made, actually. We followed it up. Seems like Mr Magnusson has his own private jet.'

Maggie's eyebrows rose. 'Impressive,' she remarked.

'Well, we all know he's a multi-millionaire,' Lorimer replied. 'But' – he paused, looking his wife in the eye – 'what we didn't know until today is that Henrik Magnusson was in Glasgow the night his daughter was murdered. And that his jet took off from Glasgow airport shortly after two a.m. on the Saturday.'

'This changes everything.' Jo Grant ran her hand through her newly gelled hair.

'Yes,' Lorimer replied. 'As far as we knew, Magnusson was in Stockholm that night. Even told Dr Fergusson that he couldn't get a flight out straight away. Something's not right.'

'No.' The DI's sigh seemed to come all the way from her thick-soled boots. 'How long will you be gone?'

Lorimer shrugged. 'As long as it takes. Might have to hook up with some of the local police in Stockholm, we'll see. Depends on what I find.'

'And Colin Young?'

Lorimer caught sight of her face, eyes flicking away from his own. She was feeling it now, all right, a sense of unease that she had arrested the wrong man after all.

'Up to the Fiscal. But I doubt there's anything like enough evidence to release him yet. And, Jo?'

'Yes?' She met his keen blue gaze now.

'Despite what Kirsty Wilson thinks, you might still be right.'

Professor Solomon Brightman sat back and looked at the words he had typed onto the screen. He blinked, thinking about the profiles he was creating. One was of a shadowy figure that leapt out at blonde women from his hiding places in the woods. And his chosen victims were so alike. That was significant, he thought. Why a person should suddenly take it into their head to attack and try to kill suggested some sort of trigger. Something to do with a woman who resembled his victims, perhaps? Had the killer undergone a recent trauma? Or were the attacks drug-related in some psychotic way? He would think more about that later but now he wanted to concentrate on a different man.

Solly scrolled back to read the pages that related to a previous profile: Henrik Magnusson. So far he had built up a picture of a domineering father who was trying to mould his only daughter into the sort of woman he wanted her to be. Someone in the image of her dead mother, perhaps? He stroked his beard. It was a possibility. He had asked Lorimer to find out what he could about the late Mrs Magnusson. Had she been a virginal bride? Or had he elevated her to a position of perfection as memory had faded? It happened sometimes. It was easier to forget the petty, human things that made a couple irritated with one another and only remember the good times.

And if his theory was correct then he had to ask one important question: had Eva been a disappointment to him in some way? Solly stared at the screen. He was seeing not the words now but picturing in his mind's eye the photograph of a girl laughing into the camera on the ski slopes, laughing for her father. Or, he wondered, had she been laughing *at* him? A teenage girl who had slept around as easily as Eva had in the months she had been in Glasgow was surely adept in her sexual adventures long before her arrival in the city.

None of Jo Grant's team had asked the question of where Eva's father had been on the night of her murder, assuming Magnusson to have been in Stockholm. *Never make assumptions*, he remembered Lorimer telling his team on more than one occasion when he had sat amongst the officers. But they had, and who could have blamed them for that? The fact remained that the Swede had been in Glasgow on the night of his daughter's murder. And now Solly Brightman had been asked by Strathclyde's finest to regard the man as a potential suspect.

CHAPTER 37

Stockholm.

Lorimer looked out of the window as the plane came into land, marvelling at the water everywhere, tiny clusters of houses dotted on the margins of what appeared to be islets floating down below. The sky was an icy blue, the weak sun making the snow-covered landscape sparkle; an illusion of warmth in a land in the iron grip of winter. It was like an illustration from a fairy tale, he decided as the plane banked for the final descent, these steep-roofed houses clustered together, clad in white. And wasn't this the land of Hans Christian Andersen? Memories of childhood tales came back: the Snow Queen and the fragment of mirror that had lodged in a child's heart, freezing it and turning him to darkness and despair.

No, he remembered now, Andersen belonged to Denmark. And it was quite a different Andersson that he would shortly be seeking.

Solly had been right urging him to take his warmest coat, Lorimer thought as the doors opened with a sigh, the clean sharpness taking his breath away.

It was a short taxi ride to the small hotel he had booked online and the driver was mercifully silent. Lorimer gazed out of the window as the city streets became narrower and the traffic slowed, allowing him to admire the pastel-coloured old buildings. He had read somewhere that Stockholm was called 'The Venice of the North' and now he could see why as the taxi slipped down a narrow cobbled street emerging into daylight, the water glimmering nearby. It would be a lovely city to visit properly, he told himself. Perhaps one day, with Maggie ...

A quick splash in the hotel's ample wash basin was all that was needed before Lorimer headed out once again into the streets. He had called his counterpart in the Stockholm police to let her know that he had arrived. Should anything unusual happen then he had the back-up of her force, the senior officer had assured him.

Magnusson's home was in the outskirts of Östermalm, the eastern part of the city, and that was where the detective superintendent was heading first. There were only six hours of daylight at this time of the year and already the afternoon sky had turned grey. Once more Lorimer looked out of a taxi window but this driver was eager to chat, wishing no doubt to impress the visitor with his beautiful city.

'We go through the Old Town, sir,' the man told him, his English flawless but overlaid with an American accent. 'It's called Gamla Stan,' he added. 'I'll show you our royal palace if you like.'

'I don't have time for sight-seeing, I'm afraid.' Lorimer leaned forward, seeing the disappointment on the man's face. 'I'm here on business rather than for pleasure.'

'Well, you'll see some of the best architecture in the world anyway,' the driver boasted. 'Just keep looking out the window. Best preserved city centre you'll ever see. Medieval.' He grimaced as though a bad taste had come into his mouth. 'Used to be old stuff everywhere when I was a boy. Tore most of it down where I live.'

'Oh?'

'Yeah. Place called Klarakvarteren. Ever heard of it?'

'No, sorry.'

'Huh! Famous in its own way, y'know. Urban renewal, they called it. Urban disgrace most of us think!'

Lorimer let the driver chatter on, complaining about the way developers had made their fortunes back in the sixties and seventies. Had Magnusson been part of that, he wondered? Had he made his money out of that particular part of the city? He dismissed the thought at once: Henrik Magnusson would also have been a child back then. But perhaps his own empire had been built on the success of such developments?

'Posh part of town, here,' the driver snorted, looking up at the massive apartment buildings as they passed by. Lorimer nodded silently, thinking how much they reminded him of the wealthier *arrondissements* of Paris.

Soon they had left the streets and were passing a snow-covered park, heading away from the city. Lorimer bent his head to see the sun; it lingered briefly, a ghostly outline of misty gold against the pale grey skies, before vanishing once again as though afraid to be seen. Daylight was waning now and the white fields and gardens looked bruised beneath the gathering dusk.

The Magnusson house lay somewhere beyond the park, the driver had told him, though it was evident the man had not driven anyone there before today. So it came as a surprise when they turned into what appeared to be a farm road, banks of snow heaped on either side as though the snow ploughs made regular visits to keep this particular route clear. They passed frosted trees, their branches stark against the cold winter sky, then, as the Skoda slowed to take a corner, Lorimer could see the lights from a distant house. The driver muttered to himself as the car slipped and slithered on the icy road until at last they reached a set of large black gates. Beyond lay a solid-looking modern house, its lower windows shuttered against the night, though Lorimer could see light glimmering from the fanlight above the door.

'Here, sir, this is the place you're looking for,' the driver said, turning his head and looking at Lorimer with a quizzical expression. 'Expecting you, are they? Looks to me like these are locked.' The taxi driver pointed to the security box fixed against one of the two stone pillars that flanked the metal gates.

Lorimer followed his gaze. Had Solly mentioned this? For a moment he simply couldn't remember. No, he decided. The psychologist had not told him about this feature, but perhaps it was something he should have anticipated, arriving unannounced at the home of one of Sweden's wealthiest men.

'Want me to wait?'

'Just for a bit,' Lorimer said. 'See if anyone's at home.'

The cold hit him the moment he stepped from the taxi and the detective pulled his scarf closer to his chin as he stepped carefully over the frozen snow.

He pressed a call button and waited. For a long moment there was nothing, not even a crackle of static to show that the device was in working order. He half turned to the driver who shrugged his shoulders. It was all to the good if this fare was returning to the city, his gesture seemed to say.

Then a woman's voice spoke in Swedish, her tone quizzical.

'Hello, this is Detective Superintendent Lorimer from Strathclyde Police in Scotland. I'm here to see Henrik Magnusson. May I come in, please?'

There was a hesitation then the voice spoke again, this time in English. 'Mr Magnusson is not back yet, but you may come in and wait for him.' There was a loud click and the gates swung open a fraction.

Lorimer stepped back to the driver who was now leaning out of the opened window.

'How much?'

The driver told him and he thrust the fare and a decent tip into his outstretched hand.

'Maybe see you later,' Lorimer advised him.

'Maybe not.' The driver grinned ominously then the window rolled up and the car lumbered backwards as he attempted to turn and head back the way they had come. Would any taxi driver come back for him tonight or was he fated to be stranded out here in the depths of the countryside?

Taking a deep breath of the frozen air, Lorimer pushed the gates open. They swung back, closing automatically with a dull clang that made him shiver. Behind him the skies had darkened now, the lights from several eye-level lanterns on either side of the driveway making everything beyond indistinguishable shapes disappearing into shadowy blackness.

Then the door opened and he saw the figure of a woman framed against the light.

'Hello, I'm Detective Superintendent Lorimer,' he said, holding out his warrant card for the woman to see. 'I was hoping to see Henrik Magnusson. He isn't expecting me, I'm afraid.' Now that he was in the vestibule he could see that she was a tall woman, fair and slender, her hair caught up in an old-fashioned pleat across her head. Her scarlet sweater gave a certain glow to the woman's creamy skin, making him look at her face, noting the high cheekbones and steady grey eyes. A swift appraisal let the detective see that she had donned a pair of stout leather boots below her calf-length black skirt: had the woman been getting ready to leave the house? And if so, was Magnusson going to return soon?

'Marthe Lindgren,' she told him, giving the warrant card only the most cursory of glances. 'I'm Mr Magnusson's housekeeper. Please come in, Superintendent. I can let him know of your arrival.'

Lorimer stamped the snow from his shoes before crossing the threshold then stepped into a hallway full of warmth and light.

'Would you like some coffee?' Marthe asked, beckoning Lorimer to follow her along a corridor that ended in a white-painted door. 'The kitchen is warm,' she explained with a hint of a smile on her thin lips.

'Thank you, I would like that very much indeed,' he replied.

'Have you just arrived from Scotland?' She threw the question over her shoulder, smiling politely.

Lorimer strode after her, through the white door and along a second corridor that led into a vast square kitchen where a wood-burning stove threw out a welcome blast of heat.

'Just today,' he replied.

'Please, sit here,' Marthe said, sweeping a dish towel from a comfortable old-fashioned-looking wooden chair next to the stove. 'And do allow me to take your coat,' she said, holding out her hands as he fumbled the buttons open.

'Thank you.'

Marthe merely nodded as she turned away, placing the coat on another chair near the stove. 'It will be warm for you when you leave,' she said simply. 'You are here about Eva, yes?'

'I'm afraid so.'

'It isn't a surprise that you have to see him, but why come all the way to Stockholm?' Marthe asked. Her back was to Lorimer as she busied herself with preparing a pot of coffee but he could see from the tilt of her head that the housekeeper was curious.

'Please, do sit down and join me in a coffee, if you will,' Lorimer asked gently. 'Then I can explain.'

When Marthe Lindgren turned to look at him just then, he could see the tears in her eyes, tears that held a genuine sorrow for the dead girl.

'Thank you.' She moved her head again, concentrating on pouring coffee into two plain white porcelain beakers.

'Now,' Lorimer began as he took the coffee from her. 'It was necessary to come here to see two people who are resident in Sweden. And I'll explain why in a moment. But first I would like very much to talk to you about Eva. Would you mind that?'

The woman sighed, cupping the mug between her long thin hands. 'Poor little Eva,' she said, looking down at her lap. 'If only she hadn't had to leave ...'

'But surely it was her choice to study in Glasgow?'

Marthe's cheeks flushed into twin spots of colour. 'Oh!' she exclaimed. 'Perhaps I ought not to have said that!'

'I'm here to help find out what I can about several things that may lie behind Eva's murder,' he told her gently.

'But I don't understand! Surely the man has been caught?'

'There is a person in custody, yes,' Lorimer agreed. 'But there are some doubts about whether he is in fact the perpetrator.'

'My God!' Marthe's hand flew to her face, some coffee spilling onto her skirt.

Lorimer took the cup from her and placed it on the counter beside him. 'Marthe, does the name Anders Andersson mean anything to you?'

'Anders?' Her eyes widened in horror. 'You don't think *he* killed Eva? No, no, that can't be!'

'Can you tell me something about him?'

She sighed deeply, her face solemn. 'Poor, poor Anders, it wasn't fair, really, he was such a nice little boy . . .'

'Yes?'

'Superintendent, it was because of Anders that Eva had to leave home,' Marthe explained. 'When Henrik found them together . . .' She broke off. 'You don't know anything about that, do you?' she asked, looking at him gravely. 'Well, let me tell you what happened. Anders came about the house for years with his father, old Anders, the Magnussons' gardener. He and Eva played together as children. I suppose old Anders and I both felt a little sorry for the child. You see, Eva was home schooled and, well, children need other children to play with . . .' She broke off again, stifling a sudden sob. 'Forgive me, it is just that when I remember Eva as a little girl . . .' She took out a handkerchief from her skirt pocket and wiped her nose. 'Where was I? Yes, Anders.' She nodded sadly, sniffing back more tears. 'He was a beautiful little boy and he became a very good-looking young man. Oh, Superintendent, if you could have seen them together! But of course Henrik would never have allowed a relationship, even when Anders went to university and had such big plans for his future.' She sighed again. 'You have children, Superintendent?'

Lorimer shook his head.

'Well, it is a fact that the harder you try to stop a young person doing something the more determined they will be to carry out their own desires.'

'Anders and Eva?'

She nodded. 'Henrik found them in her bedroom one afternoon.' Her voice dropped. 'It was terrible. Old Anders was dismissed, the young man thrown out and Eva and her father had the most terrible quarrel.'

'So she was forced to leave Sweden? To get away from the boy?'

Marthe nodded. 'You could see that it broke his heart but I thought maybe it was also a good thing for Eva.' There was a pause as Marthe picked up her cup and took a drink of the coffee. 'She needed to get away, you know. Feel a little of the freedom for a while.'

'Did you know that Anders Andersson had followed Eva to Glasgow?'

Marthe shook her head. 'No! Oh dear, I wish ... I shouldn't have said ...'

'It's all right,' Lorimer reassured her. 'Someone would have told me this story if you hadn't, I'm sure.'

'And is he still there?'

'I don't think so. His father told me he had gone away, but he wasn't very explicit. You don't happen to have a home address for them, do you?' It was something he had hesitated to ask the Swedish police earlier, deciding in the end to make his own enquiries.

'Yes, I can give you that,' she replied, standing up and walking over to the other end of the kitchen.

Lorimer watched the housekeeper as she searched in a hand-bag that had been slung over a hook fixed to the inside of a cupboard door. He had seen Marthe Lindgren's ashen face as she spoke about Eva and now he noticed the way her fingers trembled as she wrote down the address on a piece of paper taken from her bag. Grief, real grief, was etched on the woman's handsome features and Lorimer wondered if Marthe Lindgren had played the part of a mother for the Swedish girl over the years.

'Thank you,' he said as she handed him the paper. 'Is it far from here?'

'Anders used to drive a little truck from his place. It's not that far, maybe about eight kilometres from here?'

'And you, Marthe? Where is it that you live?'

The housekeeper sat down again to face him, blushing a little. 'I have a room here that suits me whenever I choose to stay over, Superintendent. Like tonight when the weather is so bad and I have still to cook for Henrik.' She shrugged. 'But my own little apartment is in the city, in Norrmalm.'

Lorimer tried not to stare at her flushed cheeks. Was Marthe Lindgren more than a mere housekeeper to Henrik Magnusson, then?

'I am sure Henrik will ask you to stay too, Superintendent. The roads out here become very icy once the darkness has fallen.'

As if to give credence to her words the sound of a car crunching over the snowy drive could be heard.

'That's Henrik now! Oh, and I meant to call him to tell him of your arrival!' Marthe exclaimed, springing up and striding towards the kitchen door. 'Come, Superintendent Lorimer. The lounge is warm. I'm sure he will want to meet you there.'

Before he could reply, Lorimer found himself being bustled out of the kitchen, along a different corridor with large double doors that the housekeeper swept open to reveal a huge lounge with pale furnishings.

'Do sit,' she urged, flapping a hand at the enormous white leather sofas. 'I will tell Henrik that you are here.'

Lorimer glanced at her as she closed the doors behind her. There was something nervous in the woman's manner now as if she was slightly afraid of her master. But perhaps she was only fearful of his reaction upon hearing that a policeman from Scotland had arrived unannounced? He stood by the fireplace, feeling the warmth and wondering just what sort of reception he would receive from Henrik Magnusson. There were voices coming from the hall but he could not make out either words or tone of voice before the doors burst open again.

'Lorimer!'

The tall Swede was suddenly striding towards him, one hand outstretched. There was a smile on the big man's face that did not quite reach his keen blue eyes.

'Forgive my unexpected visit, Mr Magnusson,' Lorimer said politely, feeling the man's strong grasp as he shook his hand. 'One or two matters necessitated my presence here in Stockholm,' he added vaguely.

'It is a surprise, yes.' Magnusson frowned. 'But you will stay for dinner? Or have you plans to return to the city tonight?'

'No plans, and, thanks, I'd be happy to join you for a meal.'

Magnusson smiled. 'Marthe is a superb cook,' he said. 'And I am sure you will enjoy her Swedish recipes. Please, sit down and let me get you a drink. What will you have?'

'Whisky, thanks.'

Magnusson nodded, and Lorimer sensed a certain confidence in his manner as he walked across the room to a console table that held several decanters; the sort of confidence that Lorimer had seen in other men of wealth and power.

'Ice?'

'No, just a wee splash of water, thanks,' Lorimer replied. As his host poured the drinks he had time to look around at the room and remember some of the things that Solly had told him. *It had the look of a room where one entertained visitors*, the psychologist had said. *Not the sort of place where one would choose to relax*. And it was true. After all, hadn't Marthe Lindgren led him straight into the kitchen, a place that was so often the true heart of a home?

'Your good health,' Magnusson murmured, raising his glass and looking keenly at the Scottish detective.

'*Slainte*,' Lorimer replied then lowered his glass. 'You must be wondering why I'm here?'

Magnusson nodded. 'Curious,' he agreed.

'Well I'm sorry I gave you no forewarning of my arrival but I wanted to see both yourself and a young man by the name of Anders Andersson.'

Magnusson's face tightened. 'I see,' he replied stiffly.

'You shouldn't have lied to me,' Lorimer told him quietly.

Magnusson looked shamefaced.

'I know about his romance with Eva,' Lorimer went on, sitting back in the corner of the squashy sofa and crossing one leg over the other. 'I guess it wasn't completely over, though.'

'What do you mean?' Magnusson sat forward, his fist clutching the crystal whisky glass.

'You didn't know he had followed her to Glasgow?'

The Swede gave a sigh and shook his head. 'No, not at first. I thought they'd finished with all that nonsense.'

'And when did you find out?'

Magnusson looked away from him, biting his lip as though unsure what to reply.

'I do know that you were in Glasgow the night your daughter died, Henrik,' Lorimer said softly, then sipped the whisky, watching the man's reaction.

Magnusson's mouth opened but no words came out.

'What happened? Something pretty bad, I imagine, to make you keep that sort of information from the Scottish police.'

The big man shook his blond head. 'It wasn't what you're thinking,' he said at last, then gave a huge sigh. Lorimer watched him taking a slug of his drink, the air of smooth confidence gone now, the broad shoulders tensed in anxiety.

'Oh, God!' Magnusson sighed, setting down his glass on the carpet and putting both hands to his head. 'Oh, dear God!'

Lorimer waited, quietly sipping the whisky. It was the moment when a man either lied his way out of a difficult situation or decided to tell the truth. He watched Eva's father closely to see just which way he would go.

'So you know about my little aircraft?' Magnusson took his hands from his face, glancing at the tall man opposite.

Lorimer nodded.

'It was horrible,' Magnusson whispered, looking away to his feet. 'I had called her but she was at some party or other, said she'd be back at the flat by midnight. So I waited for her there.'

Lorimer gave the merest trace of a nod but did not interrupt.

'We quarrelled,' Magnusson sighed. 'About Anders. I'd found out that he was also in Glasgow.' He looked at Lorimer again, eyes pleading as if to compel the detective to understand what he had felt that night.

'I was furious with her. Said some things that I . . . now regret,' he said, his voice failing for a moment in a sob.

Lorimer watched him take a large handkerchief from his pocket and wipe his eyes.

'I'm sorry. It's just, well, we parted on such bad terms.' He looked at Lorimer with an expression of anguish in his eyes. 'And I never saw her alive again.'

'Was Eva alone in the flat when you left?'

Magnusson nodded. 'There was no one else there. I remember the last I ever heard her voice. She was shouting at me from the landing outside the front door,' he whispered, biting his lip, trying hard not to break down in tears.

Lorimer watched the man as he picked up his glass from the floor and emptied the whisky in one gulp.

Was that the truth? He wanted to believe that it was, but, looking at Magnusson's hands clasped around the crystal glass, the detective superintendent wondered if they had in fact encircled his own daughter's throat in a moment of fury.

CHAPTER 38

A self-obsessed man who needed to control his daughter at all costs. Solly looked at the words he had written. And, if that was true, had Henrik Magnusson attacked the very thing he loved most in a vicious need to bring her back into his command? It was possible. He was a powerful man in the world of business; did that power extend to ruling every aspect of his world? There could be a reason for that, Solly thought. His wife's untimely death was something that had been outside his ability to control. So had that left him determined to fashion Eva's life the way he had wanted? Perhaps he would speak to Rosie about her own impressions of the man. After all, his pathologist wife had been the first person to see the grieving father after Eva's murder.

He frowned, reading the words a second time. If he had needed to control her to such an extent, why allow her to come to Glasgow in the first place? Sure, he wanted to split her up from the gardener's son, but had Eva herself insisted on a break from her homeland? The psychologist stroked his beard as he pondered the difficult question of just who Eva Magnusson had been. That was the problem with appearance and reality, he told himself. Outwardly she had appeared to be a demure girl – yes, those were the words that Colin Young had used in his letter. And she had apparently charmed everyone she met. But Solly Brightman was beginning to create a different impression of the Swedish girl: someone who had been a passionate and sexual young woman, adept at hiding her true nature from everyone, especially from her father.

Or, he thought, leaning back in his office chair, was that absolutely the case? Magnusson had known about Anders. And Solly was pretty sure that the Swede had deliberately picked three young men as more than mere flatmates for his daughter. Were Colin, Gary and Roger simply potential boyfriends or had they been chosen to satisfy Eva's sexual lusts? In selecting these three young men Magnusson had sought to maintain some sort of control over his daughter for one reason or another. It was a plausible theory, Solly decided. But was it one that could ever be proved? Perhaps when Lorimer met young Anders Andersson today he might find an answer to that question.

Stockholm on this January morning was wreathed in a low-lying mist but already Lorimer could see the glint of sunlight attempting to force its way through from the heavens.

After an uncomfortable dinner where Marthe Lindgren had taken pains to engage him in polite conversation, Lorimer had been only too glad to call a taxi to take him back to his hotel. There had not been an offer of a bed for the night and he was sure that Henrik Magnusson was relieved to see his uninvited guest depart shortly after the meal. It was good to walk on the well-gritted pavements, to breathe in the chilly air. The big house in Östermalm had felt suffocating despite the grand proportions of the rooms. They had eaten in a formal dining room with French windows. Lorimer guessed that they overlooked the gardens but any such view was shut off by thick curtains drawn firmly against the night.

Marthe had suggested that the detective superintendent would find Anders senior at home: after all, there was little call for a gardener at this time of year and she'd heard that the old man's arthritis had worsened lately. Lorimer had glanced at Magnusson as Marthe offered this nugget of information but the Swede's face had remained closed and impassive, as if his housekeeper's contact with the Andersson family was of no interest whatsoever.

Lorimer crossed the street and stood looking out at the water. Already the mist was beginning to lift and the dappled surface had changed from steely grey to a silvery blue. For a moment he thought about his own city with the River Clyde running through its heart, severing north from south, then he recalled all of the murky things he had seen, things that had lingered in its depths. As the morning sun pierced the last shreds of vapour coating the surface of the water in a hazy brightness, Lorimer swept his gaze over the picture-postcard prettiness of the scene. It should have filled him with a sense of wonder, surely? Yet that image of Glasgow and the knowledge of so many cases in his past made the detective feel only a pang of despair. Was he always destined to look for the brutal things below the surface? And in that search had he lost the joy that came from seeing a morning sunrise?

The apartment where Andersson lived was a featureless block surrounded by glass and concrete, a savage contrast to the old medieval buildings in Gamla Stan. Standing at the security entrance, Lorimer tapped in the flat number that Marthe Lindgren had given him the previous evening. There was a crackle then a voice spoke in Swedish.

'Mr Andersson? This is Detective Superintendent Lorimer from Strathclyde Police in Scotland. May I come up, please?'

There was a momentary pause before the same voice broke through. 'Fifth floor.'

A single buzzing note accompanied the click as the door was unlocked and Lorimer stepped into the foyer.

As the lift opened Lorimer could see a short man wearing a fisherman's jersey over worn jeans waiting for him at his door.

'Mr Andersson?'

The man stared at him and nodded. 'Better come in,' he said gruffly.

The flat was warm enough, Lorimer thought as he was led along a short corridor and into a room that appeared to serve as a kitchen cum sitting room. His eyes flicked around the place, noting a table with breakfast dishes still in place: two empty mugs and a couple of cereal bowls pushed to one side.

'My son is not here. I told you that on the telephone,' Anders began. 'So why you come all the way here?'

'I need to see him,' Lorimer said simply. 'And I want you to tell me where he is.'

'Why don't you listen to me? I say he is not here!'

Lorimer turned to look pointedly at the breakfast table. 'But he *was* here, wasn't he, Mr Andersson?'

The old man followed his gaze then his mouth took on a mulish expression.

'Okay, so he stays the night sometimes,' he admitted grudgingly.

'And where is he now?'

The old man's shoulders heaved up and down in a sigh. 'At the market. He works there most mornings.'

'Market?'

'The big one. Östermalms Saluhall.' Andersson frowned. 'Surely you've heard of it?'

'This is my first visit to Stockholm,' Lorimer said. 'I'm still finding my way around.'

'One of the best markets in the world,' the old man said, his head tilting with pride. 'You'll find my Anders there.' He paused for a moment, looking more keenly at Lorimer. 'He's done nothing wrong, you know.'

'Thanks, Mr Andersson.' Lorimer nodded and turned to leave.

He was at the lift when Andersson called after him.

'Look for number fourteen, okay?'

'What?' Lorimer spun around but the door to the apartment was closed and he was left with the impression that the old man had been laughing at him.

Östermalms Saluhall dominated the corner of the street, an imposing red-stone building topped with a double cupola with the word SALUHALL picked out in gold.

Lorimer made to push open the slate blue doors but as he approached they opened with a squeak, revealing a second set of doors that admitted him into a cavernous hall full of noise and smells. He blinked for a moment, wondering which way to go. Hearing the Swedish voices all around him gave him the sense of being isolated, a foreigner, yet everywhere he looked there were men and women who could have been taken for Scots. So similar were they in dress and appearance that the detective superintendent was reminded of something he had learned over the years: that all humanity was the same when you came down to it.

For a moment he was transported back in time to his early childhood when his mother would take him into Glasgow to a well-known delicatessen grocer; the smell of cooked hams hanging from the ceiling and the whiff of freshly ground coffee brought it back so clearly he could almost feel his small boy's hand in hers. A smile played about his lips as he remembered, then he gave a sigh, returning to the here and now of one of the world's largest indoor food halls. Where on earth would he begin to find the boy in a place like this?

Standing still and taking a good look around to get some bearings paid off immediately as he saw numbers and names above each market stall. Number fourteen, Andersson had told him. Okay, then he would walk around this place until he found it.

Lorimer walked slowly past walls of chilled cabinets. Some were full of cheeses, whole ones piled high, others cut and oozing softly from their wrappings; a butcher's stall contained tiny pictures of reindeer below cuts of meat. He walked on, catching sight of rows of luscious cakes including chocolate circles decorated with fresh fruit and his favourite, Danish pastries, swirled into mouth-watering shapes. *Maggie, you would love this*, he told his wife silently, vowing that if he ever had the chance he would bring her back here for a visit.

Number fourteen proved to be a vegetable stall with rows of fresh produce heaped enticingly up to the counter level, strings of garlic suspended above it. There was only one person behind the counter, a blond lad in a short-sleeved white polo shirt crouching over boxes of leeks that had been piled to one side.

'Hello,' Lorimer called out. 'Are you Anders?'

The lad stood up, rubbing his hands down his jeans. Lorimer caught the tumble of blond curls and the frank open expression as the boy turned to look at him.

'Yes, I'm Anders, who are you?'

'Detective Superintendent Lorimer. Strathclyde Police. Can we talk?'

Anders Andersson looked him in the eye and nodded. 'Sure,'

he said. 'But I need to get someone to cover for me. I can't leave the place unattended.'

He took a swift look around then beckoned to a girl at the cheese counter opposite. Although he had called out to her in Swedish, Lorimer could understand the gist of the request from their body language. *Come over and let me get away for a bit, can you?*

'This is a friend from Scotland,' Anders lied, smiling jauntily at the girl who was already behind the counter. 'We won't be long, Brigitte.' And, giving her a wave, he led Lorimer away from the stall and into the mêlée of the marketplace.

'A coffee?' Anders asked, nodding towards one of the many seated areas that were dotted amongst the wooden-fronted shops.

'My treat,' Lorimer grinned. 'Seeing as I'm an "old friend",' he added wryly.

Anders shrugged. 'What did you expect me to tell her? That the cops are after me?' The boy laughed, showing white even teeth.

They sat down at a table for two and immediately a waitress was at their side and Anders was speaking to her in his native tongue. He looked at Lorimer questioningly.

'Want anything to eat with your coffee?'

He was about to make a polite refusal when he noticed the tempting array of cakes behind the clear plastic display counter.

'A Danish pastry, please,' he murmured to Anders. The waitress smiled and nodded, then disappeared to deliver their order.

'Well, Detective Superintendent Lorimer, here I am, you found me.' Anders gave a resigned smile.

Lorimer raised his eyebrows. 'I was beginning to think you didn't want to be found,' he replied mildly.

The young man's smile faded as he cast his eyes down. 'Know what it's like,' he said. 'You lose someone special and it's hard to want to talk about it.'

'Yes, but the manner of losing Eva *was* and still *is* a police matter, Anders. It would have been helpful if you hadn't tried to avoid talking to me.'

'But I thought you'd got someone for her murder? That boy in her flat?'

'There are ongoing enquiries,' Lorimer said vaguely. 'Things we still need to determine. Especially about Eva. And that's why I'm here: to talk to you about your relationship with her.'

Anders made a face. 'Didn't have a relationship,' he mumbled.

'Don't give me that, son, I know all about how Magnusson threw you out of the house and gave your dad the sack.'

Anders blushed, lowering his head. 'That was ages ago,' he mumbled. 'Eva and I stopped being an item shortly after that.'

'Really? So why follow her to Glasgow if you weren't seeing her?'

Anders shrugged. 'Suppose I was hoping for another chance,' he said. 'But Eva wanted different things.'

'Wasn't it awkward being around her at the university?'

The boy looked him in the eye again. 'We were just friends by then. Hung around together a bit. But no romance.' He gave a short laugh. 'Eva was having far too much fun with her new friends,' he continued. 'That lecturer for one, and then the lads in her flat. She told me all about them. Used to call me up late at night,' he added, continuing to hold Lorimer's gaze in a way that told the detective he was being told the truth.

'And you weren't jealous?'

Anders laughed again. 'This is Eva Magnusson we're talking about, right? The girl who could have anything she wanted?'

'What do you mean?'

'Look, she was spoiled rotten all her life. Daddy gave her everything she could ask for.'

'But he didn't let her have *you*, did he, Anders?'

The boy shook his head and sighed. 'You can't blame Eva. She was enjoying her first taste of freedom from that man. What beautiful girl wouldn't have wanted to play around a bit? And that's all it was, really. Eva wasn't in love with me, Superintendent. In fact, I doubt if she had ever felt what it was like to really love another soul,' he said, his voice dropping to a murmur.

'You make her sound cold-hearted.'

'No! She was never that! She was a lovely girl and one day she would have found someone she could feel strongly about, I'm sure of that,' Anders said vehemently, sudden tears springing to his large eyes.

'And if you'd waited long enough that might have been you?'

Anders shook his head sadly. 'I'll never know now, will I?'

'Tell me,' Lorimer asked, 'why did she keep you a secret from the rest of her flatmates?'

'Oh, that's easy enough,' Anders told him. 'There was no way she wanted Daddy finding out I was in Scotland. Besides' – he gave a nonchalant shrug – 'she wanted to screw these boys one after the other and having me around would've messed that up for her.' He looked up at a clock behind the counter. 'Look, I really have to get back, Brigitte isn't going to be able to stay much longer.' He stood up. 'You've got my number, haven't you?'

'Yes,' Lorimer told him, looking up at his earnest young face. 'And you will answer if I call you, won't you?'

Anders had the grace to blush and nod before standing up and turning to walk away.

Lorimer looked down at the table. His black coffee was cold and the pastry lay untouched on his plate. He sighed, wondering if his journey had yielded anything of importance that would help to free Colin Young or if what he had learned about Eva might simply reinforce his DI's suspicions.

CHAPTER 39

'The table next to the vending machine,' Sam had told him. 'That's where they'll be sitting. Just go up and say "Billy says next Tuesday".'

Colin stood with the other prisoners waiting in the cold corridor between the main prison and the annexe that held the visiting room. It was deliberately designed to disorientate the men, he had decided; a maze of narrow corridors twisting this way and that between lots of locked doors. And the visiting room itself was windowless, not allowing anyone to get their bearings at all. Despite the chill in the air he could feel sweat trickling through his hair and down the side of his face. He glanced behind him but the prison officer wasn't looking his way so he gave the offending wetness a swipe with his sleeve.

Then the doors were opened and the men trooped into the large colourful room. Colin ignored the smile from his father who was half out of his own chair as soon as he spotted his son and headed instead as if to make a purchase from the machine that held all sorts of crisps and chocolate bars.

'Billy says next Tuesday.' He bent forward suddenly, whispering the words to the man and woman sitting by the machine, then, patting his pockets as though to find them empty, he turned back and strode across to his father, heart pounding, afraid to glance up at any of the officers who might have been watching his little performance.

'Colin, how are you, son? Here, I got you some sandwiches for later.' Alec Young pushed the packet across the table. He must have been here early, Colin thought, rushed to the front of the vending queue and back to wait for his son.

'Well done, Dad, you're learning.' Colin tried to grin at his father, though he was finding it hard not to look across at the other table.

'Well, maybe we won't have to go through all this for much longer, son,' Alec Young said. 'Here, I've been thinking. Soon as you're out of this place why don't you and me and Thomas go for a wee holiday? Somewhere you can get a bit of sun about you.'

Colin saw the look of anxiety cloud his father's face.

'You're that peely-wally from being in here,' Alec added. 'Maybe we could get a wee break to Mallorca. Or Tenerife?'

'Aye, Dad.' Colin smiled at him, determined not to spoil the older man's hopes. 'Surely won't be too long till I'm out of here, eh?'

I had always imagined us on a sunny beach, somewhere like you see in these fancy travel brochures; lying under a thatched beach umbrella, miles of endless sand and blue ocean and skies as far as you can see. Just me and Eva ...

Colin's pen hovered above the notebook. *Pipe dreams*, he should add. Just a lad's fantasy of being with a beautiful girl. Eva had been everywhere, of course. She'd told him about the holidays in the Seychelles, the luxury yacht. Maybe that was why he'd had such a vision of them together, cast away on their very own desert island.

And what would Eva have made of his plight now? He imagined her face – with the smooth skin that glowed in a certain light – distorted into anguish as she looked down from wherever she was. The image vanished in an instant. At this moment Colin didn't believe in any sort of afterlife. It was here today and into a nothingness tomorrow. That was what he believed now despite the years of goodly priests feeding him their dogma along with the wine and the wafers.

If there was a God, why had he allowed this to happen? Colin thought, a sudden fury coursing through his veins. And now he was in thrall to one of the invisible men over in E Block, Billy Brogan, wheeler and dealer extraordinaire. If the passing on of that message should get back to the prison officers ... Colin shuddered. Perhaps there was no easy way out of here at all, just an endless series of events that could conspire to keep him here for years.

He looked back at what he had written, then, face twisting into rage, he ripped out the page and crushed it into his fist.

The January day was fading into darkness as the hooded man stepped out from the bushes in the park. Jogging towards him, the blonde woman ran to one side of the path, never changing her stride.

The slap slap of her trainers on the hard tarmac was the only sound as he approached. His fingers curled over the club hidden inside the heavy overcoat, his eyes fixed on the pale golden hair bobbing up and down on her shoulders as she came nearer and nearer.

The woman's scream as the heavy stick felled her made a blackbird fly upwards. Its warning cry echoed in the frosty air.

Then it was all over, just the single white cloud of breath issuing from his open mouth as he stood over her, panting, stick in hand. He turned his face up to the heavens, and, as he gazed at the first stars wheeling overhead, the world tilted suddenly into a thousand fragments, a dizzying glimpse of something like eternity.

He stopped, frozen, as other footsteps sounded around the bend on the path. Glancing to his right and left, the hooded figure slipped back into the shrubbery and forced his way back into the depths of the woodland beyond.

'Kelvin walkway,' Jo Grant told her detective sergeant as they headed away from Stewart Street. 'Woman was found badly beaten.'

'Strangled?'

Jo shook her head. 'No, not this time.' She grimaced. 'Another jogger came by pretty soon after the assault. Called 999.'

'She's dead?'

Jo nodded miserably. 'Died on the way to hospital. Massive brain haemorrhage.'

'But you think it's the same guy?' DS Wilson continued.

The DI raised her eyebrows speculatively. 'Could be. We've got a description of the man from Lesley Crawford and there are CCTV cameras near the locus so let's see what they can give us.'

Wilson's stomach rumbled noisily, reminding him of the half-eaten sandwich and mug of tea he'd left on his desk. He screwed up his face and gave a despondent sigh. 'Any joy on the medical front?' he asked as they crossed the city and headed west.

'Maybe,' Jo nodded. 'There have been a few patients that didn't turn up for their regular visits at both Leverndale and Dykebar. We're still doing house checks on them all.'

'Any of them got form?'

Jo shook her head. 'That's not relevant, Alistair. Remember we don't have this guy's DNA on our database so we can rule him out as ever having been an offender.'

DS Alistair Wilson sighed again. A dangerous nutter running around Glasgow on the loose had already elevated this into a grade A case, one that the Fiscal wanted Lorimer to oversee. And where was his boss while all this was going on? Wilson raised his eyes to the heavens. With a bit of luck the detective superintendent would be somewhere in the air between Stockholm and Glasgow.

A thin-faced man of about forty was sitting in a small room at Gartnavel hospital, a blanket draped around his shoulders and a cup of tea held unsteadily in his hands, when the two detectives arrived. The uniformed officer stood up as soon as they entered the room, laying down his own mug on a work surface.

'I'm DI Grant and this is DS Wilson,' Jo said shortly. 'I gather you were the man who called this one in?'

'Christopher Gifford,' the man told them. 'It was such a shock. That poor woman lying there … all that blood …'

'Mr Gifford's had a bad shock,' the uniform offered. 'Doctor said to let him stay here quietly till you got here, ma'am.'

Jo nodded then dragged a chair from a corner to sit beside Gifford.

'Sorry to seem so insensitive, sir, but we do need to take a statement from you. Understand?'

Christopher Gifford nodded.

'Right, tell us exactly what happened this evening.'

'I was taking a run through the park. Decided to go down towards the river. See if there were any migrants.'

'Migrants?' Jo's eyebrows shot up.

'Birds,' Gifford explained hastily. 'Migrating birds. Like red-wings. Or waxwings. Only see them at this time of year in the cold, you know,' he offered, looking from one officer to the other.

Jo Grant tried not to heave a sigh. Lorimer would love this guy, she thought; a fellow birder to share stories with.

'And you ran which way?'

'Across Kelvin Way and down the side path, the one that takes you beside the river and beyond. She was just lying there near the bushes,' he said, his voice dropping to a whisper. 'I thought she'd had an accident. Till I saw her head.' He looked up. 'Then I knew. She must have been mugged.'

Grant and Wilson exchanged a glance.

'It's the same fellow, isn't it?' Gifford asked eagerly. 'The one who's been targeting these other women?'

'Did you touch her at all, Mr Gifford?'

There was the merest hesitation before the man nodded. 'Just her wrist, mind. To find a pulse. That was when I called 999. But it was no use.' Gifford's face crumpled in despair. 'They've told me she died even before she got here.'

'I'm really sorry you've had this awful experience,' Jo said, touching his sleeve. 'But there's just one more thing. Can you remember seeing anyone, anyone at all who might have been coming up from that path before you arrived?'

Gifford pursed his lips as he thought. 'No,' he said at last. 'A bit too cold and dark for most people to be out, I'd say. Plenty of cars coming up and down, of course. Had to wait a bit before I could cross the road, I remember that now. But, no, there was nobody else on that path, Inspector. No one at all.'

CHAPTER 40

The psychiatrist put down the telephone with a sigh. Kevin had missed his clinic appointments for more than a month now and although she had written a report to his care worker, Gwen Lockhart couldn't help feeling that she ought to have done more for her patient. And now, this. The police officer had explained that, yes, they knew all about patient confidentiality, but they wanted to be made aware of anyone who might have come off their medication, someone who could consequently be a danger to themselves and to others. Gwen looked thoughtful as she twirled a pencil between her slim fingers. The death of his partner had changed the man, something that was not to be overlooked.

The last time she had seen him, Kevin had twitched and fidgeted in front of her, his OCD worse than ever. She'd talked to him about Caitlin, encouraging him to express his feelings, but the harder she'd tried, the more bottled up he'd become. Then, as if he had simply had enough, Kevin had stood up, walked out of her room and she had not seen him again since that December day.

Professor Brightman was part of the investigative team, the officer had told her, and somehow that reassured the psychiatrist.

Gwen laid down the pencil, her hand stretched out to the diary that sat to one side of her desk: all her patients' details were there, safe from prying eyes. Her face was impassive as she flicked through the notebook, coming to a stop as she reached the page with Kevin Haggarty's address.

DS Wilson turned up the collar of his winter coat as they left the warmth of the car. It had been a short drive across town, past the fancy new yuppie flats lining the banks of the Clyde over the Squinty Bridge towards the Glasgow Science Centre before reaching the old part of Govan, a remnant of the Dickensian streets that had been ripped apart and modernised in the eighties. There was still a vestige of dignity lingering on these Victorian red-sandstone tenements, at least from a distance. Close up they looked what they were: run down and dishevelled – even the graffiti was poor stuff. There was a black metal gate across the entrance to the tenement that swung open at the detective sergeant's touch. A few stairs separated the pavement from an inner door, its dark red paintwork gouged out by scores of wilful kids trying out their knife skills.

'Not exactly the place you'd choose if you were the depressive sort,' Wilson remarked to Jo Grant.

The DI glanced upwards and shook her head. 'There but for the grace of God,' she murmured.

Haggarty's flat was on the ground floor and Wilson pressed the lowest button on the metal keypad then waited.

'Could be out,' Jo Grant suggested.

Then, as though to give the lie to her words, there was a buzzing sound followed by a metallic click. She nodded at Wilson and they both entered the building.

There was a short flight of steps rising to the landing for the ground floor flats, lit only by a lamp fixed into the cement wall between the two houses.

'Would you look at this,' Wilson remarked, pointing at the door. Instead of nameplates there were several scraps of paper held by drawing pins, showing the names of whatever tenants happened to be currently in residence. One of them was Haggarty's.

'Here today and gone tomorrow,' Jo Grant remarked.

'Well, let's hope our man's here at any rate.'

A brisk knock brought the sound of scurrying feet and then the door swung open to reveal a rat-faced young man, a brown dressing gown wrapped hastily around his skinny body. He looked at the two police officers through dirty, lank hair that hung in strings across his waxen skin.

'What d'youse want?' he growled.

'Kevin Haggarty?' Jo held out her warrant card.

''S no' here,' the man replied. 'What're ye wantin' him fur?'

'May we come in?' Jo asked, stepping into the hallway before the man had time to refuse. 'Funny smell here, don't you think, DS Wilson?' she said, her nose tilting upwards as she sniffed. The unmistakably pungent smell of cannabis filled the flat.

'Aye,' Wilson grinned. 'Been having a party or do you grow the stuff in the bathroom?'

'Are youse here tae see Kevin or what?' The man stood to one side now, shivering as he regarded the two detectives.

'Och, aye, but maybe you could tell us a wee bit about Mr Haggarty, seeing as how you both live here,' Wilson cajoled. 'Is there a kitchen down this corridor? I'm fair gasping for a cup of tea, son.' He nodded towards the end of the hallway.

'Ye cannae jist come in here an'—'

'And what, son?' Wilson turned suddenly, his face darkening.

'Ask questions? Maybe if we get the right answers we won't mind that funny smell, what d'you think, Inspector Grant?'

The man eyed them in turn, then gave a resigned shrug before leading them along the corridor, his bare feet slapping against the cold linoleum.

'Which one is Kevin's room?' Jo asked as they passed several closed doors on either side.

'Wan nearest the kitchen.' The man jerked his thumb at a badly painted door that had once been white and was now edged in greying patches where countless fingers had pushed it open.

'Him and Caitlin stayed there,' the man offered. ''Fore she OD'd.' He shrugged off the girl's death in a careless manner that made the detective sergeant shudder.

Wilson let the others walk ahead so that he could try the door but it was locked fast.

The smell of cannabis was even stronger in the kitchen, he decided, but at least it was warm.

'What d'you call yourself when you're signing on, son?' Wilson asked the man as he leaned against the door jamb.

'Rab Green,' he replied, taking a dingy-looking kettle jug and filling it at the sink.

'Well, Rab, maybe you'd be good enough to give us a few details about Mr Haggarty.'

The man turned and set the kettle back on its plinth. 'Och, Kevin's no' well. Hasnae been great since Caitlin died. Ah mean, how wid ye feel, eh? Wakin' up alongside a deid body?'

'When did this happen?' Jo asked.

Green twisted his mouth as he thought. 'Cannae right mind. The funeral wis aboot the middle o' December.' He stood, a vacant expression in his eyes. 'Naw, she musta died aboot the end of November or that. Sorry, cannae mind. Ah'm not very good wi'

327

dates anat.' He grinned at them apologetically, showing uneven and discoloured teeth.

Green fished behind a bread bin where a pile of leaflets and letters were stashed, drawing out a leaflet.

'Here,' he said, holding it out for them to see.

It was an order of service for a funeral, the picture of a young smiling woman on the front page.

'That's her there. Caitlin. Least that's how she musta looked at wan time.' He sniggered. 'Wasnae like that when she lived here, poor wee cow. Junkies don't look that pretty after a while.' He laughed again, but there was no real mirth in his eyes as he gazed over Wilson's shoulder at the picture of Caitlin Alice Muir.

Alistair Wilson stared at the photocopied picture and swallowed hard.

The dead woman looking back at them bore an uncanny resemblance to both Fiona Travers and Lesley Crawford.

'What now?' Wilson asked as he fastened his seat belt.

'Find Kevin Haggarty,' Jo replied. 'Dr Lockhart says she can't predict what might happen once he stops taking his medication but he has shown erratic behaviour before when that happened.'

'You think the girlfriend's death has triggered something?'

Jo sighed. 'Who knows? You know what Prof Brightman thinks about that one. And did you see that photograph?' She glanced at Wilson. 'Something weird going on.'

Alistair Wilson looked back at the DI who was biting her lip. She doesn't want to jump to any conclusions this time, he thought. And who could blame her? But there was more than just a suspicion that they were after the right man this time.

'Aye,' he nodded, put the Astra into gear and pulled away from the pavement, glad to be leaving the dingy street behind him.

Then, as they turned away from the shadowy tenements and headed back towards the city, Alistair Wilson felt a sudden surge of gratitude for his own ordered life with a wife and home that awaited him at the end of every day.

'This is the one.' Corinne unbuckled her safety belt and turned to the old man beside her. 'Look, Dad, see how nice it is, and look at the view we'll have!'

The small white bungalow sat at an angle facing the sea, its bay windows glittering in the midday light. Derek McCubbin saw the FOR SALE sign leaning drunkenly behind a privet hedge, a victim no doubt of the recent winter storms, then his eyes strayed to a smart silver saloon car parked at the kerb.

'C'mon, Dad, estate agent's here already.'

'It's cold,' Derek complained, struggling out of the black Volkswagen Golf. His daughter had persuaded him to buy the car and after several arguments about the cost he had relented, seeing the sense in having some transport of their own. The old man sighed. It wasn't as if he was short of funds, she had wheedled, and besides, wouldn't it be nice to take him on wee jaunts once the weather was better?

Derek had continued to grumble a little but only because he couldn't bear to give in without some sort of protest.

The rain had been lashing against the windscreen as they left the city but now soft white clouds scudded across a pale blue sky, the sun glinting on the water below them.

'Come on, Dad, let's get inside,' Corinne urged him, offering him her arm.

Derek shook her off. 'Got my stick,' he grunted. 'Don't need *you* to help me to walk along a road.'

Corinne shook her head, rolling her eyes to heaven. 'Suit

yourself. I'm dying to see what it looks like inside.' And with that, she walked briskly down the path towards the front door, leaving her father to look around him.

Derek McCubbin blinked as the sunlight met his eyes. He had spent more years at sea than he cared to remember and now, looking out at the expanse of water beyond the shore, he realised that his latter years could be properly indulged with memories, memories that might take away the darkness and despair gnawing at his soul. Yet the wrench he had felt after Grace's death had not gone away, his errant daughter a poor substitute for a beloved neighbour.

They would live here together, he thought, Corinne becoming bossier as he became older and weaker. Already he was beginning to see what sort of existence they would have – the balance of power shifting from an ageing father to a daughter who was becoming bolder day by day. Corinne was already entering the open doorway, talking to the young girl from the estate agency who had arrived before them.

Derek's mouth trembled for a moment then he closed his eyes against the treacherous tears as Corinne's voice summoned him.

'CCTV footage shows a man fitting the description of Kevin Haggarty,' Jo told the officers assembled in the muster room.

All eyes were on the screen at the back of the room, the projected images sent through from Cowcaddens.

'Sir!' Jo stopped suddenly, looking up, and all eyes turned to see the detective superintendent enter the room.

'Carry on, DI Grant,' Lorimer said. 'I'm interested to hear all about this.'

Jo took them through the footage and there was complete silence from all of the officers as they watched the hooded figure of a man slip across the main road and into the darkened path beside the River Kelvin. There was no sound from the cameras but each officer imagined the sough of wind that blew the hood from the man's dark head, a flurry of leaves scattering upwards as he pulled it back up. It was a split second moment, but sufficient to let them see the man's face. And, as Jo played the image over again and again, there were nods and glances as each police officer saw the likeness between the man caught on camera and the artist's image that Lesley Crawford had described.

'I think we need to make this public,' Jo said, looking past the assembled officers to where Lorimer was standing, arms folded.

'Perhaps,' Lorimer said. 'I agree that this man presents a real danger to the public now but we need to be aware that Haggarty could slip out of our grasp if we alert him to what we know. It's a case of balancing the two risks.'

'What do you suggest, sir?'

Lorimer stepped forward and joined his DI at the front of the room. 'I'm more than happy to throw every resource we have at this one. Issue as many officers as possible with this information and comb the streets till we find him. Put a twenty-four-hour surveillance on the Govan flat. He has to come back there some time,' he suggested. 'Tell Dr Lockhart and the care worker to let us know the moment he appears, though I got the impression from your message that Haggarty has chosen to ignore the people who would normally help him.'

'Does Professor Brightman have any idea about Haggarty?' someone asked.

Jo Grant nodded. 'It was Professor Brightman who gave us the profile of a mentally disturbed man. He talked about a trigger, something like a shock that made him begin to attack young blonde women.'

'And that shock could be his girlfriend's death from a drug overdose,' DS Wilson offered.

There were murmurs from the officers; then, as Lorimer stepped forward, all talking ceased, all eyes focused on the man standing before them.

'Right, we go with this one. Find Haggarty. That's everyone's top priority. And if he's not in custody in twenty-four hours I'm prepared to let DI Grant throw this to the media,' he told them.

CHAPTER 41

Cold wind was creeping through every layer of his clothing as Kevin glanced up and down the road, waiting for a break in the traffic.

The towers of the Kelvingrove Art Gallery were outlined against a deep blue sky, an orange haze of light pollution throwing the architectural shapes into relief. He crept in there sometimes, looking at the stuffed animals with their glassy dead eyes staring back at him. But it would be closed now, the big doors slammed shut, locking him out from the warmth.

As he crossed Kelvin Way he could see the police tape still flapping across the entrance to the park but there was no uniformed officer standing guard, blocking his entrance to the walkway. Nor was there any pedestrian making their way along the road, not a dog walker or jogger to be seen at all. As he walked down the familiar path, hearing the rush of water to his left, it was as if the entire place had become his alone.

What Kevin Haggarty could not see were hidden eyes watching him from a control room deep within the heart of the city; the eyes of a police officer who, at that moment, had just identified the hooded man.

*

'He's going down the same route,' the officer spoke into his head-set. 'Definitely Haggarty.'

The man in the control room would continue to sit there but even he felt a thrill in his blood as he imagined police cars being mobilised from all parts of the city, knowing that in a matter of minutes the path along the Kelvin would be swarming with his fellow officers.

The hooded man heard the stamp, stamp, stamp of running boots.

Something was happening on the path above him.

He turned to see figures darkening the space between earth and sky then pressed himself against the railing. Only a few feet separated him from the brown river water rushing a few feet below the bank. He hesitated for a moment but it was too late. The black-garbed men were upon him, cutting off any thoughts of escape.

Kevin Haggarty's mouth opened in a soundless cry as the first two policemen caught him by the arms.

Then, hearing those awful words flung at him, Kevin tilted his head back and uttered a roar of anguish that chilled the blood of everyone who heard it.

'God, it was like some sort of wounded animal.' Wilson shook his head as he sat in Lorimer's room. 'Desperate, really desperate.'

'You sound almost sorry for him, Alistair,' Lorimer remarked.

The DS sighed. 'Well he's no' right in the head, is he? Cannae help but feel for the poor bastard. Some terrible things must be going on in that sick brain of his.'

'Where is he now?'

'In the cells. But he's to be taken to Interview Room Three just as soon as you give the word. Is DI Grant . . . ?'

Lorimer shook his head. 'I'll see Haggarty,' he said. 'But I'd like you there too. And Allan Martin's the duty solicitor. Dr Lockhart feels that the presence of a woman might unsettle him right now.'

As the detective superintendent entered the room he saw Kevin Haggarty sitting by the table, hands cuffed together. He winced, seeing how gaunt this man was, the sharp angles of his face reminding Lorimer of pictures of Japanese prisoners of war. Haggarty shared that same defeated look; eyes sunk in hollows, the bones in his long fingers protruding through a scant covering of skin. When had he last eaten? Lorimer wondered.

'Mr Haggarty?' He stood over the man for a moment, looking intently to see if he would raise his eyes. But he seemed oblivious to anyone, even the solicitor who sat beside him.

There was the merest nod from Allan Martin and so Lorimer sat down opposite, making room for Alistair Wilson beside him.

'I'm Detective Superintendent Lorimer and this is my colleague, Detective Sergeant Wilson.'

There was no reaction from Haggarty who had cast his eyes down as though reluctant to acknowledge the presence of the two men who had entered the room.

'Have you had anything to eat or drink?' Lorimer asked. Then, as the prisoner sat mute and unresponsive, Lorimer looked at the duty officer by the door.

'He was offered something, sir, but didn't take it,' the officer replied.

'You look hungry, Kevin,' Lorimer said softly, staring at the lowered head in front of him. 'I could send out for a burger, if you like? Double cheese? And a cup of tea?'

He saw Haggarty's Adam's apple rise and fall as he swallowed. The very mention of food seemed to be getting to him.

The instant Haggarty looked up he was caught and held by Lorimer's blue gaze.

'How about it? I can have it here in just a few minutes.' Lorimer shrugged as though it was no big deal to him whether the prisoner had food or not. 'It's just that we're going to be here for quite a long time tonight, Kevin, and I need you to be able to concentrate, see?'

Lorimer smiled, the avuncular schoolteacher explaining matters for his wayward pupil.

Haggarty swallowed again then his tongue traced a line across his lower lip. 'With chips?' he asked, his voice husky as if from hours of weeping.

By the time the food had arrived and been wolfed down, Lorimer had established the basic information that was required: Haggarty was twenty-nine years old, lived in rented accommodation in Govan and was in receipt of state benefits.

As he watched the man wipe away traces of red ketchup from his mouth, Lorimer decided to ignore the psychiatrist's advice to go easy on her patient.

'The women you attacked were all like Caitlin, weren't they, Kevin?'

The man's mouth opened at the suddenness of the question.

'*Weren't they?*' Lorimer insisted. 'I am showing Mr Haggarty pictures of Eva Magnusson, Fiona Travers, Lesley Crawford and Maria Campbell,' he continued firmly as he placed the photographs on the table between them, never once taking his eyes from Haggarty's.

The man glanced down as Lorimer pushed them nearer. Then, as Haggarty caught sight of the women, a whimper escaped from his bloodless lips.

The detective watched him, those eyes darting over the images from left to right and back again as though devouring them. Haggarty's body language was something the tape could not record, the shoulders hunched, arms circling the photographs of the women as though to contain them: Eva Magnusson, Fiona Travers, Lesley Crawford and his latest victim who had been identified as dental hygienist Maria Campbell.

Haggarty lifted a finger as he looked at the first picture.

'You killed these women,' Lorimer told him sternly, 'and badly injured this one. I am indicating Lesley Crawford to the prisoner,' he added for the benefit of the machine that was recording the entire interview.

He wanted to ask 'why', but such questions were best left to the medical professionals who would, no doubt, have years ahead of them to find the answer to that question.

'That one,' Haggarty said slowly, tapping the picture of the Swedish girl. 'I don't know her.'

He looked up at Lorimer. His expression was impassive as he tapped the photo again. 'I didn't do that one,' he said again.

'The prisoner is indicating the picture of Eva Magnusson,' Lorimer said, keeping his voice neutral, trying not to show his disappointment.

'And the others?'

Haggarty looked at them again and as he studied the pictures, Lorimer was struck by the man's complete lack of emotion.

He nodded at last.

'Please speak for the tape,' Lorimer advised.

'Yes, I did them,' Haggarty said, his glance shifting from right to left. 'But not that one.' His voice was firm and assured as his finger hovered over the image of Eva Magnusson.

*

337

More than an hour and several polystyrene cups of tea later, the detective superintendent kneaded the knotted muscles on the back of his neck and stifled a sigh.

'Eva Magnusson,' he said again, holding out the photograph of the Swedish girl. 'Isn't she like Caitlin?' he persisted.

Haggarty was slumped back against the seat shaking his head once again.

'Never seen her before,' he yawned.

Lorimer clenched and unclenched his fists.

'I think my client's had enough,' Allan Martin suggested and Lorimer nodded in agreement. Haggarty looked exhausted now and even in this extremity of tiredness he wasn't about to put his hand up for a crime that he hadn't committed. Besides, Lorimer thought wearily, despite what he had hoped to hear to the contrary, he really believed him.

The DNA samples taken from the man would confirm his story soon enough. Then he would have to admit that Jo Grant had been right to arrest Colin Young. Had the student murdered the girl he professed to love? Surely this was beginning to seem a real possibility?

And yet, a small voice insisted: if Haggarty was telling the truth and if Jo was wrong, then Eva Magnusson's killer was still out there.

CHAPTER 42

'Looks like Colin's going to have to face trial,' Lorimer said, looking at Kirsty's face to see her reaction.

They were at her local again, coffees in front of them, the snow falling slantwise outside the window making a small haven of the cosy pub on the corner of Merryfield Avenue.

'I thought Haggarty would tell you he'd killed Eva,' Kirsty said in a small voice.

'I know, lass.' Lorimer touched her hand gently. 'But Professor Brightman always said it wasn't the same person. Besides' – he sipped his espresso – 'the evidence points to two different killers. Eva was killed inside her own home, possibly by someone she already knew. And the other women were all out of doors, prey to Haggarty's random attacks.'

'Only they weren't quite random, were they?' Kirsty asked. A fleeting hope in her eyes. 'He wanted to grab someone who looked like his dead girlfriend, didn't he? Someone who looked like Eva? Maybe he followed her home, crept upstairs and ...?'

'Eva took a taxi home from the party, remember? And the flat was locked when you came home, wasn't it?'

Kirsty frowned, nodding. The big front door was heavy to manoeuvre and it had definitely been shut when she'd got home.

And the flat had been locked as well when she'd returned from work. Had she really heard anything? Or had it been an over-wrought imagination? 'Do you think it was Colin?' she asked.

Lorimer sighed heavily. 'A jury has to decide,' he said. 'But, no, if it makes you feel any better I don't think the Colin Young you describe was capable of murder.'

'Thanks.'

Lorimer bit back the words that he might have spoken. *There could be another Colin that you don't know, Kirsty; someone you never saw – a young man whose passions overcame his normal good sense.*

'More drinks?'

The purple-haired barmaid hovered beside their table.

'Aye, I'll have another espresso, please. Kirsty?'

'Oh, it's you!' the barmaid exclaimed. 'You're one of the students that live next door to old Derek McCubbin. "The captain", we always called him.'

'That's right,' Kirsty nodded. 'And you're Ina?'

'Aye, that's me, hen. But see auld Derek, we havenae seen him in ages. Is he awright?'

'Gone to live with his daughter,' Lorimer offered.

'Aw, thank gawd fur that,' Ina said, seating herself between the pair of them. 'When we saw thon sign up at the hoose we all thought he wis deid!'

She shook her head. 'Terrible thing that aboot the bonny wee Swedish lassie. Funny thing, though.' She dug Lorimer with a sharp elbow. 'That wis the last time I saw the auld fella.'

'The same night?' Lorimer asked.

'Aye,' Ina nodded. 'Wis in here till closing time. Staggered back round the corner as usual. Me an' Tam watched him till he got in tae the close.'

She looked at Lorimer who was frowning at her.

'What? Tam and me aye look out fur the auld bugger, him being that shoogly oan his feet.'

'Derek McCubbin went home that same night? Are you sure of that?'

'Sure ah'm sure. Mean, ye couldnae forget whit happened *that* night, eh?'

'And it was closing time?'

Ina glanced behind her, a shifty look in her eyes.

'Look, dinna tell onybody but some Fridays we have a late night, bit o' music after hours, know whit ah mean?'

'And what time did Derek McCubbin leave here?'

'Och, well, could've been after midnight. Cannae right mind. Sorry.' The barmaid rose to go. 'Better get yer coffees. Anither latte fur you, hen?'

'What is it?' Kirsty whispered, leaning forward towards the detective superintendent.

'Derek McCubbin claims to have been at his daughter's in Castlemilk that night.'

'But why would he lie?'

Lorimer's frown deepened. 'What if he saw something?'

'Wouldn't he have told the police?'

Lorimer sat for a moment, trying to imagine what could have been going on in the old man's mind. Had he heard Eva screaming at her father? And had he seen Magnusson on the stairs? Or had Eva's father really told him the truth? And had the old man seen Eva's killer slinking down the stairs?

'Thank Goad!' Corinne Kennedy opened the door wide. 'About time too! I've been worried sick!'

Lorimer stood on the threshold of the woman's home, taking in her tear-stained white face. Corinne let go the handle of the door and stepped back inside the hallway then pulled a handkerchief from her trouser pocket, dabbing at her eyes as she led the detective superintendent through to the living room. The old man's chair was empty, the walking stick nowhere to be seen.

'What's wrong?' he asked, steering the woman towards a chair, seeing her twist the handkerchief between her fingers, clearly agitated.

'Do you not know?' Corinne's head shot up. 'Did they not send you from the polis station? I called them more than two hours ago.'

'Has something happened to Derek?'

Corinne sniffed back a sob. 'I don't know!' she wailed. 'He wasn't here this morning when I got up. Thought he might have slipped out for a paper or something. But he's never done that since he came. I even phoned the flat at Merryfield Avenue when I found he'd taken the key but there was no answer. And, I mean, look at the weather. Who'd want to go out in this?'

Lorimer glanced towards the window. The snow that had been falling all morning was heaped into drifts on either side of the road, making it impossible to see the pavements. No elderly person in their right mind would want to risk a fall in those conditions. Little wonder Corinne had reported her father as a missing person.

'When did you see him last?'

'We went down the coast yesterday to see this wee hoose ...' Corinne broke off sobbing then pressed the hanky to her mouth for a moment. 'It was lovely, just what we wanted. Nice view of the water. Immediate entry. Everything.'

'He liked it?'

Corinne shook her head. 'Christ knows! Hardly said two words

342

the whole time we were there. Thon lassie from the estate agents must've thought he was no' right in the head.'

'Do you think he might have been ill?'

The woman shrugged. 'Don't know,' she said in a small voice. 'He could be dead quiet like that sometimes. Moody, y'know? Thought it was just one of his turns.'

'And now?'

Corinne Kennedy heaved a sigh. 'He's never gone out without me since he came here. Not once. It's not like him, Superintendent.' Her voice cracked, betraying the woman's anxiety.

'Tell me,' Lorimer asked, looking Derek McCubbin's daughter straight in the eye. 'Was your father really here the night Eva Magnusson was killed?'

CHAPTER 43

In the end it felt like she had betrayed me, Colin wrote. *I still loved her, of course I did. That was something I'd never felt for any girl before. She was so special, so different from anyone I'd ever met. And she'd made me think I was special too.* He paused, remembering Eva's sleepy smile as she'd rolled away from his arms, the sense of triumph he'd experienced in satisfying such a sexually adept young woman. *I thought we could make a go of it. How wrong was I about that! But of course I never knew that at the time, not until after she was dead.*

He sighed, his mouth a tense hard line. Eva had used him, used them all, like playthings. He'd sat listening to the service on Sunday, wondering why he bothered to be there at all, listening to the priest talk about forgiveness. Had he forgiven her?

He should feel bitter, but all he could think about as he crouched on the narrow bunk, notebook in his hands, was about the terrible waste of her young life.

Colin looked down, seeing the words blur through his sudden tears. He closed his eyes and clasped his hands tightly together.

He had wanted to stop believing, to tell himself that there was no God up there, no master of the universe. But now all he wanted was to pray in the hope that someone was listening.

'Hello?' Kirsty's voice sounded tinny and remote over the intercom as Lorimer stood outside 24 Merryfield Avenue.

'It's Lorimer. I need to come up.'

As reply, the buzzer sounded and Lorimer pushed open the heavy green door. Behind him were Wilson, Grant and two uniformed officers, their squad car parked several yards along the snow-covered street.

'What's happening?' Kirsty Wilson stood on the landing, peering down at the figures ascending the stone staircase, Lorimer leading them towards her. 'What's wrong?'

Lorimer was at the top of the stairs now and had turned towards the flat next door.

'Go inside, Kirsty. We'll see you later,' he told her, merely nodding at the girl's puzzled expression.

He heard the door click shut but no footsteps disappearing along the hall. She would be standing there, behind the glass door, curious yet disappointed, no doubt, wanting to be part of whatever was unfolding.

The doorbell to Derek McCubbin's flat rang out as Lorimer pressed the old-fashioned bell, the long sound drilling through the empty hall. Behind him, Wilson and Grant exchanged glances.

Lorimer hunkered down, eyes level with the shabby brass letterbox, but all he could see was the interior glass door, no shadow moving beyond.

'He's not here,' Wilson said, making to move back down the stairs, but he stopped as Lorimer stood up and knocked sharply on the storm doors.

Still there was no answer.

'Right.' Lorimer turned to the two uniformed officers. 'You know what to do.'

The booming sound reverberated in the chill air of the close as they battered Derek McCubbin's solid door. A splintering noise made them stop, the red battering ram swaying between them.

'Okay, do the other one.'

Shards of glass tinkled to the ground as they burst a hole beside the lock.

Lorimer reached inside with his gloved hand.

It was there. He caught hold of the key between his thumb and forefinger then turned, wondering who had locked this door, fearful of what might lie within.

Not a word was spoken as they entered the house, only the crunch of glass below several pairs of boots alerting anyone inside to their intrusion.

Lorimer flicked a switch inside the doorway, illuminating the long hall. He could see the walls were half timbered, the doors along the corridor a dark varnish, yellowing wallpaper testifying to years of neglect. An old man's house, he thought. Ancient mahogany bookcases and side tables cluttered with trinkets lined the walls, brass-framed prints of sailing ships above them, making the place seem narrower than it really was. All the doors along the passage were shut, except for the one farthest away, a lozenge of light drawing them towards the end of the hall.

The big kitchen was a mirror image of the one next door, even down to the roof beams suspended from the kitchen ceiling.

The body swayed slightly, the draught catching it as Lorimer pushed the door wide. Sightless eyes stared down at them, the old man's neck twisted to one side as though he had struggled at the end, his mouth agape.

Had he wanted to change his mind? Or was it the body's

natural instinct to resist the onset of death? Lorimer could imagine that throttling cough as the rope bit into the old man's throat, feet scrabbling for a surface that was no longer there.

A bentwood chair lay tumbled where Derek McCubbin had kicked it aside, the wooden stick halfway across the kitchen floor.

'Leave it,' Lorimer said shortly as one of the police officers went to pick it up. 'Don't touch a thing until Forensics arrive.'

Nobody spoke again for a few moments, the officers looking at the body swinging gently on its rope.

'We should look for a note.' Jo Grant touched Lorimer's sleeve. 'If you think he'll have left one.'

Lorimer nodded. 'I hope to God he has.'

It was all he needed to say for the four officers to begin their search, leaving the detective superintendent gazing at the body hanging there. His eyes wandered over the kitchen, noting the cup and saucer placed upside down on the draining board, a teapot laid to one side. He imagined the old man sitting drinking that last cup of tea, hand shaking as he thought ahead to that final act. What had gone through his mind? Remorse? Guilt? Who could tell?

'We've found it, sir.' Alistair Wilson stood by his side turning a sheet of pale blue notepaper in one gloved hand. 'Pretty much says it all,' he added.

Lorimer glanced down at the crabbed handwriting that filled almost both sides of the note. He would read it eventually, see if it confirmed what Corinne Kennedy had already told him and hope to understand finally what had happened on that fateful December night.

Lorimer read the photocopied letter once again. The original was sealed within a sheet of plastic, the final production in a case that had taken so many weeks out of Colin Young's life.

347

I couldn't let them keep the boy inside. It wasn't right. He had nothing to do with it.

I'd seen her looking at me whenever I passed them, laughing at me, sniggering behind her hand, thinking I didn't know she was making a fool of me. Thought she was better than them all, oh, I could see that. I used to hear them on the stairs, calling out. Noisy wee beggars. This was never meant to be a place for students. Grace would have hated all that uproar, Grace, my dear friend. I miss her so much.

That Swedish girl, she was screaming at the man outside the door. Terrible things. I'd just got home, still had my coat and gloves on so I came out to give her a telling-off. The man had gone and she was leaning over the banister, saying something in Swedish that I couldn't understand. Be quiet, I told her. Stop all this racket. But she just turned on me with that false wee smile of hers. Told me to get lost. That was when I tried to grab her but she dodged into the flat and I followed her down the hall, taking my stick with me.

'He didn't mean to hit her,' Corinne Kennedy had told him, sobbing. 'He said it just sort of happened. One minute the girl had been shouting at him to get out of her house, Grace's old house, then she was on the floor.'

I can't remember much, just that anger swelling up inside as I took hold of her throat. Then she was so still. She just lay on the carpet, not breathing any more. I knew I'd killed her. I was frightened then, didn't know what to do. Just wanted to get away.

'And did he tell you what happened then?' Lorimer had asked Derek's daughter.

'He was halfway along the hall when he heard someone at the

348

door,' Corinne had sniffed. 'Slipped into the bathroom, didn't he? Waited till she'd gone into her room. Then got out of the place as quick as he could and came to me.'

I couldn't stay there. Took a taxi to Corinne's and told her there had been an accident. Later, when she heard about the girl's death, she looked at me funny. But she didn't let on to the police, not even when they came to her house to see me.

Tell the boy I'm sorry.

It was as comprehensive a confession as the detective superintendent could have wished for. He had even written the date then signed it, *Derek McCubbin.*

Lorimer passed the copy to the girl, watching her face as she read.

'I *knew* there was something I'd forgotten. Thought I'd heard the door open and close but I decided it must have been the wind,' Kirsty muttered.

They were sitting in his office at Stewart Street. It was less than twenty-four hours since Derek McCubbin's suicide but already it seemed much longer, so much had happened.

'Why did he do it?' Kirsty asked at last, handing the letter back to Lorimer. 'And how could he do it anyway, he was such a weak old man, wasn't he?'

'Spite, probably. A moment of madness,' Lorimer said. 'His daughter told us that he had been really cut up about losing his old neighbour, especially when the flat was sold on and occupied with students.'

'But we were never bad to him,' Kirsty protested. 'We didn't do the things he said.'

'Never mocked him, even when you thought he couldn't hear you?'

'No, not once,' she said firmly. 'In fact Eva always said she felt sorry for him. "Daddy No Mates", she called him because he was always on his own.'

'And you were always together in a group.'

Kirsty nodded. 'Who would have thought an old man like that could have been capable of killing anyone,' she mused.

'He was an ex-merchant seaman,' Lorimer told her. 'Hardy type, even though he had a gammy leg, he was evidently strong enough to overpower Eva. And fury can give a person strength.'

'But why didn't he confess at the outset? Why wait all this time leaving poor Colin in prison?'

'Fear,' Lorimer told her. 'Too old to face going to prison himself. And afterwards he probably tried to blot it out of his mind.'

'So what made him . . . ?' Kirsty stopped, reluctant to put the image of the hanging man into words.

Lorimer shook his head. That was another story, one that he had pieced together in his own mind. An aged father and a grasping daughter, the one fearful of discovery, the other seizing her chance to hold his terrible crime over him for the rest of his days. Corinne Kennedy had wanted a life away from the drudgery she had endured for so many years and had seen her father as her only way out. The car, the bungalow by the seaside, the old man under her thumb as she reminded him daily that she knew what he had done. He'd never be able to prove it but the mendacious look in the woman's eyes had told him more than any confession.

The old man had faced a different sort of imprisonment, Lorimer guessed. A life with his daughter would have taken away the last vestiges of his freedom. And in the end, a life not worth living.

'Perhaps he just couldn't live with himself any longer,' Lorimer told Kirsty. It was a sort of truth, after all.

'Professor Brightman was right after all,' she said. 'He didn't think Colin had killed Eva or that it was some random stranger. He always said that she knew who her killer was. And she did, didn't she?'

Lorimer sighed again. 'Maybe none of you really knew Derek McCubbin,' he said slowly. 'Maybe that was the problem. He was an old cantankerous man who kept folk at a distance, imagining the worst of them. Not your fault,' he added as Kirsty opened her mouth to protest.

'Anyway,' he said, glancing at his watch, 'isn't it time you were getting back to the flat? Thought you'd be baking a cake for your pal when he comes home.'

CHAPTER 44

It was still dark when he awoke and for a minute or two Colin could not recall where he was. Then the bed creaked under him and he remembered. *Home.*

Outside his room he could hear the sounds of someone clattering pans in the kitchen. Of course. Dad had said he was taking the day off work. *Can't have my boy waking up all alone*, he'd murmured as they'd said goodnight.

He and Thomas had sat in the living room, drinking beers and talking till the wee small hours. Not about Eva, nor about the weeks spent incarcerated in HMP Barlinnie. No, it had just been catching up with daft stuff like how Celtic was doing in the league and what was going on in the neighbourhood. There would be a few sorry-looking faces avoiding their stares, Thomas had told him grimly. The newspapers would be full of it today: already there had been online reports about Derek McCubbin's suicide and Colin Young's release from Barlinnie.

He was surprised the phone wasn't ringing already, but then hadn't Dad said something about unplugging it to give him a wee bit of peace?

Colin turned onto his side, relishing the feel of the duvet against his skin, breathing in the fresh newly washed smell of it.

He sighed, remembering. Eva had always insisted on them using that lavender fabric softener in the laundry. Would there be any of it left in the cupboard under the kitchen sink? Funny how things like that popped into his head, wee reminders of how life was before . . .

Thomas had told him he was nuts wanting to go back to Merryfield Avenue but Kirsty and the others were there and he had to resume his lectures sometime soon if he were to stay on course. He'd texted her last night, told her he was fine. Colin's mouth twisted in a rueful smile. That ubiquitous catch-all word: 'fine'.

It would take a while, the prison governor had told him. It always did. He'd shaken Colin's hand, wished him luck for his future. Tears had smarted in Colin's eyes then, as he realised that he did have a future after all.

He'd said nothing to the governor about what he'd done for Billy Brogan or about Sam, the passman. That was all behind him now and he could forget them for ever if he wanted to.

The first rays of a cold January sun filtered through the curtains, hitting the notebook that lay on his bedside table. He had sent so many letters to Professor Brightman, opening his heart and mind about Eva Magnusson. *The Swedish Girl* would never be finished now but perhaps his weeks inside one of Scotland's most notorious jails could provide material for a different story altogether . . . ?

'You're going to do *what*?' Alistair Wilson's jaw dropped in astonishment as Kirsty faced him, arms folded across her chest.

'But you're doing so well, pet,' Betty pleaded. 'Wouldn't it be better to finish your degree first then think about it later?'

'You have no idea what sort of life it is for a lassie in the police,' Alistair fumed. 'They need to work harder, do more to prove themselves as good as, if not better than, their male colleagues.'

'I know, Dad,' Kirsty said with a sigh. 'It's not as if I haven't been exposed to the job in recent weeks.'

'We thought you wanted to get away, go abroad to work in the hotel trade,' Betty protested.

'Well, I've changed my mind,' Kirsty said firmly. 'I've already downloaded my application and sent it away.' She shrugged. 'Maybe they won't take me.'

'Oh, I bet they will. Determined wee madam like you!'

Alistair Wilson stared at her for a moment then his face changed as he nodded, remembering what Lorimer had said about his daughter: *She has a knack of getting under the skin of people she meets.* And wasn't that just like the detective superintendent himself?

He grinned suddenly. 'Ach, well, two polis in the family, why not?'

Acknowledgements

Thanks are due to the many people who helped bring this novel to fruition. As always I begin with those who gave of their time to help with research. Thank you Chief Inspector Martin Cloherty and DCI David Halliday of A Division in Strathclyde Police for letting me ask all sorts of questions and take video clips on my visit to HQ. The governor of Barlinnie Prison, Derek McGill, and several of his staff and some of the inmates were also very generous with their time, allowing me to see places and find out things about that institution that I would not otherwise have known. Thank you, all. To DI Bob Frew and DC Mhairi Milne, again many thanks for letting me ask random questions as I composed the novel. Dr Marjorie Turner is always there to keep me on the right track with Rosie, just in case my scalpel slips! Thanks, Marjorie, my turn for lunch.

Huge thanks to everyone at Little Brown, especially my lovely editor, Jade Chandler, who approved the first draft and whose editing thoughts thankfully chimed in with my own; to Maddy, and Moira for keeping my head straight and not letting me double-book myself, and dear David Shelley who is always there for me.

Bless you, Jenny, for being so supportive and always knowing the right word to cheer me up when things aren't going right. You are an agent in a million.

Finally, thanks to Donnie who reads the first draft, points out typos and tries to give me gentle advice (too many murders!!). Life would just not be the same without you to keep me going.